GW00727998

KATHERINE SCHOLES was born in Tanzania and spent most of her childhood there before moving to England and then Tasmania. She is the author of the international bestsellers *Make Me An Idol* and *The Rain Queen*. She has written several children's books including the acclaimed *Peacetimes*, and a young adult novel *The Blue Chameleon*, which won a New South Wales State Literary Award. All of her books have been translated into numerous languages. Katherine also works in the film industry. She currently lives in Tasmania with her film-maker husband, Roger Scholes, and their two sons.

Also by Katherine Scholes

Make Me An Idol
The Rain Queen

KATHERINE SCHOLES

THE STONE ANGEL

PAN

Pan Macmillan Australia

First published 2006 in Macmillan by Pan Macmillan Australia Pty Limited
This Pan edition published in 2007 by Pan Macmillan Australia Pty Limited
1 Market Street, Sydney

Copyright © Katherine Scholes 2006
The moral right of the author has been asserted

All rights reserved. No part of this book may be reproduced or transmitted in any form or by
any means, electronic, mechanical, including photocopying, recording or by any information
storage and retrieval system, without prior permission in writing from the publisher.

National Library of Australia
Cataloguing-in-Publication Data:

Scholes, Katherine.
The stone angel.

ISBN-13: 978 0 330 42285 7.

I. Title.

A823.3

Papers used by Pan Macmillan Australia Pty Limited are natural, recyclable products made
from wood grown in sustainable forests. The manufacturing processes conform to the
environmental regulations of the country of origin.

Typeset in Birka by Post Pre-press Group, Brisbane
Printed in Australia by McPherson's Printing Group

The events, locales and characters in this book are fictitious.
Any resemblance to real persons, living or dead, is purely coincidental.

CHAPTER ONE

Addis Ababa, Ethiopia, 1990

Negatu swung the steering wheel, neatly dodging potholes as he drove quickly through downtown streets that were almost deserted. Stella leaned her head against the dusty side window of the Land Rover. She could see part of her face reflected in the wing-mirror. Strands of hair had come loose from her plait – they stuck to her sweaty skin, making long black lines against her pale cheek. Her lips looked dry, and her sunburned nose was just beginning to peel. Her eyes . . . The eyes trapped her gaze, drawing her in. They looked too bright, too clear. It seemed impossible that there should be no sign of damage – no mark left behind by the things that they had seen.

The image jolted as the vehicle suddenly slowed. Stella glanced up to see a line of fuel drums and sticks placed across the road to make a barrier. Negatu cursed under his breath.

'You must find your documents,' he said, steering with one hand while he fumbled in the pocket of his shirt.

As the Land Rover pulled over to the side of the road, a soldier strode towards them. He stood by the passenger door, resting the butt of his machine gun against his thigh as Stella slid open her window.

'Present to me your papers,' he demanded. He spoke slowly, shaping the English words carefully. Then he thrust a hand into the vehicle, close to the woman's face. The pink palm was marked with a long, deep scar.

Stella offered him her press card. As he examined it, she looked into the distance, where birds circled above a grey stone statue.

'What is this?' the soldier asked, jabbing a finger at the piece of folded cardboard, colourful with stamps and signatures in different inks. '*Women's World* magazine?'

'Yes, I work for them.' Stella pointed to the nametag she wore pinned to her shirt.

The soldier leaned into the car, bringing with him the smell of old sweat and charcoal smoke. Stella watched him study the badge's lilac border and daisy motif, and the words written in pretty, lacy script. The feminine style, she knew, would remind him that she was a woman, not just a journalist. He would begin to see her as his sister, or his girlfriend – someone who should be looked after. His expression softened for an instant. But then he looked suspicious.

'Why have you come here? To write about dresses?'

Doubt grew on his face as he looked Stella up and down, taking in her worn shirt, streaked with red highland dust, and her creased skirt.

'I write news stories about women,' Stella explained. 'We are returning from the north. Welo region. Many mothers cannot feed their children. The rains did not come. It is a very bad situation.'

'Welo?' the man repeated.

'Yes,' Stella said. 'We were near Kobo.'

The man's shoulders slumped. 'That is my home. My people are there.'

Stella nodded slowly. There was nothing she could say.

'So . . .' The soldier fixed her with a piercing gaze. 'You will tell your magazine. Everyone will know. Help will come.'

'Yes. I hope so,' Stella responded.

A look of optimism flashed in the man's eyes – then died away.

He seemed suddenly weary, all feeling gone from his face, as though his muscles were too tired, too worn out, to do their job. He knew, Stella sensed, that things were not that simple.

He turned away, waving one hand behind him, and walked across to the side of the road. There, he crouched beside a muddy puddle and began to wash his boots, cupping red-brown water in one hand and sloshing it over the worn leather.

Negatu hauled the vehicle back onto the road and accelerated away. Stella heard him sigh with relief as they left the roadblock behind.

'Now to your hotel?' he asked.

'Yes,' Stella replied.

He threw her a sharp look. 'You should be at the Hilton, with the other foreigners. It is much safer there.'

Stella nodded, but said nothing. She never stayed at international hotels. Even if she wanted to, she couldn't afford them. She was paid only for each article she sold, with no wage to cover the gaps between stories. For a decade she'd refused offers to join agencies, or even to take a retainer. She'd stuck to the path Daniel had set her on. 'Work freelance,' he'd advised her. She could remember the time he'd first said it, as he handed her his camera – a Leica with a click that you could hardly hear, and every shiny surface covered in black tape so that it drew no attention. 'That's what the word "freelance" means,' he'd said, using an airbrush to puff away dust from the lens. His ageing hands were clumsy, but his voice was strong. 'Free. Free to tell the truth.' He'd looked up, his eyes bright darts across the space between them. 'That's all you have to do. Tell the truth.'

The driver turned to Stella and smiled encouragingly. 'You can have a nice time at the Hilton. There is a swimming pool, hairdresser, business centre. I have seen them all. Also, you can meet new friends there.'

He ran his eyes down over Stella's body, pausing on her breasts. She knew what he was thinking – that she was passing up chances to find a man, a husband. She'd seen him studying her passport at one of the checkpoints in Welo, so she guessed he knew her age. Thirty-one. Her time had almost run out.

'I'm not looking for new friends,' Stella said. 'I'm here to work.'

It was true. She devoted all her energy to the tasks she set herself. During the long journey back south she'd already thought out what she wanted to say about the experiences she'd just had. As always, she let the images come to her first – filling her head, each one jostling for her attention. Then the words began to gather . . . As soon as she got back to her room, she'd take out her typewriter. Finding the place to begin would be the hardest part. After that, she knew, everything would fall into line.

The vehicle pulled up outside the Ethiopian Hotel, with its white façade decorated with chipped colonnades. Children clustered around the car. They pressed their faces against the windows, smearing the glass as they watched Stella taking wads of notes from her pocket. She intended to pay Negatu well. It had not been easy to find someone who was prepared to leave the city, and the scenes he had encountered at the famine camps would not be easily erased. At least one or two, Stella knew, would stay with him forever, lodged deep in his soul.

Like the child they'd seen on the first morning . . .

Stella faltered in the midst of counting the notes.

He was there again – the fair-skinned boy, blue-eyed, standing amongst the crowd in the feeding tent. At first Stella had guessed he must be the son of an aid worker or missionary – though she could not imagine why he would be here, in a place like this. Then she saw that he was dressed in rags; his arms were wasted to the bone, his belly swollen with hunger. Stella had looked around for the official. What was the boy doing here? she wanted to ask. Where were his parents? Panic twisted inside her. It seemed to her – in the moment – that sickness, even starvation, was nothing beside the nightmare of being so lost, so separated from the place where you belong . . .

'That child you are looking at,' Negatu had said. 'He's zeru zeru. We know two reasons for this. He was conceived by a woman who

4

was menstruating. Or he was substituted for a proper child by an evil spirit.'

Stella stared, unable to make sense of his words. The panic would not fade. Her breath seemed caught in her chest.

The government official had appeared beside her then. 'You want to photograph the albino child?' he'd asked.

Stella had shaken her head. The boy's eyes were fixed on her. Every child in the tent was looking at the foreign woman, but this child's gaze seemed to cut deep inside her.

'I can summon him,' the official said.

'No,' Stella replied. 'I don't want to photograph him.'

She wanted to forget that face.

She knew she never would.

The boy's eyes had followed her. Even as she sat in the Land Rover, counting out Negatu's money, she could still feel it. She felt as if she had abandoned him there, in a place where he should not be.

But he wasn't lost, she reminded herself. He was no different from the others . . .

Negatu bowed his head politely as Stella handed over a pile of soft-worn notes.

'Thank you,' he said. 'I wish you well.'

'Shall I find you again?' Stella asked. She knew she should be making good use of her time while it was still possible to leave the city. It was not too soon to be planning the next trip. 'I am hoping to go south.'

He shrugged. 'Maybe. I hope so. Who can say?'

Stella stepped out onto the roadside, slinging her backpack up onto one shoulder and turning to wave at the driver. She glimpsed the hotel doorman approaching, carrying an umbrella made of silky cloth in rainbow colours edged with a gold fringe. As he drew near, the children melted away, leaving only a couple of shoeshine boys eyeing Stella's canvas tennis shoes with dismay.

She headed for the hotel entrance with the doorman following behind her, holding the umbrella over her head. He held it carefully, as if she were a princess – a treasure to be shielded at all costs from any kind of damage. The gesture was strangely comforting. As if here, at least, was one person who knew what she'd just been through, but also how strong she was. Just a few moments of being cared for, and she would be restored.

Pushing her way through the creaky revolving doors, Stella stepped into the foyer. She'd only been based here for a month, yet she felt a sense of homecoming as she glanced around her – taking in the scuffed terrazzo floor with its pattern of coloured marble slabs; the dust balls lying beneath a lumpy couch; the sun slanting rosy shafts through cracks in the heavy brocade curtains. Today, the usual smells of fried spices and mouldering plaster were overlaid with the aroma of freshly roasted coffee beans. There was a hint of frankincense, too, wafting on the air. Hunting for its source, Stella saw the fragrant smoke drifting from a charcoal burner – a faint blue haze.

She crossed the foyer and stood in an open archway looking into the hotel restaurant. When she'd first arrived, she'd been taken aback by the contrast between the dining room and the foyer. Now, her gaze slid easily over the lime-green vinyl booths, and the orange bench seats and matching crockery.

At the sight of a menu laid out on a table, Stella felt hunger stirring inside her. Hours had passed since she'd eaten breakfast at a country guesthouse. The memory came back to her – of the stale bread rolls and bitter coffee; the harsh crumbs, barely softened by the greasy black brew, sticking in her throat. She felt her appetite ebb away, and turned instead to the reception desk.

The assistant manager stood up to greet her. 'Your room is still available,' he said, handing her a key attached to a heavy brass tag. 'We have kept it for you.'

'Thank you. I am very grateful,' Stella replied. Upstairs, she knew, were dozens of silent, empty rooms. There had been no tourists for years.

'And post has arrived at last,' the man added. 'There are three letters for you.'

Stella watched him retrieve her mail from a long row of otherwise empty pigeonholes. She recognised one of the lilac envelopes used by her editor, Lorna, at *Women's World*. It still seemed miraculous to Stella that postal services continued to work, even in countries like this one – at war and on the brink of collapse. Lorna could send off an envelope from London – to whatever address Stella had sent to her – and sooner or later it would arrive. Faxes provided an even more unlikely link. When Stella stood by a machine, slowly feeding in her typed pages – in hotel lobbies, post offices, or aid-agency bunkers in remote corners of the world – she often found herself picturing a replica of her work rolling slowly out onto the plush lilac carpet in Lorna's London office.

As the assistant manager handed Stella her mail, he offered to lend her a silver letterknife. She shook her head. He was always very helpful, but she knew that in return he would expect a big tip when she checked out. It was one of the things she found tiring about living amongst strangers – always having to measure every favour with a reward.

Stella climbed slowly up the wide marble stairs that swept in a graceful curve to the first floor. Her bag dragged at her shoulder, reminding her that she needed a good night's sleep. She glanced at the letters in her hand. Lorna's one was on top. Behind it was a letter that had been forwarded from the hotel where Stella had lived in Nairobi. The name and address were written in a clumsy childlike hand. The third was in an Ethiopian Hotel envelope. She guessed it would contain a polite reminder about her bill, which she had forgotten to pay before setting off for the north.

Stella paused in the doorway to her room, glancing around the small, bare space. In her absence someone had straightened her sheets, refolded her meagre collection of clothes, and swept the floor between the two beds. Otherwise, everything was as she'd left it.

She dropped the envelopes onto a table and up-ended her backpack beside them. Her notepads and address book slid out, along with her radio, camera and rolls of exposed film. Then came her spare shirt and undies – all now dirty – and her toilet bag and first-aid kit. Last to fall out was an object about the size of her hand, wrapped in an old silk scarf. Stella took it across to a bedside cabinet, removing the cloth as she went.

She unveiled a stone carving of a kneeling figure with wings. An angel. She let it rest in the palm of her hand, feeling its familiar weight and shape. Then she placed the statue down on the scratched veneer of a bedside cabinet, next to a chipped saucer stained with cigarette burns. The stone face looked towards the pillow, where Stella would rest her head later on, and try to sleep.

Tepid water ran down over Stella's body, washing away sweat and dust. She rubbed a piece of bright blue soap through her hair, breathing in the cheap perfume to banish the smell of the camps – the latrines, the clinic with no disinfectant, the white-shrouded bodies laid out in the sun. The government official had handed her a sprig of rue – the herb the Ethiopians put in their coffee. He'd motioned for her to stick it up her nose – to fight one smell with another. It had only worked for a while.

Stella closed her eyes and lifted her face into the thin stream of water. Snatches of scenes flickered through her mind. An old man's hand resting so lightly on the perfect face of a little girl, who looked as if she were only sleeping. Flies feeding on wounds that would never heal. And Stella's own hand clutching secret food, to be consumed – dry-mouthed – in the green-tinged gloom of a zipped tent . . .

Through the sound of the shower came the voice of a radio newsreader: a British accent, calm and authoritative. Stella listened out for news of places she'd lived in, or the voices of journalists she'd met in the field – and maybe even something on the situation here in Ethiopia. She might find out whether the rebels really were as close to Addis as they were rumoured to be.

Stepping out of the shower, Stella used her one worn towel to wrap her hair in a turban. Sitting on her bed, the coarse blanket prickling her bare skin, she looked at her letters. She turned to

Lorna's envelope first, tearing it open and pulling out a bundle of papers: cuttings of her articles. Sifting through them she glimpsed fragments of photos and pieces of text, set alongside advertisements for lipsticks and wrinkle creams or recipes for low-fat dinner menus. She read the titles. They were always chosen by Lorna, who liked them to follow a theme.

'WOMEN WHO PROTECT THEIR DAUGHTERS BY DRESSING THEM AS MEN – A story from the hillside villages of East Timor . . .'

'WOMEN FIGHTERS WHO WEAR POISON CAPSULES AROUND THEIR NECKS – A story from the jungles of northern Sri Lanka . . .'

Reaching the back of the pile, Stella looked for her cheque. There it was, clipped to a sheet of letterhead paper. Stella sat for a few seconds, gazing down at it. The money would not go far. Living expenses were high here in Addis. And she had to be able to travel around. After paying her costs, she would hardly be able to save anything – once again. She would simply have to ask Lorna for an increase. She could not put it off any longer. She would have to pretend Lorna was a politician, a member of the military, a warlord or a chief. Then Stella would be able to ask questions, demand action – anything – without flinching.

She turned to the grubby envelope with the handwritten address, and scanned the letter inside. It was from someone she'd interviewed, recently, in southern Kenya.

'*I must inform you, and I beg for your assistance,*' it began. '*My husband has been arrested and taken away. My children . . .*'

Stella folded the letter up and put it aside. It was vital, she knew, not to look back. When she'd written a story, she let it go. She made sure to cut her ties behind her. If she did not, she knew that a group of people – a place, a life – would begin to draw her in. And then she would not be free to do her job.

Turning to the final envelope – the one with '*Ethiopian Hotel*' printed on the front – Stella braced herself. She was about to discover exactly how much her room bill had grown. Feeling inside the envelope, she drew out some folded sheets of paper. But they were not the usual typed account forms covered in neat handwriting. They were thin, shiny pages – from a fax machine. The *Women's World* logo leapt out at her from the first one: a cover sheet. Her gaze swept down the page.

TO: Stella Boyd, guest, The Ethiopian Hotel, Addis Ababa
Private and Confidential.

Urgent message attached. Please forward.

She turned to the second piece of paper. Skimming an official-looking letterhead, she jumped to the typed message beneath:

STELLA BOYD c/o WOMEN'S WORLD MAGAZINE

TASMANIA POLICE IS TRYING TO CONTACT YOU. PLEASE PHONE HALFMOON STATION IMMEDIATELY 63247789. YOUR FATHER IS MISSING AT SEA.

Stella stared at the fax. The meaning of the words refused to settle in her head. They were like phrases in a foreign language.

Missing at sea . . . Tasmania Police . . .

She fixed her eyes on the printed words – the black and white shapes.

Your father . . .

It couldn't be true. William was the most cautious man in the fleet. He stayed ashore if the weather was bad, no matter how much he needed the catch. He never varied his rules about how he worked the pots. And his boat, the *Lady Tirian* was built for safety instead of speed.

But the fax lay on Stella's lap – real paper, real words; sent across the world to her. The local policeman, Spinks, must have contacted the magazine. And Lorna's secretary had faxed it straight on.

Stella stood up slowly and reached for some clothes, as the implications of the brief message sank in. She knew well enough that 'missing at sea' often meant 'lost' or 'drowned'. Near the Halfmoon Bay wharf was a seafarers' memorial where brass plaques marked a whole list of local tragedies – fishermen washed overboard, boats wrecked, whole crews vanished. Taken by the sea . . .

With clumsy fingers she dragged on her T-shirt and struggled with the zip of her jeans. Then she fumbled on the floor for her shoes.

She forced herself to keep calm. Snatching up the fax, she checked the date. It had come yesterday, while she was in the camp. They've probably found him already, she told herself. She pictured him at home, wrapped up in a blanket; her mother hovering over him offering hot beef soup. They were in Grace's kitchen, where everything was neat and clean. There would be the smell of Velvet soap and wood smoke. Fresh-made biscuits cooling on racks. And William's 'sea cakes' lined up by the oven, wrapped in foil.

The manager was just coming in through the front door as Stella arrived at reception.

'Miss Stella!' he called to her as he hurried over. 'You are back! An urgent message has arrived for you – I put it in an envelope. I could not help reading it . . .' His voice trailed off. 'I fear you have received bad news.'

Stella nodded mutely and gestured towards the telephone. Mr Berhanu hurried round behind the counter and pushed the old black telephone across to her.

'The phone is working,' the man said. 'It's your lucky day.' He looked away, embarrassed. The word 'lucky' lingered in the air.

Stella dialled the prefix for Australia, followed by the number given in the fax, and waited for the call signal. She estimated that it must be well into the night in Halfmoon Bay. She pictured the phone ringing out into the darkness of the abandoned police station – then she heard it switching through to Spinks' house next door. She imagined him cursing as he climbed out of bed. Or – a thought came to her, prickling through her body – perhaps he was

11

not there, but out supervising a search. Did they stop at night, she wondered, or work on, with lights . . .

'Spinks here.' The voice was firm, indicating in just two words that the call had better be important.

Stella felt her throat closing up. She had to force out her voice. 'It's Stella.'

'Stella! Thank-god-for-that,' Spinks replied. 'I never thought we'd find you. Where are you?'

'I'm in Addis. Ethiopia. I got the fax,' Stella stammered. 'It said he's missing. Dad's missing.'

There was a short silence. Stella heard the man draw in a breath.

'That's correct. There's no good news I'm afraid. But the search resumes at first light.' Spinks cleared his throat. 'Now listen – you have to come home. Straightaway. You're needed here.'

Stella stared at the phone, dark and squat, smudged with greasy fingerprints. *Come home*. The phrase was so simple, short. As if Halfmoon Bay were just around the corner. As if it were a place she could just return to, like any other . . .

'Stella? You hear me?' Suddenly, Spinks was the cop who caught teenagers smoking or writing rude words in the dusty side-panels of the police car. And she was the little girl who did not know the right thing to do.

'Yes,' Stella replied. Her thoughts raced across splintered details – flight departure times, exit papers; an airport ringed with troops ready to make a last stand. 'Okay – I'll be there as soon as I can,' she promised.

'Good,' Spinks said. 'There's still no phone on out there – at your parents' place. I'll let Grace know you're on your way.'

He hung up, and the line went dead. Stella met Mr Berhanu's gaze as she replaced the receiver on its cradle.

'Miss Stella, I am sorry. Your father has not been found?' the man asked.

'I have to go,' Stella said. 'I have to go right now.'

She listened to her words as if they were being uttered by a stranger. She felt numb, unable to concentrate. Yet she knew she had to hurry. There was one flight a day to Dubai. It left in five hours' time. Before she could leave the country she'd have to get clearance at the Ministry of Information – the place where officials sat beside piles of paperwork, gazing idly at long lines of rubber stamps. A large amount of her precious cash would be spent bribing them to pick up their pens and write.

Turning on her heel, she headed for the stairway and ran up it, two marble steps at a time. Her thoughts flew ahead of her feet. She planned how she would throw everything into her bag – the angel, safely wrapped in the scarf; the clothes Stella had washed out in the shower, stuffed wet into a plastic bag; her passport, stowed ready in the outside pocket. She'd go to the airline office first, and then drive through town to the Ministry . . . The plan rolled out smoothly in her head. This was how she functioned best – her mind became steady, weighed down with strategies; her body, spurred to action, became strong; and there was no room left for feelings to intrude.

Mr Berhanu had a taxi waiting for her when she came back downstairs. Along with the money she owed, she handed him her typewriter. It was Daniel's portable Olivetti with its zip-around case – the one with the keys that kept sticking and having to be fixed – t, q and 6. She felt as though she were leaving a part of herself behind.

'Keep that for me,' she said. 'The fewer things I have, the faster I'll get through customs.'

'What shall I do with it if you do not return?' the man asked tentatively.

Stella just looked at him. She hadn't thought beyond her immediate plan. 'I will return,' she said firmly. 'Very soon. I'll want my room back.'

Mr Berhanu gave her a small smile. 'Certainly. No one else shall have it.' After a brief pause he placed his hand on her shoulder – a gentle touch. 'I pray you will find your father alive.'

His words made Stella feel like a child suddenly – lost and confused and afraid. 'Thank you,' she whispered.

She turned and walked away. She looked down at the large terrazzo tiles passing under her feet. Three, four, five . . . She found herself counting them. Six, seven . . . If there were an even number when she reached the revolving door, she told herself, he'd be rescued. Safe and sound.

She forced herself to lift her gaze before the doorway drew close.

As the plane laboured through the air, climbing steeply above the airport, Stella sat with her chin resting on one arm, looking out through the scuffed plastic window. Below her, at the end of the runway, lay the rusting carcass of an aircraft shot down decades ago when the civil war was still young. She kept it in view as long as possible. Then she began scanning the countryside beyond the edge of the city, picking out the places she'd passed through only yesterday. But soon there was nothing else she could find to fill her head and hold her thoughts at bay.

She closed her eyes. She reached for the image of William, her warm, strong father, who had once been so proud of his only child . . .

But the face that came to her had eyes that were hard and cold. And lips that were pressed together into an unrelenting line.

Stella's hands gripped the armrests as tension grew inside her. She could feel it all again: the iron strength of her father's will, and the weight of his words – so measured and sure – as he laid out his plan for her.

The plan that would tear her heart in two . . .

Old anger surged through her body like a poison in her blood. But it was mixed with pain and a daughter's stubborn love. Stella could feel the separate currents running inside her as they had done for years: love and anger, warmth and darkness.

She stared down at the rugged landscape passing beneath her.

Her stomach churned with fear. So much lay in wait for her, she knew. There was not just her feelings for William to be faced. There was her mother, Grace, as well . . .

Then there was the place, Halfmoon Bay. The old house on the point, with its garden fenced in from the wild. The rocks, the wind, the sky, the sea.

Most of all, there were the hidden coves. And memories of Zeph.

Zeph, with his windblown hair made of all the colours of the sands. His green eyes dappled with blue, like the surface of the ocean. He returned to her like a vision, bringing a glow of joy – but that, too, was wrapped in pain. The worst pain of all.

She pressed her hands over her face.

I can't go back, she told herself. I can't.

The words echoed in her head, devoid of meaning. She heard the hum of the aircraft engines and felt their power vibrating through her body, as they pulled the aircraft steadily onwards through the empty sky.

CHAPTER TWO

Tasmania, Australia

The highway wound between hilly paddocks that were dotted with newly shorn sheep. As the coach rumbled past, one or two of them lifted their heads, but the rest went on feeding on the lush spring grass. Stella looked out at the landscape slipping past. Beyond the fencelines grew tall stands of blue-grey gum and wattle. They hid the coast from view, but she could sense the ocean there: a cold presence lurking just behind the trees.

Shifting in her seat, she looked across the aisle. Steep wooded hills stretched inland to a bank of craggy mountains. On the horizon, sheer slabs of stone rose up – dark pillars pressing against the grey sky. The scene looked ominous and bleak. Stella turned her gaze back to the roadside.

As the next farm drew near, she recognised a large dam and a derelict barn surrounded by shearers' huts. Round the next bend, she knew, the paddocks would give way to a stretch of untouched bush – and soon after that she'd see the turn-off to Halfmoon Bay. Picking up her bag, she walked along the aisle and waited in the doorway.

The coach slowed down as a narrow gravel road appeared ahead, forking off to the left.

'Here we are,' the driver said.

He pulled over to the side of the road, near a wooden signpost. Stella looked out through bleary glass doors at the line of black letters painted on white – the 'H' for Halfmoon blotchy with bullet holes.

'Sure you don't want me to drive you down?' the driver asked.

Stella looked back at him over her shoulder. She saw him taking in her unbrushed hair and crumpled, travel-worn clothing. She forced a bright smile onto her face. 'No thanks – I'm happy to walk.'

The man stirred in his seat, reaching for the gear stick. 'Better you than me. It's blowing a gale.' He shook his head. 'I hate spring weather. Can't trust it at all.'

The doors hissed open. Stella waved behind her and then stepped down onto the gravel. A cold wind whipped her face and beat in through her thin jacket. She slung her bag up onto her shoulder and set off, wrapping her arms close around her body. Behind her, the coach accelerated away, spitting back loose stones.

The road was a narrow ribbon of pale grey, leading in through the dense bushland. Boobyalla shrubs and banksia bushes grew right up to its edges; their leaves were pale with dust thrown up by passing vehicles. Stella walked steadily along – down a hill and round a long corner. Then the road emerged suddenly from the trees.

She stood still, staring ahead over open heathland. The sea lay spread before her – a wide expanse of heaving grey, faintly flecked with white. The leaden hue was mirrored so closely by the sky that the horizon could barely be seen. Sky and sea were one – a vast, cold realm. She felt a slow shiver travel up her spine.

The wind carried the smell of churned seaweed and salt. It entered her body with each breath that she took. Stella hurried on, barely noticing the patchwork colours of the bushes that she passed – the familiar shades of green, brown and red. Before long, the road veered right and dropped down towards the sea. In a few minutes she would see the wharf, the pub, the shop. Everything.

Rounding the corner, she looked down. Her step faltered as flashes of bright orange leapt out at her. They were dotted around the car park beside the wharf. Orange people, orange vehicles . . . It was a sight she recognised from scenes of disaster that she'd witnessed around the world – earthquakes in Turkey and Japan, floods in Bangladesh, a bomb blast in Ireland. She bit her lip, her hands clenching in her pockets.

They were still searching.

He was still lost.

Images of broken timbers flashed before her. Splintered boards tossed in the surf. Tangled ropes. Shredded canvas. Questions tumbled through Stella's head. Had they found the boat? The life-raft? Anything . . .

She wanted to run straight down and find out, but she forced herself to stop. It was important to be ready first. She sought Daniel's voice in her head. 'It's like the boy scouts. Be prepared. Before you go in, warn yourself of what to expect. Steel yourself. Then hang back, look and listen, gather all the facts.'

She began with the sea. Closer up, she could now see the swell – waves coming in long and steep. They broke right over the rocks that sheltered the fishing gulch from the open water and spattered the air with white foam.

Small fishing boats were moored along the wharf, nudging one another as they rocked in the waves; but all the big tuna boats and deep-sea vessels were out – taking part in the search, Stella guessed. The only exception was Joe's derelict ketch *Grand Lady*. She was there in the middle of the wharf, where she always had been – right in everyone's way.

Stella saw Mick's old blue dinghy tied up at his mooring buoy, bucking in the waves. She pictured the fisherman standing on the sturdy steel decks of his tuna boat, combing the sea for some sign of the *Lady Tirian*. But it was fifteen years since she was last here, Stella reminded herself. There was nothing to say that Mick was still working out of the bay. Fishermen sometimes became farmers, or got jobs in St Louis. Boats got bought, sold; they got broken up and lost. After all this time she could not be sure of anything . . .

Shifting her gaze from the water to the land, Stella saw that there were about two dozen of the orange-clad figures – perhaps more. They were mixed with a smaller number of men in khaki work-clothes. Here and there the yellow oilskins of a fisherman stood out. At the sight of them, Stella felt a sharp stab of pain. Each one looked as if he could have been her father.

At the centre of activity was a caravan with a whiteboard set up outside it. A police car was parked nearby. Next to that was a trestle table bearing large cooking pots set on portable gas burners and stacks of bowls and mugs. A group of women were gathered there – hair blowing in the wind, skirts flapping, faces turned towards one another as they talked. Amongst them a tall slender figure caught Stella's eye. There was something about the way she stood – along-side the others, yet holding herself apart. Stella drew in her breath. It was Grace.

The sight of her mother – here, at the wharf – made the whole situation seem suddenly more real. Stella broke into a quick walk, heading down towards the car park.

She aimed for the caravan, passing unnoticed between the groups of Search and Rescue volunteers. But then, suddenly, she found her-self encountering people she knew. Familiar faces appeared in front of her – looking older but otherwise unchanged. There was Mrs Barron, her hair still a flaming red. Joe, with his weather-wizened face. Laura's parents. Lenny. Ned . . . As each of them recognised Stella their eyes widened with surprise. Then came looks of sympa-thy and concern – backed by keen interest. Stella returned their greetings but kept walking on.

Suddenly a hand grasped her shoulder.

'Stella! It's me.'

'Pauline.' Stella barely had time to utter the name before she found herself pulled into an embrace. Soft arms drew her in.

'Come here, love.'

Stella breathed the powdery fragrance of the woman's bosom. It was the cozy, safe smell of a mother who kissed squashed fingers, who made messy plates of fairy bread, and who never told children to put on their shoes.

Jamie's mother.

Stella stiffened and pulled away, but Pauline's hands stayed on her shoulders. Stella felt their weight, resting there. She saw that the woman had wrinkles now, following the pattern of her smiles.

'They're doing everything they can,' Pauline said. 'We all are. Brian's been out every minute of daylight. Jamie's not here – he's still in the Northern Territory . . .' Her voice trailed off. She sniffed, but then managed a smile. 'It's so good to see you, pet. I've missed you all these years.'

Stella tried to smile in reply. She searched the woman's face, but she found no hint of reproach there for all the pain Stella had caused her.

'Come here. I want to talk to you.' Pauline tugged Stella's elbow, leading her round behind an orange van. When they were alone there, she spoke again. 'I'm worried about Grace. Everyone is. She stands out here in the weather all day. Then she goes home and – judging by what she brings down in the morning – she must be up half the night cooking. Of course, we'd all do the same in her position. It's just that Grace has been so unwell.'

Stella looked at her blankly.

Pauline appeared embarrassed. 'Mrs Barron says you write, now and then. So I thought you'd have heard.'

Stella shook her head.

'It began with that back injury she had – when you stayed home from college to nurse her. One thing led to another. Her health's been poor ever since. We hardly see her. A lot of the time she's not well enough to leave Seven Oaks. Poor William. He's been a saint . . .'

Stella studied her hands. She could think of nothing to say. There had been so many lies told that last summer. Grace's back injury had been one of them. Stella and William had spread the story around – that Grace was bedridden, that she needed her daughter home to care for her. When all the time she had been as strong as an ox.

Perhaps, Stella thought, a lie once told was like a seed planted in the earth. It grew bigger, stronger, over time. And then, finally, it became real . . .

'At least you're here now,' Pauline said. 'Grace'll be so glad to see you. She's over there, serving out soup.' She pointed Stella in the direction of the food table, and gave a gentle push to her back.

People moved out of Stella's way as she came near them – as if she were either fragile or dangerous, and should not be touched or made to alter her path. Before long, she found herself standing in front of the table. She recognised the three other women working there. They exchanged nods with her, but said nothing. Stella sensed they did not want to greet her ahead of her mother.

Grace was bent over a pot with a ladle in her hand. She was stirring soup, moving the spoon round and round in slow, steady circles – oblivious to the attention focused on her. She looked as though she might just stand there stirring all day.

The woman's blonde hair was now streaked with grey. Knotted veins had appeared in her hands. But her face was still smooth and almost free of lines – the legacy of the deep stillness that had so often inhabited her features. Even now she looked calm, serene. She didn't look unwell.

Stella reached out and touched the hand holding the ladle. Grace jerked up her head, startled. She stared at the figure before her. The realisation of who it was, standing there, seemed to reach her slowly, as if filtering through layers of gauze.

Then, suddenly, the last veil was drawn aside. Grace looked into Stella's eyes. For an instant, nothing was hidden. A spark leaped between them. Stella caught her breath as joy surged through her. She was here, with her mother – after so long . . . But then came the pain and the anger bursting up. Stella saw the same turmoil reflected briefly in Grace's eyes before her mother tore her gaze away. Grace's face became a mask – polite and distant. Her daughter might have been a visitor who'd arrived unexpectedly for tea.

Stella stepped back, letting her hand fall to her side. Grace leaned the ladle carefully against the side of the saucepan. She wiped her hands on a tea-towel and straightened her skirt. Then she stepped round the table and walked towards her daughter.

Stella put down her bag. She braced herself for her mother's touch – for the feel of Grace's thick hair brushing against her skin. And the smell of tea-rose talc – the only perfume William liked . . .

Grace hovered just out of reach. Her face was pale but for two smudges of pink on her cheeks.

Stella pushed her hands into her pockets. 'I got the fax,' she said. 'I came straightaway. I was lucky to get out.'

Grace looked at her in confusion. 'What do you mean?'

'Everything's on the brink of collapse over there – where I've been . . .' Stella broke off. Her world seemed impossibly far away from the place where she now stood.

'It's good that you've come,' Grace said. 'William will be pleased.'

There was a short silence. The words – framed by Grace's refined English accent, still unchanged after decades of living in Tasmania – seemed to echo in the air, confident and sure. The other women turned awkwardly away.

In the moments that followed, Stella glimpsed something through the crowd: the blue of a policeman's uniform. Moving to get a clearer view, she recognised Spinks' grey hair and upright stance. She felt all the questions held at bay during the journey clamouring inside her. She left Grace standing there and strode towards him.

When she reached the man's side, she touched his arm. 'It's me. I just got here.'

At the sound of her voice, Spinks spun to face her. He searched her face briefly. 'Good to see you, Stella.'

'What's happening? Please – tell me,' Stella said.

Spinks frowned gravely. 'We need to talk.' He led her back to where her mother was still standing by the food table. He lifted a hand towards Grace, but then seemed to think better of touching her. 'Come into the caravan, both of you,' he instructed.

He walked towards the metal steps, glancing back over his shoulder to make sure that the two women were following.

The caravan smelled of fried muttonbird, cigarette smoke and wet wool. There was a sense of well-worn holiday comfort, out of keeping with the presence of a uniformed policeman.

'Take a seat, ladies,' Spinks said.

He stood stiffly aside from them. As far as Stella knew, the policeman – along with his sister, who shared his home – was one of her parents' closest friends, even though they only met socially a few times a year. But Spinks had always prided himself on being professional. Even in the privacy of the van, he was carefully neutral.

He waited while both women squeezed in behind a table littered with paper cups, maps and drawing pins. A folded newspaper lying amongst the chaos caught Stella's eye. She froze. There was an image of William's face staring up at her. Her heart clenched with pain. He had the proud look that she knew so well – the one he'd always worn when he walked his daughter into the schoolyard on the first day of each new term . . . She looked into his eyes – his gaze trapped in black and white. The photograph was blurry, as if it had been snatched long-lens by a stranger.

'*William Birchmore,*' the caption read. '*President of the Halfmoon Bay Fishermen's Association.*' Stella scanned the text that followed. '*Prominent member of the close-knit coastal community . . . reported missing four days ago . . . air search called off . . .*'

The image slid sideways as Spinks took the paper and folded it away. He tucked it under his arm and went to stand in the small space between the door and the stove.

'Two days of air search have been conducted. Nothing found, I'm afraid. No sign of the *Lady Tirian* or the life-raft.' He looked at Stella. 'I had to call it off yesterday.'

Stella nodded slowly. She was aware of Grace sitting beside her, twisting a biro tensely in her hands.

'We're concentrating on the land search now,' Spinks continued. He pointed towards a map pinned onto the wardrobe door.

Black lines were drawn in the sea, angling out from the bay and pointing south. Stella recognised them immediately: William's regular fishing runs – the routes he chose from, depending on the weather, for each voyage. The coastline was marked out in sections, with shaded areas of different colours.

'I've got people in all sectors,' Spinks said, 'checking inland as well. The trouble is, we've known all along where to look. Starting with his runs, we've plotted out drift zones – taking into account wind and current. And there's just nothing there.'

Stella sat perfectly still as the meaning of his words sank slowly in. 'What happened?' she asked finally. 'What went wrong?'

Grace put down the biro and looked intently at the policeman's face, as if hoping to hear something new.

Spinks shook his head helplessly. 'I wish I had an answer for you. There was a storm. Gale-force winds up and down the coast. Nothing out of the usual, though. The other boats made it in okay, or took shelter behind the islands. But you know how the sea is down here. You can get a freak wave that smashes one boat and leaves another untouched. Whatever went wrong, it must've happened suddenly. There was no May Day call. No flares. And your dad never went out without everything in good working order. Not like some . . .'

Stella eyed Spinks in silence. He was talking too fast – keeping the air full of words, she sensed, to hold the grim reality at bay.

'What's the window of survivability – that's the question,' Spinks went on. 'Well, in these conditions, it depends. If he was in the sea, then I'm afraid . . .' The man let his voice trail off. 'Of course, if he was in a life-raft it's another story altogether. They should have spotted it from the air, but it's much harder to see things in the water than people think – you can miss a sizeable vessel in a big swell. Even so, we think the best hope is that he's made it to shore. I have to be honest, though, and say the situation is very serious.'

'He's not dead.' Grace's voice cut the air, sharp and clear. A sudden gust of wind rattled the door of the van.

Stella turned to look at her. The woman's chin was lifted defiantly. 'He's not dead,' Grace repeated. 'I'd know if he were.'

Stella looked at Spinks. He nodded faintly, as if acknowledging that her mother's words might be true. After all, everyone knew how close Grace and William were. They were almost like one person.

'Remember those other boats,' Grace continued. 'The ones in the photos at the pub . . .'

'Yes. Miracles have certainly happened,' Spinks agreed. 'There was the *Briar Rose* in 1974. Three survivors walked into a bush-walkers' camp after ten days. Then there was the wreck of the *Ella Jane*. And old Joe out there – we'd given up hope of ever seeing him or *Grand Lady* again.'

Stella looked down at her fingers tracing circles in the fake wood pattern printed on the tabletop. The man was reeling off local history as though she were an ignorant stranger – when she'd been right there at the wharf when news of the *Ella Jane* came in. Had he forgotten? Or did he want to remind her that she no longer belonged here – that she'd stayed away too long, turning her back on them all?

Spinks stepped forward to peer through the window. 'I think they could do with your help out there,' he said to Grace. He quietly signalled for Stella to remain.

Grace eased herself out from behind the table. She looked relieved to be going – like a schoolgirl released from the head-master's office. When she'd gone, carefully shutting the door behind her, Spinks leaned against the stove. He seemed to be weighing up what to say next.

Stella stared out through the window. Up near the pub she caught the bright flash of a neon sign: words in looping letters, shining red against the grey sky. HALFMOON BAY HOTEL.

'I need to talk to you about Grace,' Spinks said. 'I'm concerned about her.'

'Yes, I know,' Stella broke in. 'Pauline's already told me. Surely it's up to Mum to decide what she can manage.'

'It's not just that,' Spinks said. 'She's been driving herself down here in the ute.'

Stella frowned at him in disbelief. Her mother had never been able to drive. The Birchmores lived way out on the point and Grace had always had to rely on her husband for transport to and from Halfmoon Bay.

'When did she learn to drive?' Stella asked.

'She didn't,' Spinks stated. 'I watched her arrive this morning – she can hardly change gears, and she almost hit a boat trailer trying to park. It's got to stop.'

'Okay,' Stella said. 'I'll talk to her.' She could feel the weight of responsibility gathering around her.

'Good girl,' Spinks said. 'Now, you go out there and help your mother.' As Stella took a step towards the door, he held up his hand. 'Wait a minute. I just want to say something. I know you've got a very important job working for that magazine. My sister Mary's got all your cuttings in a scrapbook. Two scrapbooks. But you've done the right thing – coming home.' He paused and looked into Stella's face. 'I'm sorry it's taken something like this to bring you back. Don't take this the wrong way, Stella, but I think it's long overdue. When someone stays away for years – doesn't come back even to visit – something must need fixing.'

Stella looked down at the ground. He doesn't know, she told herself – he can't know. William and Grace would never have told. But she felt a thread of doubt. Spinks had always seemed able to discover things he was not meant to know. It was like a sixth sense that he possessed.

Stella lifted her face and looked the policeman in the eyes. 'I won't be staying long,' she said firmly.

Spinks made no response for a moment, then he reached into his pocket. 'I took the liberty of removing this.' He held out a single key. The end that fitted into the lock was shiny, but the rest of it was corroded with salt. 'It's from the ute,' he explained. 'I had a job getting it out.' He pushed the key into Stella's hand. 'You keep it, from now on.'

Stella felt its shape printed on her skin. The key was a symbol, she knew. A transaction had taken place. It was her job to look after Grace now – and it would remain so until . . . until William was found.

He might never be found.

Stella breathed in sharply. Beneath the pain of that thought lay a stream of questions – about what it would mean for Grace; for her . . . Stella could see similar concerns reflected in the policeman's face. She shoved the key deep into her pocket and walked past him, out the door.

A team of volunteers had gathered around the food table, almost hiding it from view. Stella began pushing her way in through the crowd, towards the place where Grace had been standing. But as the woman's grey-blonde head came into view, Stella's step faltered. Suddenly she felt unable to face her mother again. She felt a twist of sickness at the thought of what lay between them – the potent emotions that were being held at bay. She needed some time alone, she knew – to take control of her feelings and prepare herself for what was to come.

Veering off in the opposite direction, Stella strode back up through the car park, dodging vehicles and boat trailers. She kept her eyes fixed ahead to give the impression that she was on an urgent mission and should not be interrupted. She was aiming for the sandstone ruins of the old whaling station. She knew it offered a place that was sheltered from watching eyes. Teenagers used to smoke and kiss there. They scratched their names in the soft stone. Stella's own name was there. '*Jamie loves Stella 1972*.' Or was it '*Stella loves Jamie*'? She could not remember.

Reaching the gaping doorway of the old building, Stella ducked inside. The seaward end of the building was gone, and the wind blasted in unchecked. It beat against Stella's face as she stood with her back to the wall, resting her head against the sandy stone.

She stared down over wind-stunted grassland towards the boulders that edged the sea. The waves crashed hard against them and then reared up into the air. Her gaze was drawn across to the headland, jutting into the strait – and on, out to the islands, squatting like animals on the horizon.

She found herself tracing the outlines of distant rocky hills. Their shapes were so familiar to her that they might have been imprinted on her soul. She knew all the smells, the sounds and colours as well. It was as if she had been here only yesterday.

Too late, she saw that it had been a mistake coming in here, leaving herself alone with the sea . . .

She stood still, her body pressed against the wall, as though she were trying to disappear inside it. The wind battered her face, flinging the ends of her hair into her eyes. Her lips were whipped dry; her hands ached with cold.

But she didn't notice. She was lost in the sound of the gulls and the scream of the wind blowing in from the west. It held her in its grasp, powerless, as it wrapped itself around her – and carried her back . . .

CHAPTER THREE

FIFTEEN YEARS EARLIER

Halfmoon Bay, Tasmania, 1975

It was only nine o'clock in the morning, but the sun was already warm against Stella's back as she rode her bike along the foreshore. She pedalled slowly, looking down over the beach. Black kelp-weed flopped about in the shallows, prodded gently by a lazy sea. Pacific gulls stalked the sands, leaving long lines of footprints behind them. The sea was an open plain of clear bright blue, stretching away to the horizon.

When the track petered out, Stella rode over bumpy grassland until she met the gravel road that led down the hill towards Halfmoon Bay. She could see all the houses clustered together there around the wharf and gulch – their tin roofs painted in shades of red and green, and the occasional sheet of bare metal glinting in the sunshine. Picking up speed, she lifted her face, letting her long hair stream out behind her.

As she rounded a sharp corner, the blue and white awning of the shop suddenly came into view. A blur of colour near the doorway caught Stella's eye. Drawing nearer, she saw that it was Mrs Barron, the shopkeeper – the woman was perched halfway up a stepladder, arms outstretched as she struggled to hold up a large brown shape cut out of plywood. It was the Christmas reindeer. The animal had adorned the shop façade since early November, but now it had come free at one end and hung down at an angle. Silver tinsel dangled from its antlers.

'Who's that?' Mrs Barron called, without turning her head, as Stella brought the bike to a standstill.

'It's me, Stella.'

'Come and hold the ladder steady for me, love. The bloody wind's been at it again.'

Stella climbed off her bike and hurried across. She smiled to herself. Mrs Barron was always doing battle with the wind. As well as tearing down her decorations it blew salty spray onto her windows, ripped her newspaper posters and knocked over her 'specials' blackboard. And the sun was just as bad – it bleached her window displays and wilted the fruit and vegetables.

Bracing herself against the wall of the shop, Stella held the ladder firmly while Mrs Barron hammered in four large nails, attaching the plywood shape to the weatherboard cladding.

'That should hold him,' the woman said with a nod of satisfaction. 'Can't have Rudolph letting us down on Christmas Eve!' She peered down at Stella. 'Come to see the photos, have you?'

Stella looked blank. 'What photos?'

'The ones from the leavers' dinner.' Mrs Barron gestured towards the community noticeboard mounted on the wall just inside the door. Stella glimpsed a row of colour photographs pinned there on top of the collection of handwritten 'For Sale' notes. 'The photographer sent them from St Louis. They arrived yesterday. Go and look. I'll be there in a tick – I'll just put the ladder away.'

Squeezing past Mrs Barron, Stella went to stand in front of the pictures. The first photo was a group shot of the Grade 10 girls standing in a line. They all wore long dresses made of pastel floral fabric decorated with lace and frills. Their hair was piled up on their heads or looped into elaborate curls, and their faces were bright with eyeshadow, lipstick and blusher.

One figure stood out amongst them. A dark-haired girl wearing a dress of plain bold orange – simply cut, with no lace, no frills, no sash. Her makeup was barely visible, and her hair hung loose, draping her shoulders.

She looked beautiful.

Stella's lips parted as she gazed at the image. She could hardly believe it was her – Stella Birchmore.

She relived the moment of arriving at the school gym with Jamie at her side – walking past the climbing bars draped with muslin and streamers and on towards the stage, where a live band had been set up in the place where the headmaster usually stood. She'd been aware of eyes following her from every part of the room – and of Jamie's admiring glances. Her friends had greeted her with looks of envy. They'd all tried so hard to transform themselves for this one special night – to become new creatures and not just old friends who had been sharing lunch snacks and secrets since kindergarten. But Stella alone had succeeded.

She had sent a silent message of thanks to her father. It was he who had made this happen. He'd known better than she what was best . . .

All the other girls had gone with their mothers to Hobart to choose their dresses, but William had insisted that his daughter's be made at home. She had protested, but to no avail.

'You don't want to look like everyone else,' William had stated. He was standing in Stella's bedroom – the girl-sized things making him look bigger than he was. Stella had opened her mouth to argue again, but William had left the room, making it clear that the discussion was over.

Later that day, Grace had appeared with a bundle of orange satin folded into a parcel and tied with ribbon. 'I brought this with us, from England,' she said. She spread it out, filling the air with a mothball smell. Her hands hovered over the cloth as if half-inclined to gather it up again and hide it away. She gave Stella a quick, tentative look. 'I know it's old, but it's very good quality. I think it will suit you.'

Stella had barely glimpsed the swathe of orange as she'd turned her face away.

In the weeks that followed, the orange satin kept appearing in different parts of the house – lengths and snippets of it, and long trails of thread. Stella still wished she could have bought her dress in a shop like the other girls, yet she felt herself being seduced by the smouldering beauty of Grace's cloth. Stella could imagine it in an oriental bazaar, being displayed by a merchant with a curved sword at his hip and a striped turban on his head – a shimmering reflection of the blended colours of tangerines and spices . . .

When the dress was finished, Stella had put it on and walked cautiously into her parents' bedroom to look in the big dressing-table mirror. She'd gasped with relief. She'd not understood, then, how perfect the dress was. But she knew she was safe. It was good enough, at least . . .

Stella stared in through the dusty glass of the noticeboard. Behind her, the fly-strips in the doorway swished as Mrs Barron came inside. She looked over the girl's shoulder.

'I wouldn't have believed it was you!' the woman said. 'You look like someone in a film. Where did you find that dress?'

'Mum made it,' Stella said. She could hear the note of surprise in her own voice. She had no idea how it was that Grace – who never sat around with the other mothers looking at the fashion pages of magazines – could have created such a dress.

'I didn't know she could sew,' Mrs Barron said.

There was a moment of quiet. Stella understood its meaning from years of experience – not just with the shopkeeper, but with other people as well. Grace could only make it to social events – like meetings of the Fishermen's Wives Association – when William was home to drive her. And then she always had to leave early, because – being a fisherman – her husband liked to go to bed soon after tea.

Occasionally, when he was at sea, Grace resorted to cycling into Halfmoon Bay when she needed something from the shop – but it always took her so long and wasted so much time that she usually ended up sending Stella instead. As a result, Grace was not well-known in the community in the way that other women were.

Mrs Barron pointed at another of the photographs. 'But this is my favourite of you.'

She'd chosen one of the 'couples' pictures – an image of Stella standing beside Jamie. The two had been snapped in the midst of sharing a joke, their eyes meeting, smiles on their faces.

Jamie looked as striking as Stella. His dark hair matched the dark jacket of his hired suit; his teeth were white like his brand-new shirt. The colour of his skin – tanned olive – bridged the two extremes.

'You make a beautiful pair,' Mrs Barron said. 'Change the colour of the dress and you could be a bride and groom!'

'We're only sixteen,' Stella protested. But she smiled proudly.

'I was engaged when I was sixteen,' Mrs Barron responded. 'Oh, I know it's different these days. You have to go away and study all kinds of things.' She walked off across the room. 'I've got mail for you, by the way.'

Stella followed her. When she reached the counter, Mrs Barron was shuffling through envelopes in the pigeonhole marked 'B'. After a short while she produced a postcard.

'From Laura,' she said, handing it over. 'Sounds like they're having a good time.'

Stella glanced at the picture of girls in bikinis by a tropical poolside. A sense of loss came over her. Laura's family had set off for the Gold Coast the morning after the leavers' dinner, depriving Stella of her best friend for the whole of the holidays. They'd invited Stella to travel with them, but she'd declined without even asking her parents. William would have refused permission, she knew – he didn't think Laura's parents were strict enough. And anyway, Stella could not imagine what kind of Christmas William and Grace would have with no relatives around and their only child not there.

'And look what arrived just this morning –'

Mrs Barron dumped a parcel on the counter. Stella ran her eyes over the brown-paper wrapping, smiling as she recognised her god-father's elaborate handwriting. Ever since she could remember she'd received a Christmas gift from Daniel. It was the only contact that the man ever made with her, and she looked forward to its arrival each November or early December. This year, as the weeks had gone past with no sign of it, Stella had begun to wonder what might have happened – to the parcel, to him . . .

'I thought you were going to miss out,' the woman continued. 'He was cutting it a bit fine.'

Stella pressed her lips together. She didn't mind the woman reading Laura's postcard, but her godfather's parcel was special – private. She wanted to tell Mrs Barron that it was nothing to do with her if Daniel's parcel was late, or never came at all. Instead, she just picked up the package and hugged it against her chest.

'Got a list for me, have you?' Mrs Barron asked.

Stella reached a hand into her pocket, pulling out a sheet of paper marked with Grace's careful writing.

Mrs Barron studied it for a few seconds and then moved off around her shop, picking items from various shelves and lining them up on the counter.

'There we are,' she said, checking through the list. 'Clover honey. Vanilla pods, not essence. Flour, sugar, et cetera. There's just one thing I haven't got. Gravy beef. I'll have a look in the other freezer, but I'm pretty sure the only stewing steak I've got is wallaby.'

She gave Stella a knowing smile as she headed towards the second ice-chest. 'That won't do for the Birchmores, of course!'

Stella gave no response. When she visited the homes of her friends she was happy to eat wallaby, muttonbird, native goose, fish – anything. But it was true that at Seven Oaks, Grace served only lamb, chicken or beef – and only the exact cuts that were listed in the recipes she used.

They all came from one book – a handwritten notebook bound

in dark cloth. Whenever Grace was about to bake a cake or prepare a casserole – or even to make up a shopping list – she would take the book from its place on the mantelpiece. Then she'd run her hand over the kitchen table, checking that the surface was clean before laying it down. The book was handled like a sacred text – the pages were never allowed to be splashed with milk or smudged with cocoa.

The collection of recipes had been compiled by William's mother. She had died – along with his father – in a car accident, when William was just a child. Aunt Jane had held the book in trust for William's future bride. It was now family folklore, how the older woman had given the precious gift to Grace on her wedding day wrapped in snow-white muslin. And how Aunt Jane had explained to Grace later that she'd done this so that William would always be able to eat the food that his mother – and then she – had cooked for him.

Grace's dedication to Aunt Jane's task had become legendary, too. William liked to tell Stella how her mother had practised all the recipes until she could cook each dish to perfection. The key to her success, Stella was told, lay in following the recipes exactly. Measuring quantities instead of guessing. Doing each step in the right order. And never substituting one ingredient for another . . .

Stella looked up as Mrs Barron approached empty-handed.

'Nothing but deer and roo,' the woman said. 'I'll have to send an order to St Louis.'

Stella helped Mrs Barron stack the groceries into a carton. When the job was done, the shopkeeper glanced down towards the wharf.

'Your dad's not in yet,' she commented. She threw a cold look behind her into the open doorway that led to her private sitting room. 'He's a hard worker that one,' she said loudly. 'Not like some people.'

Stella glimpsed Mr Barron's grey head there – and the flicker of a television screen.

'He'll stay out as long as he can,' Stella said, 'with conditions like this. The price is very good right now – with New Year coming.' She felt a surge of pride as she spoke about her father. She knew William was viewed by everyone as one of the best fishermen of Halfmoon Bay. His achievement was made greater by the fact that he had not been born to the sea. He had mastered the skills of boating and fishing by sheer hard work.

Mrs Barron held out the carton so that Stella could balance her parcel on top. 'Are you going to order any of the photos?' she asked. Her tone was casual, but Stella knew what lay beneath it.

The girl shrugged, wanting to appear completely uninterested. 'Not sure.'

'You just write down the number in the corner. I'm making up the list for the photographer.' Mrs Barron paused for a second, checking a list by the till. 'Let's see . . . Jamie's ordered that one of the two of you together. And that nice picture of you on your own. He's getting it enlarged.'

Stella smiled sweetly. She imagined Grace looking on, pleased with her well-mannered daughter – a grown-up girl who could hide the way she felt.

'Have a very happy Christmas, Mrs Barron,' she said. Then she turned and walked out of the shop.

In a stand of ti-tree near the rear of the shop, Stella put down the carton beside her bike and sat on the ground with her parcel. Resting her back against the papery bark of a trunk, she read the address, written in the familiar decorative handwriting.

To Miss Stella Birchmore, c/o Halfmoon Bay Store, Halfmoon Bay, Tasmania.

She turned it over and read the back.

From Mr Daniel Boyd, 125 Willowdene Street, Melbourne, Victoria.

It was four years since her godfather had moved from England, yet Stella had never met him – even though, as Grace's cousin, he was the only relative the Birchmores had in Australia. Daniel's signature was on Stella's christening certificate, but there were no photographs of the occasion so she had no image of him in her mind. She knew him only by his gifts – special gifts, which she kept safely together in a wooden box. When she was little he sent shop-bought toys, in boxes and packets with printed labels and instructions. But as she grew older he sent her unusual things from other parts of the world – chosen, she guessed, from amongst his own possessions. There was a pair of silk shoes from China, too tiny to wear. A music box with a carved lid that played 'Edelweiss'. A painted mask from Kenya. They always came with a card, hand-written in script that matched the address on the outside of the parcel. It described the object and often included a date.

'*1930s*', '*1955*' or '*pre-second world war*'.

Sometimes Daniel told her how they had been found.

'*Swapped with an Arab trader in Aden bazaar, 1967*', or '*Souvenir from Egypt*'.

Stella loved them, these gifts from afar – her own treasures that did not belong to William and Grace, but only to her . . .

The ti-tree cast a dappled shade over Stella as she turned the par-cel around on her lap to find the knot in the string. It was heavy for its size, and the shape offered no clue to its contents. As she untied the string and peeled off pieces of sticky tape, Stella focused on try-ing to guess what the present might be. She tried not to think about Daniel – not to wonder, again, what it was that he had done wrong. She knew it was something very serious. The man's name was rarely mentioned. And when Stella unwrapped the gifts each Christmas morning an uneasy silence would fill the room. Stella found it frightening to think that this was how things could end up between people – even members of the same family. A person could be cut off, like the limb of a gum tree accused of being dangerous or block-ing out the light.

The brown paper fell away, revealing a package swathed in rose tissue and tied with a gold ribbon. Daniel's gifts were always in beautiful wrappings – never ordinary paper printed with snow-flakes, Christmas trees and Santas. Stella wondered if he chose them himself; they didn't look like the work of a man. Feeling through the soft tissue, Stella's fingers met something hard and lumpy, about the size of her hand. Taped to an inner layer of plain white paper, Stella found a small card.

> *To my dear Stella,*
> *with great affection,*
> *your godfather Daniel*

He wrote the exact same words each year, as if unwilling to risk opening up a more intimate dialogue, or – it had occurred to Stella – forbidden . . . She turned the card over and read the words on the back.

> *Niche angel, from a French garden*
> *At least a hundred years old.*

Removing the paper, Stella saw a kneeling figure carved from white stone. She had a peaceful face adorned with a wide halo, and delicate praying hands. Stella breathed in with pleasure. The angel looked serene yet bold. Beautiful. The carved features were so lifelike that although she was made of bare stone there was an impression of colour. Stella could see the gold of the halo, the royal blue of the dress, the pink of her cheeks set against dewy skin. It was a dark-haired angel, she sensed, with strong brows and brown eyes lined with black lashes. Turning her over, Stella saw a pair of folded wings. They looked surprisingly powerful, tied to the girl's back with strong muscles. If she chose, Stella thought, the angel could take flight at any time and be gone.

Stella sat still for a while, gazing down at her angel cradled in her hand. Then she carefully reassembled the parcel so that no one could tell that it had ever been taken apart.

Stella pedalled her bike along the coast road, heading home. The sun was higher in the sky now – the heat stronger. In the paddock that ran along the side of the road, sheep were clustered together, trying to share the shade of the few surviving gum trees. They panted in the heat, weighed down by their thick woolly coats. There had been more shade here once – the paddock was dotted with dead trees. Their skeleton limbs, white and leafless, reached up into the sky as though they still hoped for rescue. William had told Stella that the settlers who'd cleared the land hadn't known that gum trees needed to grow in stands and would not survive on their own. They hadn't known, either, that the coastal soil – stripped of its forest cover – was stony and thin. As Stella gazed over patches of earth, chewed bare and burned in the sun, she could almost feel its tiredness. She preferred to look towards the sea. It was cool and blue – and so vast, surely, that it could never be worn out.

Sweat beaded on her face, and her shirt was stuck to her back by the time she reached the place where she turned off the road. A neat green and white sign was attached to the gate that marked the entrance to the Birchmores' property. SEVEN OAKS, it said, in black capital letters. Stella's eyes skimmed past the words as she unlatched the gate and pushed it open. They always made her feel uneasy – the bold letters looked so clear and sure. As if there were seven sturdy oak trees growing somewhere beyond the gate, when in fact there was only one. William had planted it soon after he bought the property and chose the new name. That had been back when Stella was a baby, yet the oak was still small – like the gum trees, it seemed unable to thrive on its own, even though it was watered every day.

Climbing back on her bike, Stella rode on along the dirt track. It wound down the middle of a narrow headland. Paddocks ran off on either side, sloping away to where granite boulders lay along the foreshore. Stella picked out William's six rust-coloured cows. The animals were outnumbered by the dozens of wallabies and rabbits that had come in from the bush to share the salty pasture. When the girl drew near them on her bike they bounded away, taking shelter behind stands of ti-tree.

Stella rounded a bend in the track and the house appeared ahead.

As she pedalled towards it, she traced the familiar outlines of her home – a stark shape rising up against a backdrop of sea and sky.

The house was set near the end of the headland – right next to the boulders, close to the water's edge. The building was actually quite small, but it looked grand and important standing out there all on its own. It was surrounded by a white picket fence enclosing a large garden. Stella could see Grace's fruit trees growing there, safely out of reach of the wildlife – and also the tops of sweetcorn plants and berry bushes. Near the front door was the single oak, its flimsy branches laced with summer green.

Stella put her bike away in the shed and then entered the garden, heading for the side door near the kitchen. She passed the lily patch, enjoying the thick scent that rose from the white trumpet-shaped blooms. They were Grace's favourite flowers, and the bed had recently been enlarged to make room for all the bulbs that kept multiplying each year. Stella glanced over the rest of the garden – the neatly sown vegetable plots free of weeds; the bamboo stakes standing in straight rows, like soldiers marching over the earth; and the line of dense mirror bush that protected the plants from sea spray.

By the rainwater tank, she paused, knocking on the upper rungs till she heard the change of tone that marked the water level. There was plenty there. If it had been low she'd have turned on the pump to fill it from the backup tank. While her father was away she felt responsible for dealing with things like this. She checked the fences as well, looking for loose palings, and kept an eye out for snakes in the garden. 'Take care of your mother,' William often said as he prepared to set out to sea. As though the dangers he faced – the changing currents and shifting sandbanks, rogue waves and sudden squalls – were nothing compared to the hazards of remaining at home.

As she pulled off her boots at the side door, Stella peered in through the window. She could see her mother's head bent over a mixing bowl. The woman's thick blonde hair was tied back in a low ponytail – as it always was in the kitchen. Grace worried that a loose hair might find its way into her cooking. As she stirred and poured, her hands often rose up, checking that her hair was in place.

When Stella padded inside, barefoot, Grace looked up. She was still for a second, as if startled from a dream. Then she smiled.

'Hello, darling. Did you have a nice ride?'

'Yes, thank you,' Stella replied.

'You've got the shopping. Good.'

'There was no stewing steak,' Stella warned.

Grace nodded, but made no comment. She looked distracted. 'Was there any mail?' she asked after a short silence.

Stella lifted the parcel out of the carton. As she did so she saw a look of relief, mixed with pleasure, pass briefly over her mother's face. Whatever Daniel had done wrong, Stella realised, Grace still cared about him.

Grace returned to her cooking. Stella wanted to ask her about Daniel straight out, but she knew it would be pointless. Grace had already told her that William did not want the matter discussed. Stella's parents believed in the importance of presenting a united front – unlike Jamie's mum and dad, who argued in front of their children even with visitors present. Stella suspected the rest of Grace's family might be involved, somehow, with the cloud that hung over Daniel. But Grace wouldn't say much about any of them either. If Stella asked questions concerning them, Grace always answered very vaguely. She talked about how unhelpful it was to come to a new country as a migrant and then spend your time looking back to a life that you'd left behind.

'What are you making?' Stella asked.

Grace pointed a floury finger towards the recipe book. Stella glanced over the page at which it lay open – reading neat, sloping handwriting in blue ink.

Cousin Elizabeth's Special Pudding.

It was a heavy, sweet cake that William particularly liked. Grace must have made it hundreds of times before, but she still checked the recipe before preparing each ingredient. Stella watched as the woman stirred an egg into the flour. Grace was using her favourite spoon – an old serving spoon with a coat of arms engraved on the handle. It had come from the Fishermen's Association op shop, Stella assumed – the rest of the cutlery in the house was part of a matching set, decorated with a simple scalloped edge. Stella watched Grace add a second egg. The careful way she did it made the girl feel safe, somehow. If Grace let small changes creep in, she suspected things would turn slowly wrong. And they'd know, she felt sure – all those women whose recipes had been collected in the book. Great Aunt Cecilia, Aunt Eliza, Granny, Josephine, Aunt Jane. And, of course, William's poor dead mother, whose recipes bore the title 'My Own . . .'

Though far away or dead, they would know.

'You must be hungry.' Grace waved a hand towards a fruit loaf cooling on a rack at the other end of the table. 'It's a bit overcooked, I think, but it should be all right. Shall I cut you a slice?'

Stella glanced at the loaf, which was a perfect honey-gold tone. 'I'll put this under the tree first.'

She undid the parcel, removing the brown covering – aware of Grace eyeing the prettily wrapped gift as it emerged.

'I wonder what it is this year,' Grace said.

Stella shrugged. Folding the brown paper into a neat square, she pushed it into one of the kitchen drawers, where it joined Grace's collection of loose pieces of string and old paper bags.

With the tissue-shrouded angel cradled in her arm, she walked down the hallway – entering the long room that made up most of the back half of the house. It had a bank of tall windows that ran right along the wall, opening the place to the sea. The water was so close that if you were sitting down you could see no land at all. You could be on a ship, if the ground were not so steady. The Birchmores called it 'the sea room'. They ate their meals in here – sitting around one end of a mahogany dining table; or they retired to the couch and armchairs grouped near the fireplace, to read, talk, sew or watch television.

The Christmas tree had been set up in one corner of the sitting area, as it was each year. It was a small plantation pine – a perfect triangle shape, and not too tall. The trunk was wedged in a bucket of sand topped with ocean pebbles. Finely crafted decorations brought over from England dotted the foliage. They were old, their sparkle tarnished, but they reminded William of his childhood. Stella had once tried adding decorations that she'd made at school, but they just spoiled the look of the others.

Stella breathed the fresh green smell of the pine needles as she knelt to place Daniel's package beneath the spreading limbs. The Birchmores didn't put their own gifts to one another under the tree until Christmas morning, so there were only a few presents already there. Aunt Jane's was placed most prominently – she always sent a book, elaborately wrapped in expensive paper and tied with velvet ribbon. Standing at a respectful distance from it was the tin of toffees given each year by the fish factory to the fishermen's wives. Then there was a soft bundle Laura had dropped round before going away; a small box from Jamie's mother, Pauline; and one large present wrapped in bright striped paper. 'To Stella from Jamie,' the tag on this last one said. Stella looked at the size and shape of it, trying to guess at its contents. Jamie always bought her something special. Pauline helped him choose it, Stella suspected – but he used his own money, earned by cleaning at the fish factory on Saturdays. Looking at the gift, Stella was torn between being touched by Jamie's generosity and feeling guilty. She was not allowed to get a job, and William didn't see the need for her to have an allowance – he preferred to pay for anything that he could see his daughter needed. This year Stella had made Jamie a small table for his bedroom from wood she'd found on the beach. He'd appreciate it because she'd made it, but Stella knew he really preferred neat, new things with straight edges. She wished she'd been able to buy him a proper gift from a shop.

Stella moved Jamie's present aside and tucked the wrapped angel in behind the toffee tin. She did not want to think of how, in the morning, the carving would have to be unwrapped. The niche angel was made of stone – able to withstand rain, sun and creeping moss – but still, Stella did not like to think of her laid out, exposed, under William's cool gaze.

Over by the window, Stella stood with her head resting against the glass. From here she could look straight down onto the foreshore. A flash of red caught her eye amongst the boulders. Focusing more closely, she could see that it was the remains of a buoy. Nearby was the sole of a rubber thong, tangled in weed. There had been a late spring storm, Stella recalled, about a week ago. With the end of year exams and then the leavers' dinner she'd not had time to go down to the beach and see what the waves had brought in. Now the tide was just right – almost at its lowest point. She pictured treasures scattered along the shorelines, laid out there, just for her . . .

She returned to the kitchen, leaning in from the door to speak to her mother. 'If I set the table now, and get everything ready, can I go to the coves?' she asked.

Grace glanced up, and then looked out through the kitchen window towards the sea. Her eyes were clouded with anxiety. 'I don't think that's a good idea,' she said. 'William will be coming in. He'll expect you to be at the wharf.'

'I'll keep a look out for him,' Stella promised. 'I'll still be able to see from up there.'

As she spoke, she followed Grace's gaze – looking to the south and checking the distant sea for any sign of the *Lady Tirian*. The two never knew when to expect the fisherman's return. He radioed ahead to the factory with an estimated time of arrival so that the staff would know when to expect his fish – but his messages could not be passed on to Grace because the Birchmores had no phone. William believed the benefits of being able to receive useful communication were outweighed by the disadvantages of having the family's privacy invaded by people calling for no good reason. So, when William was out fishing, Stella and Grace were used to living with one eye on the sea, guessing from the weather what day or time the man might return.

'I don't want you to miss him,' Grace said.

Her firm tone seemed to accentuate her English accent. The finely formed words raised a barrier that felt – to Stella – impenetrable. She fought to control her frustration. She was sixteen years old, after all – not a child needing permission for every little thing.

'I can be back here in half an hour,' Stella reasoned, 'that's all it takes by my track. Then it's just twenty minutes to the wharf.'

Grace looked unconvinced. 'Can't you just go somewhere nearby?'

Stella shook her head. The coves were by far the best place to go after a storm. There was something about the way the rocks worked with the currents, or perhaps it was the angle of the little bays. Whatever it was, Stella always found more things washed up there than she did anywhere else. And almost no one but she ever went there. You could get close to the coves by car, but it was a roundabout route from Halfmoon Bay, and when you got there the road met a dead-end. People just didn't bother to head up that way unless they were cutting firewood or shooting.

'He won't be back early,' Stella said. 'Look at the day.' She waved an arm towards the window – the clear sky and flat sea.

Grace eyed her uncertainly. She began to knead a lump of dough she'd laid out on a scattering of flour, pushing at it cautiously, her eyes fixed on her hands as though the task demanded all her attention. Stella watched her in silence. The pale mixture, lightly tinged with brown, was a perfect match for her mother's freckled skin.

'Use the green tablecloth,' the woman said finally. 'And the Sunday plates.'

Stella smiled. 'Thanks.' She turned away slowly, knowing there would be more instructions to come.

'And tidy up in there.'

Stella knew what Grace meant by this. Put the two loose cushions side by side on the couch. Smooth the protective cloths that were draped over the armrests. Make sure the curtains, bunched up at each side of the windows, hung in straight folds. And – of greatest importance – dust the sideboard, making sure not to miss any of the little nooks and ledges. The piece of antique furniture was William's most precious possession: it had belonged to his Aunt Jane, and to her mother before her. Whenever he returned home he went went straight to the sideboard to put down the logbook he brought in from the *Lady Tirian*. As he did so, he always glanced around the room. Stella understood that he liked to see everything in its right place. Her father worked hard out at sea. The least he should be able to expect was to return home to a house that was peaceful, tidy and clean.

Leaving her bike in the bushes, out of sight of the road, Stella picked her way through the low-growing heath to the place where her hidden track began. The path started with a short section that Stella had cut for herself, but then it joined a wallaby trail – a narrow band of earth worn free of vegetation by the passage of countless little feet. The first trail joined another, which then led all the way to the edge of the she-oak forest.

Stella bowed her head as she stepped in under the first tree. She had no idea why it was called a she-oak – it was nothing like William's English oak. Instead of leaves it had long draping fronds, similar to over-sized pine needles, but with a surface that was less smooth. They were her favourite trees. From the outside the canopies looked like hairy heads with uncut fringes. From the inside they were like tents left behind by nomads. The floors were thickly carpeted with dropped needles, laid down over centuries. They crunched lightly under Stella's boots as she walked.

Reaching the edge of the forest, she pushed out through the last veil of fronds. As the needles brushed past her cheeks she saw the shoreline spread out in front of her. Huge pale boulders edged the land – a necklace of giant beads. She looked along the chain of rocks to a small headland. Beyond it she could see the first of the white beaches. Hidden from view were another three of them – each a perfect crescent moon. Her secret coves.

Lured by the sight of seaweed scattered on the beach, Stella ran down over the rocks, jumping expertly from one boulder to the next. Within minutes she was down on the sand – walking along, her eyes trained on the tideline.

She paused to bend over the dark body of a seabird. It lay on the sand, tangled in seaweed. Something had already eaten the eyes, leaving small blank hollows; the claws were curled as if still grasping at some last hope of survival. Stella looked up, turning towards the line of islands on the horizon. Out there, in one of the rookeries, would be the bird's family burrow. A furry-feathered baby would be sheltering there. At dusk, the loyal mate would return. Stella imagined the two of them waiting for the lost bird to come home and make the triangle complete – mother, father, baby. She tipped the carcass over with the toe of her boot. On the underside, lice crawled in the feathers.

Halfway along the beach she picked up a piece of wood. It was a section of deck timber. She could see it had been tumbled around in the sea for years – its corners were worn off and its edges smoothed. As she walked on she used her sheath knife to pick at the paintwork. Beneath a blue layer she found orange. Under that was dark green. Stella studied the colours, guessing at the life story of the boat. Was blue the colour of its end, she wondered? Was it smashed up now, and sunk? Or had the deck simply been renewed, and the old planks tossed away? She'd never know. That was what she loved about these walks along the edge of the sea. Each thing she found told a story – several stories – and all had a chance of being true.

Stella peered ahead along the rest of the beach. The sand was bare from here on, without even clumps of seaweed to offer the hope of hidden treasure. She continued towards the small rocky headland that cut off this little cove from the next. The day's find had been disappointing so far, but she had not given up hope yet. The beach she was aiming for was narrower, with a deep channel running in from the sea to meet the outlet of a freshwater creek. Anything that found its way in there became trapped. Bottles, buoys, ropes and driftwood always collected where the creek met the sand at low tide. It was here that Stella had made some of her best discoveries.

She'd once found a high-heeled shoe – lost, she guessed, from the deck of one of the luxury yachts that occasionally sailed into Halfmoon Bay. The shoe was pink, with thin straps and gold buckles and a label marked 'Made in Milan'. She'd tried the shoe on – standing there in her bikini, the heel sinking deep into the sand. The angle of her foot made her leg, honey-brown from the sun, appear long and elegant. The leg of a princess dressing for a ball. Or Cinderella, perhaps, as there was only one shoe . . . Another time, Stella had found a bamboo pipe with Chinese lettering down one side. These treasures were displayed – along with the rest of her collection of artefacts – on a panel of driftwood she'd nailed together last summer. It was about the size of a farm gate, but higher, and objects were tied onto it with pieces of salvaged rope. Stella called it her Sea Wall. It looked good, leaning up against the side of the shed. But there were lots of bare spaces on the frame, still waiting to be filled.

Reaching the jumbled boulders of the headland, Stella quickened her step, conscious of the time passing. But the sky was still clear. She pictured William winching in his pots, counting the crays as the water drained away.

Music came to her first. Drifting on the breeze, entwined with birdsong. She stopped to listen, tilting her head. Someone was here! With a radio turned up loud . . . She frowned. Her day – her place – had been invaded. As soon as she'd found out who it was, she decided, she'd give up on her search and go home.

She hurried on towards the source of the music, hopping from rock to rock and then turning inland to avoid a crevice too wide to jump. As the music grew stronger she picked out the voice of a man, backed by a guitar. He was half singing, half talking. It didn't sound like the kind of music they played on the radio.

Climbing round the tall stones that marked the high point of the headland, she peered down into the next cove. A she-oak thicket fractured the view of the beach, but between the drooping branches she could see splashes of bright colour. Yellow. Orange. Purple. She took a few steps on, and then jolted to a stop, staring down.

The sand was littered with clothes, boxes, ropes, sailcloth – spread everywhere . . .

It was a wreck, Stella realised. Alarm spiked through her body as she scrambled down towards it. She remembered television dramas where radios played on after cars had crashed and no one was left alive to listen. There could be drowned people down there, she told herself, lying amongst the wreckage, their eyes already gone . . .

Then she saw a mast – a dark line cutting the sky, straight and tall.

She slid to a stop, leaning to get a wider view. There was a yacht in the channel. A rope ran from its bow, out across the sands to the thick trunk of a gum tree growing near the creek. It was tied up there. Moored.

Stella scanned the hull, the cabin, the rigging. It was an ocean-going yacht, at least thirty feet long – perhaps forty. An old-style vessel made of wood – the kind William approved of. Not one of the flashy fibreglass ones with cocktail bars and swivel chairs on deck. Two flags flew from the mast, rippling out in the sea breeze: a plain yellow one, and an Australian flag.

There was no sign of any crew.

Stella eased herself closer. She could see now that the things on the sand had not just been tossed there – they'd been laid out to dry in the sun. An orange lifejacket. Yellow oilskins, top and bottom. Blue sleeping bag, unzipped. T-shirt. Jumper . . .

They were the belongings of a solo sailor, Stella guessed – there was only one of most things. The jacket was large enough for a man, but there were several long pieces of cloth printed with bright patterns – surely belonging to a woman.

Stella began to climb down over the rocks towards the beach. Prickly bushes grew in the cracks between the boulders and they scratched her legs as she pushed her way ahead. She knew she had to see who was here. The yacht had been through some bad weather – seas that had doused everything in salt. The sailor may not know how close they were to a port, and they may need supplies, a doctor – anything . . .

Reaching the point where she could jump down onto the sand, Stella paused, looking across to the yacht. Should she call out from here, she wondered. Or walk closer and wait for someone to come up on deck?

Then she heard, close behind her, a rustle in the bushes. Fear shot through her. In a flash she saw her mother's face, and heard her warning words. 'You shouldn't be off on your own, a girl of your age. You never know who might be about . . .'

Her hand moved to the knife at her hip. She turned around – and then froze. On a flat rock, level with her face, lay a black snake. She glimpsed the flicking tongue as the head rose, ready to strike.

She yelled out, jumping away. She fell onto the sand and scrabbled backwards on hands and feet. The snake came after her, looping over an exposed tree-root, then sliding down the rock.

Stella got to her feet and ran. A voice inside her said the creature was just taking its usual path to the creek for a drink. But sometimes, Stella knew, tiger snakes chased you, bit you – and you died from the venom.

After a few seconds, Stella looked back over her shoulder – just in time to see the snake slide into a crevice and disappear. She slowed to a halt and took a breath to calm herself. Then she turned to face the yacht.

There was a figure standing on the deck, near the entrance to the cabin, looking straight at her. It was clear from the way the person stood – hands spread open – that they were as surprised to see Stella as she had been to find a yacht moored in her cove.

There seemed no choice now but for her to approach the stranger.

Stella walked tall with her head held high – wanting to suggest that this was her domain. As she came nearer, she focused on the yacht, snatching only glimpses of the sailor. Tall, long-limbed. Hair tied back. The face strong, even-featured. Faded denim shirt, sleeves rolled to the elbows.

'Are you all right?'

A man's voice came to her.

She kept walking on, ignoring the image of Grace's face warning her away. She was not afraid. There was the knife at her hip. She was strong, and fast.

Stella strode across the sand and up onto the rocks closest to the yacht.

'I just came to see if you need any help,' she called back.

The music was loud now, competing with her words.

The man reached back into his cabin and the song faded. Then he moved to the side of the boat, jumped down onto a rock that stuck out of the water nearby, and waded over to where Stella stood.

She watched him approach. The frayed ends of his shorts dipped in the sea as he walked. Loose strands of salt-sticky hair hung down over a face that was deeply tanned. He was young, Stella realised – at most just a few years older than she was. More a boy than a man. She looked past him towards the cabin. Surely he was too young to be travelling alone – and in a big, valuable boat like this one . . .

He came to stand near her. Water dripped from his shorts.

'What was wrong back there?' The man – the boy – gestured to the place where Stella had scrambled down onto the beach.

'A snake chased me,' Stella said.

He raised his eyebrows. 'Bloody hell. No wonder you jumped.'

Their eyes met. At the same time, they both laughed. The warm sound seemed to fill the air between them. Stella saw the boy watching her face. His eyes were green, flecked with blue like the sea rippling over white sand.

They were quiet, then. The music was still playing, drifting softly around them, blending with the lap of the waves. Stella caught the words of the song – something about the wind . . .

'Bob Dylan,' the boy said.

Stella nodded. 'I'm Stella.'

The stranger looked puzzled, then he laughed again. 'No – that's who's singing,' he explained. 'My name's Zeph.'

Stella looked down at her boots, scuffing the sand. Then she lifted her sleeve to wipe her nose. 'What are you doing tied up in here?'

As she spoke, she moved her gaze slowly over the yacht. It was a well-kept vessel. Ropes were coiled neatly on the foredeck. The hull looked to be free of weed near the waterline. The woodwork gleamed with fresh varnish. Her eyes moved up the mast with its shining fittings. She stopped on the Australian flag, puzzled by the look of the Southern Cross. The minor stars were missing. It was not a proper flag, she realised then – rather, it was a rough replica, hand-painted in red and blue onto white sailcloth.

'I got caught in a storm,' said Zeph. 'The self-steering gear was damaged. Everything got pretty wet. Came in here to sort myself out.'

He spoke slowly, almost lazily. There was something unusual about the way he framed his words. He didn't speak like an American, or someone from England, or anywhere else that Stella could name. It took her a few seconds to work out that he had no accent at all. Or perhaps it was a blend of many, all rolled in together.

'Haven't you got charts?' Stella asked. 'There's a port not far from here. Halfmoon Bay. You could have gone in there.' His quiet manner made her want to keep talking. 'There's a pub, a shop – you can get take-away food – a telephone . . .'

'But I wanted to come in here,' Zeph said. 'I prefer to be on my own.'

Stella fell silent. She liked being on her own, too. When she walked along a beach with Laura she resented having to hold one side of an endless conversation, instead of just looking, thinking . . .

'And it's beautiful,' Zeph added.

He waved one arm, taking in the sea, rocks, sky. Stella saw the scene through his eyes. The painter's colours: milky-grey rocks daubed with orange lichen; white sand washed by a sea that was turquoise in the shallows then deepened to an inky purple in the channel. She felt a stirring of pride, as if all that they could see was the work of her own hand.

'No one comes here,' she said. 'Only me. I made my own track in.'

Zeph nodded. 'I haven't seen anyone else – on land or sea . . .'

'How long have you been here?' Stella asked.

'A couple of days. I've been drying out the cabin. Washing stuff in the creek – getting it dry. Making repairs. We're nearly back in order now.'

Stella glanced across to the cabin again. 'Where are the others?'

'There's just me,' Zeph replied. 'And Carla, the cat – inside, sleeping as usual.' He grinned. 'And *Tailwind*, the boat. I think of them as people, I guess. I spend so much time with just them.'

His smile lingered on his face, curling the corners of his lips. He could have been a child talking about his toys. Stella wanted to ask if he wasn't lonely, with just a cat and a boat for company. And what it had been like, in the storm. Was he afraid, on his own? But she knew better than to ask such personal questions of someone she did not know.

'Where are you from?' she asked.

Zeph screwed up his eyes as he followed the flight of a seagull past the face of the sun. 'Hard to say.'

Stella stared at him. Aside from asking someone's name, she couldn't think of a more straightforward question.

'I was born in Goa – India. I've lived in lots of places. Right now, I live . . . here.'

His gaze travelled over the beach. His possessions, dotted everywhere, seemed to prove the truth of his words.

Stella smiled. Imagine if this were really true, she thought – that he had no home but one that kept moving around . . .

'Are you a local?' Zeph asked.

'Yes,' Stella answered. 'Well, no. Not really. My parents came from England when I was only a baby. So I've lived here most of my life. But they say, round here, before a family really belongs you have to have a baby born in the hospital and someone buried in the cemetery.' She let her voice trail off. She'd said these very words before – but here, now, they sounded quaint and old-fashioned. 'I'm leaving soon anyway,' she added. 'I'm going away to finish school. You can only go up to Grade 10 in St Louis – that's our nearest town. I'll be moving to Hobart in February. All my friends are going, too.'

Suddenly, a whistling sound came from the direction of the yacht.

'Kettle's boiling,' Zeph said. 'I'll make us some chai.'

Stella eyed him uncertainly. He said 'us' so easily, as if they were friends.

'I've got two cups,' he added.

'I should go, though.' As Stella spoke, she scanned the sea. She knew William would be working near the islands to the south, yet she could not help imagining him appearing here – finding her chatting to a stranger, far from home . . .

'No, please,' Zeph responded. 'Stay.'

As she turned back to his face, Stella glimpsed something in his eyes – a bleakness, unveiled only for an instant. How long had he been at sea, she wondered, with no one to talk to?

'Okay,' she agreed.

It was, after all, only polite to accept a refreshment when offered.

Left alone on the sand, Stella wandered amongst Zeph's things – displayed on the beach like exhibits in a museum. The printed cloths, she guessed, were Indian – or from some other foreign place where he'd been. There were a few socks, but not many of them seemed to have matching pairs. Laid out on a rock were some books, their damp-curled pages opened to the sun. Moving closer, Stella saw several children's picture books. She bent over a coloured illustration of a fairy – a delicate creature with fine hair and shimmery wings. The text was not in English. Looking at it carefully,

Stella recognised a few words from the label on the bottom of Daniel's 'Edelweiss' music box. German . . .

Turning to another rock, she saw more books. One might have been Indian from the drawing on the cover. Pink dye from the jacket had bled down through the pages. Beside it lay a fat novel. The title jumped out at her. *Anna Karenina*. It was Grace's favourite book. Stella loved it, too. She was not sure why. The heroine's life was so tragic, yet the reader still envied her. The extraordinary love that she found – even when everything was lost as a result – seemed enough to make up for all the pain.

She heard Zeph coming back, the dry sand squeaking under his feet as he walked. He handed her a blue pottery cup speckled with chips. It was wet on the outside from being rinsed but not dried. A scent rose up in the steam.

Zeph closed his eyes and took a sip from his own matching cup. 'I've got to make the most of this. I used up the last of my supply.'

They sat down on a rock, side by side. Stella stretched her legs out beside Zeph's. The fine hairs on her legs were already beginning to turn gold, bleached by sun and salt. Her toenails, freshly painted for the leavers' dinner, were shiny pink. Zeph's legs were a deeper brown. His feet looked tough, accustomed to being bare and cold.

Stella sipped the pale honey-coloured brew. The first taste was salty from the seawater on the rim, but the second was spicy and sweet.

'What is it?' she asked.

'Cardamom, cinnamon – and black tea, of course. Then there's Bakti's secret ingredient: vanilla. It's not traditional, but she's always made it that way, ever since I can remember.'

'Bakti?' Stella repeated the name. It sounded awkward on her lips, made of two sounds that didn't fit together.

'My mother,' Zeph explained. 'She sends me packages of chai, if she knows where I'm headed. I try and let her know.' His tone was casual, as if he were not a teenager but an adult, living his own life.

'Tomorrow's Christmas,' Stella said suddenly. 'You won't be with her!'

'No,' Zeph said. 'I haven't been with her at Christmas for years.' He sounded neither sad nor pleased. It was just a fact.

'But what will you do?' Stella asked. 'You should . . . go to the pub in Halfmoon Bay. Just sail round there for the day. They do a three-course turkey roast.'

'I've got a tin of fruit saved up,' Zeph said. 'And the last of my rice. I'll see if I can catch a fish for a treat. Carla would like that, too.'

Stella glanced at his face. She sensed that behind his brave tone he was lonely. But perhaps it was just that she couldn't imagine how a person would not be.

'You won't get much on a line,' Stella said. 'Have you got a spear?'

Zeph shook his head. 'Not any more. Had to swap it for mooring fees in Bali.'

'You must have a knife?' Stella suggested.

He looked down at her sheath knife. 'I've got one just like that.'

Stella blushed, remembering how – just a short while ago – she'd been ready to use it. 'Then get some abalone. You don't even need goggles at low tide. You can see them in the gullies – over there.' She pointed to the rocks on the other side of the yacht.

She turned back to Zeph. He wasn't watching to see where the abalone could be found. He was looking at her, his eyes travelling over her face, her hair, her body. He studied her openly, as if he had as much right to look at Stella as he had to enjoy the sea, the sky, or a pretty shell lying on the sand.

Stella looked down into her cup. Under his gaze she felt an impulse to toss back her hair from her face and to bite her lips, making them look a deeper red. Her shirt, she knew, hung open, showing off Laura's old bikini – the low-cut, skimpy top that Stella was only allowed to use as underwear.

A tiny petal floated on the surface of the tea. Caught in a small eddy, it turned slowly round and round. Stella breathed the fragrant steam. She thought of the mother, Bakti, far away, mixing spices and tea, and packaging it in plastic bags for her son. She pictured a fine-boned woman with long dark hair and a red spot on her forehead.

'You don't look part-Indian,' she said, looking up at Zeph.

'I'm not, as far as I know,' Zeph replied. 'Bakti was the name Mum took when she joined the ashram. She's French. And my father . . . Well, we don't know much about him. But she thinks he was an Englishman.'

Stella picked at a chip on the side of her cup as she pieced together the meaning of his words. She wished she'd anticipated where her comment might lead. Surely it was painful, embarrassing, for him to have to tell her this.

'I'm sorry, I didn't mean to – ask about that,' she said.

Zeph shrugged. He didn't seem upset. He just looked out over the water. Stella saw him tracing the outlines of the islands as she so often did.

The stillness grew between them, broken only by the movement of hands and cups, the small sipping sounds. It was a comfortable quiet, though, as if they were not strangers but old friends reunited after years apart. A Pacific gull glided past them, then wheeled out to sea, heading in the direction of Halfmoon Bay. The movement drew Stella's gaze away to the south. It was then that she saw it – just a mark on the ocean: a tiny cross shape above the dark bar of the hull. There was only one boat that looked like that and came in from that direction. The *Lady Tirian*.

'I have to go,' she said, standing up. 'I have to get back.'

Zeph looked at her in surprise. 'What's wrong?'

'My dad's coming in from sea. He's a cray fisherman. I have to be at the wharf when he arrives. I mean – I want to be there. I like to wait for him.'

Stella fell quiet. How could someone like Zeph, who sailed the seas alone, understand what it would mean for her to miss meeting her father – especially when it was holiday time and she had nothing important to do. She had to be there at the wharf, standing ready as the *Lady Tirian* came into view.

'Stella.' Zeph said her name slowly. She watched his lips. 'I have to ask you a favour.'

She waited, guessing. Did he need her to return with some supplies – more tea, and rice, perhaps? She could do that for him, but not tomorrow. Not Christmas Day . . .

'Don't tell anyone I'm here.'

Her hand tightened round the cup. She glanced across at the yacht, moored here, out of the way. And too valuable, surely, to be owned by someone only seventeen or eighteen years old . . .

'It's not a big deal,' Zeph said quickly, as if he could see the doubts forming in her mind. He pointed at the mast. 'I've got my quarantine flag up, in case anyone does see me. I'm not breaking the law. Well, I am – but only by giving you a cup of tea.'

Stella kept her eyes fixed on the *Lady Tirian*, far away.

'I could go into port. All my documents are in order – there's no problem there. It's just that I'm not staying long. I don't want to bother with customs and all that stuff – checking in with the police. Especially in the middle of Christmas.'

Stella nodded slowly. She understood how some people hated formalities. William liked to do things correctly, setting a good example by taking into account every by-law and regulation. But there were other fishermen who tore up letters they didn't like, and dropped council notices between the planks of the wharf and refused to license their guns. They drove Spinks mad. Thinking of the policeman, Stella almost smiled. She tried to imagine what he would have to say to Zeph. 'But where are your parents, young fellow? Bakti? What kind of name is that? India? Where?'

'I won't tell,' she said. 'I promise.' She handed him her cup. 'Thanks for the . . .'

'Chai,' he finished.

She hovered uncertainly. She wanted to ask if she should return. Would he still be here?

Would they ever meet again?

'Goodbye,' she said.

He nodded. 'Happy Christmas.'

'You, too.'

Then she was walking away. Leaving him behind. She pictured herself as she would appear to him – her hips swaying just a little with each step, her hair falling long and dark halfway down her back . . .

But she did not know if he was watching. She kept looking straight ahead. The singing still came from the cabin, a faint voice following her along the beach – then fading to nothing.

⤷

The Seafarers' Memorial was an ugly cream brick wall dotted with brass plaques. It stood right near the wharf, serving as a warning to all who set out in boats that this part of the coast was especially dangerous. William had explained to Stella why this was: there was not a single landmass to break the momentum of ocean swells all the way between here and faraway South America. There was just the vast Southern Ocean – home to the wildest stretches of water on the planet.

Stella sat at the far end of the wall, where there were, as yet, no engraved words – no names. Her legs ached from riding her bike. After leaving the coves she'd raced home to Grace, to let her mother know that she had seen the *Lady Tirian* coming in. Then she'd headed on to the wharf. The ride was mostly downhill, but still, it had been hard work. Now, at last, she was here . . .

She tried not to think of Zeph. He'd become too . . . big, she realised. Too important. For someone she might never see again. To distract herself, she glanced along the wall, scanning the plaques. There was a game she played: she had to recite all the epitaphs without missing any. Then everyone she loved – her parents and all her friends – would be safe forever.

The first plaques in the line had been placed there by the St Louis Historical Society. The brief notes, in letters of raised metal, bore witness to old tragedies. There was the captain's wife and her five children, who had all been drowned in sight of the shore. The entire crew of a cutter bound for South Africa, lost near Standaway Island. Then there were the wrecks of the *Birmingham*, the *Valiant*, and the barque *Enrico* . . .

Next came the more recent disasters – a cluster of plaques in the middle of the wall. They were more varied in size and shape, having been chosen by the grieving families, but the words had in common a sense of personal grief still raw.

James Maitland
Fisherman of Halfmoon Bay
Lost overboard from the Ellen Jay while setting a cray pot
'The Sea Giveth and the Sea Taketh Away'

Michael Maitland, father of James Maitland
Fisherman of Halfmoon Bay
Washed overboard from the Sandra Lee in terrible seas
'The Sea Showeth No Mercy'

David Grey
Fisherman of Halfmoon Bay
Son of Mary Grey (deceased)
'Taken by the Sea'

Stella paused on David Grey's plaque. Until recently there had always been fresh garden flowers here – lilies, roses and forget-me-nots tucked into decorative holes in the surrounding bricks. Stella could still see the last stalks and petals, dried up and dead. No one in Halfmoon Bay knew the woman who had brought the flowers, week after week. She never spoke to anyone. She just climbed out of her car, placed her flowers near the plaque and then drove away. When they stopped appearing, Laura said David Grey's true love had finally turned to another. But Stella believed she was dead.

Stella jumped off the wall and started across the car park towards the wharf. Then she paused, catching sight of a figure coming down from the shop and heading in the same direction. It was Jamie. Stella recognised him by the way he walked, up on the balls of his feet. And from his blue and white checked shirt. Stella had been with him in St Louis when he'd seen the shirt in the window of the agricultural store. It was smarter than the usual style of workshirt, having a button-down collar. Jamie had bought three of them the same, so that he would always be able to wear a shirt that he liked.

Stella veered left, slipping in behind the old whaling station, hoping she'd not been seen. Jamie would be able to tell, she felt sure, the instant he looked into her eyes, that her head was full of pictures, thoughts, dreams of Zeph. It didn't matter that they were crazy things, with no place in reality. They should not be there. Stella belonged to Jamie – everyone knew that. She'd belonged to him since as far back as she could remember, and maybe even before.

His parents – Brian and Pauline – had been the Birchmores' first friends when they arrived in Tasmania from England. Brian had taught William how to work the crayboat he'd bought from a retired fisherman in St Louis. In those days there had been plenty of crayfish to go around, and there was none of the competition between fishermen that had grown up more recently. Still, Brian had been generous with his knowledge, and William had appreciated his help. William had told Stella the story of how he'd been so impressed with Brian's honest, straightforward ways that he'd encouraged the two wives to make friends.

Pauline was as disorganised and impulsive as Grace was careful and neat. But, apparently, the differences between them were made up for by the fact that they were both first-time mothers with babies of nearly the same age. When William was home he used to drive his wife and daughter to Pauline's house – leaving them there while he went to do business at the fish factory or to keep other appointments. Grace and Pauline had cups of tea and chatted as they played with their babies.

From this early start, Stella and Jamie had grown up together – sharing everything from toys and clothes to chickenpox and birthday parties. The parts of their history that Stella didn't remember lived in her mind through the dozens of photographs Pauline had taken of the two children over the years. Stella had her favourite pinned on her bedroom wall. It had been snapped at one of Brian's barbecues. Stella and Jamie were eight years old, with matching smiles and the same teeth missing. They were holding identical buckets and spades, bought from the Halfmoon Store. Pauline had already had three more babies by then – all boys. They were crammed into the picture, clustered around their big brother and his friend. Grace was there as well – standing in the background, looking very neat beside all the scruffy children.

When she grew old enough to ride into town by herself, Stella started going to Jamie's place nearly every Saturday – leaving Grace behind at Seven Oaks, working in her garden. By then it was not just Stella's friendship with Jamie that drew her to Pauline's place. The girl enjoyed the noisy chaos of the growing household. She liked watching television and eating at the same time. She liked cooking in Pauline's untidy kitchen, safe in the knowledge that her own mess would never be noticed. And she liked the freedom that came from being in a house that was full of people.

When the summer months came, Pauline let Stella and Jamie go to the beach by themselves. She didn't follow them around as Grace would have done – warning them to look out for sharks and not to go out too deep. They swam and dived together all day – staying in the water until their skin was wrinkled and their toes and fingers numb. When they were hungry they took bites from the same soggy sandwiches, gritty with sand. They unzipped one another's wetsuits, freeing trapped hands from tight wet sleeves. They lay side by side in the sun, getting burned, and – days later – peeled long, papery strips of dead skin from each other's backs.

Their bodies were toys, then, or weapons – used for handstands and pin jumps, wrestling and aiming rocks.

When their bodies started to change – hers before his, her nipples becoming swollen and tender – they took no notice at first. Until, one summer – after a winter of being covered – they began hiding from each other, undressing behind trees or rocks. Their new bodies were secret now, unfamiliar to themselves as well as each other.

The first kisses had been games, played in groups. Spin the bottle on the sand, lips touching briefly, eyes closed . . . When the time came to make up couples – to move off in pairs and lie in the dunes – they'd first chosen other partners. But, eventually, they'd been drawn back together.

Now, they were girlfriend and boyfriend – and yet still best mates as well. Even as they kissed, they laughed at the idea of romance and mocked scenes of passion. That kind of thing was for strangers in TV soapies. Not for people who hunted crayfish together. Who hooked fingers into fish guts and ripped them out. The same fingers they used to explore the secrets of their grown-up bodies . . . Stella sucking in her belly to make room in the front of her jeans to let his hand in. Holding her breath so that he wouldn't stop. Leaning forward, her bra unclipped, so that her breasts hung free under her shirt.

They never took off their clothes. That was the unspoken rule. It meant Stella could go home and face William knowing that she was still a good girl. His good girl – returning to him safe and sound.

Stella peered over the ruined wall to see where Jamie was. He was standing down on the wharf now, looking intently into the distance. Stella followed the direction of his gaze – past the rocky island that sheltered the gulch, and out to the open sea. There, poking up from behind a pile of rocks daubed with white bird droppings, was the tip of the *Lady Tirian*'s mast.

She stumbled over the uneven ground as she ran towards a gap in the walls, and out into the car park.

Jamie turned to watch Stella as she hurried along the wharf. He grinned as she drew near. It was the same grin he'd always had, wider on one side. She smiled back – too quickly, she suspected, too brightly. But he didn't seem to notice.

'I'm meeting him, too,' he said. 'Thought I'd make myself useful.'

'That's good,' Stella responded. 'It's nearly five o'clock. They'll be wanting his fish unpacked as soon as possible.'

She looked across to the fish factory. She could see Sharon and Noel sitting in the sun near the entrance, sharing a can of beer, already in a holiday mood.

Jamie draped one arm over Stella's shoulder as they walked along the wharf. It felt heavy, pressing into her bones, and she made an excuse to pull away.

She headed to where a rusty fishing ketch was moored. The vessel's name – *Grand Lady* – was painted in flaky letters on the dented hull. Through the open door of the wheelhouse, Stella could see a tangled sleeping bag on the floor. Joe was living here again, she realised. He was not really allowed to – and Spinks issued warnings every now and then. But the old sailor's other dwelling – a disused boat-builder's shed out on the other side of the bay – had no kitchen or bedroom.

She followed Jamie on towards the far end of the wharf. They reached the place where *Cassandra* – Brian's cray boat – was moored. The boat looked neat enough, viewed on her own. But Stella knew that when the *Lady Tirian* came into port, *Cassandra* would instantly appear shabby.

Jamie walked past his father's boat without a glance and went to stand at the vacant mooring where the *Lady Tirian* would tie up.

Stella stood a little apart from him. She waited for William to appear – looking forward to the moment when he would see her standing there. He always waved, just once. Then he smiled as he came near, his eyes meeting hers. Even if the wharf was busy – the weather closing in and boats from other ports crowding in to take cover – Stella always felt, under his gaze, as though she were the only person standing there . . .

'Here she comes,' Jamie said.

The *Lady Tirian* glided into the gulch. The sun shone on the bright red and green paint of her hull, and on her bare wooden decks, scrubbed clean.

As the boat came near, Stella fixed her eyes on her father. He was in the wheelhouse – a steady, upright figure dressed in overalls of yellow oilskin. His hair stood up, stiff with salt. His face was ruddy, his eyes a deep bright blue. She felt a thrill of pride. He looked more like a good-looking actor playing the part of a hero seaman than a fisherman from the real world.

When William saw Stella, he lifted one hand. She smiled in return. She could see on his face that the trip had been a success – the catch good. He looked pleased, too, that there were two people there to meet him – a special Christmas welcome.

Stella moved forward, ready to catch the mooring rope. But Jamie was already there, in front of her – waiting with his hands outstretched. The boy caught the rope and placed its looped end carefully over the bollard. Stella ran her eye along the line to where the other end was knotted firmly to the *Lady Tirian*. She guessed her father had taught Jamie the same rule he'd taught her. Tie the rope to the boat, but never to the wharf. Make sure you can leave in a hurry . . .

When the boat was secure, Jamie gave the skipper a nod. William nodded back. Stella watched the exchange with a sudden stab of envy. The gesture was more intimate, she sensed, than the one-hand wave. More exclusive. A private salute between men.

William went into the wheelhouse and shut off the motor. Then he emerged with Grace's esky: the one she filled with food for him, for each voyage. It was a battle-worn box, its metal sides dented all over and the tartan print almost worn away. It swung light in his hand – all the pies and cakes and stews eaten up.

'Here you are, then,' he said, handing it to Stella. This was what he always did first thing when he arrived back. But with Jamie here, Stella found herself resenting the gesture. It linked her with Grace, with the task of staying at home and preparing provisions – as though Stella had no place on the *Lady Tirian*. When, in fact, every holiday since she'd been old enough to be useful she'd gone out with William, working in all weather, long and hard. She could chart a course to Standaway Island and back without putting the vessel up on the sands. She'd scraped and varnished and painted the pine timbers. And she'd worked on the diesel engine with William so many times that she knew even before being asked which tool he would need next. 'She's as good as a young fella,' Joe had said once. And her father had agreed.

William leaned over to Stella again – this time to hand her a bucket of fish and a small foil-wrapped package.

'Take these to Joe,' he said. 'He'll be glad of a good meal.'

This was another of Stella's tasks – giving away any of Grace's food that was left over at the end of the voyage, along with any good eating fish that William had caught in the bait trap. Seafood was never brought home to Seven Oaks. William didn't like the taste of it, or even the smell of it cooking.

Stella heard William and Jamie talking together as she crossed the wharf to the old ketch. She strode up the gangplank, dumped the bucket and the cake inside the wheelhouse, and then returned to the place where the *Lady Tirian* was moored.

A heap of wet-weather gear now sat on the wharf beside the esky. Jamie had joined William on board – the two were standing by the piles of pots on the foredeck. Stella waited for them to notice her, but they appeared to be deep in conversation. Finally, she gathered up the gear with one arm, picked up the esky with the other, and walked away. The esky bumped against her leg as she strode along the wharf and up towards the car park – where William's ute was waiting under a tree.

Wrenching open the passenger door, she shoved the esky in onto the seat. She dumped the wet-weather gear beside it. Then she rested her elbows on the faded roof, avoiding the seagull droppings, and looked down at the *Lady Tirian*.

Jamie and William stood side by side, peering into the fish well. They both had their legs braced apart, as if – even moored here in the gulch – they wanted to be prepared to ride a sudden swell. As Stella watched, William put out his arm and touched Jamie's shoulder. The boy laughed, his teeth showing white against his tanned face; and the older man joined in.

Stella turned away. She pushed shut the door of the ute, scattering fragments of rust onto the ground – then she walked back past the memorial to find her bike.

Stella settled back into the armchair. The curtains were drawn over the sea-room windows, and the air still carried the comforting smell of roast lamb. William was writing at his desk – a fold-down section of Aunt Jane's sideboard. His pencil made small scratchy sounds as he copied out notes from his fisherman's log into a thick hardbacked notebook. Grace was sitting near the fireplace with its display of Christmas pinecones. She was darning her husband's favourite navy blue jumper. Her head was bent low over her work, and a small frown of concentration marked her face. It was a peaceful scene – the quiet broken only by the sea murmuring outside, and the drone of radio voices coming from the kitchen.

A worn copy of *Anna Karenina* lay open on Stella's knee. She scanned the long list of Russian names and titles printed in the front, refreshing her memory of the characters – working out who belonged to who, and where they came from . . .

After a while she gave up on the complex genealogies. Her gaze wandered back across the room, settling on William. He turned his head from side to side as he shifted his attention from one book to another. When he was at sea he recorded all the information in his log that the authorities required – the number of fish caught, the location of the pots, the total weight of the catch. He also wrote down notes of his own, based on his weather observations. He liked to keep track of wind direction, tides, wave action, clouds, air temperature. The mysteries of the sea and sky were a constant challenge to him. Knowledge is power, he sometimes said. And William knew so much about the local weather patterns that people often asked him for forecasts. Fishermen would listen intently to his detailed predictions. Stella had heard people say that if not for the way he spoke – his round English vowels – you would think William had been born here.

After each voyage, William brought the official log back to the house with him. In the evening he transferred all the information he'd gathered into his own notebook, kept safely here in the locked drawer of the sideboard. The big blue book offered more room for his comments. Stella sometimes stood beside him, reading them. His phrases were longer and more detailed.

Cumulus cloud, drifting to the northeast – common at this time of the year. Rain gauge showed one and a half.

He wrote about sightings of dolphins, whales and seabirds. They were a part of the puzzle, he explained to Stella. If you kept notes for long enough, about anything, a pattern might emerge.

At dawn, a family of dolphins passed to the starboard side, just off Standaway Island.

I was followed by an albatross. Not the usual local species – a Wanderer.

Sitting forward in the armchair, Stella watched the way William's work-toughened hands cradled his pencil as he wrote. She pictured his neat, even writing stretching out across the page. It reminded her of how careful and competent her father was in everything he did. This was what attracted Jamie to him, she knew. Even though Stella had felt excluded down at the wharf, she could not blame her boyfriend for wanting to take her place. When you were with William, you felt important – as though all the extra care that he took was somehow because of you . . . You felt safe in his presence. There was something about the way he spoke – his words measured out slowly and evenly, each one offered as a gift. And his steady movements. Even in a storm, he never started shouting and running around. He was always in control.

Stella stood up and wandered across to the window. It was dark outside, but she could just see the white foam of the waves breaking against the rocks.

She watched their constant movement. Night and day, they kept rolling in from the south. She liked to think of them as being the same waves – or perhaps children of the same waves – that had rocked icebergs and brushed the backs of giant whales.

The same waves that had brought a stranger here. A boy in a boat, hiding in Stella's cove . . .

She pictured Zeph sheltering inside his cabin – lying in his blue sleeping bag, unzipped in the warmth, showing its yellow lining. Reading *Anna Karenina* by the light of a candle. Wearing the T-shirt with 'Bali' printed on the front . . . The picture surprised Stella with its detail. She hadn't realised how much she'd noticed about Zeph's possessions spread out along the beach. She wondered what he'd been eating while Grace had served up 'My Own Roast Lamb with Honey', followed by 'Aunt Jane's Half-hour Pudding'. Had he opened a tin of something, or cooked a handful of rice? Stella wished she'd had a cake, or something, to leave with Zeph. She hoped he'd caught a fish, somehow. It had not been all that helpful of her – showing him where to find abalone, without telling him how to prepare them.

Was he thinking of her? Stella wondered. Hoping she'd find a way to get back to him, perhaps even tomorrow?

She laughed at herself. If he gave a second thought to the girl who had disturbed him today, she knew it would only be to worry about whether she would keep her promise, and tell no one that he was there.

William put down his pencil and stood up. Stella heard the delicate tinkle of fine crystal as he took some long-stemmed sherry glasses out of the sideboard cupboard.

'Time for a Christmas drink,' he announced. He filled a glass with golden liquid and handed it to Grace. Then he brought a second one over to Stella. She looked at it in surprise. She'd only ever been given a tiny serving of sherry, but this glass was full to the brim.

'You're sixteen now,' William said generously. He looked across to

Grace, as if the woman had uttered an objection. 'If they can learn to drink sensibly, at home – it's the best approach. And I know we can trust her to do the right thing.'

He smiled down at Stella. As she felt his warm gaze resting on her, she could not help imagining what he would think if he had seen her with Zeph today. Alone, in an isolated place, with a boy that no one knew. When he turned away, she licked a drip that was running down the outside of her glass.

'Happy Christmas!' William held up his drink.

Stella and Grace followed suit, repeating his words in unison. Then quiet settled again over the room. From the radio in the kitchen came the distant sound of a choir singing. The words floated in the air, disembodied, like voices of angels coming out of the dark.

'Away in a manger, no crib for a bed, the little lord Jesus laid down his sweet head . . .'

The words drew Stella's eyes across to where the nativity set was laid out on the mantelpiece – sharing pride of place with Aunt Jane's large, gilt-edged Christmas card. The wise men, shepherds, angels and animals were in two little groups, with a space between them. Joseph stood there, upright and strong. Mary knelt by his side, her face serene and calm. In front of her was the manger with the little baby Jesus, wrapped in swaddling clothes, waving bare chubby arms. Stella smiled at the scene. When she'd been younger she'd thought the holy family was a reflection of her own. Father, mother and one precious child.

CHAPTER FOUR

A bulging shoulder bag bumped against Stella's hips as she jumped from rock to rock. She was breathless and sweat trickled down her back, but she didn't allow herself to pause. At the most she had an hour and a half before she should be back at Seven Oaks. She pictured William and Grace returning home and finding her note on the door. '*Feeling better*,' it read. '*Gone for a walk to get some fresh air*.' The thought of the words, spelled out so clearly, made her feel both nervous and guilty.

William hated lies more than anything.

There had been plenty of times when Stella had decided not to tell the truth – not to confess that Laura's parents had let them come home after midnight, not to say that all the kids had drunk too much . . . But what she'd done this afternoon was something else altogether. Constable Spinks and his sister always invited the Birchmores to Christmas afternoon drinks – both families were outsiders to Halfmoon Bay and had no relatives with whom to share the celebrations. Today, Stella had feigned sickness. She had lain on the couch, enduring William's sympathy. She'd mouthed quiet assurances to Grace that she would be all right as her parents had prepared to leave. She'd felt cold inside as they'd driven away. It had been so easy to lie . . . But it had not been a selfish lie, Stella told

71

herself. She was bringing food to a stranger, who had come from far away and had only a cat for company. Surely that was not wrong. It was like something out of the Christmas story itself.

As Stella climbed around a pile of heaped boulders the top of the yacht's mast came into view. The two flags fluttered there against the sky – a patch of yellow and the red, white and blue. Stella breathed out with relief. Zeph was still there, hiding in her cove.

She hurried on towards the place where the snake had been, and then jumped down onto the sand. The tide was low, and the beach a wide arc of white. All the clothes and other possessions that had been strewn along it yesterday were gone. There were no footprints on the sand. No strains of singing floated on the air. The only sounds were the gentle pinging of metal rigging being blown against the mast, the slapping of quiet waves against the shore, and the shrill peeping of oyster birds.

Stella walked round to where the shoreline came closest to the side of the yacht. The cove offered a perfect mooring place, she realised – the deep channel met a row of rocks with almost sheer sides. And the cove was narrow at this point. Zeph had lines running out from each side of the hull, holding the vessel safely in place.

'Hello!' Stella called out. She felt awkward again, as if she were invading someone's privacy – even though this was her beach; Zeph and his yacht were visitors just passing through.

A long arm reached out from the cabin, followed by a face framed with tousled hair. Zeph squinted for a moment, into the sunshine. Then a quick, bright grin chased the drowsiness from his face.

'Stella!'

He hauled himself up onto the deck and stood there, stretching as he looked at her. He was dressed only in one of the coloured cloths, wrapped loosely around his waist. Stella shook off her shoulder bag and busied herself searching inside it – fumbling amongst the packages of food that she'd brought. An image of him stayed with her – the languid ease of his movements, lean arms moulded with muscle, the way the cloth draped from his hips. When she glanced up he was looking straight into her eyes.

Stella felt his surprise – his pleasure – that she'd come. It was there in his eyes, his mouth, even his hands.

She smiled at him. 'Happy Christmas.'

'Oh, yes . . .' Zeph looked as though he'd forgotten it was a special day. 'Come on up.'

He pointed to where she could step onto a rock only just submerged, then jump onto his dinghy. He stood at the stern of the yacht ready to help her across to the deck from there.

As Stella launched herself onto the small craft she was aware of Zeph watching her. You could read a person's history with boats when they stepped into a dinghy: if the action was unfamiliar to them they clutched at the gunnels and edged sideways like a crab. But Stella stood tall, her balance sure, even as the little boat rocked beneath her.

She reached out to take hold of his waiting hand. It closed warm and strong around hers. As she gave him her weight he pulled her up towards him. Her second foot found its place on the deck, but then she stumbled, falling against him. He grasped her shoulders to steady her. For an instant he held her there. Then he let her go, pulling back from the touch. He looked young, suddenly – unsure. Not a man of the sea, but just a kid, like her . . . It made Stella feel brave, in control. She began to walk along the side of the yacht.

'Have you just woken up?' she asked, looking back over her shoulder. 'It's after three.'

Zeph followed her. 'I was up for a while, earlier on. I sleep in short bits. Out at sea, on your own, you can't afford to be asleep for hours at night, especially in the shipping lanes. A freighter will drive right over you – won't even know you're there. And last night the moon was so bright . . . I went for a long walk.' Stella paused, turning to watch him as he continued. 'It was like a dream – everything silver and blue.'

Stella smiled. She knew exactly how it would have been – the moonshine laid over the sea like a great highway to another world. And the waves all edged with silver lace.

Coming up beside her, Zeph gestured towards a pair of cushions. They were set side by side on the back deck – almost as though he'd been expecting company. The covers were made of bright yellow silk, densely embroidered in matching thread and inset with tiny round mirrors that danced in the sunshine.

Stella sat down, with her bag beside her. Close-up she saw the white pattern of dried salt overlaying the silk designs. The cloth was flecked with black and orange cat hair. It was Carla's cushion, she realised. It was the cat who sat beside Zeph out here on the deck, watching the sunset . . .

'I've brought you some food,' Stella said.

Zeph raised his eyebrows in surprise. Then he fixed his gaze on her bag. He looked more like someone who was hungry, Stella thought, than someone hoping for a treat.

She began bringing out the things she had brought. Zeph watched intently, nodding over each item. There was a packet of tea, some rice, tinned beetroot, cheese, apples. Stella felt like a magician pulling tricks out of a hat. She put down one of Grace's foil-wrapped cakes.

'Aunt Eliza's Cut and Come Again Cake,' she announced.

Zeph looked puzzled. 'What did you call it?'

'Cut and Come Again,' Stella repeated. 'That's just the name of the recipe.' She paused, glancing at Zeph. 'Don't worry – my mother won't miss it. She makes them six at a time and puts them in the freezer for Dad to take to sea.' She laid out some oranges and a packet of dry biscuits. 'And a tin of tuna, for Carla.'

As if hearing the name, a brindled cat poked its face out of the cabin. Carla stalked across to Stella, hesitating only briefly before jumping onto her lap.

Zeph stared at the creature. 'She hates strangers,' he said.

Carla kneaded Stella's legs, pushing sharp claws through the denim of her jeans. Then the cat circled once before curling up in the girl's lap. Stella smiled, feeling pleased – special. She leaned over the cat to take the last things from her bag. There were three jars of dark gold honey.

'We've got stacks of this out in the shed. It's bush honey. We only use clover honey, from the shop, but Joe keeps giving it to us. We don't like to say that we don't want it.'

Zeph opened one of the jars and scooped a fingerful into his mouth. He licked his lips, savouring the taste. 'What's wrong with it?' He reached into the jar again. 'It tastes fine to me.'

He held it out to Stella. She dipped her finger in and sucked the sweet syrup. Zeph's enjoyment was catching. The honey tasted better than it ever had before. The flavour was deep, like well-cooked caramel, and only slightly smoky.

The two leaned over the jar, taking turns to dip fingers into it and carry sticky blobs of honey to their waiting mouths. Honey wound through the air in long strings; golden drops fell onto the cushions. A drip ran down Zeph's chin, and Carla licked at Stella's sticky arm with her rough pink tongue.

When the jar was half-empty, Stella and Zeph shared an orange, the tart juice driving away the sweetness. Stella looked up the tall mast as she licked her lips. She knew enough about yachts to recognise the quality of the rigging. No expense had been spared in preparing the boat for ocean sailing. She wondered again – uneasily – how it could possibly belong to Zeph.

'It's a beautiful yacht,' she said. She added nothing more – just left the comment hanging, to see where it might lead.

Zeph smiled proudly. 'Yes, she is. She handles beautifully, too. The two things go together, you know, with yachts. If all the proportions look right then you can be pretty sure she'll sail well. I'd trust *Tailwind* in any kind of sea.' He pointed up the mast. 'See that second sail-track that stops about a third of the way up? That means I can get a storm sail up in five minutes. And see the spreaders – four of them. That mast would stand up to anything.' He swung his arm towards the cabin. 'And look at the shape of the cabin – in big seas the waves just roll right over her.'

He fell silent, his gaze travelling over the yacht. 'She's not mine, of course. I'm looking after her for a friend. He was the one who designed her . . .'

His voice trailed off. Stella tried to read the look on his face – he seemed wistful, almost sad.

'I'll make some tea for us,' Zeph said, getting to his feet.

'No,' Stella replied. 'I can't stay. I'm expected back.'

He looked at her blankly.

'It wasn't easy to get away,' Stella explained.

Zeph nodded. 'Without telling them I was here,' he finished for her.

She paused for a second and then replied, 'That's right. I had to keep your secret.' She spoke as if she could otherwise have simply told William about Zeph: 'Hey, Dad – I met a sailor from India. Out at the coves, where no one else goes. I'm just going back to see him again . . .'

She stood up and slung her limp bag onto her shoulder. She wanted to ask *How long are you staying? When are you leaving?* But she remained silent. She felt, somehow, that if she said the word 'leaving' it would happen. He'd weigh anchor and sail away over the horizon.

'Wait,' Zeph said. He crossed the deck and swung himself down into the cabin. Stella peered after him, wanting to steal a glimpse of his home, but the curtains must have been closed down there. She saw only a shadowy gloom marked by vague shapes.

Zeph reappeared a few seconds later with a small package in his hand. It was wrapped in a piece of faded cotton cut from one of the printed cloths. Instead of being tied with string or ribbon it was bound by a long strand of fresh seaweed. The edges of the weed were just beginning to dry out, curling into decorative frills.

'Open it,' Zeph said.

Stella pulled off the seaweed string. The cloth fell open, revealing a small woven grass basket. It was decorated with feathers, shells,

76

and wispy fronds of pink and yellow seaweed – all collected, she knew, from this area. She looked up at Zeph. Here was someone like her, she realised, who still loved to gather treasure and make things, even though he was no longer a child.

'It's beautiful,' she said.

'I made it for you,' Zeph told her.

Stella bit her lip. How did he know she'd come back? Was he used to this – meeting girls and making them into his friends straight-away . . .

'I was going to leave it behind,' Zeph continued, 'up there where the driftwood gathers by the pool. With a note inside. "*For Stella. Happy Christmas from Zeph and Carla.*"'

'I'd like to have that note.' Stella smiled. The moment of doubt had been abandoned, and now she felt reckless with relief. She handed the basket back. 'I'll come and collect it tomorrow.'

He held out his hand for her to shake. 'It's a deal.'

Stella laid her hand in his. He didn't grasp it as he had done when helping her on board. He just let it lie there, gently cradled in his palm – as if it were not the hand of a girl who could fillet a king flathead in under ten seconds, or hold the tiller firm till her fingers were stiff and blue with cold; as if it were, instead, a fragile thing, rare and precious.

Leaving Zeph still standing near the yellow cushions, Stella jumped ashore and crossed the rocks to the sand. She walked away along the beach. This time she felt certain that the boy was watching her. Under his gaze, her arms swung gracefully. Her neck was straight, holding her head high. Her hips curved below her small waist. And her hair, freshly washed for Christmas morning, swished across her back like a silk mantle, shiny in the sun.

The smell of baking drifted into the room as early morning light filtered between cracks in the curtains. Stella lay in bed, listening to the sounds of her parents walking about in the kitchen – Grace's soft tread and William's heavy footfalls – and the murmur of gentle conversation. They were familiar sounds, comforting.

Everything was as it should be.

Stella's eyes moved slowly around her room, taking in the pink walls, the curtains printed with ballerinas and the old cupboard with all her school athletics ribbons pinned on the side – more than a dozen of the blue ones for first place, and just a few red ones for coming second. She looked at the stone angel sitting in her new place on the shelf, in the company of Stella's dolls. There was the baby doll with soft, lifelike limbs, the Aboriginal doll with curly hair and dark skin, and Stella's childhood favourite, Miranda, the walking doll with long, red hair.

William had bought Miranda for Stella when she won a statewide essay competition in Grade 4. At the toyshop in St Louis you could buy extra clothes for her – and on several occasions when Stella had done something else that pleased William he'd brought home another outfit as a reward.

Stella glanced across to where the doll's clothes were kept in a neat pile on the lower shelf. There was a pair of jeans, a tennis dress made of cream linen, a pantsuit with a little gold chain belt, a navy blue jumper that looked a bit like the one Grace had knitted for William – and, most beautiful of all, a bride's dress. Grace had made it herself from a fragment of silk left over from her own wedding gown.

As Stella looked at all her possessions spread around her, a dull fear gathered in her chest. Soon she would be leaving everything behind her. Moving away to the city and going to a much bigger school. Jamie and Laura and the others would be with her, but still – she would have to deal with so much that was new and strange . . .

An image of Zeph came to her then. She pictured him setting sail – alone, but for a cat – heading for adventure and not looking back. That was the answer, she thought. She would have to be more like Zeph – brave, and unafraid of taking a risk. It occurred to her then that this approach to life was the exact opposite to William's. She pushed the idea away, feeling guilty and exposed, like a child who had scribbled on a textbook in biro and could not now rub it out.

She listened again to the sounds coming from the kitchen. There was the clunk of metal against metal – Grace washing up saucepans. Stella could picture exactly how her mother would be standing, her tall frame hunched over the sink . . . A new thought came to her with a twist of sadness. How would Grace manage when William went to sea, without her daughter to keep her company? Would she have another attempt at learning to drive, so that she could go out more often? Stella knew William had tried to teach his wife, years ago, but it had not gone well. The dent was still there in the back of the ute, where Grace had slammed into the gatepost. It was hard to imagine her wanting to tackle driving again.

Stella rolled over, gathering her bedclothes around her body, and turned her thoughts back to Zeph. She pictured him out at the cove, lounging on his yellow cushions with Carla, waiting for Stella to return. She saw his sun-streaked hair hanging long around his shoulders. She saw the stone pendant that he wore hanging from a leather cord around his neck – a teardrop of clear red. It lay against skin that was burned a deep brown. But the undersides of his arms were still pale, she recalled – the touch of the sun had been laid over skin that was born fair, like hers . . .

There was a brisk knock on the bedroom door – then it banged open. William strode across the room and flung back the curtains.

'You're wasting the day,' he said. 'It's almost breakfast-time.'

Three places were set at one end of the dining table: William at the head, Grace to his right and his daughter to the left. Everything was laid out ready for the Birchmores' Boxing Day breakfast. The fine bone-china teapot rested on a cork mat next to matching cups and saucers. Linen napkins, rolled inside silver rings, lay next to gleaming cutlery.

Stella leaned into the middle of the table, placing two jam pots there, side by side. William sat in the armchair, facing out to sea. He looked thoughtful, almost a little uneasy. Stella felt a twinge of anxiety that grew into a creeping fear. Had she been reported peddling at speed yesterday along the road towards her hidden track – looking very unlike a girl who was ill? Or had someone, passing out to sea, taken a look at the moored yacht through binoculars and seen her there with Zeph? Stella had been caught out before – she'd been discovered in the wrong place at the wrong time. But she'd never been found guilty of telling a bare-faced lie.

In the silence, Stella gazed blankly at the Christmas tree. It looked tired already – bereft of gifts but still weighed down with decorations – as though its magic had begun dwindling the instant the clock struck twelve on Christmas night. The baby Jesus on the mantelpiece looked pale and cold in the early light.

Grace came in from the kitchen with a plate of My Own Griddle Cakes and a third pot of home-made jam. She hovered by her chair, her eyes darting over the table, checking and checking again that everything was in place.

Stella looked at the golden cakes, glossy with melted butter. She knew William loved them – he had been served them every Boxing Day since he was a child. Yet, today her father hardly seemed to notice them. Stella eyed him nervously.

Finally, he spoke. 'If the weather holds,' he addressed his wife and daughter, 'I'm going out tomorrow, first light.'

Stella pretended to study her plate. Tomorrow! William always stayed home between Christmas and New Year. He didn't go back to work until the first of January.

And when he did, he took Stella with him.

Stella pressed her lips together. No, she wanted to say. I can't come tomorrow. I've promised a friend . . .

'I thought this year' continued William 'I'd take you on a later trip, Stella. Your mother would like you home for a while.'

Stella caught her breath. It seemed too good to be true – as if whatever she wanted would happen, like magic . . . She glanced at Grace, offering her a silent thank you.

But her mother was staring at William in surprise. Grace opened her mouth ready to speak, then just turned her face away.

'And,' William paused to clear his throat, 'I'm taking Jamie. The lad's asked, and I think it would be good for him.' Stella looked up. William refused to meet her gaze. 'We'll be back before New Year's Eve, so we can all go to the dinner dance as usual.'

Stella nodded but said nothing. She did not trust herself to sound disappointed.

'I knew you'd approve,' he said. 'And by the way, Jamie asked me to say goodbye to you for him. They've got their family barbecue at Nautilus Bay today, of course. He'll need tonight to get ready and we'll be off before dawn. So you won't see him.'

'That's okay,' Stella said. 'I want to be off early tomorrow, too. I promised Joe I'd check the tide lines for timber.'

Another lie – so easy . . .

William rubbed his hands together, smiling to his left, then to his right. 'Good – that's all settled. Now, Gracie, pass me one of those griddle cakes. And some of that jam. It all looks delicious!'

Stella looked at her father's face. She knew he'd expected his daughter to be upset about not going to sea, and he was happy now. His plan had been accepted. She felt a flicker of anger – not with William, but with herself. Because she knew she could always be relied upon to go along with him, her feelings formed by his.

William pointed at Stella's T-shirt. 'Is that your Christmas shirt? It suits you . . .'

Stella felt the warmth of his praise poured over her. 'Thank you.'

'Eat up, then. You too, Grace,' William said.

Stella glanced across the table at her mother. Grace sat looking down at a single griddle cake that had barely been touched. For all her interest in cooking, she never ate much. If William commented, she always said she was full. She never said what it was that she was full of.

Stella watched Grace lift a morsel of food to her lips and chew it in short bursts. There was a line in her cheeks, near each corner of her lips. Stella stared at her. A realisation came to her – alien, yet unavoidable: Grace was angry with William.

Full of swallowed anger.

Stella turned back to her father. He was taking a second griddle cake from the plate. Noticing his daughter's gaze, he winked.

Stella's hand looked large and pale in the undersea light. Strands of hair drifted in front of her mask. She held onto a rock as a swell came through, swirling the weeds. When the sea became still again she pulled her knife from the sheath strapped to her leg. She reached towards one of the pink and brown abalone shells that lined a rocky ledge. Digging the tip of the wide blade under the shell, she twisted it firmly, flicking the shellfish away from the rock and catching it with her hand. She worked quickly. Once an abalone got a chance to clamp on, she knew it was almost impossible to prise it free.

She had brought no diving bag – just her mask and snorkel – so she surfaced with each shellfish and handed it to Zeph. He stood on a rock with a bucket, reaching out to her as she appeared with her catch in her hand. She felt a surge of pride each time. It took skill to pick them off without dropping them, and she sensed that he knew it. When she had collected six large abalone she swam in to the beach.

She sat there enjoying the heat of the midday sun. She felt her skin warming, drying – her bikini top becoming two cold wet triangles over her breasts. Zeph walked round towards her, the bucket swinging in his hand. He wore just a cloth wrapped round his waist. Only two days ago, Stella remembered, it had been strange to see a man in a skirt, yet now it looked normal. Things could change so quickly.

'What do we do with them now?' Zeph asked. He sat beside Stella, looking down into the bucket. The abalone squirmed out from their shells, searching for the familiar touch of rock, and finding only smooth plastic or the shells and bodies of their companions.

'You don't want to know,' grinned Stella. They had to be cut from their shells, their guts ripped away, and then all the black slime scraped off. Only then could they be sliced into thin strips, ready for frying.

Zeph learned quickly how to clean and prepare the abalone. Soon he was working alongside Stella so efficiently that he might have been doing it for years. Stella watched the way his hands gripped the shell and held the knife. She pushed aside an image of Jamie's hands carrying out the same tasks in exactly the same way. She felt disloyal, as though the cleaning and slicing were an intimate ritual that she had no right to be sharing.

Zeph held one of the abalone in his hand, observing the way the shellfish twisted in its shell – glistening wet, changing shape. Watching him, Stella felt a warm blush on her cheeks. The boys often laughed about the abalone, saying they looked like girls' fannies. 'How would they know?' Laura liked to say. 'They've never had a good look.' It was true, the boys got to feel rather than see their girlfriends' bodies – reaching down inside their jeans then pushing up into the softness. If anyone went as far as undressing they always did it in the dark.

Stella glanced at Zeph. She imagined him standing naked in the bright light of day – not feeling the need to hide anything. And not expecting a girl to hide, either . . .

'They cook best over a fire,' Stella said, wanting to fill the air with words. 'Just for a few minutes, very hot. But I'm not sure where to light one. If anyone sees the smoke, they'll come.' In fact, she knew the whole volunteer fire brigade might come – headed up by Jamie's uncle Bill.

'I've got a little spirit stove,' Zeph said. 'For emergencies. I'll bring it across with a pan. What else do we need?'

Stella gestured towards her shoulder bag. 'I've got butter and lemon, salt and pepper. That's everything.'

Zeph nodded and turned away. As if spurred by hunger, he ran towards the yacht. The way he tied his sarong allowed his legs to move easily. Stella watched the muscles flexing in his calves and across his back. He had the body of a man – even though his hair, streaming back behind him, and the careless way he moved, made him look like a boy.

They cooked in the shade, fronds of she-oak dangling over their heads. The slivers of white flesh curled and spat in the hot butter. The sea air was laced with the tang of cut lemon and the smell of burning methylated spirits.

'How long are you staying?' Stella had to ask. She wanted to know when it was going to be time to say goodbye.

'I should leave soon,' Zeph replied. 'I've fixed the self-steering gear now. I made a plan to meet Bakti in New Zealand. I have to be there.'

'How long will it take for you to sail that far?' Stella asked. She tried to keep her tone light.

'I'll have to get going tomorrow. Next day at the latest.'

The two were silent. Butter hissed in the pan. Then Zeph spoke again.

'Why don't you come with me? Bakti wouldn't mind. I could bring you back – a few weeks from now. In time for school.'

Stella laughed.

'No, I'm serious.'

She shook her head. Did he really imagine that she could just leave with him on his yacht, she wondered. 'I've got – things to do – you know, I've got to pack up . . .' She looked at him. He probably thinks I'm older, she told herself. People often did, because she was tall. 'I'm only sixteen.'

'Sixteen . . .' Zeph repeated. 'I was living on my own by then. Bakti moved to another ashram. I stayed in Goa.' He looked over to the yacht. 'That's when I met Wolfgang. He was looking for someone to take care of his children. His wife, Lotte, had hepatitis – she was really sick. I lived with them. They had six children. Three girls and three boys. The youngest was only a baby. Nina . . .'

Zeph sifted dry sand through his fingers as he talked. When he mentioned the baby's name, he paused, his hand hovering in the air. A smile curved his lips briefly – then it was gone.

'There was some problem back in Germany – one day they all just left. I looked after *Tailwind* in case they came back. Wolfgang said they would. I hoped they would – I liked living with them. I really missed the kids.' His voice softened. Stella saw him surrounded by little blonde-haired children, a baby in his arms. 'I waited for them – nearly a year. Living on board. They never came back. So I sailed her away. And here I am . . .'

'Don't go tomorrow.' The words fell from Stella's lips unplanned. 'I want to come back once more.'

'You'll have to,' Zeph said straightaway. 'I haven't written your goodbye note yet.'

Stella smiled at him. She wrapped her arms round her knees, hugging them against her body. One more visit, she told herself. Then it would all be over. She would go back to being the girl she used to be. Jamie's girl. William's girl.

Just one more visit.

It was nothing.

But at the same time – she knew – it was everything. A gift that would stay with her forever, whispering in her heart like the hush of a quiet sea.

Chapter Five

The sun gleamed off the polished table in the kitchen. The clothbound recipe book lay open there beside a steaming pot of tea. Harsh early light picked out every neatly inscribed word on the yellowed pages. Grace sat on a stool, leaning over a golden-topped steak pie wrapped in a plastic bag. With a straw in her mouth she sucked out the last pocket of air. Then she taped the package closed. Finally, she wrote out the date and the name of the recipe on a piece of card and attached it to the wrapped pie. The process was repeated with five more pies. Stella watched from the door, waiting for the last item to be ready. Then she loaded them onto a tray and headed out to the shed.

She shouldered open the big wooden door and stepped inside, breathing the smell of diesel and pine. She crossed to the corner, where the large chest freezer stood out, white and sleek in the dingy air. Lifting the lid, she peered inside. The chest was nearly full – if Grace stopped cooking, she calculated, there would still be enough food for six or seven voyages. Yet Stella knew her mother would always keep on cooking. Once, years ago, Grace had become distracted by her garden, and when William was ready to go to sea he'd discovered that no food had been prepared. He'd had to set off with only half a loaf of bread, a bag of onions and potatoes and a few jars of chutney. Stella remembered how the weight of his disappoint-ment had lain like a heavy shroud over the household long after the *Lady Tirian* had disappeared from view. She was not surprised that Grace never wanted to be caught short again.

Chilly air wafted up into Stella's face as she leaned over the freezer, laying the packages carefully in their correct places. Grace insisted the rules of the freezer manual be followed meticulously. Everything had to be stacked in the right order, so that the oldest items could be found and used first.

Stella glanced towards the door to check that Grace was not com-ing – then she began removing some frozen packages for Zeph. She could easily take a pie or two, some casseroles and some soup, along with several cakes – enough to at least provide fresh food for the first week of his journey. Grace would never miss them.

When she'd assembled a collection of frozen food, she went over to an old bookcase that stood against the shed wall. Its shelves were loaded with row upon row of jams, preserves, pickles and all the jars of Joe's honey. She picked out a few samples and rearranged the shelves so that there were no gaps. Then she began to search for something in which it could all be carried.

William's shed was tidy and well-organised. His benches were bare of sawdust and his tools hung on the wall, matching shadow shapes painted in black. After only a quick search, Stella found some calico oat bags folded in a neat pile on top of some tarpaulins stacked in the back corner. She reached across to one of the bags, pulling it towards her. But as it came free it snagged on another sack further down in the pile. The whole column of sacks and tarpaulins toppled sideways and fell to the floor. An oblong case with brass handles was revealed – leatherbound, and glowing a deep red in the dim light. Stella leaned forward for a closer look. She had never seen it before.

Pushing past the tumbled bags, she stood beside the box. It looked solid and heavy. Grasping the brass handles with both hands, she managed to heave it out of the corner – sending earwigs and silverfish scuttling for cover.

She laid it down flat on the floor. Kneeling beside it, she unclipped some metal clasps – corroded in the salt air and scratchy on their hinges. Then she raised the lid. Inside were long lines of spoons, forks, knives, teaspoons, soupspoons – all laid out, gleaming, on a bed of royal blue velvet. It was a huge cutlery set, several layers deep; there must have been at least twenty of each utensil.

Stella knew straightaway that it went with the dining table in the sea room. The table was not especially large as it was set up at present, but there were eight extra leaves that could be added to it. With them all in place, the table would be long enough to seat a large number of guests.

Or a big family. One with seven children – 'Seven Oaks'.

Stella could see the dusty wooden panels over near the freezer, leaning against the wall. She knew they had been brought all the way here from England because William had pictured himself sitting at the head of the long table, with children placed down each side. It had been Pauline who told Stella of William's dream of raising a large family, here in his new homeland. Grace had once shared this information with her friend, but she'd regretted it later – it was private family business – and Pauline made sure Stella understood that she must not let her father know the subject had ever been discussed.

There was other proof of William's plan as well. There was the sketch Stella had found in the cabin of the *Lady Tirian*: a design for an extension to the house at Seven Oaks that had never been built. Also, not long after arriving in Tasmania, William had bought a family burial plot in the Anglican churchyard. He'd chosen it with care, selecting a prime plot with a good view over the sea and enough room for plenty of graves.

But his dream had failed to come true. Grace had never fallen pregnant again. Stella suspected her mother might not have minded all that much – Grace always shrank from the sticky fingers of Pauline's youngest child. And everything about Grace's house spoke of adult order and calm. She just wasn't the kind of mother who liked cuddling little children or wiping up their mess; it didn't fit with her careful English manners. Whereas William enjoyed the sorts of things fathers did. He was so good at offering advice and teaching people useful skills. Stella felt sorry for him, that he had only one child – a daughter.

Stella picked up a fork, holding it towards the window to catch the light. Now, she saw that the handle was engraved with a coat of arms. She looked at it in surprise. It was the same emblem as the one on Grace's cooking spoon. There was the cat, the flower and the star . . . Lifting out the top tray, Stella saw that there was indeed a serving spoon missing. She could see the empty place where it belonged – its contours pressed into the blue velvet.

The set belonged to Grace's family, Stella guessed, because the sea-room table was the one family heirloom that had not come from the Birchmores. Stella turned the fork over in her hand. The heavy silver and the coat of arms all suggested that this was the possession of a wealthy family. Perhaps that was why the silver was hidden away in the shed, Stella thought – apart from the one spoon that Grace had borrowed to use in her kitchen. William didn't like people who showed off their wealth. It was one of his complaints about Laura's father, who had made a fortune as an abalone diver.

Stella put the fork back in its velvet-lined niche. She was about to close the lid of the box when she noticed something more about the coat of arms. Now that she knew it was linked with Grace, she recognised that the flower was a lily. She studied it more closely. It was exactly like the ones Grace grew in her garden. Stella stared at it. She'd never imagined there was any meaning in Grace's choice of a favourite flower.

She glanced around her uneasily, wondering what else appeared random, ordinary – and was not . . .

She looked back down at the lily. Opposite the flower was the cat. Though small, it looked brave. Carla. Stella remembered the warm weight of the brindled cat lying on her lap. The purring that could be felt as well as heard.

One last visit.

Stella jumped to her feet. She closed the lid of the case, then hauled it back into its place in the corner and covered it up again. Returning to the freezer, she filled the oat bag with food and left it just inside the entrance to the shed.

She hurried back towards the house. When she reached the door she met Grace coming outside with a bucket of soapy water in her hand.

'I can hardly see through that kitchen window,' her mother said. 'Those spiders have been at work again.'

Grace crossed to the window and began sloshing water onto the pane with a sponge. Next, she dried the glass with a cloth before finishing off with newspaper and methylated spirits.

'That's a bit better,' Grace said, standing back to check her progress.

The window sparkled in the sun – every trace of cobweb gone. Grace seemed able to manage without the special cleaning products that other women used. William thought they were a waste of money. He liked his wife to use simple things – vinegar for cleaning toilets; Velvet soap and bicarbonate of soda instead of detergent; eucalyptus oil instead of stain remover. He always praised her results. He knew the floors in his home, the glass in his windows, the sheets on his bed were cleaner than those of any man in Halfmoon Bay.

Grace leaned close to the window again, breathing on a smudge and then wiping it away. Stella saw the woman's face reflected in the spotless glass. Grace studied her handiwork intently, then stood back with a smile of satisfaction on her lips.

'I think I'll head out to the coves then,' Stella said casually.

Grace nodded. 'You might as well make the most of the day.'

When William was at sea, Grace stuck to her busy schedule of cooking and cleaning – but she was happy for Stella to leave her alone with her work. In fact, as long as she approved of what the girl was doing, she seemed to like the idea of her daughter enjoying herself. Today, Stella had avoided having to make up an elaborate lie about her plans. It had been easy to strap a few pieces of salvaged timber onto her bike when she'd gone out earlier to pick up the shopping. And easy to say, when she'd returned without them, that Joe had asked her if she could find some more. Grace had even packed up some fruit and date loaf for her daughter's lunch.

Stella waved goodbye, and then returned to the shed for her sack. When Grace was safely occupied with the next windowpane, Stella slipped away down the path. Near the gate, she paused and looked out to sea. The *Lady Tirian*, with William and Jamie on board, was just visible on the horizon.

Then the boat sailed away out of sight.

The point of the stick sank into the firm sand. Stella dragged it easily, making a long, curving line. First she drew a capital S. Then she added the rest of the letters that made up her name. STELLA. She handed the stick to Zeph. He began writing his name next to hers. His letters were bigger; each line pushed deeper into the sand.

As she stood watching, Stella draped a silky sarong that she'd borrowed from Zeph's clothesline over her head and shoulders, making a shelter against the sun. It was not yet noon, but already hot.

'There,' Zeph said, when his name was complete. 'This beach belongs to us.'

As if in response to his words, Carla ran out from behind a rock. She skipped lightly across the writing, leaving a faint pattern of prints behind her. Then she sat down between the two names and began to lick one of her paws.

Stella watched the pink tongue working over the dark fur. Carla looked so at home here that it was hard to imagine that she would soon be gone, never to return. *Tailwind* would be gone. And Zeph.

Zeph.

Stella traced the shape of his name on the sand.

'I've never met anyone with your name,' she said to Zeph.

'It's short for Zephyrus,' he replied. 'The West Wind.'

Stella looked at him in surprise. It seemed an odd name for a mother to choose for her child. Westerly winds were cold and blustery; they whipped up white horses out at sea and turned the sky into slate.

'Bakti always said I was true to my name,' Zeph continued. 'Easy-natured, no trouble . . .'

Stella frowned, puzzled. 'When we get westerly weather it's not quite like that,' she ventured.

'That's in the south,' Zeph explained. He bent to scratch Carla behind the ear as she rubbed her body back and forth against his shins. 'Zephyrus was a Greek god. In the northern hemisphere everything's the other way around.'

Stella eyed him cautiously. Could that be true, she wondered? You might as well call the winter warm and the summer dark and chilly.

'It's true,' Zeph insisted. 'The stars are all different, too. The constellations are upside-down, in the wrong part of the sky.'

Stella found his words unsettling. She looked down at her feet. The very sand beneath them felt as though it might begin to shift.

'You can get lost if you're not careful,' Zeph added.

'Did you ever get lost?' Stella asked.

'Plenty of times,' Zeph laughed.

'What did you do?' Stella watched his face, imagining the nightmare of being lost on a boundless ocean.

Zeph shrugged his shoulders. 'I ended up in a different place from what I'd planned. That's how I discovered Samoa. Which was a good thing – I loved it there.'

A seagull squawked loudly as it flew overhead. Stella looked up, tracing the path of its flight. The sky was a wide empty blue, a blank palette on which anything could be written. She felt, suddenly, the excitement of not knowing, not caring, just letting things happen.

Zeph moved away a few steps and stood gazing at the water. Sunshine danced on the surface, but below the sea looked cool and still.

'Come for a swim before we eat.' He turned back to Stella. His eyes were small pools of the same emerald green as the ocean, his hair the colour of the sand.

Walking to the water's edge, he dropped his sarong on a rock. He paused, facing the sea. His naked form looked so natural there. His body was tanned evenly all over, with no area of pale skin to suggest a forbidden zone usually covered by bathers or shorts.

Zeph ran into the sea, shouting as the cold water shocked his skin. Turning towards Stella, he grinned and beckoned.

Stella looked across to the yacht, where her bag containing her bikini wrapped in a towel lay on Carla's yellow cushion. She took two steps towards the boat, but then paused. To make a point of going to get her bathers when Zeph had none seemed almost rude – a false modesty that bordered on vanity. She hovered uncertainly, her thoughts racing. Was she ashamed of her body? Or did she want to keep it from him? Either way, the act of hiding herself would make a division between them. It would be a reminder of their difference.

When what Stella wanted was to become more like Zeph. To live in a world like his. A world in which the west wind could be warm if it chose; and the stars could dance in the sky.

Anything could happen.

She took off her clothes and wrapped herself in the borrowed sarong. When she moved she felt the soft folds brushing her hips. At the edge of the water she unwound the cloth and let it drop beside Zeph's, a whisper of silk settling onto the rock.

As she walked into the sea she glimpsed the stark skin of her breasts: white skin, never burned, set against last summer's linger-ing tan, mirroring the outline of her bikini top. Her nipples stood out in the cold. She raised her hands to her neck, covering herself with her arms – light brown skin pushing against the white.

She looked down at the water as it rose up her shins to lap at her knees; then travelled up her thighs to reach the dark triangle of hair.

Lifting her gaze she found Zeph looking at her. He was close to her – almost within reach – standing waist-deep in the sea. There was a stillness to his body, like that of a wild creature frozen in the glare of a hunter's light. The look in his eyes – something almost like fear, overlaid with wonder, admiration – made Stella feel suddenly strong and free. She laughed and splashed water towards him.

Instantly, salt water was flung back at her face. She blinked it away. Then, using both of her arms, she began heaving water towards him, ducking as he aimed more back. Gasping with laughter, Stella swam away. She headed for the deep channel, making the distance in long, fluid strokes.

As Zeph appeared beside her, Stella slowed her pace. Treading water, she looked down. The sea was clear. It wavered the lines of his body, but hid nothing. She knew he was looking at her, too. Their bodies were close. Her leg brushed once across his – skin sliding over skin. Their eyes met and held one another for a long moment. Then Stella laughed to break the tension.

'Race you back,' she said.

Diving underwater, she swam towards the shore. Zeph sped up behind her and they were side by side when they reached the shallows.

They lay there in water that was just a foot deep, resting their chins on their elbows – looking up at their names written on the beach. Their bodies settled into the welcoming contours of soft, large-grained sand. As low waves washed into the cove, warm sea swirled through the narrow gap that lay between. Drifting strands of seaweed draped their skin.

'I could stay here forever,' Stella said.

Zeph smiled, but shook his head. 'No, you can't stay anywhere forever.'

'Are you never going to stop and live in a house?' Stella asked.

'I guess I will, one day.' Zeph looked at his yacht, rocking slowly at its mooring. 'But where – I don't know.'

'Tell me about the best places you've been in the world.' Stella lowered her voice as she spoke. She felt disloyal to the gleaming sand, the lichened rocks of sunset orange, the deep azure of the ocean. Surely nowhere was as beautiful as here.

'I love the beaches in the Pacific,' Zeph said. 'Palm trees grow all along the edge of the sand, leaning out over the water. They look like people standing there – tall, elegant people . . . You can just pick up a green coconut, cut off the top with a knife, and sip the juice.' He ran his tongue over his lips as though the memory of the taste was still fresh. 'I love India as well – for different reasons.'

Stella listened intently while Zeph told stories of the land where he had spent most of his life. He described the way the desert looked from the swaying back of a camel. And told of sleeping on the rooftops of ancient forts, gazing up at the stars.

She felt herself drawn to his pictures. William had told Stella she need not bother with travelling. He'd looked around and found the best part of the whole world was right here. Tasmania. But Zeph made India sound like a magical place, full of colour and light.

He described the ashram in Goa where he'd lived as a child – a big rambling place set beside the sea. Then he began to talk about the German family – Wolfgang and Lotte and the children. He spoke most about the baby, Nina.

'I used to carry her against my chest,' he said, 'tied up in a cloth. The Indian women always teased me. They said, "Where is your wife? Where is your sister? This is not the work of a man!"' Zeph laughed at the memory – then his face became serious. 'But I didn't care. I knew Nina was safe carried there.'

Stella nodded. She pictured Zeph's tall figure moving through a crowd, a little blonde baby held in his arms.

A wave washed in then – slightly bigger than the ones that had come before. It reached up over their shoulders. Stella shivered suddenly – the water that had seemed warm when they first moved into the shallows now felt cool against her skin.

'You're cold.' Zeph turned to her with a look of concern. 'You need to get out and lie in the sun.'

Stella smiled, seeing herself through Zeph's eyes. She was a fragile, precious creature. She might be able to dive five metres underwater, or run faster than any girl in her school, but she must not be allowed to catch a chill.

Stella followed Zeph towards the rock where the two sarongs lay. Zeph picked them both up and held one out towards her. He wrapped the other expertly around his waist. Then he watched while Stella wound hers across her body, under her arms, covering her breasts. She smelled Zeph on the cloth, a spicy cardamom smell faintly touched with fresh sweat.

'You're beautiful,' he said when she was finished, as if it were now safe for him to speak. He looked into Stella's face, his eyes a deep brooding green. She held her breath, wondering if he would touch her now – kiss her. Instead, he just reached out one hand towards her face. He lifted a strand of salty hair that had fallen over her eyes, and gently moved it aside.

She stared at him, trapped in his gaze. The places where his fingers had touched her – on her forehead and her cheek – seemed changed somehow. As though an imprint had been left behind there, a pattern on her skin.

They lay on the beach, warmed by the sand from beneath and bathed in the sun from above. At the edge of her vision, Stella could see a she-oak tree leaning out over the rocks. Its fringe of blue-green fronds nearly swept the ground.

Carla lifted a tentative paw up onto Stella's bare shoulder, and then snatched it away, shaking off drops of water. Stella laughed. She knew Zeph was watching her – seeing how her lips revealed her teeth. Perfect teeth, brushed twice a day and not even one filling.

Zeph raised himself onto one elbow and looked down into Stella's eyes. She felt her heart beating loudly in her chest as she waited for him to speak.

'I have to leave tomorrow, first light.' Zeph's voice was soft with regret, yet at the same time firm and clear. 'I have to go to Bakti. She'll be waiting.'

'I know,' Stella said faintly.

His words circled in her head. *I have to leave. Tomorrow . . .*

In a flash it came to her – that this was the reason he hadn't touched her body, hadn't kissed her. He knew it would not be right when he was leaving her.

The thought was a song in her heart. Zeph was good. He was a good person.

But soon he would be gone. The knowledge drove out the warmth she'd felt. How many hours did they have left? Two – three . . .

She sat up, so that her eyes were level with Zeph's.

'I really don't want to go,' Zeph said. 'I'd rather stay here with you. But I promised her.'

Stella looked down at her hand, digging in the shell-speckled sand. She unearthed a tiny purple crab, which scuttled sideways under her leg. Please – don't go, she wanted to say. Don't go to Bakti. I want you here. But she just smiled, to show that she understood.

'I'll probably spend a couple of weeks working up there,' Zeph said. 'Just to get some cash.'

'What will you do?' Stella asked.

'I can usually find some work at a marina. Not always – a few times I've run right out of food and kerosene. It gets desperate then – there are a few things you've just got to have. But something always turns up in the end. I look around for a yacht that needs some work done on it – and I offer my services.' He paused, seeming uncertain whether to continue. When he did, he sounded almost shy. 'I'm good at fixing things. Making things. That's what I'd like to do as a job one day.'

Stella nodded. She could see from the way he kept the yacht in such good order that he was skilled with his hands.

'I'm going to study medicine,' she said. It was a firm plan. When she'd finished school she'd go straight on to university.

'Why?' Zeph asked.

Stella looked at him blankly. She'd had her dream for years. It was all mapped out in her mind. She would graduate with honours and return home to Halfmoon Bay as a doctor. 'The' doctor. Everyone would come and ask her advice. Birchmore would become one of the names most spoken, most written, here in this place where the family was so new that no Birchmore had yet been born or buried.

'What made you choose medicine?' Zeph asked again.

Stella frowned as she hunted back to find the place where it had all begun. William's face came to her. It had been his idea, she realised. His plan first – and then hers.

'I don't know really,' Stella replied. She was unnerved by her discovery. And annoyed that William had found a way into her thoughts – here, now. What did the future matter anyway – to her and Zeph? All they had was the present. Stella felt something almost like panic growing inside her. Soon there would be nothing. Their time would be over.

She began to study Zeph's face so that it would live on in her mind. She saw the sparse golden spikes of his roughly shaved beard. And a curved pink scar on the left side of his chin. At his temples, strands of fine hair formed little whorls and ringlets. She saw how his lips curled, even when he was serious.

The feeling of panic gave way to sadness. Dragging her gaze away, Stella stared bleakly over Zeph's shoulder. Then, as she looked towards the western horizon, her eyes widened. She breathed in slowly, deeply.

Clouds were forming there, dark and grey.

A storm was brewing.

She looked again to make sure. The day had been so clear. And William, who always checked the forecast, had set off only this morning, expecting several days of good weather.

But it was true.

Stella stared at the darkening sky. If the storm continued to build there would be no way the yacht could venture out from the safety of the cove.

She fixed her eyes on the clouds, willing them to grow. She sent a wordless plea to summon the west wind. And, as she lifted her face to the sky, she sensed the first whisper of a reply.

Hope burned bright inside her, bringing a small smile to her lips.

She was a goddess, in league with them all – the sky, the wind, the sea. These elements that she knew so well – and who, surely, knew her too – would come to her aid. A wild sea had brought Zeph here, to shelter in her cove – and a wild sea would keep him here.

For just a little bit longer. That was all she asked.

⌒

Rain drummed on the tin roof of the house, and gurgled as it ran from the spouting into the tanks. Almost lost beneath these sounds – but still there – was the steady pounding of a triumphant sea, showing off its power.

Stella stood near the open kitchen window, tasting the salty air and the smell of wet grass. She hugged herself with secret joy as the rain drove down onto Grace's lilies, battering the delicate petals.

Behind her she heard footsteps entering the room. She turned to see Grace lifting a large jam pan onto the table, and dusting it out with a tea-towel.

'A perfect day for making jam,' Grace announced. 'Luckily I picked the boysenberries yesterday.'

Stella heard the reproach in her mother's voice. It was Stella's job to pick fruit, but when she'd returned home yesterday two buckets full of berries were standing on the kitchen table. Grace's hands were stained purple with juice, and her forearms patterned with white scratches.

'I'll wash the jars,' Stella offered. She took them from the cupboard near the stove, and placed them in a sink full of hot soapy water. Suds slopped up her arms as she scrubbed each jar, removing every speck of dirt. Now and then she lifted her gaze – looking out through the window – checking on the progress of the storm.

When she had parted from Zeph, late in the afternoon, it had not yet become clear how fast the clouds were approaching, or how strong the storm would be.

'I have to go, if I can,' Zeph had said. He'd sounded as if he were talking to himself as much as to Stella.

They had said goodbye, keeping it quick and simple to hold confusion at bay. After all, what could be said when two people had known one another so briefly and yet so deeply? When what lay between them was at once boundless and small.

Stella had kissed Carla. 'Goodbye little cat,' she'd said. But, even as her lips had touched the soft fur, she'd raised her eyes to Zeph. He could see, she'd felt certain, that her farewell words were hollow. That she did not believe in the parting. She had placed her trust in the storm.

The storm.

The storm had swept into the bay before nightfall, whipping up steep waves. It had strengthened during the night. And it still raged now – steady and strong . . .

Zeph wouldn't have left, Stella felt sure – he couldn't have. *Tailwind* would still be there, moored safely in the hidden cove. She burned with impatience to get back there, to see him. But she had not yet thought of an excuse to go out into the storm. For now, she could only take comfort in the thought of Zeph being there – separated from her, but still a part of her world.

'That's quite a storm,' Grace said.

Stella glanced back over her shoulder to find that her mother was looking out through the window as well.

'They'll be okay,' Stella said.

Grace nodded. 'Of course they will.'

They both knew that at the first sign of a change in the weather William would have taken the *Lady Tirian* into shelter behind one of the islands. He'd be waiting there now for the storm to pass.

Stella pictured William and Jamie sitting in the cabin – rosy-cheeked and surrounded by the smell of wet wool, diesel and fish blood. William would be checking his rain gauges and barometer, entering notes in his log. The storm would make them hungry. She saw them sharing slices of Grace's beef pie, heated up on the gas burner. They were eating in silence, words closed out by the rain slashing against the decks. Eating and thinking. Thinking of Grace and Stella at home, waiting patiently for their men to return.

Stella emptied the water, grey and slippery with soap, and ran another sinkful. She pushed William and Jamie's faces from her thoughts. Soon enough, she knew, this dream she was in would be over. It would be time, then, to return to her real life. For now, she wanted only to think of Zeph. He'd be closed up in his cabin, too – in his secret realm that Stella had still not seen. She played a game with herself, naming all the things she knew Zeph possessed – beginning with that first day when his things had been spread out on the sand. If she could remember everything, Stella told herself, she'd see him again. If she missed something, he'd begin to fade away . . .

The jars were all filled to the brim with hot jam. They glowed quietly in the light of the bare electric bulb that hung from the middle of the room. Stella stood by the kitchen table, looking down at a small pool of red juice that stained the scrubbed pine. It looked like a splash of fresh blood, but she knew that if she dipped her finger into it and sucked the redness she'd taste the summery flavour of berry syrup.

She breathed in air sweetened by hours of boiling jam. She felt as if she were enveloped in a sugary haze, wrapped in the warm cocoon of Grace's kitchen. Suspended in time, waiting . . .

Grace returned from the laundry having put away the jam pan, and proceeded to make a pot of tea. Stella drew out a chair and sat down. She watched her mother's hand turning the teapot, one circle to the left, two turns to the right. Was it the other way around in the northern hemisphere, she wondered? Or did other mothers, born here in the south, do it differently to Grace?

Leaving the tea to brew, Grace poured milk into a small jug and returned to the table. As she placed it down, she jolted it against the sugar bowl, spilling milk.

Stella looked up, surprised by Grace's clumsiness. She saw then that there were tight little lines around her mother's lips. She watched uneasily as Grace mopped up the mess. Stella felt tempted to speak – about anything, nothing – just to break the quiet.

Silence was normal between her and Grace. Grace treasured peace – she wrapped it around herself like a warm cloak. Sometimes, when William was at sea they hardly spoke for days. But the silence was always calm, empty. Not tense, like this.

At last, Grace spoke. 'I was just thinking of William – being out there, with Jamie.'

Stella frowned in confusion. The words seemed unimportant, yet Grace's voice sounded strained and sharp. Then Stella understood: Grace thought her daughter felt hurt – jealous. She knew how Stella treasured her times alone with her father – precious interludes like this one, when fishing was not possible and William had spare hours to spend teaching her how to draw seabirds on the wing, or to recite verse after verse of 'The Rime of the Ancient Mariner'.

'It's all right, Mum,' Stella said. 'I don't mind about it.'

Grace said nothing for a time. When she spoke, her voice was quiet, as though she hardly dared let out her words. 'You don't see what he's doing.'

'What do you mean?' Stella's eyes widened with shock. She held her breath, waiting for the reply. Even the wind outside seemed to pause and listen.

Grace kept her head bent over the teapot as she replied. 'You're going away to Hobart and he wants Jamie to look after you – that's why he's taking him under his wing.' Grace paused, glancing anxiously towards the window as if she imagined that her husband – though held captive out at sea by the storm – might somehow be listening. 'You can't blame him. You're his only daughter. He wants to make sure you're safe. But . . . ' She looked into Stella's eyes. 'If you want to stay with Jamie, that's fine. But don't do it just because your father approves of him.' There was a short pause, and then Grace's final words came out. 'I want you to make your own choices. Do what you want. Study whatever you like. Travel the world. I want you to be free.'

Stella stared at her. Grace sounded like someone else. In all the conversations that had been held about Stella's future – about her education, her career plans – Grace had let William talk on her behalf as well as his own. What had made her speak out in this way now? Stella looked across to the window. It was almost as if Zeph's presence, his magic, which turned things upside-down, had somehow found its way here. Had she brought it home with her, Stella wondered – a spirit trailing behind her like an invisible Carla. Or had it been carried in the wind, blown in under the door . . .

Whatever it was, Stella wanted to catch hold of it, to stretch it out.

'Did you travel – before you married Dad?' She threw the question into the air, and waited.

Grace gazed out through the window. 'My parents had a holiday house in Aquitaine. Southern France. We went there twice a year. There was a goose farm next door. I used to go and watch them being fed. You know, they fatten them up by pouring grain straight down their throats.'

Stella smiled encouragingly. She wanted to ask, now, all about the family. About Daniel. The lilies. The banquets for two dozen people . . .

But Grace turned her attention to wiping up the spilled milk. She pressed her lips together into a firm line. It meant she would add nothing more, Stella knew. Her mother had already gone further than she should have – talking about her husband behind his back.

Stella picked at a splinter on the table-edge, peeling it back in a long, wooden curl. Grace's words circled in her mind.

I want you to be free. Make your own choices. Travel . . .

There seemed to be some special meaning to them, linked with Zeph. But that wasn't possible, Stella knew. Zeph was her secret. Grace knew nothing about him.

But still . . . Thoughts jostled in Stella's head. She found herself wanting to tell Grace everything. She imagined them talking and laughing together, like Laura and her mum often did, while the tea grew cold in its pot. How would she describe Zeph to her mother?

But then Stella shook off the fantasy. The Birchmores had high standards of behaviour. Grace would be horrified by Stella's accounts of visiting Zeph at the coves. She would forbid her daughter to set foot outside the house until her father came home. The only safe thing, Stella knew, was to keep her secret hidden inside her.

She stood to pour out the tea, and offered a cup to Grace. 'Where are the jam labels?' she asked.

'In the second drawer,' Grace replied. 'Don't forget to write the month as well as the year. And sharpen the pencil before you begin.'

As the woman picked up the recipe book, Stella watched from the corner of her eye, willing Grace to put it away. Sometimes, when it rained, Grace rested. She liked the sound of the rain drumming on the roof. It often sent her to sleep.

The pages rustled as Grace flicked through the book. She laid it carefully down on the table, open at a page headed 'Aunt Jane's Pickled Walnuts'.

Stella watched mutely as Grace measured out salt to make brine.

'The walnuts are in the pantry,' Grace said, 'I filled half a bucket yesterday. You can start pricking them.' She handed her daughter a pair of rubber gloves. 'Don't get the juice on your skin,' she warned.

Stella brought the bucket into the kitchen and put it down by the sink. Then she pulled the gloves on, and gingerly picked up an unripe walnut. The smooth-skinned ball was soft and green now, but she knew that as soon as she began pricking it, the juice – touched by air – would turn black. Once, Stella had not bothered to cover her hands and they'd been deeply stained. They had not looked clean for months.

Stella turned the walnut slowly in her hand, pushing a fork into its flesh. She did not like this task. There was something sinister, she thought, about the way the walnuts turned from a light spring green to pitch black. As if they were transformed by magic – dark magic that did not belong in a kitchen.

The hallway was murky with shadow, lit only by a small lamp set on a table near the kitchen. Stella stood by the entrance to Grace and William's bedroom, her ear pressed against the white panelled door, listening. The hem of her nightdress, stirred by a draught, fluttered lightly around her legs.

At last, through the sound of wind rattling the guttering and bushes being shaken against the weatherboards, she heard what she was waiting for. The creak of the mattress springs as her mother climbed into bed. Then the click of the lamp being turned off.

Back in her own room, Stella went to stand at the window, the curtains draping softly behind her back as she looked outside. The verandah light had been left on. It threw a glow into the night, making gold needles of the slanting rain. Straining her eyes beyond their reach, Stella could just see the white-topped waves rolling in and breaking close to the shore. She rested her fingers against the cold glass, feeling the power of wind and sea, a deep vibration travelling through her body.

Her storm. Calling her out into its presence.

She dressed quickly, pulling on the crumpled clothes she'd taken off only an hour before. Soon she was ready – her boots held in her hand and her oilskin bundled under her arm.

As she crossed the room, she paused, looking at her reflection, caught in the dressing-table mirror. It was a strange black and white image, leached of colour by the thin light. Her hair was a blanket of darkness draping her shoulders. Her lips were stained deep red with berry juice. In contrast, her face, her neck, might have been carved from pale stone – like Daniel's niche angel, sitting on the shelf with the dolls.

Only the eyes looked alive. Wide and bright. Reckless and brave . . .

Moments later, Stella was standing in the garden amongst the beaten lilies. Rain streamed off her oilskin, soaking her boots. She looked up into the sky, squinting through the rain. The cloud was breaking up, letting patches of moonshine through. She glanced once at the dark square of Grace's window, and then switched on her torch. She angled its thin beam ahead of her, and followed it into the night.

It was as if he had been waiting for her. As if he knew already how she'd ridden madly in the dark along the bushy path, and then picked her way over the boulders, only slipping once. How she'd pounded along the sand, boots sinking with each step, her gasping breath overtaking the clamour of the sea. And how deeply she'd feared that when she finally got to the cove, the yacht would not be there.

He was standing on the deck as her torchlight scanned the cove. As she ran along the last stretch of sand she saw him jump from yacht to dinghy to shore, led by his own small beam – a dancing spot of yellow.

Then he was there, in front of her. All the light of the moon breaking through the clouds seemed concentrated in his smile, his eyes. He didn't say anything, just put his hands lightly on Stella's shoulders, as though testing to see that she was real. Then he wrapped both arms around her, pulling her against him.

Stella pressed her face against his neck, warm and smooth. Beneath the oilskin smell of his coat was the fragrance of incense and coffee. Rain beat onto her cheek. It ran down her neck, under her shirt, and trickled over her chest. She didn't move. Held inside their embrace was the sound of her heart, her breath, mirroring his. She felt the strength of his arms tight around her. And the firm shape of his back beneath layers of clothing, as she pressed her hands against him.

There was nothing else in the world – just her and Zeph. And the storm, surrounding them. The rain, the wind, the darkness – and the faraway moon, turning a blind eye to the world as it came and went behind the inky clouds.

A kerosene lantern swinging from a hook shed a yellow light over the cabin. Stella glanced around her, taking in the chart table, the galley, the bunks. Like the outside of the yacht, the interior was orderly and clean – oddly out of keeping with Zeph's bare feet and sarongs, and his long, unruly hair.

Stella bundled up her rain jacket – wet side facing in so that it would not drip – and lodged it in a storage hammock. Zeph hung his in the doorway.

She stood with her back to Zeph, then – unsure where to sit, what to do . . . In this new place, with light on their faces and the air around them so quiet and still, their meeting out in the rain as the sea reached towards them over the sand seemed to belong to another reality.

She heard Zeph behind her, turning on the stove. 'I was making coffee,' he said, as if she were an ordinary friend who'd just dropped in.

Stella filled the moment by studying the cabin more closely. The yacht had been furnished with great care. Everything was latched, clipped, or set into tailor-made holes – no matter what the conditions, nothing in here would roll around or come loose. A dustpan and brush was fitted into a niche in the cabinetwork. Pencils lay in specially placed runnels on the chart table. There were matching mugs, with *Tailwind* printed on their sides, in a cabinet mounted on the wall.

There were just a few things Stella saw dotted around the space that spoke more of Zeph. A collection of shells, a carved wooden mask with cowrie shells in place of eyes. The sarongs, of course. And the little basket woven from grass and seaweed. Her basket.

The yellow cushions from the deck caught her eye. They felt familiar, welcoming, in this new place. Stella moved towards the one with cat hairs on the cover. She was about to sit down there when a soft weight landed on her shoulder. Carla. Claws pierced Stella's skin momentarily as the cat caught her balance.

'Ow!' Stella cried out. Then she laughed as Carla turned innocent eyes towards her and leaned to rub her face against the girl's cheek.

'She loves doing that,' Zeph said, turning with a grin on his face. 'She hides on top of the lockers and pounces.'

Stella smiled at Zeph as she lifted the cat down into her arms. Suddenly, the awkwardness was gone.

Stella sat on the cushion with Carla stretched out on her lap. She watched Zeph taking the two blue pottery mugs out of a cupboard. He shook powdered milk into a jug and added water from a bottle. She recognised the light brown water of the creek, stained with tannin but clean and clear. Her water. No, she thought – our water. She pictured their names, written large on the sand. What was it Zeph had said? *This beach belongs to us* . . .

On the wall behind Zeph's head was a framed drawing – a detailed diagram of something – perhaps the work of an engineer.

'That's one of Wolfgang's inventions,' Zeph said, following her gaze.

'The German man – Nina's father?' Stella asked.

Zeph nodded. A smile touched his lips. 'He was always inventing things. He taught me to draw, like that. I used to help him with his blueprints.' He gestured towards the chart table, neatly laid out with sextant, sharpened pencils, dividers. 'He was the one who showed me how to read charts, navigate. He taught me – everything.'

Stella leaned forward to look at the chart. She saw Zeph's course plotted there. All the little crosses marking each position taken, joined together with lines. They were like footsteps over the ocean – a map of the journey that had brought him here, to her.

'I try to look after everything in the yacht, all their stuff,' Zeph said. As he spoke, Stella looked across to a bookcase built into a bulkhead. She could see the German picture books there – now dried and pressed flat again. 'I've left Bakti's address for them at the yacht club in Goa. I still . . . I still hope they'll come back.'

Stella turned to Zeph. Pain showed openly on his face. He looked young, lost. She wanted to put her arms around him again, to hold him as if he were a child. But what words would she have to offer him? A girl who had been loved and cared for by two parents for her whole life? A girl who had never lost anything?

'He would not be pleased to see a tub of earth on his boat,

though,' Zeph said. He pointed at a plant growing in a ceramic pot – a thick-leafed plant with a few withered stalks where flowers had recently bloomed. 'That's my garden.'

Stella saw a fragment of dried petal lying in the soil, a dark red husk. It was strange to think of a plant at sea. Sailing from one season to another, in different parts of the world, yet belonging only in the little world of this cabin. Like us, Stella thought. This cabin, this cove, is all we have.

'I went looking for you today,' Zeph said.

Stella's eyes widened. 'What?'

'I went to see if I could find you. I walked for ages, but there were no houses to ask at.'

Stella sat upright, pushing Carla off her lap. She stared at Zeph. 'You mustn't do that! No one knows you're here.'

Zeph waved one hand to push aside her words. 'It doesn't matter that much. By the time they send anyone to check on me, I'll be gone.'

Stella looked at him in confusion for a time – then she realised Zeph was talking about having broken the rules by hiding *Tailwind* out here in the cove.

'It's not that . . .' Stella began. She let her voice trail off, but Zeph was watching her face, waiting for her to continue. 'If they knew you were here, they wouldn't let me come to see you. It's nothing to do with who you are – really . . .' Now that she'd begun there seemed no choice but to lay it all out. 'They don't know you, or your family. You don't live like we do. They just wouldn't understand. And if anyone else knew I was here, with you, they'd tell my father. That's how it is round here. There are no secrets. Everyone knows everything.'

Zeph looked puzzled. 'You're sixteen. You said you're about to go away to Hobart.'

'Yes, but – I'm still . . .' Stella faltered. Still what? Still William's daughter. Still Jamie's girlfriend. One of the Halfmoon kids. 'It's not a bad thing.' Stella found herself wanting to defend her home, her life. 'Everyone looks out for each other, that's all. But – I really mean it – you mustn't come looking for me.' She lifted her face towards

Zeph. 'I'll come to you. I don't care about the rain, or the dark. I know the way here like the back of my hand. I'll keep coming here, whenever I can, for as long as you stay. I want to be with you. That's all I want . . .'

She heard the tremor in her voice, failing under the weight of her emotions.

Zeph came across to where she sat. He seemed drawn by the power of her words. The lost, sad boy was gone. Healed. His eyes were soft with joy. Stella felt his weight on the cushion beside her, tilting her towards him. He took her hand in his. His skin was damp from the rain, the tips of his fingers still cold – but his palm, tough-skinned from working the boat, pulsed with a deep warmth. She felt his touch echoing through her body.

He leaned close to her. Stella shut her eyes. She felt his hair brushing her cheek. His lips touched hers – gently, at first, as if tasting the last traces of red berry juice. Then his hand came up behind her head, fingers tangling in her hair. He pressed his lips harder against hers, searching, pushing open her mouth.

It seemed timeless – a kiss that would last forever. Then Zeph pulled away. Stella opened her eyes. Zeph smiled, his lips shining wet in the lamplight, his eyes glowing a deep warm green. He looked into Stella's face, his hands cupping her cheeks. Slowly, he lifted her chin. She felt his lips against the skin of her neck. They travelled down until they met the edge of her shirt, resting against her collarbone. They stopped there, as though the cloth formed a boundary that could not be crossed.

Stella felt his hands tracing the shape of her shoulders, and then moving down her back. They travelled over the bump of her bra strap and followed the curve of her waist. But when Zeph came to the end of her shirt, hanging loose over her jeans, he did not reach up underneath it. Nor did he press his hands against her breasts, feeling her through the soft cotton of her bra. Stella rested her head against his shoulder, grateful that he should treat her with such care. It made her feel precious; safe. Loved.

'I wish you didn't have to go,' she said.

'So do I.'

He drew her close and held her tight.

They clung together, listening in silence to the storm.

The wind whistled in the rigging. Rain beat onto the decks. Out in the open sea, waves thundered towards the shore. But the rocks shielded the little cove, with its secret mooring. In the quiet water the yacht swayed gently, rocking to and fro, like a mother holding her children safe, for the moment, from all the pain and troubles of the world.

CHAPTER SIX

Through the next day, and into the night, the storm made sure the sky remained dark with clouds, and the winds maintained the fury of the waves. Stella visited the cove after dark again, when Grace was safely asleep. In the cozy cabin she lounged in Zeph's arms, talking with him, sipping black tea from one shared mug, kissing – and talking again. Some strange magic was at work – Stella seemed to know Zeph more deeply after just these few hours than she did Jamie after years and years . . .

On the third morning of the storm, Stella woke to the sound of light rain whispering against the roof. By the time she'd had breakfast the rain had eased and died away. The skies had lightened and cleared. Only the sea still roared, waves pounding the rocks.

As she was sweeping up her toast crumbs, her mother came in from the sea room.

'The windows are covered in salt again,' Grace said. She crossed to the sink and stood looking out over her garden, where rain-trodden plants sprawled across the beds. 'I'll have to rescue those poor things, too.' She turned to Stella. 'What are you going to do?'

'It's a good morning for beachcombing,' Stella responded.

Grace was already putting on her gardening apron and heading for the side door.

From the kitchen, Stella took a loaf of fresh bread. And a jar of the boysenberry jam; a warm red jewel in her hand.

Mid-morning sunshine slanted in through the cabin windows. It lit up the dust in the air, and sparkled on traces of salt on the varnished tabletop. Stella reached out to touch the leaves of Zeph's plant. They were turning towards the light, she saw – lifting themselves to the warmth.

Zeph lay close beside her in the narrow bunk, his limbs matching hers length for length. Stella felt a stab of regret at the thought that they would never stand back-to-back with a book balanced on their heads to make certain who was the tallest. Just as they would never swim together under a full moon, the sea looking thick like oil all around them. She could hear the sound of the sea. It was still too wild for boats to venture out, but she knew it would calm down within hours.

Then Zeph would sail away.

'I'm coming back, you know that, don't you?' Zeph said, as if he could read her thoughts.

Stella fixed her eyes on the string hammock swinging above her, tracing the criss-cross lines, the diamond shapes of the holes. She'd longed to hear Zeph say this. She'd dreamed of it. But she could not forget how – not long after they first met – he had suggested taking her with him to visit Bakti. He'd made the offer so easily. Too easily, perhaps . . .

'When do you have to leave for Hobart?' Zeph asked.

'February twelfth,' Stella said. William and Grace were going to drive her all the way there in the ute, and see her settled into the hostel.

'That's about six weeks away,' Zeph said. 'I can be back before then, for sure.'

Stella bit her lip. She had to know, to be certain. She could not bear to wait – and just hope.

'Promise me,' she said.

She breathed in and waited. If he made a promise to her, he'd keep it, she knew – just as he was going to keep his promise to Bakti.

Zeph got up on one elbow and looked down into her eyes. 'I promise,' he said. 'I promise to return.'

The words sang through Stella's head like a blessing.

'Carla promises, too,' Zeph said with a grin. He prodded the sleeping cat. 'Don't you?'

Then he grew serious. He touched Stella's cheek gently, running his fingers over her skin and on down her neck to the edge of her shirt. When he spoke, his voice was quiet yet firm.

'Stella, I haven't felt this way about anyone – ever. Nothing could stop me from coming back to you.'

Tears filled Stella's eyes as she looked up at him. She reached for his face and kissed him – gently first, then her mouth pressing hard against his, her tongue reaching past his lips.

She felt his hands behind her back, easing in under her shirt, creeping up towards the clasp of her bra. The barrier that had stood between them – the knowledge that their time together was soon to end – was gone.

I promise to return.

Stella sat up to take off her shirt, and then her bra – dropping them in a soft heap on the table. Zeph didn't touch her for a while, he just looked up at her intently – as though he were trying to fix in his mind the exact pattern of the shadows that played over her skin. Stella saw her body through his eyes – her flat stomach, her lean thighs. The skin of her breasts looked like velvet, the fabric of lily petals, bathed in the soft sunlight.

She lay down beside him. She could see his erection pushing against the cloth still wrapped around his hips. He rolled to lie on top of her, his legs interleaved with hers, his weight held on his arms. Salt-stiffened strands of hair fell forward, brushing her nipples.

'Have you?' Zeph whispered.

Stella knew what he was asking. She shook her head.

'I haven't either,' Zeph said.

Closing her eyes, Stella felt relief wash through her. He was hers. He had belonged to no one else.

Suddenly, Zeph arched away from her. He sat up, swinging his legs down onto the floor. 'We can't. We mustn't.'

Stella swallowed, her heart pounding in her chest. Now was the time to agree with him, she knew – to rescue herself. But she'd worked it all out. She knew.

'We can. I'm safe.'

Zeph stared at her, unmoving.

'My period's almost due,' Stella added. 'I'm always regular.'

'Are you sure?' he asked.

Stella could tell by Zeph's face that he was not certain exactly what she meant. It was up to her. She was the one who could say.

'I want to,' Stella replied.

As she looked into his eyes – dusky green in the light of the cabin – she reached over to where his sarong was tied at his waist. She undid the knot and eased the cloth aside. Then she lay back, waiting for him to return to her. She let her legs fall apart, leaving her body open.

He stretched out over her, raised up on one elbow. His erection lay hard against the front of her hip. He touched her first with his fingers – spreading her wetness. Then he shifted so that he was poised between her legs.

Stella closed her eyes. She felt every nerve in her body being drawn together, meeting in the place where he was about to enter her. She drew in her breath as he moved suddenly, pushing up inside her. He pressed deep and hard. There was a moment of stillness as he held her close. Her body, her heart, her soul felt full – made one with him.

The *Lady Tirian* was a dark shape against the glistening sea. Stella screwed up her eyes to pick out the two figures on the deck. William and Jamie. As she watched their steady progress towards her she felt numb, like a person trapped in a dream and unable to move their limbs – just watching, waiting, helpless.

She wrenched her gaze away and instead scanned the car park, littered with gum bark and leaves snatched away by the winds. She glanced over at the Memorial Wall, with David Grey's abandoned plaque. Then she looked across at the façade of the Halfmoon Hotel with its cracked-paint sign.

Everything looked diminished, somehow – as if she were viewing the scene from far away. As if she were not really here any more.

As if the real Stella had left with Zeph, hours ago – and was, at this minute, sailing away into the strait.

She heard someone approaching behind her – heavy steps along the wharf. Joe, she thought. Coming over from his mooring to await William's arrival – to make sure he was not forgotten if there should be any leftover food or some fish.

But then a faint perfume came to Stella, carried by the breeze. She stiffened, recognising at once the sweet, flowery fragrance. 'Allure'. It was what Jamie always bought – soap, talc or eau de toilette – for his mother at Christmas.

'I thought you'd be here, pet,' Pauline said. 'I'm going in to St Louis with Brian for tea, but I want to see Jamie before I go.' Her bright pink lips stood out against the rest of her face. 'You'll be glad to have him back!'

'Yes,' Stella replied. She tried to say something more – something casual, normal. But the best she could do was smile.

As she came to stand by Stella, Pauline fiddled distractedly with her hair. It had been curled into a loose bun on top of her head, but was now falling down on one side. She pulled out bobby pins and tried to push them back in. She leaned towards Stella.

'Help me with this, love.' She spoke through pins sticking out of her mouth.

Stella's hands felt stiff and clumsy as she tried to scoop the loose locks back into place. She thought of all the times she'd sat in

116

Pauline's kitchen having her own hair pinned up. She remembered the touch of the woman's fingers against her scalp and the way the hair brushing against her skin sent her into a trance. Pauline often tried out new hairstyles, consulting a magazine laid open on the table. 'You're my pretend daughter,' Pauline liked to tell her. And Jamie would always smile at her words. He expected he would marry Stella, one day. He did not imagine he could lose her to a stranger passing by in a yacht.

'I was a bit worried about New Year's Eve,' Pauline commented. 'It would have been a quiet old time for us girls if that weather had lasted any longer.'

Stella looked at the woman in silence. Was it New Year's Eve tonight? Or tomorrow night? She saw herself dressing for the dinner dance as she did each year. William would complain about her clothes, her makeup – reminding her that she was only sixteen. Meanwhile, Grace would spend ages choosing a dress from the collection of eveningwear she'd brought with her from England – and then end up changing at the last minute into one that her husband preferred. Finally, they'd set off in the ute, the three of them – the air close with perfume, aftershave, and an undercurrent of mothballs. When they arrived at the hall, Jamie would already be there waiting, his face pastel-painted by the glow of coloured fairy lights.

Stella froze, her fingers still twisted in Pauline's hair. She knew, suddenly. She would not be able to pretend with Jamie. Not even for a minute. She would have to tell him straightaway that she didn't . . . didn't what? Love him? Belong to him? After all these years, and all the plans that had been made . . .

She swallowed on a knot of fear – a sense that a wave was gathering, rising beyond her control.

'Are you done? Thanks, pet.' Pauline straightened. 'Look. Here they come.'

Stella turned her face in the direction of the boat, but she gazed past it – only glimpsing the waving figure on the foredeck and the dark blur of her father's head and shoulders inside the wheelhouse.

She focused on the rocks beyond, the ones that sheltered the gulch. The seabirds that usually congregated there were gone, hunting for food now that the seas were calm. The layer of white droppings that topped the granite boulders had been washed thin by the days of rain.

She wouldn't tell anyone about Zeph, Stella decided. Not Jamie, not William, not anyone. She would keep him to herself. She did not want to expose him – her memories of him – to anger, hurt, disbelief. Some part of her felt that if she did, she might not see him again. Like the prince in the fairy tales, he would vanish with the coming of daylight. She must hide him in the shadows of secrecy – safe, until his return.

'I have to go.' The words escaped Stella's lips before she had time to think. She had no excuse, no plan.

Pauline frowned with concern. 'What on earth's wrong? Are you sick?'

'Yes,' Stella lied. 'Just a bit.'

'I'll drive you home,' Pauline said firmly. 'St Louis can wait.' She nodded towards the boat, already drawing near. 'They can wait, too.'

'No,' Stella said. 'No, thanks. I'll be okay. I've got my bike.'

Before Pauline could say anything else, Stella turned and hurried away. Her boots hammered loudly on the decking of the wharf. She knew without looking that the woman was staring after her.

In the shelter of a she-oak thicket, well along from the main beach, Stella sat looking down at the sea. Where the rocks cast shadows over the water she could see down into the green depths – in which seaweed fronds wavered above the white shapes of empty oyster shells. Where there were no shadows, the sea was a mirror, reflecting an untarnished image of a clear blue sky.

The ground beneath Stella was layered with she-oak fronds, dropped over centuries. Prickly seed pods dotted the soft bed. Stella picked one up and held it in her hand. Tightening her fist around it, she pressed its spikes into her flesh. She savoured the small points of pain. They were signals from a body that was more sensitive, more alive than before, she was sure. The sea smelled fresher in her nostrils. The trees rustled more loudly. She wrapped her arms around herself, hugging her body.

Everything was changed.

Stella stared at her hand, still gripping the seedpod, the spikes printing their shape on her skin. She remembered the burning, afterwards; the ache. The green-leaf smell of sperm, sticky and damp on her thighs. And the feel of it leaking from her body, running down to stain the sarong that was bunched between her legs.

Now, on the bed of she-oak needles she moved her hips, feeling for the faint echo of the pain still lingering in her body. She cradled it inside her. Her secret. Her power. The knowledge that she was no longer a virgin. She and Zeph had made love. And it could never be undone.

CHAPTER SEVEN

A small pool of spilled lemonade lay on a wooden tabletop scarred with cigarette burns. Stella looked closely at it, watching tiny bubbles rising and bursting into nothing.

Jamie took a swig of his beer. The publican, Griggs, had given it to him in a mug – so that if Spinks came in he would not see what it was. Now Griggs was in the saloon, watching television. There was a strange, timeless feeling to the place – it was mid-morning, mid-week. Stella felt as though she must have skipped school to be here.

Jamie leaned across to Stella, resting his arm comfortably over her shoulder. His hand, hanging down, brushed the side of her breast.

'Want another one?' he pointed to her drink.

She shook her head.

'Mum's a bit worried about you,' Jamie commented. 'She said you were sick. That's why you weren't there when we got in yesterday.'

'I'm fine now,' Stella replied.

Avoiding his gaze, she pretended to study the framed photographs hanging nearby on the wall. There was a picture of the gulch, taken during the worst storm in living memory: one of the fishing boats had been swept up and dumped on the wharf. There was a shot of a well-known English yachtsman who had called in on a round-the-world solo voyage. A few newspaper cuttings were there, too – stories about the miraculous survival of three fishermen after the wreck of the *Briar Rose*. Then there was the line of portraits: all the presidents of the Fishermen's Association. William was amongst them, his chin lifted proudly as he faced the camera.

'Your hair smells funny,' Jamie said, holding a lock of it against his face. 'Incense. You've been burning incense.' He wrinkled up his nose.

Stella turned from the photographs to look out through the salt-crusted windows down towards the wharf. She could see the Memorial Wall. She counted along until she came to the plaque of David Grey – the lost sailor who had been loved so loyally. He would give her strength, she felt: the courage to speak. Because he was a part of the plan . . .

When Zeph returned in *Tailwind* he was going to sail in and tie up at the wharf. He wouldn't stay long enough for Spinks to see him there, or even for Joe to come over and start chatting. He'd just wander across to the wall, and go round to the back. There, directly behind David Grey's plaque, he'd push his hand into the decorative hole in the brickwork. Deep in the cavity, he'd leave Stella a message. It would not be a note; nothing as dangerous – or as ordinary – as that. Instead, it would be some kind of token, the meaning of which only Stella would recognise. A drawing of a cat, perhaps, like the one on Grace's spoon. Or a tiny basket, woven from tropical reeds . . .

'There's a party at Ryan's place,' Jamie said. 'We can walk from here – after the dinner dance.' He looked over at a hand-drawn poster of a dancing couple with New Year's Eve 1976 written in a square above their heads. 'We don't need to stay here till midnight. A few hours will be enough to please everyone.'

'I'm not coming,' Stella said. Her voice sounded small in the room full of empty chairs and tables.

'What do you mean? What are you talking about?' Jamie said.

Stella looked sideways at him. She could still see the line of paler skin, untouched by wind and sun, where his hair had been cut short for the leavers' dinner. Only a few weeks ago they'd stood together telling jokes, and kissed behind the muslin and crepe-paper drapes.

'You look like someone else in that dress,' Jamie had whispered in her ear.

I am, Stella thought. I am someone else.

She had to speak, now – to draw the line between the past and the future. She closed her eyes, unwilling to look at his face. She knew exactly how his lips would begin to curl at the corners as he fought to control his feelings.

'I don't want to come . . . with you.'

'Yeah, good one, Stell.' Jamie grinned, his teeth white against his wind-burned face. He pretended to push her off her chair, but held her arm to keep her from falling.

She turned to face him, staring at him in silence, waiting for him to grow serious.

'What's the matter?' he asked, frowning with confusion. 'What's wrong with you?'

Stella glanced over to the bar. Griggs was not there. From the saloon came the sound of snooker balls clinking. 'I don't want to . . . be with you. Any more.'

The words hung in the air. As their meaning sank in, Jamie flinched. His hand clenched his mug. He bent over it, as though studying it closely to see if it was real.

Outside, a car radio could be heard, growing louder as the vehicle approached, then quickly fading as it sped away. The sound of heavy footsteps reached them from across the room.

'You lovebirds staying for lunch, are you?' Griggs called over.

He began writing with squeaky chalk on a blackboard next to the bar. '*Special today: Surf and turf.*' He looked back over his shoulder. 'That's steak topped with oysters. It's from the new menu.'

Stella stood up, bumping the table. 'Let's go,' she said quietly.

In the shelter of the whaling station, Stella leaned her back against the soft stone wall. All around her were the carved names of her and Jamie's friends. And, further along, their own love heart, carved only a few years ago, the lines deep and clear. *Stella loves Jamie 1972.*

Jamie stood in front of her, his hands hanging at his sides. He looked young, suddenly, like a child unable to make sense of the world. Stella swallowed, forcing the words from her lips.

'You're my best friend. I care so much for you. But I can't be your girlfriend any more.'

He put his hands on her shoulders. 'You don't mean it.' But he could see that she did. He knew her so well. That, at least, made it easier.

'Why?' Jamie asked. 'Tell me why. At least . . . tell me why.'

'I can't,' Stella said.

It was true. She could not add the pain of jealousy to the hurt she was already inflicting on Jamie. She knew she would not be able to tell Laura, either, when she got back from Queensland. She had to keep her secret. As long as she said nothing, no one would guess that she had met someone else. How could she have? There wasn't anyone.

'It's nothing you've done,' Stella said. 'It's just . . .'

She paused, hunting for words. Then she remembered Grace speaking out under the cover of the storm.

'I want to be free.' Her mother's words fell from her lips. 'I want to make my own choices. I want to travel.'

Jamie stared at her. He shook his head, as if to clear his thoughts. 'But I'd never stop you from doing whatever you wanted. I never have. Have I?'

Stella shook her head numbly.

'So – what is it?' he asked. 'You don't want to go on studying? We can take a year off. Mick's sister did that.'

'No.' The single word seemed to have a weight that broke through Jamie's disbelief.

'You don't love me any more,' he said. His voice caught in his throat.

Stella shook her head again. Her lips were trembling. Tears gathered in her eyes. She looked through them at Jamie, his dark eyes wavering in the watery blur. Then her tears spilled down her cheeks.

'Stell – we can fix it, whatever it is.' He lifted a comforting hand towards her face. 'You don't have to do this.'

'I do,' Stella said. 'I have to.'

He let his hand drop to his side. Walking a few steps away, he turned and stood looking out to sea. The swell was long and slow – the white horses all gone. Stella watched his shoulders slump. Then, after a few seconds, they rose as he took in a deep breath. Trying not to cry. Trying to be strong.

Stella pressed her hands into the gritty surface of the sandstone wall. She longed to go to him – not to leave her friend standing there alone. She was the girl who'd punched a boy in Grade 4 for being mean to him. She'd been there that day in the rosy dawn when he caught his first big wave standing up on his surfboard.

But she did not belong to him any more.

She had to go; it was the only thing to do. She fixed her gaze ahead – on the ti-tree canopy rising behind the shop. If she just kept walking and did not stop, she would reach it. And there, in the forest, she could hide amongst the spindly trunks with curling paper bark, sheltered by foliage so thick that the sun could not get through. In the gloom, surrounded by the smell of ants and the musky scent of the leaves, she could be alone. She would not think of Jamie. And she would not think of Pauline – the woman's kind eyes widening with shock; her laugh-lined face mirroring the pain of her favourite son as he wept in front of her. Or William.

She would, instead, picture *Tailwind* sailing bravely over the sea, her sails bulging with wind and her keel rising and falling with each long swell.

She would treasure the joy of her secret lover. She would curl up on the dry earth, and rest.

William steadied the log with his hand, holding it upright on the splitting slab. Then he lifted the axe high above his head and brought it down hard. The dry wood cracked apart and the split pieces fell to each side. William stood back for Stella to pick them up. As she scurried forward, bent over, she could feel the cold silence spreading out from him, stiffening the air.

He was angry, she knew. Angry about what she'd done to Jamie.

Stella carried the firewood across the yard, holding it against her body. The long splintery pieces spiked the fabric of her shirt and pressed hard into her breasts. Through the kitchen window she could see Grace standing at the table, rolling pastry. As Stella drew near, her mother glanced up, meeting her gaze. Grace looked guilty – almost afraid – as if she knew how Stella had made use of her rash words of advice. Turning back to her rolling, she pressed long, jerky tracks into the dough.

At the side door, Stella dropped her load onto a heap of firewood. Then she knelt by the woodbox and began stacking the pieces inside. A spider ran over her hand, tickling her skin, but she barely noticed. She tried to focus all her attention on the task of finding the right combination of pieces to make a perfect row. She wanted to keep her mind busy, full – so that the days would pass, one by one. And Zeph's return would come closer.

Through the open back door she smelled onions frying – tonight's dinner. Stella's stomach turned at the thought of how she would have to force down a plateful of beef stew followed by rich oily pastries, amidst William's cold silence and Grace's new, uneasy quiet. When she had succeeded in swallowing the last mouthful she could escape to the kitchen and do the washing up. Only then could she go to her room, and lie with a novel opened but unread on her bed.

She would lie there thinking of Zeph, feeling the sweet pain of longing. She would share it wordlessly with the stone angel, who looked down on her from the shelf. And with the dolls, lined up beside her. Stella trusted them all with her secret. The angel's chiselled features and the painted eyes and pursed lips of the dolls gave nothing away.

One night, Stella had taken Miranda, the walking doll, down from the shelf. Resting the doll on her crossed legs, she'd pulled off the little fisherman's jumper, dragging it over the stiff arms and dropping it onto the candlewick bedspread. For a time, the doll had lain in her lap naked – the plastic body looking boyish and sexless. Then, Stella had taken the white wedding gown from the pile of doll's clothes, shaking out the silken folds of the skirt. The fabric had brushed Stella's bare legs with a soft whisper as she tenderly dressed the doll.

The bride now stood on the shelf, a little apart from the others – all alone, waiting.

Near the doll's bare feet, hidden behind a stack of books, was the woven basket that Zeph had made for Stella after the first time they'd met. The grasses had dried, turning stiff, and the seaweed had become brittle. When Stella took it out she cradled it carefully in her hands, as though it were a nest with a fledgling held inside it.

Zeph had given it to her in the last minutes before they parted – a folded note tucked into the side between the woven strands. Stella had not read it then – preferring to wait until he was gone: keeping one last piece of the story yet to come . . .

In her room, she'd stood with her back to the door, her breath catching – a sob of joy bound with pain in her chest. The rustle of the paper under her fingers was like a scratch over sunburned skin. The words, written in blue ink, were faintly blurred with damp.

Dear Stella,
I love you.
I love you forever.
I promise to return.
Zeph (and Carla)
xxxx

Stella knew the short message by heart – she knew the shape of every letter, and the slight dip in the line of words. Her fingers memorised the ragged outline of the paper – a page sacrificed from the logbook. The torn fragment was like an island, lifted from one of Zeph's charts. Holding the paper to her nose, she smelled seaweed and grass.

She sat with it often, on the bed, reading it over and over. Hugging her body to herself, aware of every fold of her skin, every muscle that moved beneath her flesh. She admired them all, loved them – because they belonged to him.

When she tired of reading the note and examining the basket, Stella took out her *Student's Atlas*, opening it up at the page for New Zealand. She traced the rugged outline of the South Island, reading strange Maori place names. Zeph had told her the name of the post office that was nearest to the coastal farm where he was to meet with Bakti. He'd said he would write it down, so that Stella could send a letter to him there – but if he had he'd forgotten to give it to her in the midst of preparing *Tailwind* for departure. Zeph understood that it was too risky for him to write to Stella, care of Mrs Barron's shop, so Stella knew that unless she managed to recall the name he'd mentioned there would be no contact between them in the weeks that lay ahead.

'Tuatapere. Waihoaka. Otatara. Wakaputa . . .' She rolled the sounds on her tongue to see if any of them felt familiar. But none of them did. Or rather, they all did. Stella studied the map, time after time. But it was a pleasurable rather than a despairing occupation. The fact that no contact was possible made the separation feel more potent – as if the aching pain that she felt would somehow only contribute to the joy of their reunion.

Stella leaned over the side of the boat, looking down into the water through a wide plastic tube with glass mounted in the end. The sea was murky with stirred-up plankton, but she could still see the dark pattern of seaweed on the ocean floor. Straightening up, she signalled to William in the wheelhouse: this was a place to set a pot.

He eased back the throttle. As the boat slowed, it began to wallow in the swell. Engine fumes tainted the air. Stella gripped the engine mounting with one hand as a wave of nausea churned her stomach. She heard William come up behind her, grabbing a pot and beginning to lower it over the side.

'Come on, girl,' he called to her. 'Give us a hand.' He glanced quickly at her face as he let the rope run through his fingers. 'What's wrong with you?'

Stella shook her head. 'Nothing. I'm a bit seasick.'

Usually she could cope with any conditions at sea without feeling ill, as long as she was up on deck in the fresh air. But occasionally, if the motion of the boat was wrong, she felt queasy.

'You've been ashore too long!' William responded. 'You need to get your sea legs back.'

Stella forced a smile, picking up a kind tone in his voice. This was how it often was with her father – after days of silence he would suddenly become warm again, his disappointment or anger forgotten. It was as hard then to recall his face looking closed and distant as it was to believe in the chill of winter once summer returned.

As William hurried into the wheelhouse to adjust the throttle, she clambered to the foredeck and dragged back another pot. A flathead had been left behind in the bait-holder. She glimpsed its pale, sea-washed carcass and caught the smell of rotting fish. She only just managed to reach the side before she vomited into the sea.

'You want to eat something now,' William said, as she stood up and wiped her mouth with the back of her hand. 'Nothing worse than an empty stomach.' He nodded towards the wheelhouse. 'See what you can find.'

The air in the wheelhouse was still and close. It smelled as it always did – of diesel, tar, wet wool, fried eggs and bacon. Stella tried to calm herself by taking a long, deep breath. She sat down on the padded bench. As she did so, the straps of her bib and brace overalls pulled her trousers up into her crotch. She felt wetness there – and closed her eyes in relief. Her period had come at last. Standing up with her back to the window, she reached into her overalls, her hand shaky with pent-up tension. She pushed one outstretched finger in between her legs. She could feel the blood, slippery on her skin. Wriggling her hand back out, she checked her finger. But there was no trace of red. Her finger had the clear silvery sheen of a fish pulled fresh from the sea. She stared at it, her body rigid with panic, as the knowledge she'd tried to keep at bay closed in around her like a dark cloud.

She'd counted and re-counted the days, her pencil leaving dots on the calendar as she searched for an error in her calculations. She and Laura had the same system. They didn't want to risk being caught unawares on the school bus or in class, so they always marked their first day of bleeding on the calendar.

December 3rd.

Stella had circled the date with a careless hand, all those weeks ago – unaware of how many times she would later stare at it. Unaware of how she would count on from it – to 28 and 29. Then stretch it to 30.

This morning, before leaving for the wharf with William, she'd marked day 36. It was too late. She'd known it – but refused to think about what it meant.

Movement outside drew her attention: William was gesturing for her to steer the boat further away from the shore. She acted mechanically, swinging the wheel as she pushed the throttle. She watched herself as if her mind were separate from her body – measuring swells, judging speed, checking for rocks.

From the outside, she knew, she looked normal. Inside, she reeled like someone who had been hit hard and now barely had the strength to stand up.

The suitcase smelled of mothballs and old clothes. Grace wiped it out with a damp cloth and then took a step back to let Stella inspect it.

The girl nodded. 'It's fine. I'm not taking all my things anyway.'

'I wish they had a uniform,' Grace commented. 'It makes things so much easier.'

Stella went to her chest of drawers and began taking out shirts and jeans. There were still two weeks to go until it was time to leave for Hobart, but William wanted to see that Stella had everything ready well in advance.

Not two weeks. Thirteen days.

In that time, Stella knew, Zeph would come. Any day now she would reach into the brickwork behind David Grey's plaque and find something placed there at last. Not just the husk of a dead caterpillar, a scattering of sandy grit, a long-dead petal . . .

Stella did not picture what would happen when Zeph returned. It was impossible to imagine him here, in the house, dealing with William. But she knew he would rescue her. He had sailed the oceans of the world, all alone, unafraid. He would know what to do.

Her hand hovered over a blue and white checked shirt. It was one of Jamie's. As she picked it up his smell came to her – familiar, safe. She longed suddenly to be with him. To tell him everything and ask for his help. She glanced up to see Grace looking at her. Stella dropped the shirt into the drawer, pushing it to the back, out of sight. It was too late to return it now. Jamie had gone away. Not to Hobart, to continue his schooling, but to work as a farmhand on a property on the mainland. Stella felt a dull pain at the thought of his chosen exile – a boy who loved to surf living a thousand miles inland on the edge of the desert. Because of her.

The back door banged loudly. There was the thud of footsteps in the hall, then William came into the room. He stood there looking at the empty suitcase.

'I can't believe you're going.' He shook his head sadly. 'My little girl, all grown up . . .' He rubbed his hands together. 'You'll be home at Easter though. It's not so long. By the way, I saw Laura at the shop. I didn't think they were due back for another week.'

Stella felt a rush of fear at the thought of meeting up with her friend. Laura would have new bikinis and a deep tanned body to show off. She'd summon Stella immediately to the main beach. There, they'd lie in the sun, skin glistening with coconut oil. They'd compare bodies, as they always did – seeing who had put on weight over Christmas, and how much. Stella's body was still unchanged to the eye, but she felt so different – like someone who'd crossed a threshold into a parallel world. How could she act as if nothing had happened? She knew it would be impossible to keep her secret.

Stella drew in her breath. She watched herself with a horrified fascination. She was going to do it – here, now.

'I'm not going,' she said. 'I'm not going to Hobart.'

William sighed. 'Just because Jamie has –'

'It's not that,' Stella said. She backed away from them to lean against the wall. There was no going back. It was begun. 'I'm pregnant.'

She looked down at the floor, her body tensed as if it expected to be struck. She heard Grace gasp. She sensed William, motionless, staring at her. Then sounds came from his mouth – the beginnings of words, cut off and abandoned.

'He'll have to come back.' When William finally spoke his voice was firm and strong. 'What was he thinking of, going off and leaving you?'

Stella frowned at him in confusion. She tried to think, to make sense of his words – but everything seemed to come to her in small, disjointed bits; they refused to line up in order and make sense.

'I thought we could trust you,' William said. 'And him . . .' He moved towards her. His face was rigid. His lips barely moved enough to let out his words. 'Who else knows? Do – they know? Brian and Pauline?'

Stella looked past his shoulder. She fixed her gaze on the stone angel, on the carved hands, praying.

Help me. Please.

'It's not him. Not Jamie.'

William's eyes widened. 'What?'

Stella swallowed on a lurch of sickness. 'It's someone else.'

'Who?' William's voice cut the air. 'Tell me.'

'No one you know,' Stella said. 'He's a sailor. He came in here after a storm . . .'

She turned towards Grace to see if she might find some sympathy there.

Make your own choices . . . Be free . . .

But her mother was staring at her in open horror. The look frightened Stella with its intensity. It was nothing like any expression she'd ever seen on Grace's face.

William strode to the window, looking out to sea as though he expected to see the culprit there.

'He had to go,' Stella said. 'But he's coming back.' She lifted her face. A thin shaft of sun fell on her cheek, a stroke of warmth. She felt tears warming her eyes. 'We love each other.'

William laughed, an ugly rasping sound. 'You're just a child!'

In the tense quiet, the sea sounded loud – too close – as if it had drawn near to listen in.

William cleared his throat. 'And who is he, then? Where does he live?'

'He doesn't live anywhere. He just sails around. All over the world.'

William was speechless for a few seconds. Then he shook his head like someone trying to wake from a dream. 'Spinks will tell me who he is,' he said. 'I'll find a way of asking so that he doesn't wonder why.' He spun round to Grace. 'No one must know. No one.'

'He didn't come in to Halfmoon. Spinks doesn't know,' Stella said. She felt a small thrill of pride as she spoke. 'No one does.'

She glanced at Grace. Her mother's lips moved slowly – she seemed to be hunting for words. Her eyes were still wide with mixed shock and dismay.

'Well . . . Does he have a name?' William demanded. 'We'll start there.'

Stella looked down at her hands.

Zephyrus, the West Wind, kind and gentle . . .

She would not share his name.

She lifted her eyes, meeting her father's gaze. 'Robert.'

'Robert.' William repeated the name. It was a solid, sensible name – not one that went with stars turning upside-down and a boy finding paradise by mistake. 'Robert who?'

'I don't know,' Stella replied. 'He never said.'

'He never said . . .' William echoed her words again, as if struggling to find their meaning.

'How far gone are you?' Grace asked. Her voice was sharp, strong. William looked at her in surprise.

'A few weeks,' Stella answered.

'You're not certain, then,' Grace said.

William turned from his wife to his daughter, hope breaking over his face.

'I'm certain,' Stella said. 'My period was nearly due when it happened – and that was weeks ago. I thought I was safe.'

'You thought you were safe?' William broke in. 'What about being the decent, respectable person we brought you up to be?' He rubbed his hand over his face. 'Does Jamie know?'

Stella shook her head.

'Well, that's something to be thankful for. He doesn't deserve this from you. He's a good lad.'

Stella winced under his words. She knew what he meant.

You are not a good girl any more.

She glanced over at the stone angel sent to her by Daniel. Whatever her godfather had done, it could not be worse than this. Would she be cut off, thrown out – her name never to be mentioned again?

'You have ruined your future,' William said. 'You won't be able to finish school. You'll never be a doctor.' Stella stood with her head bowed, letting her father's words flow over her. 'And it's not just you. You've ruined Jamie's plans, too. Pauline's devastated. And that was without – this!' A sudden catch in his voice made Stella look up. 'Everything I've worked for . . . Coming here from England to begin again . . .' He turned from Grace to Stella and back, with something like panic in his eyes. Stella felt an answering fear rising inside her. 'I won't have people talking about us. I won't have it . . .' William lifted his hand to his brow. His fingers trembled like leaves hanging from a branch, stirred by a brisk wind. 'You'll stay here, in your room,' he said. 'Is that clear?'

Stella nodded. 'Yes.'

Grace followed William out into the hallway. Stella breathed out with relief as they disappeared from view. The first step was over. She'd told them. And now she was going to be punished. For a brief, mad moment she imagined she had committed some ordinary crime. She'd be grounded, given extra chores. And then all would be forgiven.

But it was not like that, she knew. Something irrevocable had been begun. In nine – eight – months' time she'd have a baby. It would be her and Zeph's baby. She shut out the sound of William's voice, a low angry drone coming from the other bedroom. Instead, she thought of little Nina, carried in a cloth tied close to Zeph's body. He'd loved that German baby. He still missed her.

He'd love Stella's baby, too – the baby that was half him and half her.

It would be a dark-haired baby, with fair skin that needed to be sheltered from the sun. They'd wrap him in a soft sarong of rainbow colours and lay him down in one of *Tailwind*'s storage hammocks.

There he would swing gently, lulled to sleep by the sea.

Stella lay on her bed, pressing her hands against her abdomen. It was so flat and firm – it was hard to imagine that anything inside

134

there could have changed. She recalled a plastic model of the female body that her science teacher had once shown the class. Beneath the removable outer skin were mauve intestines that looked like bunched sausages. They lifted neatly away, and, tucked inside, were the reproductive organs. As the teacher talked and pointed, the kids had whispered and made jokes. All Stella could remember was how hard and cold all the pieces looked. And how they rattled against one another as the model was reassembled.

She did not know how long she had waited in her room, but she guessed it must have been hours. She'd heard William slam the side door, and the sound of the ute departing and then coming back.

As the day wore on, the tin roof of the house creaked, as if to break the tense stillness.

At a sound in the hallway, she sat up. Her fingers closed into fists; her toes curled in her shoes as she braced herself.

William entered the room and stood in front of her.

'Getting rid of it is out of the question,' he said. 'Just because we don't go to church every Sunday doesn't mean we don't know what's right and what's wrong.'

Stella stared at him. She knew people in other countries – on the mainland, perhaps – often had abortions. Girls at school told stories of women having coat-hangers pushed up inside them, then bleeding to death afterwards, all alone in their hotel rooms. And Laura had heard of a schoolgirl from Hobart who went to a clinic in Melbourne – a grey-walled place with an unmarked door, where she was given a number and her name was never mentioned.

But all this had nothing to do with Stella. She was waiting for Zeph.

'You will stay here for as long as you can hide your – condition. And as long as everything seems to be going along as it should,' William continued. He was calm again now, dealing out his words slowly and carefully. But he avoided Stella's eyes as he spoke, clearly embarrassed by having to talk about her body – her woman's body.

'Then you will go away. I've made some phone calls. There's a place on the mainland – country Victoria. The Salvation Army Home for Unmarried Mothers.' He glanced quickly at Stella before going on. 'It's attached to a hospital. The . . . inmates work in the hospital while they are able. Then they give birth there. Everything is arranged by the Home – the adoption, the recovery. They bind up the girls' bodies so that within days no one can tell anything has happened.'

Stella bowed her head, and said nothing.

William stepped towards her and put his hand on her shoulder. He was trying to be kind, she knew – to reach out to her across the gulf of anger and disappointment that her actions had brought into being.

'Then, we've arranged something else – something for you to look forward to. I've spoken to Aunt Jane. She's agreed to let you come and live with her, to finish your schooling in England. She's even offered to pay your fees so that you can go to a top ladies' college. She doesn't know about – this – of course. I simply raised it with her as an educational matter.' William looked at his daughter with a faint gleam in his eyes. 'It'll give you time to get over it all. Then you can come back here and do medicine, as you planned. No one need ever know what happened.'

There was a long silence.

William leaned closer to Stella. A grim smile stretched his lips.

'What do you think?' he asked. He sounded like someone who'd just outlined plans for a birthday weekend or a wedding.

Stella picked at the candlewick bedspread, pulling out pale yellow fibres and twisting them in her fingers.

'I won't give my baby away.' Stella looked up at her father as she spoke. She sensed Zeph standing beside her, invisible but strong.

William's mouth hardened again. His chest rose as he sucked in his breath, the anger about to blow.

'It's not "your" baby,' he burst out. 'It would have been "your" baby, if you had been married, and old enough to be a mother.' He broke off, and then continued in a calmer tone. 'When you've had time to think it through, you'll see that. A baby deserves to have a proper family. A proper home.'

Not just Stella, Zeph, Carla and Tailwind.

'Anyway,' William continued, 'there are other issues for now. It'll sound odd if we suddenly announce you're not going to school in Hobart. We need a reason for the change of plan – and an excuse for you not going off to the beach with Laura and the others between now and when they leave.' He paused, as if to let Stella try and guess what he was going to say next. She stared at him blankly. 'We'll say your mother is ill,' he announced. 'She can't be left alone in the house. Starting from right now, she'll need you to be here all the time. When you go to the shop, you'll come straight home.'

'What's wrong with her?' Stella asked. 'I mean – what should I say to people, if they ask?' She tried to hide the brightness in her voice. She wanted nothing more than to stay here at home, alone with her secret, until Zeph arrived.

'It's her back,' William stated. 'A slipped disc. She can't get out of bed without help. She can't cook or clean. We don't need Doctor Higgins to come out here and tell us what's wrong – because she's had it before.'

The words fell so smoothly from his lips. Stella felt a chill of remorse. Her father had always valued honesty above everything. When he was president of the Fishermen's Association he'd upset the treasurer by refusing to let beer be called bait. He wouldn't even say he liked a new dress, or one of Pauline's cakes, when he did not. It might be polite, it might be kind, he explained, but a lie was a lie. And now, here he was, weaving an elaborate lie that he was going to spread abroad. Because of her . . .

'What does Mum think?' Stella asked. She could hear Grace moving around in the kitchen, and the clink of crockery being stacked in the sink.

'She's got plenty to do with her garden, her cooking. It's lucky we live out of town – we don't have people just dropping in. It won't affect her really.'

'No, I meant about the . . . rest of the plan,' Stella said.

She remembered Grace's face when she'd first heard her daughter was pregnant. Where William had been outraged, Stella's mother had appeared deeply distressed. There was a look in her eye that Stella had only identified later: it was the incredulous gaze of one person watching another pass up a golden opportunity.

Make your own choices. Study . . . Travel . . .

'She thinks the same as me,' William replied. 'Of course, she understands more than either of us what a huge responsibility it is to have a child.' William was quiet for a time, his face bleak – then he spoke again. 'You know, they start the academic year later in England than here. When you leave for Victoria we can say you're going to visit your Aunt Jane, to settle in before school begins. The timing works out quite well.' He sounded almost pleased with himself. He rubbed his hands together briskly. 'Now, it's lunchtime. The important thing is for you not to let yourself dwell on it all too much. I have explained to Grace that the subject should not be discussed. It's a case of least said, soonest mended. We've got a difficult few months ahead of us. But they will pass – and we can make a fresh start.' A note of optimism entered his voice. 'By spring it will all be over.'

When he left the room, Stella went to stand by the window. She looked out over the bright blue ocean. She knew that wherever Zeph was, he would not be far from *Tailwind* – and that the waves that lapped the side of the yacht were joined in an unbroken stream to those washing against the rocks just a stone's throw away from her. She imagined the sea running between her and Zeph, carrying all her thoughts and feelings to him – her fear, her hope, her love.

Screwing up her eyes, she almost convinced herself that she could see *Tailwind* there – a black shape on the horizon, drawing closer and closer.

CHAPTER EIGHT

Stella walked barefoot along the beach, feeling the warmth of the late sun on the surface of the sand and the damp chill rising up from beneath. Ahead of her lay the narrow channel where *Tailwind* had been moored. She could imagine the yacht still there, bobbing in the gentle sea. A light breeze rustled the papery heads of a bunch of everlasting daisies that she held in her hand. She glanced down at their stiff petals. They would hold their colour, she knew, and would not wilt. When Zeph returned they would be here to greet him. A bright splash of yellow.

She walked across to the place where the little freshwater creek flowed out into a pool – not far from the rock where the snake had surprised her, the day she'd met Zeph for the first time. When he arrived he would want fresh water, she guessed. He would come straight over here – and see her welcome gift.

A jumble of driftwood patterned the edges of the pool. Stella took her time, choosing the pieces that she liked. Grace was gardening and William had gone to sea. Before leaving, he'd given Stella and Grace strict instructions about listening out for the vehicles coming along the track. He'd explained to Mrs Barron, and to Laura as well, that what Grace needed was rest and quiet – not visitors. But you could never be sure that people would listen to what they'd

139

been told. And if anyone did turn up, Grace had to make sure she was out of sight – resting in her room.

Stella gathered up the pieces of wood that she'd chosen – along with some bits of rope – and took them over to a rocky ledge to study them more carefully. Bending down for too long made her feel faint.

She laid them out side by side. They looked like the bones of an unknown creature – smooth and white and elegantly curved. After examining them for a few minutes she could see how they could be interlocked and tied together to make a shape that would hold the flowers – a cross between a frame and an altar.

She assembled the structure carefully, tying the ropes tightly so that even if a wallaby coming for a drink knocked against it there would be no damage. When it was finished, she carried the object over to a sheltered position not far from the pool. After lodging it there, on a flat boulder, she added the daisies – pushing the bundled stalks firmly into an empty knothole in a piece of weathered timber.

Standing back, she viewed her handiwork. The flowers, displayed so prominently, looked brave and strong. The sight filled Stella with hope. She felt the nightmare of William's anger and Grace's dismay fall away. She was certain that Zeph would soon be here. Something had delayed him, but she knew he would still come – even if he thought that she'd already gone to Hobart. He'd leave her a message, as they'd agreed, behind David Grey's plaque – knowing she'd find some way to get it. He would make a new plan. She just had to wait.

She smiled at the gulls that had gathered to watch her. Don't worry, she told them. Everything is going to be all right.

Mrs Barron leaned over the freezer, sorting through bags of meat.

'Here, hold this.'

She handed Stella a large oval package. The meat behind the plastic was a deep red.

'What is it?' the woman asked.

Stella searched the frosty lump for some kind of marking, but found none. 'It doesn't say.'

Mrs Barron sighed with frustration. 'I've told Laurie, he must always write on the bags. If he's in a hurry he just piles it in here – bird and beast – and leaves people guessing. One day I'll just throw it all out the door.'

Stella nodded, but made no comment. Mrs Barron liked to complain about Laurie, but the fact was she relied on the man for most of the meat she sold. The hunter brought in all kinds of game: deer, rabbits, wallaby, wild birds, fowl that had gone feral, goats that no one seemed to own. There were some customers who, like Grace, would never eat any of it. But many families, struggling to stretch their budgets, found it was the only meat they could afford. They swapped recipes with one another, and discussed the best ways of cooking it.

Laurie was a friend of Brian's, and on several occasions when Stella had been at the house for dinner the hunter had been a guest as well. Unlike other men – who drank beer in the lounge or on the verandah while dinner was being prepared – Laurie liked to stay in the kitchen, helping Pauline cook. Whenever he was there, the meal was especially good.

Jamie and Stella had always been fascinated by him. He was the same age as William and Brian, yet he wore his hair long, tied back in a ponytail. He dressed in jeans and wore boots like a cowboy. People said he could shoot a moving target at twenty feet, with a rifle held in one hand.

When they were young, Jamie and Stella used to hang around his Jeep, looking at dents and stains and speculating about their causes. They peered in at the dashboard, where there was a collection of different shaped wishbones stuck into the air vents. They thought then that Laurie was a dangerous person with a dark and secret past.

Their view of him changed when they became teenagers. They

began to see him as an ally – an adult in their midst who challenged the authorities: the council, government departments, everyone . . .

He was always in trouble with Spinks.

Stella had been at the wharf one morning when Spinks confronted Laurie in the car park. The policeman had taken his notebook out, and was threatening to issue Laurie with a fine.

'You've got no respect for the law,' Spinks had said.

'That's where you're wrong,' Laurie answered calmly. He stood by his Jeep dressed in bloodied trousers. Behind him lay the still body of a deer. 'It's just that my laws don't match up with yours.'

My laws don't match up with yours.

Stella gazed blankly past Mrs Barron's bent figure as the statement lingered in her head. Laurie had spoken easily, almost casually, that day – but Stella now understood that they were brave words.

It was not easy to live by making up your own rules – especially if you had to keep up a pretence of doing otherwise. To outsiders, Stella was a dutiful daughter who had interrupted her schooling to look after her sick mother. To William and Grace she was a girl who had made a terrible mistake, but who was at least grateful for their help in trying to resolve the situation. To Laura, she was a friend stuck at home with nothing interesting to write about, while her old classmates were busy joining sports teams and choosing exciting new subjects. And all the time, while Stella played these roles, she was just waiting for Zeph to sail in from beyond the horizon and rescue her. She felt like an actor performing in several different plays: there was always the risk she'd mix up her lines.

'Here it is!' Mrs Barron straightened up. She held a polystyrene tray of meat in her hand. It had a printed label on the front and the name of the butcher in St Louis. 'Beef brisket. I knew they sent me some. Just throw that back in, love, and shut the lid.'

Mrs Barron shuffled across to the counter in her soft-soled slippers. She picked up a pencil, licked the tip, and ticked off the last item on Grace's shopping list.

Stella joined her there. The wooden surface was cluttered with baskets of Easter eggs wrapped in coloured foil. Some of them were decorated with little chicks made of yellow fluff; they had orange feet made of wire and paper beaks.

Stella touched one with her finger. The baby birds were a sign of spring – new life. But, like Zeph's upside-down stars, they belonged to the northern hemisphere. Easter in Tasmania marked the very end of summer – the last camping trips, the last barbecue parties, and the last quick swims in chilly seas. As soon as it was over, people started looking out for the muttonbirds setting off in vast flocks – crossing the globe to escape the cold.

Stella felt a shiver travel up her spine. Winter was just around the corner.

And still, Zeph had not returned.

Mrs Barron added up the cost of the shopping and entered it in the accounts book. Stella willed her to hurry. She tried not to breathe in the stale-sweat smell that came from the pie-warmer, or even to let her gaze settle on the dried-up pastries that had sat in there all day. If she had to rush outside suddenly, Mrs Barron would definitely start wondering why.

'Now, before you go, I want to talk to you,' Mrs Barron said.

Stella froze, staring down at her hand resting beside a paper bag full of mixed lollies. Had she made a mistake? Let something slip?

'It's about the thirtieth anniversary of the Fishermen's Wives Association,' Mrs Barron said. 'We had the idea of doing a cookbook, like the CWA ladies do. But we want it to be different. The plan is that we'll all contribute one recipe that we have made up ourselves.' She paused to let Stella respond.

'That sounds interesting,' Stella said politely. She looked at a packet of potato chips. Salt and vinegar. She imagined the tangy taste easing the churning of her stomach.

'It doesn't have to be completely new. It might be one that we've improved in some way. But nothing that's just copied. The Christmas section is still under discussion. We can't agree on whether to include cold main dishes. Betty thinks they should go in

"Tasmanian", because it's not traditional. Anyway, I can let you know.'

Stella nodded absently. She ran her gaze along the pigeonholes, each marked with a hand-painted letter. Some were stuffed with mail; others were empty. There was one letter in 'B', but Stella could see the St Louis Council emblem on the front – it would be someone's rates notice or dog licence renewal.

She imagined how it would feel to see a letter lying there and to know that it had come from Zeph – that he'd decided to throw caution to the wind and just write to her anyway. She let the fantasy play out. Perhaps Mrs Barron would have kept his letter aside, guessing its meaning. 'Something special for you, Stella,' she'd say with a secretive smile – and slide an envelope over the counter.

Crinkly with salty damp. A black and orange cat's hair caught in the glue.

'So next time you come in,' Mrs Barron continued, 'it would be nice if you could bring something from Grace.' She gave a sad smile, as if she'd just spoken of someone who was dead. 'You can write it down for her if it's just in her head. We don't want to bother her. But it would be a shame for her to miss out – especially when she's such a good cook. In fact, if she can't decide which recipe to contribute, I could suggest the one she sent along for the church cake stall. Everyone said it was –'

'But they're not her recipes,' Stella broke in. 'They come from a book of family recipes, written out by my dad's mother.'

'Ah yes,' Mrs Barron said, 'the mother-in-law's recipes. Passed on to us so we can cook our dear husbands the food they have been accustomed to.'

Stella studied Mrs Barron's face. There was a cynical curl to the woman's lip – suggesting she held a very different view of a gesture Stella had always thought of as being kind and helpful.

'Grace must make other things, though,' Mrs Barron said, 'that aren't in the book.'

Stella shook her head.

Mrs Barron smiled knowingly. 'I suppose he wouldn't eat it if she did. Some men are like that . . .'

Stella looked at her in silence. She knew it was disloyal to be discussing her father, but the woman was right. It was impossible to imagine William sitting at the dining table, fork poised over a meal that he did not recognise. There were enough surprises to be faced out at sea, he often said. When a man came home, he liked to know what he could expect.

Mrs Barron tapped her cheek with one finger, looking thoughtful. 'Well, I don't know. Perhaps she could pretend. After all, no one else will know – if all the recipes come from England.' She glanced quickly at Stella's face. 'I don't mean to suggest she'd tell a lie.'

'Of course not,' Stella replied. She smiled, wanting to end the conversation. 'Look, I'll just tell her you asked for a recipe.'

Mrs Barron nodded. 'Thanks, dear. You let me know.' She settled herself comfortably, her back resting against the wall. 'I hear you've become quite a little cook yourself.'

Stella studied her hands, unsure what the woman meant. Anxiety stirred inside her again.

'Miss Spinks said she called in to see how Grace was getting on, and you had a whole rack of fresh biscuits and a casserole on the stove.'

Stella offered no response. She remembered the urgent rush there'd been that day, to get Grace safely into her bedroom before Miss Spinks' Volkswagen made it to the house.

Mrs Barron smiled warmly. 'You're a good girl. It's not every daughter that would look after her mother so well.'

Stella still gave no reply. She looked past the woman's shoulder, down towards the wharf.

'I have to go,' she said. She picked up the box of groceries and hurried outside.

Salt lay powdery-white in the lines of David Grey's name. Stella rested against the wall, next to the plaque – postponing the moment when she would go round to the back and seek out the hole in the brickwork.

She rubbed at an ache in the small of her back, then pulled at the strap of her bra. It cut into her shoulder, dragged by the weight of her breasts.

The bra was not the soft-cupped kind she'd always worn, but a new one that William had bought for her in St Louis. He'd appeared in the doorway to Stella's room one afternoon, and handed her a brown paper parcel without saying anything or meeting her gaze. When she saw what it was, Stella realised Grace must have known she'd need a bigger one and had spoken to William. Stella couldn't bear to think of how the fisherman must have stood awkwardly in Knight's Ladieswear – having to quote, once again, the predicament of his wife, confined to her house.

The assistant had picked out an ugly old-woman's bra with thick straps and four hooks at the back. It was covered with lumpy lace in a grubby beige tone. Stella tried to forget it was there, hidden beneath the old workshirt of William's that she was wearing. Like the bra, the shirt had been handed to her by William a week earlier – without any comment. She'd understood she was to wear it when she went out in public, to cover the fact that her jeans would no longer do up properly. She had to leave the button above the fly undone, like Laura did when she put on a bit of extra weight.

But it was not fat that pushed against the denim waistband. When Stella lay on her bed and pressed her fingers into her abdomen, she could just feel her womb, a hard round bump set deep into her pelvis. Inside, she knew, was a little curled creature that looked like a newborn rabbit – hairless, with an over-sized head. Stella had studied drawings of foetuses – one for each month of pregnancy. They were cross-sections, as if a series of wombs had been cut open and the contents exposed.

The diagrams were in a paperback book called *Your Pregnancy* that Stella had discovered in the reference section of the mobile-library van. The girl had hidden with the book by the shelf at the back. As she'd flipped through the pages, phrases had lodged in her head.

. . . nourished by the placenta . . .

. . . sucking and swallowing reflexes . . .

. . . the liver produces bile . . .

. . . it looks almost human now, but could not survive outside the uterus . . .

. . . the appearance of tooth buds . . .

Stella had struggled to memorise as much information about the different stages as possible. Then she'd noticed there were whole chapters on diet, health, labour and birth. So many things she needed to know. A sense of panic grew inside her. The books in the van got changed every month. Next time she came back, *Your Pregnancy* might not be there.

Stella couldn't remember deciding to steal the book. Her hand seemed to move of its own accord – slipping the object under her loose shirt and pushing it down inside the front of her jeans, pressing the hard lump back into her body. Then she'd walked towards the librarian's desk at the front, her heart hammering in her chest.

'I didn't know you read crime,' Miss Morrel commented as she stamped the borrowing card. Her ageing hands fumbled with the inkpad.

Stella looked blank. She had grabbed a couple of novels from the shelf without even reading the titles.

'I'll have to recommend some more for you.' The librarian wrote herself a note.

Stella. Crime.

By the time Miss Morrel looked up, Stella had reached the door. The girl smiled her thanks at the old woman, and disappeared.

The brick wall pressed firmly into Stella's back. She used both hands to push herself away from it, then she walked slowly round to the other side. She closed her eyes so as not to start searching for clues, omens . . .

If an ant crosses my path, the hole will be empty.

If a seagull squawks . . .

If I can just keep breathing evenly, slowly . . .

She pushed her hand inside the hole in the brickwork, and felt around in the space behind the plaque. She knew the shape of every crack in the bricks, and the width of every line of mortar.

She knew the feeling of a space that was utterly empty.

Turning to face the sea, she curled her hands into fists. He'll come, she told herself. He will. Something has delayed him.

She blamed Bakti. Zeph's mother had made him stay longer.

She blamed *Tailwind*. The yacht had become damaged in a storm and could not be sailed again until she was mended. She imagined Zeph working hard, sanding and varnishing on a stranger's boat, to get the money for sailcloth, rope, timber.

But there were other voices in her head – ones that were growing stronger with each day that passed. They muttered that Zeph would have been here by now if he were really coming. Or he would have found a way to contact her and let her know what he was doing.

If he were still safe, alive.

If he truly loved her.

A small crack opened up inside her, a chill of doubt leaking slowly into her heart. She turned her thoughts consciously against it.

Deep down, she knew he would come.

I promise to return.

CHAPTER NINE

Stella rang the little brass bell that stood beside the cash register. She heard the creak of the couch, out in the sitting room, then Mr Barron appeared in the doorway. He wiped crumbs from his mouth with the back of his hand.

'What do you want?' he demanded. A week ago his wife had left Halfmoon Bay, to visit her sister who was in hospital in Melbourne. The man made no effort to hide his displeasure at having been left in charge of the shop.

'Is there any mail?' Stella asked.

Mr Barron gestured towards the pigeonholes. 'William's already picked it up.'

'Was there a letter for me?' Stella asked. She looked at the mixed-lollies display as she spoke, and tried to make her voice sound light and casual.

'How should I know – I just stick them in the holes,' Mr Barron said.

Stella glanced up at him. 'I just thought you might have noticed – by chance.'

Mr Barron frowned, puzzled. 'Why don't you ask your dad?'

'Oh, I will,' she said quickly. 'I just forgot.' She forced a smile.

Mr Barron tapped his hands on the counter impatiently. 'Want to buy anything?'

The girl shook her head.

'See you, then.' Mr Barron turned back towards the doorway, his eyes already seeking the coloured flicker of the television screen. He paused as a sudden gust of wind rattled the window frames. 'Bloody wind,' he said. 'Close the door on your way out, will you?'

Before Stella had a chance to respond, he was gone.

She pulled the door shut behind her and stepped out into the wind – holding her hands over her body while she checked to see if anyone was coming. The place appeared empty of people, and she paused, breathing in the fresh smell of rain in the air. Then she crossed to where her bike was leaning up against the wall. She was about to reach for the handlebars when a figure appeared – a woman, hurrying round the corner from the pub.

Stella recognised her instantly from a dozen small details of movement and shape. Pauline. The girl stood still, frozen with dismay. Then she glanced around urgently to see how she could avoid a meeting.

It was too late.

Pauline's face, as she came near, was torn with mixed emotion. The two looked at one another, caught in a tense silence. Stella could not bring herself to ask about Jamie – how he was managing so far from home, and how Pauline was coping without him – and yet she knew no other subject was possible. Pauline seemed lost for words as well. Her eyes were watery, and her hands moved helplessly at her sides.

Finally, Pauline spoke. 'I haven't seen you for ages. I've been meaning to come out and see Grace, but it's been one thing after another. Brian went to the mainland to visit Jamie. Then the two little ones got ill . . .' She broke off, searching the girl's face. 'You look tired. Are you all right?'

'Yes, I'm fine,' Stella said. She fought to put a smile on her lips.

Pauline's expression softened. 'Look,' she said, 'I don't understand what happened between you and Jamie. But I want you to know – I don't blame you for it. You were honest with him. I can't pretend I'm not sad . . .'

Stella felt tears aching behind her eyes. She took a breath to steady

150

herself. She had to be cool, calm, distant. She could not afford to start talking to Pauline. Jamie's mother was one person she could not lie to with any certainty of success . . .

Suddenly, Pauline spread her arms, ready to take Stella into an embrace. 'Come here, love.'

Stella stiffened. In that instant she pictured how Pauline would draw her in close to her soft bosom – close enough for the woman to know that Stella's body had changed.

The girl backed away, as if to avoid something dangerous or unpleasant.

A tremor of shock passed over Pauline's face – followed quickly by a look of deep hurt.

Stella stared at her, trying desperately to think of a way of explaining herself. But there was none.

'I'm in a hurry,' the girl murmured. 'I'll see you . . .'

She grabbed her bike and wheeled it quickly away, veering sideways to pass Pauline. As she climbed onto the seat and began riding, she sensed the woman still standing there, unmoving.

Rain poured from the sky. It ran in small streams along the furrows between the cream bricks of the Seafarers' Memorial. Stella felt it beating against her bare head and soaking in through her clothes, chilling her skin.

She gazed out to sea, her mind empty. She was only vaguely aware of movement behind her, and jumped in surprise when a hand came down onto her shoulder, pulling her around.

William stood there, frowning with concern. He wore his oilskin jacket but he had no hat and his hair was plastered onto his forehead; drops of rain fell from his eyebrows.

'What are you doing here?' he demanded. 'Standing in the rain . . .'

Stella gave no answer. She rubbed one finger over David Grey's plaque, smearing white bird-droppings over the letters.

William sighed in exasperation. Then he turned to look along the wharf, scanning the line of fishing boats and the empty moorings. 'It's that – Robert! You still think he's coming back!' He stared at his daughter, lips parted with amazement.

Stella looked at him in silence. Rain drummed on the tin roof of the shelter shed. It hissed into the sea.

'There must be a reason he hasn't come,' she said. 'Something's happened to him.' She paused, steeling herself to push on. 'I have to know. Has a letter ever come for me? At the shop?'

She held her breath. She was accusing her father of something akin to dishonesty.

William pulled away from her, shaking his head in disbelief. Then he looked into her eyes. 'If it had, I'd have given it to you. You know that.'

His words were firm and clear, cutting through the rain. Slowly, Stella nodded her head.

'He's forgotten all about you,' William said. 'You have to accept it.' He was quiet for a moment. When he continued, there was a softer tone to his voice. 'It's for the best, anyway. We have to deal with this ourselves.'

He put his hand on Stella's shoulder. She felt herself drawn to him. It was the first time he had touched her like this – gently, kindly – since she had let him down so badly.

'It'll be all right, Stella. Trust me. I know what's best for you. We just have to stick together.'

There was a pained look in the man's eyes. For an instant Stella glimpsed the depth of his hurt and disappointment.

'I'm sorry, Dad,' she said.

He nodded – a heavy, weary gesture. 'So am I.'

They stood in silence, the rain falling between them. Then, from over near the wharf came the sound of someone calling. They both turned to find its source.

It was Spinks, standing in the door of Joe's wheelhouse. 'Is everything all right?' he shouted across.

William raised one hand, waving away the man's concern. His expression hardened again. 'Now look what you've done!' He glanced up towards the pub and over to the fish factory. Then he grasped Stella's arm and marched her away. 'People are watching us!'

⌇

Stella closed the lid of the esky and put it down by the back door beside a pile of oilskins. Then she returned to the kitchen table and began wrapping up cakes and loaves of bread in the crumpled squares of foil that William always brought back from the boat to be washed and dried and used again. The kitchen was bathed in yellow light, shed by a bare bulb that hung down over the table. It was still dark outside: the thin grey dark that signalled the waning of the night.

Stella stifled a yawn as she placed the silver packages into a cardboard box. She was aware of Grace watching – making sure her daughter checked each item for tiny gaps that would let moisture escape. The last thing William would want to eat out at sea would be a slice of bread or cake that had turned dry and hard.

Though it was not yet five in the morning, Grace was fully dressed in a skirt, shirt, shoes and stockings. Her hair had been brushed and tied back. Some fishermen's wives stayed in bed while their husbands got up to go to work – or they shambled into their kitchens wearing stained dressing gowns and old slippers. But Grace always rose when William did, to prepare her husband a proper breakfast and pack up the food for his voyage. Now that Stella was neither on holiday nor going to school, she sensed that she should do the same.

She had been out to the shed twice already this morning, to fetch pies and cakes from the freezer. She'd welcomed the chance to escape William's cool silence. As she walked through the garden she felt her body awakening to the brisk air – picking up the timid fragrances of the fading night, the first stirring of birds in their nests. She could almost feel the night withdrawing, the day about to march in over the horizon. After the weeks of feeling sick and exhausted, a new energy coursed through her body with a power that was almost tangible. She could see it in her face – reflected in the dark rectangle of the kitchen window. Her skin glowed, pale and clear. Her cheeks were pink, her lips were sleek and red.

In the second trimester you will feel invigorated, full of life and energy. Enjoy this time with your husband . . .

Stella imagined herself like a piece of fruit: clothed in perfect skin; glowing with health; promising softness, sweetness. But, hidden away at the core, the flesh was hard. The heart was coated with steel.

Hope had died inside her. Zeph was not coming back. And there was no one else to rescue Stella from William's plan. The only relative she had in Australia was Daniel, and, apart from his gifts, he was a complete stranger to her. And what help could a man – who, as far as she knew, was a bachelor – be expected to offer a teenage girl and her baby?

Stella leaned against the metal edge of the sink – cold pressing into her belly. As she watched, the sky began to separate itself from the sea, growing a faint shade lighter. There was no warm tinge to it, though. The sun, when it rose, was going to be locked away behind bleak grey clouds.

William stomped his feet into his boots. By the back door he stood with a bucket in one hand and the esky in the other. He looked across the small room towards Stella. He kept his eyes on her face, as if the sight of her body offended him. Glancing down, Stella saw that the T-shirt she'd grabbed from the drawer and put on was stretched too tight over her breasts and rose up over the small mound that strained the top of her jeans. She half-turned to hide herself.

'There's everything you need in there.' William tilted his head towards the pantry. 'I'm going to padlock the gate behind me, so that there's no risk of visitors.' He gave Stella a warning frown. 'You are not to leave.'

'I won't,' Stella said.

After the scene at the wharf, William had decided his daughter was to stay at home. She could not be trusted to keep a low profile. And anyway, all it would take would be for the wind to blow Stella's shirt against her body and their secret might be given away. It was not worth the risk – especially when there was only about a month left for them to get through. Stella had to leave for the mainland while she could still hide her condition – in case she were to be seen by someone at the airport or on the plane. Soon it would be time for Grace's bad back to improve, and for Stella's plan of going away to school in England to be modified to allow for a European holiday – a reward for her being such a good and caring daughter.

But, for now, Grace's slipped disc had to take a turn for the worse. William had told Mr Barron that while the crisis lasted he would do the shopping for the house and get the mail between voyages. He'd begun by taking down a large shopping list from Grace, and laying in a good supply of groceries. Stella had stacked everything away in the pantry: there was enough fresh food to last the week that he would be at sea; and enough dry stores for a month.

William opened the back door. A light breeze came in, stirring the unused pieces of foil wrapping that had been left behind on the table. Grace hurried to gather them up. Then she flicked a quick glance around the rest of the kitchen.

'I'm off, then,' William said.

He waited for Grace to kiss him on the cheek, and then he picked up the last of his things. He did not ask Stella to take care of her mother, as he had done since she'd been old enough to stand on a chair and help wash the dishes. Instead, he gave his daughter a doubtful look. Stella knew he would have preferred to stay here and keep an eye on her – to make certain she stayed safely at home. But he had to go on working. Already the female crays were spawning and could not be taken; only the males were fair game. And he still needed to earn more money to add to the savings locked away in the metal cashbox in Aunt Jane's sideboard. There had to be enough to pay for

Stella's trip to England; and before that there was the expense of her secret journey to countryside Victoria and the Home for Unmarried Mothers. William simply could not afford to stay at home.

As he turned towards the lightening sky, Stella caught a last glimpse of her father's face. He wore an expression of grim satisfaction. It was the look of a man who knew that things would get worse before they got better. But now, at least, he could see the beginning of the end.

As the sound of the ute died away, a dense quiet seemed to descend on the house. The supplies William had brought in, and the knowledge that he was going to lock the gate behind him, made Stella feel as though she and Grace were cut off from the world – Seven Oaks was like a boat adrift from its moorings.

From her place at the sink, Stella glanced over to the table where Grace was stacking up dirty teacups. If the woman felt the same strange sense of isolation she gave no sign of it. She was already eyeing her recipe book, up on its shelf.

Stella swished the soap-saver through a tub of hot water so that the surface frothed with tiny bubbles. The sight was reassuringly normal. She put the plates in and began to rub off the crumbs with a mop.

'Put some gloves on.' Grace's voice came from behind her. 'You'll dry out your hands.'

'I never wear gloves,' Stella protested.

'Yes, but . . .' Grace carried the cups to the sink. 'It's different for you – now.'

Stella held the mop still.

Different because you're pregnant.

That was what Grace meant.

Stella turned round. 'Why? Why is it different now?'

'Your skin changes, that's all,' Grace said. She'd retreated to the table, where she busied herself scrubbing at a spot on the polished surface. 'I never had dry hands till . . . then.'

Stella fixed her gaze on her mother's face. This was the first time Grace had spoken about her daughter's pregnancy in a way that acknowledged it was a state she'd once experienced for herself. Grace always made it sound more like an exotic disease from which Stella needed to protect herself. She'd given the girl some cream to help prevent stretch marks, and told her not to risk straining her back. If Stella took care, she'd explained, she would come through this with her body unscathed.

'What else happened to you – when you were expecting?' Stella asked.

Grace gave no reply. It was clear from the set of her mouth that she wished she could retract her remark. But Stella refused to be put off. The small morsel Grace had thrown to her had awakened a dormant hunger. Stella could feel it in her body, urgent and strong. The book – *Your Pregnancy* – was not enough. She had to talk to a real person, someone who had been in her place before. A woman. A mother.

'Please tell me.' Stella didn't try to hide the pleading in her voice.

'I don't think it's helpful for us to talk about it,' Grace said firmly. 'I agree with your father. Least said, soonest mended.'

Stella plunged her hands deep into the hot water. Her skin smarted. She watched it begin to turn pink.

It will never be mended.

She closed her eyes, pressing away tears. She could hear Grace behind her, still rubbing away at the same stain on the table. She turned to face her.

'I've been thinking about – everything.' Stella fought to keep her voice steady. She didn't want to break down, like a child. She could still remember how William had flung those words at her.

You're just a child.

She wrapped her arms across her body to offer herself some comfort. 'You know – about going away, having the baby. The adoption.'

She saw her mother stiffen, the woman's eyes narrowing with caution.

'I know I won't see it, after it's born. I know that's for the best.'

She took in a long, shuddering breath. What could she say next? That she had given up hope of Zeph ever coming back? That she knew now that she would be going away to the Home. She would be giving birth to her baby there – and handing it over to strangers.

It was too much – too terrible to put into words. The thoughts alone were hard enough, churning in her head. They turned round and round like the treacherous waters of the Potboil, where sandbanks shifted and the sea swirled into dark spirals that threatened to suck you down.

Stella stared mutely at her mother. She could see her own pain mirrored in Grace's face. For a moment it seemed the woman was about to speak – but then she shook her head, as if to break free from her feelings. She was going to walk away, Stella saw. The curtain of silence would fall back down. Stella felt desperate. There was no way to stop it.

Then an idea came to her. It arrived fully formed, as though it had been sent from somewhere else.

'I want to give it a present,' she said. 'Something that can go with it – to the family.'

Grace responded with a faint nod, a guarded look in her eyes.

'It has to be something I've made . . .' Stella added, '. . . myself.'

As Grace took in the meaning of her daughter's words, the tension eased from her features. 'I don't see what harm that could do,' she said tentatively.

'I want you to help me,' Stella said. The words circled in her head. *I want you to help me.*

'I need you to help me. Please.' Pain tightened Stella's chest. She felt as if she were drowning in a dark sea. Grace was her only hope of rescue.

'All right,' Grace said. 'What do you want to make?'

'I don't know.' Stella heard the words coming from her mouth – all stretched out and dark in colour – like a moan in the night. She clasped her hands together to keep them from trembling.

Grace avoided meeting Stella's gaze. She smoothed the front of her apron with her hands. When she finally spoke, she kept her tone light.

'Well, perhaps a receiving blanket,' she suggested. 'Made with flannel, or woollen cloth. Or . . . a crocheted bonnet. That wouldn't be too difficult.'

Behind the bright voice, Stella picked up a note of doubt. Grace knew her daughter had never before shown any interest in learning to knit or sew. Home economics was the one subject at school in which Stella had always performed poorly.

'I don't want it to be easy,' Stella said. 'I want it to be something . . . really good.'

'I understand,' Grace said. Her voice was gentle, kind. Now, at last, she seemed to realise how much her daughter needed her. 'Let's begin with choosing some wool, then. I'm sure I've got some put away.'

Stella clung to the voice, wrapping the words around herself, feeling their touch against her skin. She looked towards the sea room where Grace's sewing chest sat by the fireplace. She could picture all the bundles of fabric and balls of wool tucked away inside. The thought of them there, neat and in order as they always had been, made her feel calm and safe.

'Not in there,' Grace said. 'Wait a minute.'

She left the room. Stella heard her footsteps heading into the main bedroom, and then returning. She beckoned for her daughter to follow, and walked towards the side door.

The freezer hummed quietly in the corner of the shed. Early sun slanted in through the windows, making patches of brightness on the dusty floor.

Grace crossed to the far corner of the space and bent down to look under William's workbench. Following her, Stella saw an old trunk with metal-bound corners. She knew it was there – she'd tried to open it once, to see what it held. But it had been locked.

'You'll have to give me a hand.' Grace moved aside to let Stella help her drag the trunk out. It was not heavy, but it was awkward to manoeuvre between the legs of the workbench. Finally the box stood out in the open.

Grace took a small brass key from her skirt pocket. She looked at it for a second, and then she knelt down on the floor and inserted it into the rusted lock. Watching her, Stella was reminded of the cutlery box hidden under the sacks and tarpaulins in the opposite corner. She glanced around the rest of the shed. How many other things belonging to Grace were hidden here, she wondered – in this place that she'd always thought of as being William's domain.

Grace lifted the lid, letting a faint woody fragrance escape into the air. She closed her eyes, breathing in deeply. Then she bent over the trunk and began to sort through the contents.

Stella peered over her shoulder, catching glimpses of objects as they were lifted and laid aside. A pink ballet slipper; a bundle of letters tied together with a white ribbon; mysterious packages, shrouded in tissue paper. A record, with a photograph of a dark-skinned woman on the cover; and a folded tablecloth embroidered with the Boyd family coat of arms. Stella eyed them all hungrily as they came briefly into view and then disappeared, like flotsam tossed in a choppy sea.

'Here it is.' Grace tugged at something deep inside the chest, and drew out a bulging bag made of blue cloth. The sharp end of a knitting needle stuck out through a hole in the side.

Stella pushed twigs into the grate, feeding blue-tinged flames that rose from the long curls of dried orange peel that the Birchmores used as firelighters. She was aware of Grace setting down cups of tea on the dining table, and then beginning to unpack the blue bag.

By the time the fire was burning properly, two dozen balls of fine wool had been laid out. Grace grouped them according to their colour. White. Pink. Cream. Delicate shades of yellow and green.

'There's no blue,' Stella said, taking a seat at the table opposite Grace.

Grace's hands became still, poised over the wool. 'I didn't make anything blue.' A thoughtful, wondering look came over her face – as if she were remembering something extraordinary. 'I knew you were going to be a girl.'

'How did you know?' Stella asked.

'I could see you,' Grace answered. 'I could see your face in my head.' She used the same confident tone as she did when reading out the ingredients of a recipe.

Stella looked at the balls of wool. She remembered her vision of the baby swathed in a sarong, lying in the hammock – gazing up at her with Zeph's green eyes, framed in a face that was pale like hers.

She pushed the image aside. Who could say what this lump inside her would turn out to be? Or what kind of face it would have? Perhaps it would take on the features of its new parents – in the same way that horse-lovers grew big teeth and lips. Stella found the idea strangely reassuring. It was not a real baby then, inside her – just the makings of one. Its life would truly begin when its mother held it in her arms.

'White's the safest choice,' Grace said. 'Or cream. And you could finish the edges in lemon.' She lifted up the bag to shake out the last of its contents. A crochet hook and some knitting needles clattered onto the table. Then a soft bundle fell out – something wrapped in white muslin. Grace looked puzzled as she opened it, then her hands froze. Beneath them was a folded piece of crochet work. Pink. Stella saw that Grace was about to snatch it up and hide it away. She reached over and took it. She held up a tiny jacket – stretching out its arms, letting the body hang limply between them.

Grace looked at the jacket in silence. In the fireplace a burnt twig subsided into ash and fell to the hearth.

'It's mine, isn't it?' Stella asked. 'You made it for me.' She swallowed on a lump in her throat. It was like a fairy's dress – the stitching so fine, the pink so subtle, the satin ribbons at the neck shimmering like moonshine. Made specially for her . . . Then she frowned as a thought came to her. 'Why is it here – in the knitting bag? Didn't I wear it?'

Grace pressed her lips together. She became very still. Her brow furrowed – she seemed to be weighing up a decision. Finally, she spoke.

'I didn't want to give it to you. Before you were born, I was looking forward to it so much. But then, when it happened, it was all different.'

Stella felt her stomach turn cold. Dropping the jacket, she looked out at the sea, her gaze travelling over the flat grey plain. Waves washed in and out, untroubled by what was coming . . . Turning back, she faced her mother. 'What do you mean?' she whispered.

Grace chewed tensely at her lip and looked down at her hands as she replied. 'I'll try to explain to you how it was. While I was expecting you, William was studying for his final exams. He was at medical school.' She glanced up as Stella's lips parted in surprise. 'I know, he always says he could never work inside. But fishing wasn't William's first choice. He wanted to be a doctor. We've never spoken of it – you'll see why in a minute – but your grandfather had been a doctor. When he was killed, he was on the path to a very promising career, according to Aunt Jane.' A frosty note entered Grace's voice – faint, but discernible. 'She encouraged William to follow in his footsteps. The only problem was that William just didn't have the head for that kind of study. When I met him he'd already failed his finals once – this was his second try. His last chance.' Grace shook her head slowly. 'He was working night and day, locked away in his study. I've never seen anybody apply themselves to a task the way he did. I just admired his determination. I spent my time learning to knit and sew – and cook . . . I barely saw your father, except for meals. But I didn't mind because I knew that when the exam was over he would be a doctor. And then he would be happy.'

Stella raised her eyebrows. It was hard to imagine William wanting to be anything but a fisherman.

'He had everything planned out,' Grace went on. 'Colleagues of his father used their influence on his behalf. After he graduated he was going to do his internship in a hospital in Gloucester. After that

162

he was to join a practice in a village nearby. We were going to live above the surgery. I was going to help with the patients, too – as much as I could, with a baby to care for.'

Stella stared at her. 'But you don't like noise and people coming and going. That's why you decided to live out of town.'

For a brief time, Grace was quiet. Then she continued. 'I wanted to be useful – to help people. In fact, that's how I met your father in the first place. I was a volunteer at a Salvation Army hostel in Bristol. William was helping there, too, one night a week – as a medical student. We met in the cafeteria.' She smiled fondly. 'I fell in love with him straightaway. He was so handsome – all the other women watched him wherever he went. It wasn't just his looks, though. There was something special about him – a kind of strength, a certainty about himself. Everyone looked up to him. He always knew exactly what to do.'

Grace paused, the warmth draining from her face. 'He failed his exam. It was awful. I was there at the college when he went up onto the stage to receive his results. It's a cruel system. The students who've passed stay up there, but the ones who fail have to turn round, in front of everyone, and walk back down. That's what William had to do.' Grace shuddered. 'I'll never forget the look on his face. He stayed in his study for days – with all his books and notes still spread out on the desk. He wouldn't eat or come to bed. I tried to help, but nothing I did or said made any difference.

'A month later, you were born. The birth was difficult, but you were a good baby. Quiet. It was almost as though you knew how things were . . . As soon as I came home from hospital we had to find somewhere else to live. William had given notice on the flat we were renting because we were to move to a hospital flat. He didn't like anything that we found. He just wouldn't accept that everything had changed. His dream was over. It was a terrible time. My family tried to help. They offered William a position in Boyd Shipping. There was a manager's house at Avonmouth that my father said we could have. He offered money as well, but that only made things worse.'

'Why?' Stella asked. 'If you needed help . . . That's what families are for.'

Grace rolled a ball of wool lightly under her hand. 'My family was very different to William's. The Boyds are an old family – and quite wealthy. William felt inferior to them.' She glanced at Stella. 'It's different in England. People think that way, even today . . . Anyway, my father persisted. William got very angry. He refused even to go to their house. He thought they all despised him – the whole Boyd family.'

'Is that why he doesn't like Daniel?' Stella asked.

Grace's hand grew still, resting on the wool. 'It's only one of the reasons,' she said. 'William doesn't – we don't – approve of the way he lives. I don't want to say any more than that.'

Stella nodded her head. She would have liked to push for more information about Daniel, but didn't want to risk bringing the conversation to an end.

'The next thing that happened,' Grace continued, 'was that William went to London, to look for work. On the way to an interview he saw a display in the window of Australia House. He decided we'd emigrate to Sydney. Then he found out about Tasmania. He said it was about as far away from everything as anyone could go.' Her lips twisted into a wry smile. '"Next stop, Antarctica" – that's what he said.'

Grace made a small circle with one hand – taking in the room, the house, the sea.

'And so – you came here, and found this place,' Stella said. She smiled.

A strange look flickered briefly onto Grace's face. It took Stella a second to work out what it meant. She gasped.

'You weren't pleased! You didn't want to come here!'

'No,' Grace replied. So simple. Just – no.

Stella felt a surge of anger. That one short syllable contained a rejection of all that surrounded them – the life that they shared.

'Well, if you didn't want to come here, why did you?'

Grace shrugged. 'It was 1960. Women went where their husbands went. They didn't question things like they do now. And I had you to think of. I just wanted your father to be happy. I made the right choice. It was harder than I thought it would be, but I succeeded.' Grace looked up at Stella with a proud tilt to her chin. 'He is happy here.'

'But what about you?' Stella asked. She twisted a ball of wool in her hands, wrenching the soft strands.

'A wife and a mother puts others before herself,' Grace said in a quiet voice.

'But that's not fair,' Stella said.

'Lots of things are not fair.' Grace reached her hand towards the pink jacket – a rosy mound lying on the polished tabletop. 'Look at Pauline – five children in eight years, two of them accidents. And all I could manage was one.'

Stella leaned towards her. 'Did you want more children as well – not just Dad?'

Grace drew in a long slow breath. She looked into Stella's eyes. 'I wanted lots of things.'

Stella flinched under the intensity of her mother's gaze. The words echoed in the air between them – blunt and bleak.

Grace turned away, looking out through the window in the way she often did, checking the horizon for the *Lady Tirian*. She squared her shoulders as if bracing herself for trouble.

'William would be so angry if he knew I'd said all this to you,' she said. 'I promised him I would never tell anyone why we left England. He's made a new life here. He wants the past left behind. But I have to speak now. I want to make sure you understand how important it is to – get through this difficult time – and leave it all behind you.'

She faced Stella again. Her grey eyes matched the sea outside. 'After you've finished school in England, you don't have to come back and live in Halfmoon Bay. I'll miss you terribly and I hope you'll return often for visits, but you mustn't feel tied to us. I want you to be free – to choose the life you want. Do you understand?'

Stella looked down at the floor. What had William said? By springtime she would be free.

Free to come and go. Free to stay away. Like Zeph.

Lifting her eyes, Stella nodded slowly. 'Yes,' she said. 'I do.'

Grace reached across the table to Stella and laid a hand on the girl's arm.

'I'll help you,' she said. 'I'll help you to get through it.' She picked up the blue bag and drew out a bundle of crochet hooks. 'Now, let's make a start.'

The white wool seemed to move of its own accord in Grace's hands. Stella watched mesmerised as it jumped from the freckled fingers to the crochet hook and back. A long line of stitches appeared, trailing down. She wanted the moment to stretch on forever: a stillness punctuated by little movements and all the small sounds Grace made – licking her lips, or pausing to brush back a loose strand of hair.

Eventually, Grace handed the crochet to Stella and sat watching while her daughter tried to replicate the movements of fingers and wool and hook. It was harder than it looked.

Grace came to stand behind Stella, leaning over the back of her chair.

'Just copy me,' she said. She put her hands over Stella's and led the girl's clumsy fingers in a slow and careful dance. Stella tried hard to keep up, but she was distracted by the touch of her mother's skin, the closeness of their bodies. She breathed in Grace's smell – the scent of rose-perfumed talc and Velvet soap.

'There you are – you've got it,' Grace said.

Stella looked up. There was an encouraging smile on her mother's face. Grace didn't appear to notice that Stella kept winding the wool the wrong way round the hook. She didn't comment on the fact that the stitches were of uneven size, or shake her head when the hook fell on the floor. It was as if all the words that had flowed out of Grace had left the woman feeling more open and relaxed – failings and careless actions no longer seemed to matter any more.

The next day dawned with a light steady rain that looked likely to set in. There was no wind with it – nothing that would cause William to abandon his voyage and come home – but it kept Grace and Stella indoors, wrapping them in a cozy quiet.

After lunch, Grace suggested that Stella have a rest, lying down on the sea-room couch – something she had only been allowed to do in the past when she was unwell. Grace even brought the mohair travel rug from her bedroom and draped it over Stella's legs. Then the woman returned to the kitchen to do some baking.

Stella had the copy of *Anna Karenina* at her side, but she soon gave up trying to read. She just lay still, listening to the peaceful sound of the rain pattering against the roof.

She was drifting off to sleep when Grace entered the room, holding the two velvet-covered cushions that went with the armchair in the main bedroom. 'I brought these for you,' her mother said as she approached. She leaned over Stella and wedged them behind her shoulders and hips. 'Now you'll be more comfortable.'

Grace spoke in a gentle, soothing tone – as though she were addressing a child. Her manner reminded Stella of someone. After a while, she realised who it was – Pauline. She savoured the thought as she nestled gratefully against the cushions.

Grace disappeared back to the kitchen, returning shortly carrying a tray. She set it down beside Stella. There was a glass of milk and three slices of cake on a plate. Stella recognised Aunt Jane's Best Family Sponge.

Raising herself on her elbow, Stella picked up one of the pieces and bit into it, cupping her hand under her chin to catch the crumbs. Licking her lips, she took another bite. Then she paused, looking carefully at the texture of the sponge. It looked different from usual – darker, heavier.

'I added some malt,' Grace said. 'And some lecithin.'

Stella stared at her – then she glanced over to the sideboard, as if the spirits of Aunt Jane's ancestors might be watching . . .

'It makes it a bit heavy,' Grace added. 'But it's much better for you.

And the baby as well.' She smiled a little awkwardly, as though she'd said something she hadn't meant to. 'Now – why don't you watch some television?'

'There won't be anything on,' Stella said. 'Only sport.' She was almost unaware of replying. She kept thinking of how the word *baby* had fallen from Grace's lips – the way it had stood out, bold and clear, like a landmark on the horizon.

'I've got an idea,' Grace said, looking thoughtful. Then she quickly left the room again.

When she reappeared this time her face was shiny with rain. She held a record in her hand. Stella recognised it as the one she had seen in the trunk. It didn't look like any of the other records Grace owned. Stella glanced at the neat pile of albums that were stacked on a shelf nearby. They were all of classical music. William bought a new recording each year for Grace's birthday. His wife was always delighted with his choice. Stella had heard Grace say to Miss Spinks that William knew what music she liked better than she did herself.

Slipping the record from its sleeve, Grace went over to the record player. She glanced at Stella – giving her a small, mysterious smile before lifting the lid and placing the disk carefully onto the turntable. She set in place William's special device that cleaned records while they played.

Stella heard the needle coming down onto the record, and the scratchy quiet that preceded the first notes. Then she lifted her head in surprise as a rich, strong voice erupted into the room.

A woman singing.

The voice was velvet-smooth – deep and strong, and charged with emotion. Stella could not pick out any words, but it didn't matter.

The voice was the song. She felt it entering her body, playing straight into her soul. Wild and free . . .

Stella looked across to her mother. Grace was in the middle of the room. She seemed lost in the sound, her eyes closed, her hips moving slightly to its rhythm. The song was taking her back, Stella could see – to another life. The one she'd left behind.

The hook was small and the wool so fine that Stella knew the crocheted jacket would take her an impossibly long time to complete. She felt like the fairy-tale princess locked in the tower and told to spin a whole roomful of hay into silken yarn. Without a miracle, she knew the task could not be accomplished.

Stella drew comfort from the thought – as if it meant this time-frozen interlude would somehow continue. For as long as the jacket remained unfinished, the baby would grow, untroubled, inside Stella's body. Grace would find new, special ways of taking care of her pregnant daughter. The *Lady Tirian* would stay out at sea.

The future would never arrive . . .

But in reality, Stella knew, there was no way to stop the passing of time.

Every morning, when she got up, she made another mark on the calendar – the same calendar where she had once counted and re-counted the days 29, 30, 31, 32 . . . The day of her departure – when William would drive her to Hobart and put her on the plane to Melbourne – was not far away. If they stuck to William's schedule, Stella had exactly two and a half weeks left. She would be twenty weeks pregnant by then.

Halfway through.

The fifth month heralds a time of exciting change. By now, the whole world can see that you are expecting a baby!

Hair begins to grow.

The baby has tiny eyelashes and brows . . .

Stella gripped the crochet hook more tightly and worked on until the end of the row. Then she looked back over the small piece of the garment that she'd made. She noticed where she had picked up two stitches at once, two rows back. And she saw that the tension was uneven – some rows were tighter than others. She felt a wave of desolation. The jacket would not be good enough, she was sure.

169

The baby's mother might not even bother to take it home with her. Stella closed her eyes on an image of her gift abandoned in the corner of a green-walled room that smelled of disinfectant – a shadowy place with no windows where they put the newborn babies while they waited for their lives to begin.

Did they leave them alone in there? Crying in the dark . . .

She stood up and began pacing round the room. There was a tightness in her chest that felt like fear. Her hair prickled on the back of her neck. Suddenly, she could not bear to be alone.

She went into the kitchen, where she found Grace preparing another cake mixture. She was using her silver spoon – the one with the Boyd family coat of arms.

The lily, the cat, the star . . .

Looking at the engraved handle, Stella imagined, suddenly, that there might be some meaning in the symbols – some comfort . . . She pointed at the spoon. 'What does it mean? Your family coat of arms . . .'

Grace looked up in surprise. 'How did you know it was ours?'

'I found the cutlery set out in the shed. I guessed it went with the big table that came from your family.'

Grace lifted the spoon from the bowl, dripping batter.

'The lily is a symbol of purity. The star goes with our family motto – "*Super Sidera Votum*". *Aim for the stars*. No one seemed to know the meaning of the cat.' Grace smiled, glancing up. 'When I was little, I used to think it was our pet. Silky. I think that's why I brought this one spoon inside – to remind me of her!' Grace crossed to the sink and turned on the tap to wash her hands. 'We've got no use for the set, of course – it's for two dozen people! William wanted to sell it. But I couldn't do that. It's not really mine, you see.' She turned round to face Stella. 'For hundreds of years it's been handed on to the oldest daughter – or niece, if there's no daughter – in each generation. I'm keeping it for you. You'll pass it on to your –'

She broke off. The water kept running into the sink. Outside, the tank pump hummed.

'I mean,' Grace added hastily, 'when you're married one day. Then you'll have – another baby . . .'

Stella stared at her mother. The moment lasted for only a few seconds, yet suddenly everything looked different – as though a light had been shed into a darkened room.

Stella saw how wrong it was, this plan of William's. How crazy. You don't give a baby away. You keep heirlooms for a baby. You plant trees to celebrate its birth. You knit jackets and make blankets that you handwash in eucalyptus oil and dry in a soft light . . .

Grace tore her gaze away. She returned to the table and bent over her mixing bowl.

But before she did, Stella saw that her mother understood all this as well.

She knew.

Stella waited. She let the new reality set firm and steady in her mind. Then she took a deep breath.

'We can't give our baby away. It's a part of our family. A part of us.'

A tremor passed over Grace's features, like a whisper of wind over the face of the sea. The woman's hands tightened on the edge of the mixing bowl.

'We have to keep him, or her, here with us,' Stella said.

There was a long silence. Stella felt that her life, and her soul, were laid out on a knife-edge – poised on the brink between hope and darkness.

Grace looked up. 'Yes,' she breathed. 'I know. We do.'

Her voice was thin and soft. But Stella caught the words, one by one, and held them safe in her heart. She turned to the window as if to make the sky her witness. The sun was breaking through the grey, shining out from a small patch of blue. The brightness blurred, as tears of relief gathered in Stella's eyes.

CHAPTER TEN

Stella leaned across a bed of bare earth, poking holes into the ground and dropping in cabbage seeds. She followed a string line that Grace had pegged out, so that each row would be straight and parallel to its neighbours.

From inside the house came the sound of Grace's record – turned up loud so that the song drifted out through the open kitchen door. The rich voice seemed to weave a spell, making the simple gardening scene feel like a piece of an epic film.

Not far from Stella, Grace was working in the lily patch. She stood with her legs apart, bracing her body as she lifted a shovel heavily loaded with compost. She was not wearing her gardening skirt. Early that morning, she had appeared in the kitchen wearing a pair of trousers. Stella had stared at her in surprise. She had never seen her mother in trousers before – Grace had always agreed with William that a grown woman should wear a dress. Stella knew without asking where they must have come from . . . They weren't the kind of trousers that were meant for gardening – they were made of velvet; a deep ruby red. They followed the line of Grace's long legs.

As Stella sowed the cabbage seeds she kept stealing glances at her mother. She watched Grace wielding her shovel, muscles tightening in her forearms as she fought its weight. Her mother looked so different from usual – taller, stronger. It was more than just the trousers, Stella realised – there was something new about the way Grace moved her body. As if the power of the woman's song had found its way inside her. Making her bolder and more free.

The two had been outside since early morning, working in the garden. They had exchanged only a few words in that time, but the quiet that surrounded them was bright and charged with energy. They did not need to speak, Stella understood – enough had been said. Grace had agreed that the baby could not be given away. The simple words that she'd uttered still echoed in Stella's ears – as enduring, in the girl's mind, as if they had been carved in solid stone and placed on a mountaintop. They had not yet discussed how they would raise the subject with William, but there was plenty of time for that. The conditions were perfect for fishing, and he would not be home for at least another couple of days.

For now, Grace seemed focused only on her gardening. As she worked, her hands moved quickly, and she paused often to throw brief, sharp looks up at the sky and out to sea. She'd not even stopped to eat breakfast – instead she'd brought a cake out from the kitchen. She and Stella had broken it in half, and eaten hunks of it with bare soiled fingers.

'Winter is coming,' Grace had commented to her daughter by way of explanation.

Stella had nodded knowingly. She was not a child, unaware of the demands of autumn in the garden; she knew how much work there was to be done.

Before the soil became heavy with rain, six more garden beds had to be prepared. Annuals that had flowered over summer and were now just spent stalks had to be pulled up and thrown away. Then the vacant earth had to be broken up and dug over. And finally, a blanket of dead leaves, straw and wallaby dung would be piled on top – to nourish and protect the earth during the long months of winter.

Months of resting, and waiting . . .

Stella looked up from her lines of seed holes, turning towards the bare earth of the lily bed. She pictured the bulbs buried deep underground. They would bide their time hidden there, till the warm weather returned. Then, green shoots would appear, thrusting up into the cool air. Gulls would lay eggs in their cliff-side nests. Buds would form on the hanging fronds of the she-oaks.

It would be springtime.

The baby would be born.

Stella stood up to stretch her cramped legs. She leaned against the fence and – lifting her face to the sky – she closed her eyes. Though the sun was not strong enough to burn now, she could still feel its warmth. The light glowed rosy through her eyelids.

Stella pictured the baby lying in her arms, wrapped in the white crocheted jacket. She could feel its soft skin against hers. A smooth cheek against her breast.

Then, with a shiver of pain, she remembered another touch. Zeph's hand, cupping her breast – his fingers, cool and salt-damp, brushing her nipples . . . His arms around her body had felt so strong. He had held her so tightly. As if he would never let her go. Never abandon her . . .

She laid one hand over the place where the baby was growing.

Never, she whispered to it.

Never.

The seaweed was banked along the back of the small beach near the house – left behind there by the storms and high tides of the equinox. Stella walked along to where it was thickest, trailing an empty chaff bag behind her. As her boots sank into the soft weed, a rich smell rose up to her – the tang of fresh shellfish, damp sand and salt – like the essence of the sea distilled. Amongst the dark stalks she could see the tiny cone-shaped shells that Aborigines used to collect for making necklaces. Joe had told Stella how his aunties still knew the secret method of removing the outer coating – revealing an iridescent sheen of deep mauve and green. Stella smiled at the thought of such beauty, concealed by nature. It reminded her of her own body, containing a hidden life . . .

Grace had sent her to gather the seaweed – enough to spread all around the apple tree. It was a big tree now, but Stella remembered when her mother had planted it, about eight years ago. When Grace had finished patting down the earth over the small bundle of roots, she'd sent Stella off on her bike, to go fishing at the wharf.

'It doesn't matter what kind, but I need a lot of fish,' she'd said. 'At least twenty.'

'Why don't you ask Dad to bring some from the bait trap?' Stella had asked, knowing it would take her days to gather a catch of that size.

'Your father does not believe it is necessary,' was all that Grace would say.

The fish had been buried in a big circle around the sapling. The roots, Grace had explained, would be drawn by the powerful presence of the fish rotting in the earth – they'd reach out towards it, and grow wide and strong.

'How did you know to do that?' Stella had asked.

'I've seen it done,' Grace had replied, and said no more.

When William came back from sea, he had scowled at the circle of newly turned earth around the tree. He'd barely spoken during the evening, clearly still offended by what he'd seen.

He refused to eat the apples from that tree. He said they tasted of fish. Joe was given most of them each year; he never complained of the taste. And, even as a child, Stella had suspected it was impossible for the fish to have tainted the fruit. But neither Grace nor Stella argued with William. If he said the apples tasted of fish, they did. Once he decided something, it became fact. Nothing could change it.

Stella stood still, looking down at the weed – the feathery fronds speckled here and there with tiny shells. A shudder of anxiety passed through her. She pictured her father's face – his bottom lip pushed up hard against his top lip, his features rigid as stone.

She shook her head, pushing the image aside. This time it would be different. When William returned from his voyage the new, strong Grace would make him change his mind. Stella would be there at her side when she spoke. Stella imagined how they would look, the two of them shoulder to shoulder, their hands even touching, perhaps – a current running between them, fusing them together and firming their resolve.

William would come to understand, as Grace and Stella had. The baby could not be given away. It was his grandchild. The first Tasmanian Birchmore.

Stella bent over, using both hands to scoop up a big mound of weed. As she did so, she felt the delicate weight of the baby rocking inside her.

The book said it would now be about twenty centimetres long. Stella had found a ruler and measured it out. It was a bit bigger than her hand. She pictured it surrounded by water.

Amniotic fluid. A colourless liquid, which protects the baby inside the sac . . .

She smiled at the thought of a hand-sized baby – a little fish, swimming in her womb. An under-size fish – like the ones she sometimes caught from the wharf. She could always tell when the fish was too light, even as she reeled it in. She knew how it would dangle on her line, sparkling in the sun: a perfect miniature – but too small, yet, to keep.

Still smiling to herself, Stella stuffed the sack until it was full, then she dragged it behind her, up towards the house.

She headed for the back of the shed – near the place where her Sea Wall was propped up against the fence. As she dropped the sack of weed, she bumped the wooden frame, setting the objects jangling on their strings. They seemed to be calling for her attention, but as she cast her eye over them, none of her old treasures trapped her gaze. They were part of another world that had nothing to do with now . . .

Scanning the garden, Stella looked for Grace's blue sunhat – but it was not visible near the lily patch or over by the compost heap. Realising her mother had gone inside, Stella guessed she was preparing some lunch. She felt suddenly hungry. The evening before, Grace had cooked My Own Lamb Pie. She'd set it out to cool on a rack by the window. Stella's mouth watered at the thought of it there: the mound of pastry, baked golden brown; and – sticking out of the middle – the sprig of rosemary, its tips blackened by the heat of the oven.

Stella eased off her boots at the side door and padded into the kitchen. The record had ended and the house was quiet. A dressed chicken lay on the table. Stella faltered at the sight of it lying there, with its goose-bumped skin bare and white. They were having a roast for dinner. She knew what that meant. A tingle of fear ran through her body. William was coming home. Grace, keeping an eye on the sea, had seen the *Lady Tirian* heading in to the bay.

Stella remembered the uneasy look that she'd seen on William's face as he'd prepared to leave. He was returning early, she guessed, to reassure himself that everything was as it should be. Stella took a deep breath to calm herself, and hurried into the sea room.

The extra cushions were gone from the couch. There were no balls of wool on the table and the bulging blue bag had disappeared. She crossed to the record player. The turntable was empty. Grace's record was gone.

She heard a light step behind her and turned to see her mother standing there. The woman had changed into a freshly ironed shirt and skirt. She held her recipe book open in her hands.

'He's coming back,' she said. 'We need to get ready. Pick me some sage and some parsley for the roast.'

Stella stared at her mother's face. The woman appeared calm – as if nothing unusual were about to happen. As if nothing had changed. Stella felt a wave of panic rising inside her.

But then, as Grace turned to go back to the kitchen, Stella glimpsed the page at which the recipe book lay open. Cousin Elizabeth's Special Pudding. William's favourite. The girl breathed out with relief. Now she understood. Grace was making a special effort. She wanted everything to be perfect, beyond reproach – so that William would be in the best possible mood. Before they spoke, before it all began . . .

⤻

Stella forced mouthfuls of food between her lips. Her cutlery clattered clumsily against her plate. Half of a potato slid sideways as she cut through its baked skin. It tumbled down her shirt, printing a trail of gravy.

'Sorry,' Stella said.

'Lean closer to your plate,' William responded. 'Pull your chair in.'

He looked tired, as though the elements had sapped his energy – when, usually, he seemed to return home from the sea looking healthier, bigger; emboldened by his conquest of the sea, the wind, the fish.

Stella glanced at Grace. The woman's plate of food was all but untouched. She kept sipping water, as if afraid to be still.

'I came back early,' William announced, 'because I think the time has come for Stella to leave.'

Stella stared at him. He met her gaze briefly, and then turned to his wife.

'I'm going in to St Louis tomorrow, to arrange the air tickets. It's not worth taking the risk of something going wrong now. The truth getting out.'

Stella looked at Grace, waiting for the woman to open her mouth – to speak. The silence lengthened. Even the sea seemed still. Then she realised – her mother was not going to speak. Not yet. It was up to her to begin.

'We've been thinking, me and Mum . . .' Stella began. She heard Grace catch her breath. 'While you were gone . . . We don't want to give the baby away.' Stella swallowed. 'We want to keep it.'

William frowned at Grace in confusion. 'What on earth is she talking about?'

Grace seemed not to have heard him. She looked past William's shoulder, out towards the sea.

'We want . . .' the words died in Stella's mouth. She took a breath. 'I've changed my mind. I want to keep my baby.'

Once she'd said it she felt strong, as if triumph already lay in her hands. The words flowed out.

'I'm not going away to the Home. I want to stay here. With you. It'll be our baby. You wanted more children. It'll make you happy. Everything will be changed. Mum will be happy. She'll like living here.'

Stella paused to let Grace speak. The woman was staring down into the gravy boat at the brown sludge with a skin of congealed fat.

Stella looked back at her father. He sat still, frozen to his chair – trapped in shock, or anger. She quailed at the sight, snatching her gaze away. She kept on talking, saying the first things that came to her – desperately piling up words like sandbags against a rising tide.

'We don't need anyone else. You can look after me. You're almost a doctor.'

William turned to Grace. His eyes were wide with outrage, but when he spoke his voice was quiet and low. 'What have you been telling her?'

Grace gave a little toss of her head, as if to shake away a fly.

William stood up, scraping back his chair.

Grace's face grew pale as she stared up at her husband. She raised one hand to touch her temple. Her fingers were shaking.

Stella opened her mouth to speak. 'It's not her fault.'

William spun to face her. 'You've said enough. Your mother and I need to talk in private.'

Grace stood up instantly, like someone being pulled by invisible strings. Stella reached a hand towards her. 'Mum . . .' The woman flinched at the touch on her arm. 'It's all right. Just tell him. Please . . .'

Grace glanced at her daughter. Stella forced an encouraging smile onto her lips. But her mother's face was blank, a mask. Stella wanted to scream, to slap her cheek. At the same time she felt empty and hopeless. She knew what was going to happen. William was going to take Grace into their bedroom. He was going to make her go back to supporting his plan.

'No!' Stella jumped to her feet, jolting the table. A glass of water tipped over, spreading a wet stain onto the cloth. 'You have to listen to me. I'm not a child. Mum – please!'

William took Grace's arm and led her from the room. Stella heard their shoes on the bare timber of the hallway, then their muffled steps as they entered the carpeted bedroom. The door shut behind them – a quiet, careful sound.

Stella stood alone by the table, waiting. She heard William talking and the faint creak of the floor as he paced up and down. Then she heard Grace's voice, breaking in. The woman's tone sounded firm and strong. Stella's hopes rose. She imagined the words her mother was saying.

Stella must make her own decision.

It's what I want, too.

I'll never agree to giving the baby away.

Never.

But then the woman's voice grew thinner. William's deeper tone cut it off, again and again. There was a long quiet. Stella felt a twist of pain inside her. She could feel Grace disappearing into silence. Retreating to a place where no one could reach her. Leaving her daughter behind, alone.

Then there were footsteps again in the hallway. Only one pair now – the heavy tread of William wearing his inside boots. When he came into the sitting room, his face looked grave, like a television doctor about to deliver bad news.

'Your mother and I know what's best for you, Stella. You've got your whole life ahead of you. We can't let you destroy your future. We've made our decision. The same decision we all made in the first place.'

'I never agreed,' said Stella. She tried to put some life, some spirit, into her voice – but it sounded hollow and weak. 'I was waiting for –' she stopped herself in time. She still wanted Zeph's name to be her secret. It was all she had of him. His name, and his baby . . . 'I thought he was going to come back. I thought – Robert – would know what to do. Now I see – it's just up to me.'

'It's not up to you,' William said patiently. 'You're not eighteen yet. It's up to us.'

He folded his hands as he spoke. Stella felt a cloak of panic fall over her. He looked like a priest – a man who knew everything and could never be argued with.

'She doesn't agree with you,' Stella said. 'Mum wants to keep the baby. I know she does.'

'How do you know?'

'She said so. And she meant it. I could tell.' Stella looked at him. She imagined trying to explain how she had seen Grace change – come alive. And how it had all been begun by talking about the baby, about Stella being pregnant. Something so simple and yet so powerful . . .

'Let's ask her, shall we?' William said. He put his hand around Stella's shoulder. It might have been a gesture of kindness, except that she could feel the steel in his flesh. If she pulled away, she sensed the hand might close around her bones like a vice.

The air in the bedroom smelled of tea rose and stale lavender. A dusting of talc coated the polished surface of the dressing table, where Grace's silver-backed hairbrushes and pots of face cream were set out in a line.

As Stella walked into the room, her eyes fell on a heap of red cloth near the end of the bed. The velvet trousers. She felt a faint stirring of hope. The last few days had not been a dream.

She turned to look at her mother. Grace was sitting on the side of the bed. She looked small, her shoulders bowed, her head hanging. William came to stand beside her. She leaned towards him almost instinctively, like a flower turning towards the sun.

William put a hand on his wife's shoulder as he faced Stella.

'Ask her, Stella. Ask your mother what she thinks is right.'

Stella looked at Grace. The woman met her gaze, but there was no spark of complicity – just the mute resignation. Stella forced herself to speak. 'Mum. Do you want to keep the baby?'

Grace lowered her face.

'Answer her,' William instructed.

The woman raised her eyes. She looked like a young girl – pleading, but powerless.

'Please – just tell him,' Stella said. 'We need to tell him now.' She tried to smile. She felt like the grown-up tempting a wilful child.

'Your father is right,' Grace said. 'You've got your whole life in front of you.'

Stella stared at her. 'But you said. You agreed.' She threw herself down at Grace's feet. 'Don't you remember? Everything we talked about – the things we did? The baby jacket, the record.'

Grace just shook her head.

Stella got to her feet and backed away. She grasped at the window ledge behind her. Fear invaded her body like a cold fog. If Grace did not help her, how could she stand against William? Where else could she turn?

She drew in a long, slow breath – gathering up pain, fear, hope and longing. She wove them all together to make a single strand, thick and strong. She imagined it wrapped around her words like a rope lashing them together. But her voice, when it came out, was thin and sad – a wind whining through a small gap in a fence.

'Mum. Don't give in to him. Remember the other day?' She felt her voice rising, out of control. 'Tell him! Please! You've got to! I'm not going away!'

'It's for the best,' Grace said quietly. 'One day you will agree.'

William patted the woman's shoulder.

'Don't do this!' Stella screamed. 'You have to stand up to him! What's wrong with you?'

Her hands stretched out towards her mother, fingers flexed. They wanted to grasp Grace by the hair, to bury their nails into the woman's scalp and shake her hard, until life returned to the wooden face.

'That's enough, Stella. I forbid you to speak to your mother like that.' William's voice was harsh, as cold as the winter sea.

Stella's hands fell to her sides. Suddenly the air was gone from her lungs. Her legs became weak. She felt the power of her father's presence, built up over all the years of her life. And she felt Grace's meekness, practised over decades. She knew he would win.

Grace's arm rose towards Stella. 'Please – try to understand . . .'

Stella turned away and stood facing the window, resting her head against the cool, hard pane. Out in the paddock, beyond the garden fence, the cows chewed silently at the bitter grass. A raven pecked at the furry mound of a dead wallaby lying amongst the rushes.

Away to her left, Stella could see the oak tree. Its limbs were bare but for a few dead leaves still clinging to the stems. Grass grew thickly around its slender trunk – and in the long space that had been kept empty, ready for the six other trees.

In that moment, Stella knew. The single oak would stand there forever, with nothing by its side.

CHAPTER ELEVEN

A collection of evening dresses were draped over the couch and armchairs – long swathes of satin, velvet, brocade and chiffon. Their patterns and colours glowed in the lamplight. By the fireplace, pairs of shoes were lined up – high-heeled slippers in gold and silver, and different shades of black, brown, blue. Pieces of jewellery were displayed on the dining table: brooches, strings of pearls, gold chains, and a necklace sparkling with diamonds. William walked up and down, looking intently at everything, like a merchant in a bazaar. Grace stood in the middle of the room, dressed in a long petticoat. Her hair was already pinned up into an elaborate coiffure, her lips painted a deep pink.

Stella observed the scene from her place by the window. She cast her gaze over her mother's body. Grace had the shape of a young woman – her breasts were firm and her abdomen flat. But there was a hardness to her form: beneath the ivory silk, Stella could see the rigid lines of a long-line bra and roll-on girdle. The garments made Grace look powerful, impenetrable – vaguely inhuman. But they meant she could still wear the evening gowns of her youth.

Stella had always been proud of how her mother looked in the dresses she'd brought with her from England – each of them was beautifully tailored, and made from expensive fabric. Some were surprisingly revealing. For eveningwear, William was prepared to tolerate low necklines and barely covered shoulders – styles that he would despise if worn in daylight. On special occasions he seemed to enjoy transforming his wife into a younger and more glamorous version of herself. When Grace walked into the pub dining room, all the other women would suddenly appear overdressed and ordinary.

But tonight, as Stella watched Grace, she felt her lips curling with contempt. This evening Grace had not even attempted to choose what to wear. She'd just stood there passively while William picked over her timeworn clothing. She was like a doll waiting to be dressed, so that she could be led out into the world, to play the part she had been given.

Tonight was to be Grace's big step back into the world – her re-appearance in the community after having been so crippled with back pain that she had barely been seen by anyone in months. She was to sit at the dinner table, chatting happily while the meal was served. Then, as soon as the band began to play, William would take Grace by the hand and lead her into the middle of the dance floor. They would waltz together – expertly and elegantly, as they always did – showing off the fact that Grace's spine was now healed.

Everyone would be told that the cure was all due to the uninter-rupted rest that had been made possible by their daughter – their wonderful daughter – who was now about to depart for England. Stella could picture the nodding heads, hairdos stiff with spray, as the women clucked over the girl's good fortune. She was to take up her studies again, under the care of her Great Aunt Jane. She'd be living in London. Going to one of the top English schools for young ladies.

The lies had all been picked out for the evening – everything matched up as carefully as the gown, shoes and jewellery. Fortunately there was no need for a story to explain Stella's absence: the Rotary Club Annual Dinner Dance was not the kind of function that young people were expected to attend.

Grace held out her arms as William passed his chosen items to

185

her, piece by piece. A record had been playing earlier – the one William had bought this last Christmas. The music had ended now, and dusty crackles played on through the speakers.

'There's a steamed chicken fillet in the fridge,' Grace said. 'And some barley custard pudding.' She turned to Stella as she waited for a response to her words.

'I don't feel like eating,' Stella said.

It was true. She had sat in the shed earlier in the day, eating hard green apples from a box. Their tartness had felt good on her tongue. But she had eaten too many, too quickly, and her stomach had rebelled. When her parents had gone, she planned to go to the bathroom and be sick.

Grace tightened her lips into a small smile. When she spoke again, there was a pleading tone in her voice.

'You should eat. Try a little taste.'

Stella just looked at her.

In this last week before her daughter was due to leave for the mainland, Grace had abandoned cooking for William and turned all her attention to Stella. She'd made every dish in the section of her recipe book called 'Meals for Invalids' – using arrowroot, gelatine and semolina. She'd coddled eggs and prepared twice-minced meats, and cut thin fingers from plain toast. She carried her offerings to Stella's room and placed them down in front of her. Later, she cleared them away, untouched.

Stella fed herself on scraps from the fridge and whole jars of smoky honey scavenged from the shed. She ate in her room. She let sticky strings of the syrup fall onto her clothes and she wiped her hands through her hair.

William had kept watch on his daughter, his eyes following her movements with a blend of pity and dismay. The man had not left the house since his return from sea, except to go to St Louis to collect the air tickets. He carried with him an air of injured kindness. But even Stella could see that – underneath – he, too, was scared.

Darkness had invaded the house. No one spoke unless they had to. Television programs sounded empty and glib; and even the most sombre music seemed heartless. When the skies were grey, they matched the mood that pervaded the place. When the weather was clear and the sun shone, the colours of the sea and sand looked falsely bright. The three stepped around one another if they met in the hallway. They spoke in strained, unnatural tones. As if someone were dead. As if everyone were dead.

Stella spent all the time she could in her room. She lay on her bed, picking at the candlewick bedspread. She pulled out the tufted threads and rolled them between her fingers, leaving a large patch plucked bald. She had not even the energy to hide the bride doll away in the drawer, or to remove a dead moth that had landed on the stone angel's shoulder. She felt tired, and sick with swallowed anger. She could feel it inside her like a cold stone. She blamed Grace for being weak, and William for being strong. She blamed Zeph for breaking his promise. She blamed herself for the fact that somehow she'd ended up at the mercy of them all.

And she blamed the baby as well.

It had begun slowly: the thought that the baby inside her wished her ill – that it did not care who Stella was, or whether she kept it or gave it away. The creature was just a parasite feeding on her from within. It was insatiable, intent on sapping the energy from her bones as it grew. And it had robbed her of her real girl's body – exchanging it for something fat and ugly. Stella could no longer fit into her own clothes – she wore old trousers of William's with the ends rolled up and a belt biting into her skin. She showered in the dark so that she could not see her breasts – swollen and patterned with blue veins – or the belly that she could no longer hold in, even for just a few minutes, so that she could pretend to be normal.

Stella could see now how she had been made to sacrifice everything to the faceless presence that inhabited her body. William and Grace – the mother and father she'd loved – seemed like characters out of a book that would never come to life again. She'd lost her friends – they'd all gone away to school. Soon she would lose her home as well. She would be sent to a place she'd never heard of – far from the sea – and work for strangers, like a prisoner. Her body would swell until it was ready to be torn open. The baby would begin its life, separate from her. She'd be left behind, spent, a worthless husk.

She turned her thoughts inward, bitter cold shafts probing her flesh. She was like a fisherman hunting in the shallows, armed with a light and a long sharp spike. She wanted to destroy this hidden presence – to wind back the clock and unmake its very beginnings.

She thought often of how time might be reversed, and history replayed.

If she had not gone to the coves that first morning, she would not even have met Zeph.

If she had not gone back again, to take him food . . .

If she had not kept the secret, and instead had told Spinks that *Tailwind* was there . . .

But, somehow, the coldness inside her evaporated when she tried to take this course. She forgot the Zeph who had failed to return, and saw instead the boy with the green eyes. Hair the colour of sand, mingling with her own. His lips pressed against her cheek. The way he smiled into her eyes.

And then, as she lay looking up at the ceiling, tears welled in her eyes. They flowed out from the corners, running back over her temples, making hot tracks into her hair. She felt then that the boy was the only human in all the world who could offer her comfort.

But he no longer existed in space and time. He was a spirit person, locked inside her.

She clutched her pillow close to her body, and let her tears fall onto its cotton case.

William stood at the bedroom door with a rug folded over his arm. He always covered the seats in the ute when people were wearing good clothes, as a protection against fish scales and loose flakes of rust. He had his hair smoothed down with cream. His tie, pulled tight, puckered the skin of his throat.

'We'll be back at eleven,' he said. He peered into the gloomy room, lit only by the glow from the hallway. Stella was lying on the bed. 'It's late, I know, but there will be speeches after the dancing and we can't leave before they finish.'

He snapped on the light. Stella blinked at him. Her hand went automatically to her shirt, making sure it was pulled down.

'Why don't you get up and do something?' he suggested. 'There's that nature program on television soon.'

'I might, later,' Stella replied.

William looked at her in silence. 'We have to go out,' he said. 'You know that, don't you? I'm accepting a service award on behalf of the Fishermen's Association.'

'I want you to go,' Stella said. 'I'll be fine.'

She thought of the hours stretching ahead – five whole hours. She imagined Grace and William driving away from her, dragging the darkness with them – leaving her in peace. She smiled.

Tension eased from William's face. He smiled back. 'Good night, then.'

He turned to go, leaving the light on.

'A giraffe never lies down,' the man in the safari suit explained as he strolled beneath an acacia tree. His hands moved in front of him while he spoke, dancing in time with his words. 'If it were to try, the weight of its long neck would mean that it would never get back up on its feet.'

The camera panned across a savannah plain. Giraffes grazed in the canopies of more acacia trees.

'This means the giraffe mother must give birth standing up. The calf begins its life by falling at least six feet, down onto the ground.'

A newborn giraffe tottered into frame, barely managing to control its gangly legs. Its mother's head appeared close behind it, keeping watch over its awkward steps. She bent her elegant neck, lowering her face to meet that of her baby. She looked at the colt with huge dark eyes edged with long lashes. She nudged the little giraffe with tender lips.

'The mother giraffe knows her job,' the man continued in his sing-song British voice, 'as animals always do.'

Stella reached to switch off the set. As she leaned forward she felt a wave of nausea. She had managed to make herself vomit after William and Grace had left – but the pain in her stomach had not eased. In fact, it had grown stronger.

She stood up, stretching her back as if to pull loose a knot inside her. Instead, it tightened; the pain grew stronger. When it eased a little, Stella headed for the bathroom, where Grace kept aspirin in the cabinet.

Halfway across the room, she faltered as the pain sharpened again. She clutched at her abdomen. The ache had sunk lower, she realised. It was nothing to do with the green apples. Something else was wrong.

She hurried to the bedroom, pressing her hand against her side, where the pain seemed to be worse. Switching on the lamp by her bed, she searched around for the pregnancy book. She had not looked at it since William had returned from his voyage, and it took her a few minutes to find it, stuck down between the mattress and the wall.

She opened it with clumsy fingers, tearing a page as she fumbled for the right section. She told herself she should turn the main light on, so that she could see clearly – but even that short journey across the room seemed impossible. Then she found the page she was after: 'When to Seek Emergency Help'.

If in doubt, don't take any chances – make a phone call.

Call the doctor, or the ambulance.

Call a friend.

Call your husband at work.

She could not stay here, Stella realised. Leaving the book behind on the bed, she made her way to the kitchen.

As she stepped into the room, she breathed in warm baking smells and heard the steady ticking of the clock on the wall. Her gaze rested on folded tea-towels and the chairs pushed in around the table. It all looked so normal, so safe.

Then she felt the pain beginning to build again. She opened the back door, staring over the dark garden to the shed, where she knew her bike – unused for weeks – was propped up beside the freezer. She looked at the sky. It was splotched with clouds, thick and dark as ink. But the moon shone down between them, shedding a grey light. She would not even need a torch in order to see the track. She leaned against the doorpost for a time, deciding on her plan. The closest neighbour was the Lincoln family. The couple would be out at the pub with everyone else, but they had a phone that Stella could use. Should she call Doctor Higgins' home? Or ask for him at the pub? She tried to calm down and think clearly. She should phone the pub anyway, she told herself, but she should not ask for the doctor – imagine if she were just overreacting and nothing serious was wrong? She should ask only to speak to her father. Make up another lie.

She bent over, holding onto the door handle as the pain gripped her again. This time it lasted longer, and bit deeper inside her. When it passed, she stood still, gulping breaths of damp night air. The smell of rotting seaweed and wet compost made her stomach heave. Her legs were shaking. There was no way she could ride her bike over the rough track and then along the road. She could barely stand.

Back in her room, Stella unbuckled her belt, letting her trousers fall to the floor. She stepped out of them and lay down on her bed. When the next pain came, she raised herself up on her hands, her body writhing in its grip. As she did so, she saw blood leaking onto the bedcover – a bright red blot, spreading out. She would have to soak the cloth later, she told herself, before it set. Using cold water, not hot. This was a good bedspread. Grace had brought it with her from England.

The thought made Stella want to laugh. Maybe it used to be a good bedspread. Before it was picked bare in the middle – all the tufts pulled out like a potato patch after the harvest.

She didn't laugh, though. She felt that if she did she would not be able to stop. And at the edges of laughter she'd find panic, wrapping her in its grasp.

She felt sweat breaking out on her face. Her heart was beating fast.

She looked up at the stone angel as she struggled to breathe steadily.

Help me, she prayed. *Make it stop.*

But she did not expect it to stop. The pains were only getting worse. She was being torn apart inside.

She tried to make sense of what was happening – her thoughts kept turning round and round, tangled with pain. What were the chances of her being alone like this, and something going wrong? She had not spent an hour by herself in months. This was no random event, she knew. It was her punishment.

This was what happened to girls who got themselves pregnant.

This was what happened to a girl who hated her baby.

She closed her eyes as another pain wrenched her abdomen. It was like the worst period cramp she had ever felt, but magnified. As if all the pain from each of the months that she'd missed – the numbers on the calendar that she had not been able to circle – was now coming at once. She grasped the sides of the mattress. She had to get up, she knew – she needed to go to the toilet.

There was no time. When the pain tightened across her body, she had to push down. The impulse came from inside her, a force beyond her control. She felt as though her body were trying to turn itself inside out – like the pale-skinned spiky fish the trawl-fishermen brought in. As they were hauled up from the deep, the air pressure inside them changed: their eyes bulged; their guts exploded from their throats . . .

The bed was now stained with a large patch of blood. In the light of the single lamp it looked dark, like oil.

As her body eased its struggle for a few minutes, Stella lay on her back, dry-mouthed, exhausted. Then the pain began building again, like a wave, carrying her away. She gave in to the need to push. This time it would not stop. It went on and on. Stella ran out of breath, and gasped for more.

Then, after all the effort and pain, a solid weight slid smoothly and easily from her body. She propped herself up on her elbows, looking down.

A grey shape – a bulging oval, smeared with blood – lay in the middle of the bed. Recoiling from the sight of it, Stella scrabbled backwards, her heels pushing into the mattress.

As the space between her and the grey lump widened, a thought came to her, bright and clear. It was over. She was free.

She wiped her hand over her face, spreading wet, salty blood. She began to tremble.

She tore off her shirt, ripping the buttons through the holes. She wanted to throw something over the mess – to hide it all away.

Then she paused, looking back down at the bed. The grey shape was the half-formed baby, she knew, still held inside its sac. According to the book, a birth sometimes happened this way – the sac was delivered unbroken, with everything inside – the placenta, the cord, the baby.

Jamie's dad had been born like this. Pauline called it 'in the caul'. It was a good start in life for a fisherman, the woman liked to say. The baby born inside its caul would never be able to drown.

Stella stared at the little bundle wrapped in silvery membrane. She felt tears stinging her eyes, then running down her cheeks. This baby would never drown, she knew – because it was already dead. Too small.

Too small to keep.

These days, a baby born prematurely after the thirty-fourth week has a good chance of surviving outside the womb.

This baby was only eighteen weeks old.

Stella shuddered, imagining a pitiful creature with stumps for arms and a body made of bloody pulp. She spread out the shirt, ready to hide it from view.

Then she paused. The moon shone in through the window. Merging with the yellow glow of the lamp, it painted the scene silver and gold. The sac gleamed, translucent, its surface stretched into a pattern of fine folds. Against the darkness of the bloody stain beneath, it stood out pale, almost glowing.

Suddenly it seemed a thing of beauty – wrapped up like a gift, and laid out for her to take.

Edging closer, Stella drew in a breath. She could see a row of tiny furled fingers. They lay against the sac, as if frozen in the act of trying to break out. There was the outline of a foot, too, pressing against its covering.

Stella's hands seemed to reach out of their own accord. They grasped the filmy membrane and tore it open. Clear liquid gushed out, spreading a sweet nutty smell into the air. The sac collapsed, lying like a shroud over a pale, still form. The spine was gently curled, like that of a kitten sleeping in a basket. Stella stared at it, her lips parted in wonder.

Her hands continued their work, stripping away the torn remains of the sac. The cord was revealed, and the frilled underside of the placenta. But the girl barely noticed them. Her gaze rested on the face. The bowed lips. The snub nose. The eyes peacefully closed.

Her perfect, tiny baby.

There was nothing but gentleness in the tranquil face. It might have been sleeping. Except that there was no movement – no little fluttering breaths, no rising of the chest.

She lifted it up, cupping its head and body in her two hands. It lay there, limp, warm. She saw a fuzz of hair on its scalp. White eyelashes. Fingernails. And she saw, between the folded legs, that it was a boy. A son.

A sob rose up from deep inside her chest. She looked up, staring around, as though hoping to find someone to help her, comfort her. Her eyes found only the stone angel, kneeling on her shelf. The

194

carved eyes – closed in prayer – and the finely moulded features mirrored those of the little baby.

Help me, Stella pleaded.

The angel was silent, her hands folded in a passive, pious pose. But there was the promise of strength in her wings . . .

Stella laid the baby gently down on the pillow. The cord – blue-white and thick – draped across its tummy, tying it to the placenta and the sagging remains of the sac. She climbed off the bed slowly, her legs weak and shaky. As she walked to the chest of drawers she was aware of a thin trickle of blood running down the inside of her thigh, and splashing onto the rug. She took her penknife from the drawer – the same sharp knife she used to cut abalone from their shells and to slice up their flesh into strips.

Grasping the handle in a sticky hand, Stella cut through the cord, parting the baby from the placenta. Then, at last, she was able to throw the shirt over the bloody remains of the birth.

Laying the baby on the pillow, she let the watery blood seep away from the wound on its tummy. When it was all gone, she used her pyjama top to wipe the little body until it was clean and dry.

Then she stood there, looking down at him. He looked so bare and cold – with nothing to protect him from the world. Stella glanced at the angel, seeking her strong presence again. It was then that she noticed the bride doll standing there on the shelf beside her. The moon gleamed softly on the white silk gown.

With trembling fingers, Stella undid the fiddly hooks and clasps and lowered the doll's dress over Miranda's plastic body. Trying not to smear the cloth with the blood on her hands, she carried the gown over to the bed. Then, she put the dress onto the tiny form, easing it gently down over the head, and pushing the floppy arms in through the sleeves.

She bent over the little boy, tenderly arranging the folds of silk around his body. He looked like a prince adorned for his christening in an heirloom gown passed down through generations.

Cradling the child in her arms, Stella crossed the room and sat down on the floor near the window. Moonshine bathed the delicate face. The baby's skin was almost transparent. Dark pink veins made a lacy pattern over the head, the hands and the feet. The rest of the baby was now hidden by the long white dress.

Stella shifted the small bundle until he was held in one arm – leaving her hand free to stroke the downy head and trace the shape of eyes, lips, cheeks. She pushed her finger between the soft lips – into the moist mouth to feel the little tongue.

The tongue that would never move to shape a sound.

The sealed-shut eyes that would never see.

The throat that held a voice which would never be heard.

Stella longed to speak to it. To pour her words into the shell-shaped ear glued against the head.

She wanted to say how sorry she was. How she could see now why the baby had to leave. Why wouldn't he? He had no father. His grandparents intended to give him away. And his mother, who had carried him inside her, had let her love for him turn cold.

She had not understood who he was.

This little perfect boy.

As she held his body in her arms, Stella sensed, beyond the still-ness, a deep, almost tangible, absence. The essence of her child had gone.

'Where are you?' she asked the silent body.

You've gone back, she thought. Back to where you came from. She pictured a place of angels, in a garden, perhaps – a French garden.

She let her tears fall down onto his face, bathing his smooth cheeks. The wetness shimmered there, like summer raindrops caught on lily petals.

She tilted his head, showing his face to the moon, the distant stars. It was the best that she could offer him. He would never know the touch of sunshine on his skin. The taste of the sea on his lips. Or hear the sound of a mother's song drifting into his dreams.

Chapter Twelve

William sounded like a stranger as he came down the hall, treading lightly in his best shoes. Stella edged backwards into the corner of the room and wrapped the blanket more tightly around her bare shoulders. She looked down at the baby, held against her breasts. The moonlight did not reach this part of the room, and his tiny face, painted with shadows, looked mysterious – as if he possessed secrets that Stella could not even begin to imagine.

She tried not to hear her father's approach – she tried not to believe that the spell she had woven, the web of peace and calm that bound her and her baby together, was about to be torn apart.

She kept her head bent, her face hidden, as the man came to stand over her. She felt his alarm transmitted through the air, but she ignored his questions. She glanced up only for a second, glimpsing her mother standing in the doorway as still as stone, glittering with diamonds like a queen.

She heard their voices as though from a distance – the urgent, fearful tones of the words and phrases that ricocheted between them.

Finally, William moved away. Lifting her gaze, Stella watched him go over to the bed. Pulling aside the shirt, he picked up the placenta. He held it under the bedside lamp, turning it over and over.

The doctor will examine the placenta to make sure that it is intact. A partially retained placenta poses a serious threat to the mother.

Grace came over and knelt down beside her daughter. Her tea-rose perfume drove away the sweet nutty smell of the birth. She picked up strands of hair, plastered against Stella's cheeks by blood and tears, and tucked them behind the girl's ears.

William moved to stand behind Grace. His voice floated down over her shoulder.

'There must have been something wrong with it. That's nature's way – to get rid of something that's not right.'

Stella looked up at him.

'It's for the best,' he said gently. 'It's all over now.'

The girl heard in his voice the veiled note of triumph. All over now. No need to go away to the Home. The shameful secret kept.

'It's not your fault.' It was Grace speaking now. 'It's nothing you did. William's right. There was some reason why it died.'

'You can't shake a good apple off the tree,' William said. 'That's what they say about a miscarriage.'

Miscarriage. Stella turned the word over in her head. She'd read about that, too – the causes, known and unknown. They had nothing at all to do with her baby. He had simply chosen not to stay. She picked up the baby's hand – a perfect miniature, smaller than her thumb. She spread the fingers, making a little star.

She saw William nudge Grace forward to take a closer look.

'It's a little boy,' Stella said. She smoothed the silk skirt and settled the lace around the tiny feet. Then she held him out for her mother to take.

As Grace leaned forward, her necklace swung out towards the downy head. Stella's hand flew out, just in time to push the stones aside.

Grace held the baby away from her body in her outstretched hands. Stella watched her face. The woman seemed torn between shock and distress – as if she could not see the beauty that lay before her. Stella reached to take him back.

'Give it to me.' William spoke in an undertone, but his words were like spikes, piercing Stella's consciousness.

'No!' Stella cried.

Grace froze, looking from Stella to William and back. Then she drew the baby towards her, as though she would keep it from them both.

'Give him to me,' Stella said. Her voice was sharp with alarm. She saw William's hands outstretched, ready. 'Mum! Don't let Dad have him!'

'It's dead, Stella,' William said. His voice was harsh, as if he hoped to jolt sense into her. 'I'm going to take it away.' He turned to his wife, motioning for her to hand the baby over.

Stella looked at her mother. 'Mum – please. Give me my baby.' Her words choked in her throat. Her eyes widened with panic.

'It's not a baby,' William said. He adopted a different tone – calming, reasonable. 'It's a foetus. Just an eighteen-week foetus. That's all it is.' He bent to look at his wife. 'Grace! Here.' He reached closer.

Grace ignored him. 'We need to get the doctor,' she said. She glanced down at the baby as she spoke.

'No, we don't,' William replied. 'Not this early. Legally, it's a foetus. We can deal with it ourselves.' He looked across to his daughter, and then back to Grace. 'If I thought there was any need, I'd take her straight into St Louis. But there's no sign of excessive bleeding.' He gestured towards the bed. 'And the placenta's intact. There's really nothing to worry about.' He pointed at the silk-wrapped bundle in Grace's hands. 'But the sooner that's out of sight, the better. You can see how upset she is.'

Grace looked at her daughter – her eyes moving over the girl's naked body, only half-covered by the blanket. She avoided meeting Stella's gaze.

Stella saw her mother begin to turn towards William. She lunged to her knees, ready to snatch back her baby. But then she stopped, her hands outstretched. He looked so fragile, lying there – with his transparent skin so finely traced with veins; his tiny limbs. If she grabbed him roughly, she feared he might tear apart into fragments, like the sac in which he'd arrived.

'Don't. Please,' she moaned. 'Give him to me.'

In a sudden movement the baby passed between Grace and William – given and taken in the same instant.

Stella opened her mouth in a silent cry. But it was too late. William was halfway across the room – then he was gone.

Grace stared at the space where her husband had been. 'It's for the best,' she said. 'It's for the best.' She kept repeating the phrase, as if by multiplication it would acquire meaning.

Stella began to cry. Great wrenching sobs made the blanket fall from her shoulders. Grace tried to lift it back again, but Stella pushed her away.

Grace shook her head helplessly.

Stella buried her face in her hands. She only raised her head when she heard the sound of the back door opening – and then banging shut.

'It's all over now,' Grace said. Her voice trembled. 'Everything's going to be all right.'

Long strips of light showed between the boards that made up the outside walls of the sleepout. William had used green timber when he'd closed-in the end of the verandah. In the years since then, the wood had shrunk and warped. Mosquitoes, spiders, even mice went in and out through the cracks.

Stella lay on the lumpy bed, looking up at a spider hanging in its web. Trussed flies made black lumps around him. She had an old blanket, coarse and scratchy, pulled up under her chin. She seemed pinned to the mattress by its weight. A helpless creature. Her body was drained of life – a leaking vessel.

Her womb leaked blood into the pads that Grace gave her to lodge between her legs. Her eyes leaked tears, day after day, drawing from an endless reservoir within. Even her breasts leaked; not milk, as a mother's might, but drops of clear liquid – shiny on her nipples like tears.

She kept her hands away from her body, not wanting to feel how her belly had shrunk – how quickly her flat girl's shape had returned. Already she looked as if she had never been transformed.

How many days had passed since she'd left her bedroom, taking refuge in the sleepout? She did not know. Time was marked only by waking and sleeping, getting up to go to the toilet, and the arrival of meals set out on trays with pretty cloths.

Grace had given up on the invalid recipes, and instead prepared all the dishes that she knew her daughter liked best. Stella sat up in bed and ate them – opening her mouth, chewing, swallowing. But she seemed to draw no sustenance from the food, as if her body had become dislocated from itself, and the links between stomach, blood, skin, hair, eyes, smiles were all broken.

William stayed home. He came often to stand in the doorway of the sleepout. He did not try to speak to his daughter, because he would not say the one thing she wanted to hear.

'Where is he?' Stella had asked, the first morning after the birth – and every day since.

'Buried.'

'Where?'

You don't need to know. It's not healthy. It's best forgotten.

Now is the time to look forward.

I won't tell you. I know best.

Somewhere in the garden. That's all I'm going to say.

And it's not a grave.

It wasn't a baby.

Stella turned her back to the window and covered her head with a blanket to shut out the sound of the sea. She could not bear the way the waves murmured on and the tides continued to rise and fall, as though nothing had changed in the world. She hated to think of the garden outside – the freshly dug beds where seeds were resting in the earth.

And where the baby was buried.

She imagined him hidden in some dank, forgotten corner. Earth clamped heavy over his face, pressing down on his fragile form. When she slept, she dreamed of him. She saw that the white skirt was wrapped up over his face, choking the air from his lungs. She saw him naked, his dress stripped off and lost.

∽

Grace came into the sleepout, holding the grey suitcase. She lifted it up for her daughter to see.

'It's funny to think of this old suitcase going back to England again,' Grace said. Her voice sounded thin and false, its surface brightness belied by the bleak look in her eyes. 'You won't need to pack much – just a few things. We've had another letter from Aunt Jane. She's going to take you shopping in London as soon as you arrive.' She paused, pressing her lips firmly together. 'She'll know best what kind of clothes you'll need.'

Stella said nothing. Life was going on around her, she knew – but it all seemed unreal. Nothing to do with her.

Grace left the sleepout. Stella heard footsteps entering her old bedroom – then her mother moving around in there, opening and closing drawers as she picked out items of clothing. The girl tried not to picture the room – with its bed of bare springs and its blank wooden floor.

She knew that the mattress, the candlewick bedspread, blanket and rug had all been burned. William had carried them well out into the paddock before shaking a can of petrol over them and standing back to toss a match. Grace had closed all the doors and windows. But still, the acrid smoke had found its way inside. The smell lingered now in the very fabric of the house. Stella breathed through the blanket – mothballs and dust – to escape it.

Before long, Grace's footsteps approached the verandah again. Then she appeared at Stella's side. As the girl looked up at her, the woman held something out in her hand. It nestled there like a fledgling – fluffy with feathers and wispy weeds. The little grass basket that had been woven by Zeph.

'Did you make this?' she asked.

There was a pleading note in her voice. Stella understood her mother was using the object as an excuse to try and begin a conversation. There was too much silence in the house now – even for Grace.

Stella shook her head wearily. She had nothing to say to her mother. Nothing to say to anyone.

Throw it away, she thought, turning her face to the wall.

Throw everything away.

As Grace retreated from the room, Stella studied a crack that ran between the sheets of hardboard panelling. It was black and deep, leading into the very bones of the building. Stella imagined being small enough to slide into it. To disappear into nothing. The vision was calming. Stella tried to lose herself in it, but the sea was too loud – the crash of tumbling surf reached her ears through the blanket. She tried to ignore it, but the steady thudding kept drawing her back. It raked her nerves like fingernails over a blackboard.

Then she heard the wind moaning as it whipped round the eaves. It sounded like someone wailing. Her body stiffened, her hands lying rigid by her side. She strained to hear the sound more clearly. It was someone lost, calling for help.

She knew what it was . . .

Her baby, searching for his true home – the place where he would belong.

I don't belong here either, she realised. Not any more. Never again.

Throwing off the blanket, she sat up and reached towards a pile of clothes that lay tangled on the floor.

Never.

Stella found the wrapping from Daniel's Christmas parcel in the place where she had left it months earlier – folded away in the kitchen drawer. Checking that neither William nor Grace was around, she grabbed the wad of brown paper and took it back with her to the sleepout. There, she tore off the return address – a cloud-shaped fragment with torn edges and words written across it in blue ink:

Mr Daniel Boyd, 125 Willowdene Street, Melbourne, Victoria

She stuffed the remains of the wrapping down the back of the chest of drawers.

Then, while Grace was preparing dinner and William was chopping wood, Stella made a hurried raid on her old room, snatching up a few pieces of clothing and a spare pair of boots and throwing them into her schoolbag. On the wall near her bed she noticed a splash of blood – a tiny black star.

Spinning round, she fastened her gaze on the stone angel – still kneeling there on the shelf, waiting. As she grabbed the statue, her elbow knocked against the doll, Miranda. The stark pink body fell to the floor and rolled over.

Stella stared at the naked doll for a moment – at a dark stain that sullied the red hair. Then she turned away and half-ran from the room.

While it was still dark the next morning, and William and Grace were fast asleep, Stella crept through the quiet house by the light of her torch. She had a note, ready in her hand. As she made her way through the kitchen towards the side door, she slipped it under Grace's recipe book, which was lying out on the table.

> *I have taken your money.*
> *I will let you know where I am.*
> *Do not come after me.*
> *I am never coming home.*

What else should she have written? *I love you. I hate you.*
Both were true. Neither were true.

Out in the garden, she kept her torch fixed on the pathway ahead. She knew that she could not begin to search the garden – sweeping her torch in an arc like the beam of a lighthouse, looking for places where the earth had been disturbed. If she did, she would be here forever.

Autumn was a busy time in the garden. Most of the ground had been dug.

Fresh bullet holes clustered around the letter H on the signpost to Halfmoon Bay. The blasts had splintered the timber and blown off the layers of paint. Stella counted them – one to eleven – as she waited for the sound of another vehicle coming down the hill. Though it was early in the morning, a car and a ute had already come into view. Stella had hung back out of sight, peering through the boobyalla bushes, to see if she recognised them. The first to reach her had been the yellow Holden owned by the Barrons. Mr Barron drove lazily, slumped back in his seat, an elbow sticking out through the window. Stella ducked out of sight as he drew near, and then watched as he slowed down and swung off the main road. The ute had come next. Stella had hidden while it approached as well, because it reminded her of one she'd seen parked outside the fish factory.

As the second vehicle disappeared along the road to Halfmoon, Stella sat down on a small granite boulder. She lowered herself carefully, her body still tender. On the opposite side of the road, a crow swooped down and landed in the verge. Its long black beak began tearing into the furry carcass of a possum. Stella noticed a trail of blood leading back to the middle of the road. The animal had been hit by a vehicle, she realised, then crawled away towards the bush to die.

Shifting her weight on the hard stone, Stella felt the crackle of paper inside her pocket. Daniel's address. It was a talisman – her only hope of survival.

She looked up at the sound of another engine. Grabbing her school bag, she slung it over her shoulder, then stood ready, watching. A light-blue sedan was approaching. As it drew nearer, she saw that it had Victorian number plates. She stepped into the road and waved.

The car slowed and came to a halt, the tyres crunching the gravel. Stella closed her eyes as a dust cloud rose. When she opened them again, the driver was winding down the window. It was a woman, middle-aged and dressed in city clothes.

Stella pushed back her hair and forced her lips to smile. 'Are you heading north?' she asked, 'or are you turning off?'

The driver took a drag from a white-tipped cigarette. She blew smoke through painted lips. 'Turning off where?' she asked.

Stella gestured towards the sign. 'Halfmoon Bay.'

The woman shook her head. 'Good God, no – never heard of it. I'm going to Hobart.'

'Me, too,' Stella said.

'Hop in, then. I'm in a hurry.'

As Stella walked round to the other side of the car she caught her reflection in the window. She looked normal, just like any other girl hitching a ride to the city. Opening the door, she swung herself down onto the seat. As she did so, she tried not to wince or move too carefully. She tried to appear bright and happy.

She didn't want the stranger to know she was a girl whose body had been injured – whose heart had been torn in two.

CHAPTER THIRTEEN

FIFTEEN YEARS LATER

Halfmoon Bay, Tasmania

Waves reared up along the shore, then crashed in a tumult of foam and tumbled seaweed. Gulls wheeled above the water, their urgent cries piercing the roar of the surf.

Stella stood near the edge of the wavewash, staring out towards the horizon. The wind buffeted her body, whipping back her hair and stinging her eyes. She leaned into it, feeling its power as it hurled against her. She imagined it entering her body – a numbing chill invading her blood.

She would become a statue made of cold stone, standing here forever . . .

A gull landed near her feet. It tipped back its head and squawked at her loudly. Then it ran off, spreading its wings and flapping into the air. Stella watched it rise up, wheeling above her. The grey sky was darkening, the daylight beginning to fade.

She looked back past a stretch of rocky foreshore to the wide sweeping beach of Halfmoon Bay. In the distance she could just see the walls of the whaling station, and beyond them the masts of the boats moored in the gulch. Checking her watch, she saw that it was after five o'clock. Grace would be wondering where she was. Spinks as well . . . She had not realised that she'd come so far, and stayed away so long.

She turned inland, walking up the beach. She remembered there was a track nearby that led to the road. Going back that way would be much faster than picking her path between the rocks and then walking over the soft sand.

The track was narrow and closed in with bushes. As Stella pushed her way along it she breathed the smell of lemon boronia, gumleaf and ants. Emerging onto the gravel road, she walked quickly, her gaze fixed ahead. The bushes grew high on each side of her, shielding her from the wind; but she shivered as she hurried along and wrapped her arms around her body. She felt vulnerable – exposed to the world – as if her skin had been stripped away. The memories that had returned to her, sweeping her along in their wake, had left her feeling raw and defenceless.

Hearing a vehicle approaching from behind, she stepped onto the verge. Looking back, she saw an old red station wagon approaching. She raised one hand – automatically making the small salute that was always exchanged between locals. Then she turned away to avoid the dust.

The car slowed and pulled over. Stella crossed to the open passenger window and peered in. She recognised the driver straightaway. Laurie wore the same leather hat – dark with sweat and gun oil – that he'd had years ago. His hair was now grey, but he still wore it long, tied back in a ponytail. Stella felt sure he knew who she was – but if he was surprised to see her here he did not show it.

'Want a lift?' he asked. He pushed a pile of old ropes off the passenger seat onto the floor. Stella climbed in, ducking under a long piece of driftwood that poked forward from the back of the car. As she sat down, her leg pressed against the barrel of a rifle, angled towards the floor between the two seats.

The car lurched off while Stella was still pulling shut the door. It rattled loudly as it bumped over corrugations in the road.

Laurie looked over to Stella. 'When did you get here?'

'Today.' Stella gave her answer with a sense of disbelief. It seemed so long since she'd arrived at Hobart airport.

'You've seen Spinks? Been at the wharf?' Laurie asked.

Stella nodded.

'I've been up at Sloop Rock,' Laurie said. 'They searched out there a day ago, but I thought it was worth another look. Didn't see anything. I was going to join the search party, but Spinks wouldn't let me – unless I left that thing behind.' He gestured towards his rifle. Then he glanced at Stella. His eyes were like chips of sapphire – hard and blue. 'Typical bloody Spinks. Didn't stop me, though. I'm just doing it my way instead.'

Stella wound up her window, cutting out the sound of the wind. The engine droned in the sudden quiet.

'Will they find him?' she asked.

Laurie stared out through the windscreen. 'We've just gotta keep looking. It's all we can do.' He was quiet for a while. When he spoke again, his voice was gentle. 'I hope he's still alive out there. I've had my differences with your dad, over the years. But I respected him.'

Stella looked down at her hands, twisted together in her lap. She could think of nothing to say in response.

Laurie braked suddenly as a wallaby lunged from the bushes and hopped onto the road. There was a grating sound as he changed down a gear.

'Takes a bit of getting used to – this car,' he commented. 'The old Jeep let me down last week. Blew the head gasket. I got a loan of this from a mate. Goes okay, when you can find the gears.'

He braked again as he reached a corner. A piece of driftwood slid forward past Stella's shoulder. As she pushed it back out of the way, she glanced into the rear of the car. There was more driftwood piled up there – a whole stack of it. Stella's eyes followed the criss-cross of silver-grey timbers – recognising bits of old decking, planks daubed with remnants of paint, and the curving limbs of trees. They were good pieces, she realised. Whoever had collected them knew where to look. They knew which of the fragments would keep their beauty when taken away from the shore, and which would not.

'Whose car is it?' Stella asked. She felt an irrational jealousy – as though this were still her place, and the treasures of the sea still belonged to her.

'New fella,' Laurie replied. 'Only been here a few years. I like him. Everyone does. He's not like some of them that have been moving in. Mainlanders have taken over the pub, you know. They don't do meals any more. I've lost my biggest customer. Used to take a lot of wallaby to make patties for a room full of people.'

Laurie slowed down as he reached the edge of town. Stella looked out at the houses passing by – the single-storey homes made of wood and tin, with only the fireplaces built from brick. They seemed small to her now, after being away. Many of them seemed shabby as well. Even in the fading daylight, Stella could see peeling weatherboards and rust patches on the roofs. But, as if to belie any sense of decay, the gardens looked even more abundant than they used to. The verandah of one house was almost lost beneath a tangle of passionfruit vines. In front of another, a square of ground where a lawn might once have been was a jungle of potato plants.

Before long the wharf came into view. The car park was half-empty – most of the boat trailers had gone, and only a few of the orange vehicles were still there. Volunteers dressed in orange remained dotted around the area. From the casual way they moved, it was obvious to Stella that there had been no breakthrough in the search.

The car drew to a halt. Laurie pointed to the passenger-door handle. 'Give that a good hard pull.'

'Thanks for the ride,' Stella said.

'Any time. It's good to see you back.'

As Stella opened the door, the wind flung it back on its hinges. When she climbed out she had to use both hands to force it shut.

Stella walked down through the car park, heading towards the caravan. A light had been switched on near the door, shedding a yellow glow into the gathering dusk. As she drew near, Stella saw that the food tables were still set up outside – but all the crockery had been packed away, and the women were gone.

Stella scanned the surrounding area. Over near the slipway, a tall figure caught her eye. She recognised Grace's hair, and her long, dark coat flapping in the wind. Near the woman's feet, Stella could see her own bulging backpack lodged against a rock. Grace held herself upright and very still – she might have been carved from wood, like the figurehead on a ship. She stared out past the rocky edge of the gulch towards the open sea.

Stella hurried towards her, wondering how she would explain why she had disappeared – and for so long. As she reached Grace, her boots crunched on some loose gravel. The woman spun round, startled.

'Oh, it's you,' she said. She gave a thin smile as she bent to pick up her basket. 'I've been waiting for you. It's time to go home.'

Stella tried to return the smile, but her face, chilled by the wind, felt as if it belonged to someone else.

Stella carried a large cooking pot across to the ute. The remains of the soup sloshed around inside it with each step that she took. Her backpack was slung over her shoulder – she welcomed its familiar weight, resting against her spine.

Grace walked along next to her, one arm hooked under the handle of a basket, the other hanging stiffly at her side.

Reaching the open back of the ute, Stella lodged the pot and her bag in between a pile of plastic bins and a fishtrap. Then she moved round to the driver's side – opening the door and sliding onto the seat. Grace climbed into the passenger seat and sat with her basket resting on her knee.

Stella switched on the ignition and pumped the accelerator, in the way she remembered William always did. The old engine kicked into life. She drove off, up past the pub and the shop and then on towards the coast – the route to Seven Oaks. Reaching the open road, she picked up speed.

After a few minutes she glanced quickly at Grace. The woman was sitting still and quiet beside her. In the small, closed space, Stella could pick up the scent of her tea-rose perfume beneath the smell of stale soup.

Stella turned back to the road and tried to look as though she were concentrating hard on driving. She felt trapped in here with her mother. It was not the place to begin talking – begin anything . . .

Stella steered the ute carefully along the track dodging bumps and potholes. They were revealed by the headlamps of the ute – twin shafts of light that made the surrounding gloom seem darker than it was. It was late twilight – the nowhere time, when the day was just gone, but night was still on its way.

The track curved through the paddocks leading on towards the sea. Peering ahead Stella could see a collection of dark oblong shapes and the outlines of trees. Her old home. She felt her hands tightening on the steering wheel as she drove steadily towards it.

Suddenly she was there. As the ute came to a standstill near the shed, Stella turned to Grace. 'You go in. I'll keep the lights on until you get to the house.'

Stella watched Grace hurrying over to the path and then disappearing into the garden. A short while later, Stella switched off the headlamps and climbed out. The smell of wet seaweed and salt surrounded her. She went to the back of the ute to retrieve her bag and pick up the cooking pot.

Then she turned to face the house.

It seemed bigger than she'd remembered it to be. The pitched roof rose boldly against the darkening sky. The windows were tall and wide – blank spaces backed by closed curtains. Stella looked along the façade towards the front door. Something moved there, in the shadows. Taking a few steps closer, she saw that it was a tree – thrashing and writhing in the wind.

William's oak.

It had grown tall, Stella saw. Even bent by the wind, the tallest branches reached almost up to the eaves. But the trunk of the tree was spindly. The branches were stunted and the foliage looked sparse. Stella turned her back on it and headed for the path.

Grace's garden was a pattern of blurry grey shapes – trees, shrubs, hedges – constantly shifting in the wind. As Stella walked amongst them she held her step steady and kept her eyes focused on the doorway ahead. She felt shadows gathering about her like ghosts.

And, behind them, she sensed a creeping darkness. It reached out towards her – rising from a hidden source, buried in the earth . . .

She was glad when a light came on in the kitchen window, shedding a yellow glow over the lily beds. Stella hurried towards it, pressing the pot against her body like a shield.

The kitchen was warm, the quiet air touched by the yeasty fragrance of the morning's baking. Grace stood by the table, still wrapped in her overcoat, turning pages in her recipe book. Her brow was furrowed with concentration.

'Can you wash up?' she asked, raising her head briefly to look at Stella. 'I'll start on tomorrow's soup.'

Stella carried the soup pot over to the sink and lifted it onto the draining board. 'That's a good-sized pot,' she commented. 'Where did you get it?'

'Joe brought it down to the wharf,' Grace responded. 'He got it from the pub when they did up the kitchen. It was being thrown out.'

'What a waste,' Stella said. As the words were exchanged, she felt a sense of relief – their tone was so calm and polite. That was how it was going to be, she realised. She and Grace would stick to safe, easy subjects – or say nothing.

She turned her attention to the task she'd been given. She picked up the rubber plug – pink and perished on its steel chain – and placed it in the sink. As she did so, her gaze skimmed over the two pot-scourers sitting side by side in a chipped blue saucer. And the neatly folded red and white wiping cloth. The dishmop, standing in its jar. The bar of yellow soap – half-used, with grey scum trapped in its cracked surface. It all looked deeply familiar to her. Turning from the sink, Stella scanned the kitchen, taking in all the other details that she knew so well. She paused on the clock in its niche above the mantelpiece. It ticked steadily, loudly – as if insisting that time kept passing.

Yet, nothing had changed.

Stella glanced at Grace – whose head was still bent over her recipe book – and then she left the kitchen. Her boots were loud on the polished boards as she walked down the hallway. When she reached the sea room, she pushed open the door and turned on the light.

The cushions were set out in a neat row on the couch. The rugs were lined up on the floor. The television set stood in its place next to the sideboard. Even the firewood was stacked in exactly the same way as it always had been. Stella's breath tightened in her chest. It really seemed that time had stopped the very day that she had left – fifteen years ago . . .

She ran her fingers over the back of a chair. William's chair. She looked down at the cushion, permanently squashed on one side from him leaning towards the warmth of the fire. Her eyes settled on his side-table – the one where he placed the little mending tasks that he brought home from his voyages. A folded newspaper lay there, still spread open, half-read.

Next to the paper was William's coffee mug – a souvenir from Lord Nelson's ship HMS *Victory*. Stella picked it up, feeling its smooth weight against her fingers. Turning it round, she read the writing stamped on the back. '*England expects that every man will do his duty*.' This famous quote was one of the first things she had learned how to read. She could remember William mouthing out the words for her. The mug had seemed much larger then, held so carefully in Stella's little hands . . .

She took the mug back with her to the kitchen. Her mother looked up as she came in. Then Grace froze – a page half-turned, poised in the air.

'What are you doing?' Her eyes were fixed on the mug.

'I'm just putting it away,' Stella said. She stepped towards the dresser.

In an instant, Grace was at her side. The woman took the mug from her hands, then disappeared into the hallway. Stella heard footsteps heading into the sea room. Moments later, Grace returned. Her cheeks were flushed pink.

'You mustn't move his things,' she said. 'Don't touch them.'

'I'm sorry,' Stella said.

'I just want everything left as it is,' Grace said firmly.

As she spoke, Grace took off her coat and hung it on the back of a chair. Then she picked up a clean apron and slipped it on. She tied the tapes behind her back, and then she turned again to her recipe book. She ran her gaze down the page, frowning in deep concentration.

Stella watched her uneasily. It was as if her mother thought that by choosing the right recipe and preparing enough food she could bring William safely home – back to his newspaper and a cup of hot tea. Stella remembered what Pauline had said – that Grace had been ill much of the time ever since her daughter had left. People had hardly seen her for years and years. With a creeping sense of dismay, Stella wondered if her mother had slowly gone mad – hiding out here, seeing no one but William year after year. She had a sudden vision of how the fifteen years might have been played out: Grace responding to her daughter's departure – and to all that had happened – by finally and utterly losing herself to her husband and her home.

Stella closed her eyes, wanting to hide from the thought. It made her feel guilty. Yet, she reminded herself, it was not her fault that she had been unable to face coming back here. Back to them . . .

Taking a wooden spoon from the drawer, Stella began scraping the pot clean. Then she ran water into the sink, holding the soap-saver under the hot stream. Bubbles began to form – a cool froth rising over her hands.

Looking up, she found her face reflected in the dark windowpane. Black eyes, white skin. Her windblown hair stood out around her face, making it look small. All the fine details were hidden – the lines around her eyes and mouth. She looked young, almost a child again.

When the washing-up was done, Grace handed Stella a knife and a board so that she could begin chopping onions.

'I'm multiplying by ten,' she said. 'That's twenty onions. There's a sack in the pantry.' She took out another chopping board. 'I'll help you.'

Stella peeled the crisp brown skin off an onion. Then she cut the pale bulb in half and began to slice it. She noticed Grace watching her.

'That's an odd way to do it,' the woman said.

'Is it?' Stella shrugged. 'I haven't cooked anything for years.'

Grace looked at her in disbelief.

'It's true,' Stella responded. 'I can't even remember the last time I went into a kitchen. People usually don't want you to go anywhere near them – in cafés or hotels, or even in homes. They think you won't eat the food if you've seen where it's made.'

'Why? Are they dirty?' As she asked the question Grace's eyes flicked over her own spotless kitchen.

'Often it's just that everything's black. People cook over a charcoal fire and there's not much water for washing,' Stella replied. She was glad to be discussing the lives of people far away. 'They have no electricity,' she continued. 'The only light comes from kero lamps. It's like camping. But when people see a foreigner, they don't imagine you'd ever cook that way. Lots of places are dirty, though. You can tell by the food they bring out – and the greasy plates and spoons. You really have to force yourself to eat.'

'Is that why you're so thin?' Grace asked. She looked down over Stella's waist and hips.

Stella felt her body stiffen under her mother's scrutiny. 'No. I eat. I just don't eat very much any more.'

'You used to like to eat,' Grace said. 'You had so many favourite things.'

Stella eyed Grace in silence, wondering how she could explain the way food had become linked – in her mind – with power and pain. Finally, she spoke.

'I've sat at tables with torturers and forced myself to eat food that's been touched by their hands. Once I could still see splashes of blood up under the sleeve of a man's shirt. Another time I ate meat that was called pork, but I knew it was too sweet and too pale . . .'

Grace's eyes widened. Then she bent her head over her chopping board.

Stella finished slicing her onion. It lay spread out in front of her in small pieces. As the vapour rose from it, tears stung her eyes. They spilled over and ran down her cheeks – then splashed onto the table.

Stella stared down at the wet marks with a sense of surprise. She never cried. People often commented on her composure in the face of tragedy. Victims seemed drawn to her, mistaking her emptiness for strength. Sometimes, Stella Boyd was accused of being a woman with a heart of stone – a journalist who had become too hard. No one knew how often she wished that she could weep.

Picking up a tea-towel, Stella wiped her eyes roughly and then continued her chopping. When she looked up after a few minutes she saw that Grace had wet cheeks as well. Tears were running freely down her face. She raised her hand and brushed them away. Her fingers were trembling.

As if feeling her daughter's gaze, Grace turned to her.

'I'm afraid,' she said. She spoke in a low voice, as if she feared being overheard. 'What if he doesn't come home?'

Stella stared at her in silence. She felt a wave of pity, but she had no words of comfort to offer. She could not imagine what Grace would do if her husband was dead.

He was everything to her. She had no one else.

Grace sniffed and wiped her eyes again. Then she went over to the sink and took the soup pot from the drying rack.

'Pass me that tea-towel,' she said to Stella. 'We need to get this soup on. It's getting late.'

Stella held a bundle of bed-linen against her chest – soft-worn sheets smelling faintly of lavender. She walked down the hall towards the verandah door. On her left was her old room. She felt it drawing nearer with each step that she took. Light spilled from the door, hanging open just a crack. Grace must have left it on, Stella realised, when she'd gone in there earlier on to get a pillow and quilt.

Stopping outside, she pushed open the door.

The narrow bed was spread with a new coverlet made of turquoise quilted cotton, edged with an orange fringe. On the floor lay a small rug – its pile unworn and stainless. All Stella's things were still spread around the room – her sports ribbons, her photos, her books . . . As if she had been expected to return. Like William.

Even from the door, Stella could see the dust furring the surfaces. The room had the timeless atmosphere of a shrine – a place dedicated to the memory of the child she once had been.

Her fingers closed around the light switch. Then she paused. A pale form caught her eye. Miranda, the walking doll. She was lying on the shelf beside the other dolls – still naked. Stella's gaze travelled over the rigid limbs, the curves of the rounded torso.

She closed her eyes on a vision of trembling fingers, smeared with blood, stripping off the white silk wedding gown.

While her eyes were shut she snapped off the light. When she looked again, the scene was transformed. Into the sudden darkness came a shaft of bright moonlight. It reached in through the window, pooling on the floor – the same silver sheen that had bathed the tiny child's face when Stella had lifted him up to show off the beauty of the stars . . .

Stella kicked open the door to the sleepout and dropped the sheets onto a small table. An old cream curtain lay over the bed. It was speckled with spider droppings and dead flies. She stripped it off, revealing a lumpy mattress covered in striped ticking. She spread the sheets over it, pulling them roughly into place. She stopped then, to listen to the wind and the sea. In the hours after dark, she realised, the strong winds had whipped up into a real storm. The waves pounded the shore outside and the iron rattled on the roof. She tried not to think of what it would mean for the search – for William . . .

Turning from the bed, she lifted her bag up onto the table and tipped out her things. She grouped them untidily into piles – clothes, equipment, toiletries. There was a chest of drawers in the corner, but the only item she packed away in there was the dusty curtain that had covered the mattress.

She stood in the small space between the bed and the table, unwinding the silk scarf that protected the stone angel. She drew comfort from the familiar weight rolling over and over in her palm. When the carving was unveiled, she placed it on the table, turning the face towards the bed. As her eyes lingered on the peaceful little face, Stella thought of Daniel. While she was between planes in Melbourne, she'd phoned him – but, to her disappointment, she'd been greeted by an answering machine. Daniel had made the recording, his voice sounding bright and pleased.

'Miles and Daniel are taking a well-earned holiday. Leave us a message and we'll call you when we get back.'

Stella felt a warm glow inside her as she replayed the message in her mind. She pictured the two of them – Daniel and Miles. Their faces . . . She remembered the way they had always looked at her: as though she were a gift that was immeasurably precious. A girl. A daughter to them both; these men who had never been fathers. She smiled at the thought of them in Bali, lying under palm trees being waited upon by graceful young men – all the while teasing one another about their own time-ravaged frames.

Pulling off her boots, Stella lay down on the bed in her clothes, trying to gather the energy to go back into the house and wash. She could feel the chill of the wind spiking in through the cracks in the walls. The regular thudding of the surf almost shook the glass in the windows. And there was a new sound, she noticed, adding to the noise of the storm. A strange, low rumble. Stella lifted her head to listen more closely, puzzled by its meaning. Then she remembered – she'd heard it once before in the fiercest of storms. William had told her what it was. On the foreshore outside, large boulders were being shifted by the waves – tumbled about like marbles in a giant's game.

'A rock-rattler,' William had called it. He'd written a long note about it in his weather journal. Stella remembered hovering at his shoulder, watching him write. It had struck her that the word 'rock-rattler' didn't seem to belong with terms like cumulus, strata, nimbus. It seemed too rough and strong.

Stella stiffened suddenly, staring up at the ceiling laced with webs.

The journal . . .

It should have been checked for information, she realised. All the details of William's most recent voyage would be recorded in the final entry – there could be some note that would help with the search. But Spinks wouldn't know the book existed – unless Grace had thought to tell him.

Stella threw back the blanket and swung her feet down onto the dusty floor. Entering the house, she padded down the hallway. She paused outside the main bedroom, listening for any sign that Grace was still awake – but there was only silence from beyond the closed door. She crept on, into the sea room.

She walked towards the dark bulk of Aunt Jane's sideboard. Only as she drew near to it did she remember that the drawer holding the weather journal was always locked. William had the only key. She paused, looking around her uncertainly. Then she crossed to the fireplace and picked up the poker. It had a thin, sharp point. Returning to the sideboard, she angled the tip of the poker into the narrow gap above the top of the drawer. She used it as a lever – leaning her weight down onto it. There was a crack of splintering wood. It took a few more tries before the drawer was freed. Then Stella slid it open and took out the heavy cloth-bound notebook.

She carried it to the dining table and switched on a lamp. As she opened the front cover, a familiar smell rose from the pages – old ink and a trace of diesel. For a painful moment it evoked William's presence. As if he were standing just nearby . . .

Stella flipped quickly through to the final entry. She scanned the descriptions of sea and wind – pausing on the number of fish caught, and the location of the pots. Stella read the entries carefully. William had been working in deeper water than usual, she noted. But he was following one of his most tried-and-true runs – off the western side of Standaway Island. There was nothing out of the ordinary.

Stella pushed the journal away. She glanced over to the damaged drawer. She knew Grace would be upset when she saw it – and nothing had been gained. Stella picked up the book to put it away. Then she paused, her eye drawn to the left-hand side of the tome – to the thick wad of pages that were covered on both sides with William's writing. He'd been using this same book ever since she could remember. There were entries covering decades of William's weather-watching, as he tried to make sense of the shifting patterns of wind, sky, sea.

It was a record of William's life . . .

Her hands seemed to begin moving all on their own – flicking back through the book, passing year after year. Searching for 1976. The month of May. Monday, the seventeenth . . .

She wanted to know, suddenly, what William had written back then – what details of weather and sky had captured his attention on the day when he knew that his daughter had gone.

There it was. Stella's hands pressed against the page, yellowed with time.

My heart is torn apart. I can barely breathe. The pain is so great. My child is gone.

Stella stared at the words. The letters were clumsily formed and pushed deep into the paper. She read the entry over and over. Then she checked the pages that followed – but they only contained the usual weather reports, couched in factual language that made the single outburst of emotion feel all the more surprising.

She leafed ahead to the entries made about a year after she'd left. It was around then, she remembered, that William had sent her his first letter. Grace had begun writing as soon as Daniel had allowed her to – when he thought the girl was strong enough. But William had been silent, month after month. Then an envelope had arrived, addressed in the same hand as the diligent weather reports. There was a single page folded inside. Sandwiched between a formal greeting and some comments on fishing was a brief message.

I can see that I may have acted in error. I think it would be best if you were to come home.

Anger had burst up inside Stella as she'd read these words. The flicker of warmth aroused by William's admission that he may have been wrong was snuffed out by his suggestion that she return home. She didn't believe he was sorry for what he'd done – he just wanted to get her away from Daniel and back under his control. She could feel him out there, waiting – ready to take over her life again.

She had thrown the letter in the fire.

The lamp cast grey shadows over the pages of the journal as Stella turned them, one by one. Finally she reached the date she was look-ing for. The seventeenth of May, 1977.

Remorse stalks my soul. It follows me through day and night, over land and sea. There is nowhere I can hide. Time and tide can never be turned back. If only I could return to that time and be someone else. Someone good.

Stella gazed down at the page. Her fingers crept over the words, wanting to feel them, hold them.

She closed the book and clasped it against her chest.

CHAPTER FOURTEEN

D awn light slid in over the sea, laying a rosy glow over the wharf. Stella stood near the slipway, with an orange jacket and a pair of matching overalls draped over her arm. She could feel the tension in her body, and a twist of anxiety in her stomach, as she waited to join the search.

She began to pace up and down, trying to ease a growing impatience. Last night's storm had passed quickly through Halfmoon Bay and now the weather was steadily improving. Several boats had already gone out, and two ground parties had left in a minibus. But the team to which Stella had been assigned had not yet been told what to do. Time was being lost.

She looked over to where some other volunteers were standing in a group. Amongst them she could see the team leader – a red-haired woman called Wendy. When Stella had arrived at the wharf this morning with Grace, there had been no sign of Spinks – and it had been Wendy who had taken down Stella's details.

'Your name?' she'd enquired, her pen poised over her clipboard.

'Stella Boyd. I mean, Birchmore.'

Wendy's eyes had flicked up.

'I'm his daughter,' Stella had said.

The woman had looked at her with mixed sympathy and doubt. 'It can be complicated, having family members take part,' she had said. 'But we understand the need to be involved. It can be a help . . .'

Wendy had been brisk and efficient then – as though every passing minute mattered to her. Now, as she waited to receive some instructions, she stood with her back to Stella idly kicking a small stone around in a circle. The man next to her appeared to be mending a tear in his jacket. Several of the group just sat on the ground, resting their heads on their hands.

Stella turned away from them – looking across to where the women were setting up their food stall amidst a murmur of voices and the faint chink of crockery. Stella could see Grace standing with them, warming her hands on the outside of one of the soup pots. Joe stood near her, cutting up slices of cake. Stella wondered if she should go over and offer to help, while she was waiting.

Suddenly the crackle of a radio drew her attention. She saw Wendy snap a transceiver from her belt and hold it to her ear. Stella hurried towards her.

'Got that. Okay.' Wendy replaced her radio and then turned to the man standing next to her. 'The blokes in Hobart have called off the search. Apparently there's some other drama going on up north.'

The man nodded. 'Yeah, well we've given it a pretty good go. Poor bloke's a gonner. We all know that. You can only spend so long hunting around for a dead one.'

Stella stepped forward. She grasped Wendy's arm. 'Who were you speaking to? Who's made this decision?'

Wendy swung round. A look of dismay came over her face. 'I'm sorry,' she said, 'I didn't know you were standing there.' She broke off, glancing at her colleagues. 'I'm afraid it's true. They've called off the search. It's over.'

'They can't,' Stella said. 'They mustn't. I need to find Spinks. Do you think he's been told?'

The woman gestured towards the radio on her hip. 'That was him, passing on the message from Hobart.'

Stella looked at her in numb silence. Then she turned away,

stumbling blindly over the rough ground. She found herself facing a wall of cream brick. The Seafarers' Memorial. She gazed blankly at the plaques.

James Maitland
Fisherman of Halfmoon Bay
'The Sea Giveth and the Sea Taketh Away'

Michael Maitland, father of James Maitland
'The Sea Showeth No Mercy'

Pain spread slowly through her. She saw the words that would soon be added here, formed in hard cold metal.

William Charles Birchmore
Fisherman of Halfmoon Bay . . .

Stella felt a sense of loss, deep and raw – not just the loss of the father she had known, but the loss of the father who had written such unimagined words – such heartfelt words – in his journal.

Someone else. Someone good.

'It can't be over,' Stella said quietly to herself.

She spun round, turning her back on the wall, and then strode away, up towards the caravan.

Stella stood in front of the maps Spinks had pinned on the van wall. She traced the black lines of William's fishing runs, standing out starkly against the pale blue sea. Then she looked at the search areas, colour-coded to denote air and ground coverage. She saw that the ground coverage was shaded to indicate two further categories: concentrated and broad. All the sectors were ticked off now – the search was complete.

She studied every detail on the maps. She could feel adrenaline running through her body, making her head clear, her eyes sharp.

The air search had covered the whole coastal area – north and south of Halfmoon Bay. The concentrated ground search covered the islands around which William fished, and the area to the south of the bay. The search to the north was zoned as 'broad'. Stella nodded to herself – that made sense: none of William's runs lay in that direction, and the prevailing currents washed south.

Then she froze, a prickle of realisation running up her spine. There was one other place that William went. A run no one knew about but her.

She'd been there with him only once. The sea had been rough, and every pot they'd hauled in was empty.

'Looks like we'll have to resort to the Larder,' William had said.

'What's that?' Stella asked.

William winked at her. 'Just a little place I keep tucked away.'

They'd motored north up the coast – well away from the areas where all the crayboats worked. They passed Stella's secret coves and ploughed on past the next headland. Then, with no warning, William cut the motor. Stella checked the charts. They were in the middle of a blank swathe of sand.

'There's no reef here,' Stella protested.

'That's right,' William smiled. 'But there's an old wreck. Uncharted. Only small. But enough to grow a bit of weed and make a home for a few crays.'

They'd caught all the fish they needed at the Larder. When they were ready to leave, William had sworn Stella to secrecy. He hardly ever went there, he said. And he'd never told a soul that it was there.

Stella stepped closer to the map. She ran her finger up the coastline – past the coves and on to the area where the Larder was. Inshore from William's secret place there was a horseshoe-shaped inlet. The map showed that it had been covered by a broad ground search. Stella guessed that meant that just a couple of people had walked the coastline. Something could easily have been missed.

Stella drove up the coast road, past the turn-off to Seven Oaks and on. Cold air laden with gravel dust blew in through rust-holes in the door of the ute. She reached for an old jumper of William's that she'd found behind the seat, and pulled it on as she drove.

Glancing down over the coast, Stella saw each landmark pass by. After the next headland she knew the road would become impass-able. When it had first been built – a hundred years ago by convicts – the road had continued for another fifty miles. But when the tin mine closed and there was no need for anyone to use it the council had closed it off, letting the bush grow back. Stella would park the ute near the road block, and proceed on foot.

She would not linger, she told herself. She would not look down through the trees and bushes and see the chain of coves – the cres-cent beaches edged with granite and lapped by the turquoise sea. She would not let her eye be drawn across to the deepest inlet – where *Tailwind* had taken refuge from the storm. Where she and Zeph had written their names on the sand.

This beach belongs to us.

The road began to peter out – there were no white guideposts now. Grass invaded the gravel, blurring the edges of the track. When she found a place where there was enough space to turn the ute around, Stella stopped and parked. She grabbed the orange daypack that she'd been given by Wendy. There was a bottle of water inside it, a raincoat, a whistle – and a wrinkled old apple she'd noticed on the caravan table amongst Spinks' papers.

Slinging the pack over her shoulder by one strap, she set off towards the place where the road officially ended. To her right she was aware of the bushland dropping steeply down to the water. To the coves . . . She fixed her gaze ahead, and hurried on.

As the last corner came into view, Stella came to a sudden halt. Ahead, a Russian minaret rose up above the she-oaks. It hovered there like a mirage – an onion-shaped dome painted blue and gold.

Stella stared in disbelief as she walked on. Gradually, pieces of timber, glass and corrugated iron became visible between the trunks. She drew in a slow breath. Someone had built a place out here – overlooking the coves. A sense of outrage flared briefly, but then she felt relieved. The place, taken over by a stranger, would be become part of the ordinary world – stripped of its power.

Before long the building came into full view. The walls shimmered with the rainbow hues of driftwood timbers – remnants of different paint tones set side by side. Large windows were edged with sea-washed limb wood: elegant grey branches stretched out along the ledges. It was not a big house – in fact, it was more like a cabin. But it was tall, rising up three storeys. The uppermost floor was crowned by the minaret. There was a window in its curved side, and a tiny balcony. Standing there, Stella guessed, you could look straight down into the coves. The sea breeze blowing up into your face . . .

Her breath caught in her throat. It was beautiful in all the ways she liked most – the kind of house she would have chosen for herself, if she had ever imagined creating a home of her own.

She skirted the side of a large garden. It was fenced around with driftwood, and festooned with old fishing nets still dangling corks and buoys. Inside, under a carport, she glimpsed a flash of red and chrome. Laurie's mate lived here, she realised. The newcomer from the mainland.

She half-ran now – wanting to be gone before she was noticed. Then the pack slipped off her shoulder and she paused to pull it back into place.

She felt a presence behind her before she registered footfalls drawing near. She spoke as she turned.

'I'm sorry. I need to get through . . .'

Her voice died on her lips.

A man stood there, looking at her.

For a moment she was lost – trapped in his gaze, held by his eyes. Green, the colour of the sea.

A current ran between them – a flash of recognition. Stella

gripped the strap of the backpack. Nothing seemed real – not the ground beneath her feet or the sky above.

'Stella.' The voice seemed to come from a distant place.

'Zeph.'

The two names hung in the air – woven into the sunlight that pushed down between the clouds.

Stella snatched a breath, her lungs crushed by the power of his presence. She could find no words. Emotions jumbled within her – shock, wonder, confusion, pain . . .

Then she found herself speaking – her voice soft, almost light. 'What are you doing here?'

Inside her, different words fought towards her lips.

You didn't come back. I waited for you.

You promised to return . . .

Stella folded her arms around her body as if to hold herself together. She felt the thickness of knitted wool closing her in, a shield around her heart.

Zeph didn't reply. He just looked at Stella – his eyes moving slowly over her face, her hair, her neck.

Stella tore her gaze away from him. Looking up the coast, she made herself picture William and the *Lady Tirian* waiting there for her. As she did so, a fresh sense of urgency moved in. She turned, and took two steps along the road.

'He's not up there,' Zeph said.

Stella stopped and looked back.

'We searched up that way three days ago,' Zeph said. 'I've been at sea looking for him – we've covered all the islands. There's no sign of him – or his boat.'

He still had the same gentle voice – the placeless accent of a boy who came from nowhere . . .

Stella faltered, feeling herself drawn towards him. But then her thoughts shifted back to William. She turned away again, and kept walking.

Behind her, she sensed Zeph still standing, watching. She stumbled, her foot catching on a tussock – then she recovered her balance and strode on. She passed the line of painted stones that signalled the end of the road, and hurried on along the rough track.

The image of his face rose before her, surprising her with its clarity: somehow, in that short time, every detail had become etched in her mind. His hair was still streaked by the sun, but it was cut shorter, falling tousled over his brow. A summer tan lingered on his skin. There were the beginnings of lines around his eyes and at the edges of his lips. His lips . . . They were still curved like an archer's bow, yet there was something firmer, stronger there.

She remembered their touch against her skin. The warm weight of his hands on her shoulders.

Something stirred inside her then – the sixteen-year-old girl she had buried so long ago awakening and struggling towards the light.

Stella pushed her back down with a ruthlessness born of fear. If she were allowed to return to life, all the pain would come with her. The long years of healing would be undone. Everything that Daniel and Miles had taught their adopted daughter – how to laugh again, how to shoot champagne corks at lily pads, how to wake up each morning and face another day – would be destroyed.

Hurrying on, Stella looked down at the ground – at the sticks and leaves and scurrying insects that she crushed beneath her feet. Her heart hammered in her chest loudly – as if the girl, locked inside her, were fighting to get out.

Caught in her power for a moment, Stella pictured herself running back to Zeph. She saw him waiting for her, his arms outstretched. She felt his body strong against hers.

But then came the silence. What would she say to him? How could she could even begin to tell him what had happened to her – after he had sailed away, leaving her so alone?

There were no words. There never would be. She knew this with a certainty that resonated deep in her soul.

All that she'd been through – the baby that Zeph knew nothing about; the shattered hope, the loss, the pain . . .

It could never now be shared.

Stella lifted her face to the wind and pushed on along the track. She felt the distance lengthening behind her. Eventually, she dared to turn back. The blue minaret, rising above the treetops, was all that she could see.

∽

The track became narrow, closed in by a dense thicket of ti-tree.

Stella walked between the paperbark trunks, breathing the fresh, sharp fragrance of the leaves. The road would emerge from the forest after a few kilometres, she knew – not far from the place where she wanted to go.

Water sloshed rhythmically in the bottle inside her pack as she kept up a steady pace. Sweat formed on her brow. She paused to pull off the jumper, tying it around her waist. Glancing down, she noticed faint tyre prints on the mossy track. Someone was using it again – shooters, she guessed, coming after geese that nested by the lagoons.

The sun was half-risen in the sky by the time she reached the headland inshore from the Larder. She struck out over the low heath until she reached the boobyalla bushes that bordered the coastline rocks.

She pushed in amongst them. Lizards and birds rustled in the undergrowth, scurrying from the path of her boots. Branches snagged her clothes and flicked against her face, but she hardly noticed them. She was aware only of fear filling her body – fear that she would find something, and fear that she would not. She held her breath as she stepped out onto a rocky shore.

Raising her hand to shield her eyes, she looked down, scanning the bay. Small stretches of water were held captive by steep mounds of granite that stretched out into the sea. Her gaze moved slowly over clumps of seaweed, rocks sticking up out of the water, patches of sand. Nothing caught her attention. Everything looked normal.

She picked her way down from boulder to boulder until she

reached sea-level. She began working her way along the rocks, looking down into all the inlets and pools.

Suddenly she stopped. A smudge of bright red showed between fronds of dark weed. She plunged her hand into the water and pulled up a piece of broken wood. Not a small fragment, but a solid length of timber. As she stared at it dripping in her hand, she knew what it was: a piece of planking, torn from the hull of the *Lady Tirian*.

She swung round, as if expecting now to find the rest of the boat. And William.

'Dad! Dad!' she shouted.

Gulls cried back at her, flapping away.

She looked along the edge of the bushland, searching for any kind of place where someone might take shelter if they were wounded or weak. A shine on the rocks near a cluster of green plants drew her eye. A seepage of fresh water.

She scrambled over the rocks, heading straight for it. Once there, she searched the bushes, calling again and again.

There was no sound but the wash of the sea and the rustle of birds in the grasses. And no sign of anyone having been there – recently, or ever . . .

Finally, she decided to climb back up to the highest point and look down again on the scene. This time she stood there for a long while, watching the weed as it washed back and forth in the swell, below the surface of the sea. She was about to turn away when she saw – just for a few seconds as the weeds parted – something pale, trapped in a wide crevice between two lines of rock. It looked like some huge sea creature wallowing belly-up beneath the surface.

She knew what it was. The upturned hull of a boat.

Stella ran down over the rocks, her eyes focused ahead and her feet skimming over tenuous footholds. As she reached the edge of the water, she flung off her backpack, untied the jumper from around her waist and pulled off her boots. She stripped off her jeans and shirt, leaving only her T-shirt and underwear. Then she lunged

233

out into the sea, bare feet slipping on weedy rocks. She gasped as the icy water enveloped her body.

She swam towards the submerged hull, her arms ploughing at the water. It was not far. She felt one foot kicking against the bottom of the keel. Panic waited at the edges of her mind, like a cat about to pounce. She made herself into two people – one was frantic with horror, but the other was calm and still. With the steady half of herself she looked at the way the sunken boat lay, and found the stern. She remembered that William kept a mask and snorkel in the side locker there. Taking a lungful of air, she dived down towards it – feeling her way blindly along the edge-rail, finding the locker room and opening the catch. With the gear in her hand she returned to the surface.

Standing on the hull, she pulled the mask over her eyes and fitted the snorkel into her mouth, tasting the salty rubber. Dragging in a deep breath, she ducked her head underwater and swam down.

Sunlight shafted in through the clear water. The scene was dreamlike – strands of weed spiralling like dancers through the depths. Stella traced the familiar line of the hull, with its deep keel like a giant shark's fin – the same keel that she'd scraped and painted each season on William's slipway. It was undamaged, and looked strangely peaceful lying there.

With the last of her breath, Stella pulled herself down further, to where the wheelhouse lay jammed against the rocky bottom.

The door to the wheelhouse had been torn from its hinges. The sea had stripped the place bare. All William's things were gone – his charts, his bedding, Stella's framed drawing of the tree in the wind . . . Washed away by the sea.

She swam back up to take another breath. She warned herself of what she might find as she searched further. She'd seen dead people pulled from the sea after a tidal wave in Papua New Guinea. A body can be transformed by sea lice in hours – all the flesh eaten away, just the skeleton and tendons remaining. Fish, too, will scavenge. Crayfish will tidy away any scraps that they leave.

Stella dived again and again. She crawled over the boat, covering its length and breadth in short sequences, broken by swift returns to the surface to gasp another breath. The mask was perished and water leaked in around the glass, a mini tide always rising, threatening her vision; but she swam on, salt stinging her eyes.

Finally, she had searched the whole of the wreck. The life raft was gone; the life-jackets and emergency ring, too. Everything was gone. The *Lady Tirian* was an empty husk.

William was not there.

As she swam back to shore, Stella told herself it meant nothing. He could still be drowned. He could still be alive. Somewhere else . . .

Stella collapsed on the stony beach, shaking with cold and numb inside. Half-thoughts tangled in her head, confused and meaningless. She sat by her clothes, her arms wrapped around her legs, pulled up against her body. Her chin rested on knees that were scraped raw and bloody.

She watched a gull circling overhead, a dark shape against the sky. She followed its flight as it swooped down and settled behind some rocks. There in the shadows was a patch of colour, visible between the boulders: almost black, yet not . . .

Rising to her feet, she stepped towards it. Then she scrambled up onto the rocks, crouching on hands and knees as she lowered her gaze.

The fisherman was lying face down on a narrow wedge of sand between two lines of rock. He wore the navy blue jumper Grace had made for him – the one with the special pattern knitted on the front and back. His feet were cased in thick woollen socks. Only his head was bare. Dark hair was matted against his skull.

Stella stared down at him, frozen with shock. As she watched, the sea washed up over the lower half of his body then retreated, leaving the green cloth of his trousers plastered against his legs. She saw then that one leg was broken and bound to a splint.

There was no room to crouch beside him so she lay over the boulder and leaned down, to touch him.

The back of his head was cold, wet.

'No. Oh no. Please – no . . .' Stella spoke quietly, as if to avoid waking a sleeping child. She reached closer, stretching trembling fingers towards his neck.

At that moment a wave washed in, reaching further up than the ones that had come before – submerging half of the man's face. Stella slid down off the rock, and then made her way round until she stood by William's head. She grasped his shoulders and pulled with all her strength. As another wave came in, she managed to shift him a little. She struggled desperately with his weight – pulling, waiting for the sea to help her, then pulling again.

At last he was free of the rocks, lying out in the open on the shingle beach. Stella held onto his shoulder and turned him over.

As his head rolled around, water ran from between his parted lips. His face, with its eyes peacefully closed, was like a mask painted in two colours. The half that had lain uppermost was white, like uncooked dough. Stella recoiled from the sight of it – patches of the pale flesh had been eaten away. The other half was a dark livid purple, but the skin – protected by the sand, perhaps – was undamaged.

Stella knelt near William's head. The knowledge that he was dead seeped slowly into her heart – a chill spreading through her. Gently, she turned his face to hide the damaged skin. His stained features looked foreign. If it were not for Grace's jumper, and the *Lady Tirian* lying nearby, she might have convinced herself that it was a stranger lying here, so silent and still and cold.

Stella laid her hand over his cheek, feeling the shape of the bone under the skin. Then she traced the outline of his nose with her finger, following it up to his forehead. She saw there the faint scar where he'd fallen against a bench in a storm. He'd refused to see the doctor, and instead had just taped the flesh together and let it heal.

Slowly, he became real to her. William. Her father. The man who had loved her, and hurt her so badly. The man who had been sorry for what he'd done to her – but who had not found a way to tell her until it was too late.

Her throat ached. Her shoulders heaved as waves of pain travelled through her body. Her eyes burned, raw and dry.

The cold crept into her, stiffening her limbs, making her teeth chatter. But she did not move. Words circled in her head, disconnected and brittle – broken scraps of thought. How long had he been dead? Had it happened before she arrived back here? Or was there something she should have done that would have led to a different end?

She looked along William's body to his splinted leg. She saw that it had been badly broken – a shaft of bone was visible where the trouser leg was torn. She flinched at the sight of it. Fragments of a story came together in her head. An accident at sea – a broken bone, a damaged boat. The *Lady Tirian* adrift, just a small speck in the ocean. William struggling to survive – waiting, hoping, for a rescue that never came . . .

She shifted her gaze back to his face. He looked so nearly alive.

Time seemed boundless as she sat there watching over him. When she heard noises behind her she registered them only faintly. Then a hand came to rest on her shoulder. She felt her body shaking under its steady touch.

Strong arms reached down and pulled her to her feet.

Zeph's face appeared, level with hers.

'You're freezing,' he said. His eyes were wide with concern. He left Stella for a short time, and then returned with her clothes.

Stella stood like a child as he took off her wet T-shirt and then dragged the thick jumper down over her head. The wool stuck to her damp skin, and he had to ease it over her hips. Then he held her steady against his body as she pushed her legs into her jeans.

'You need to get in out of the wind,' Zeph said. 'I've got the car up there. You can phone Spinks from the house.'

'No,' Stella broke in. 'I can't leave him here.'

Zeph looked down at William. 'It won't be easy to move him.' He glanced at Stella's face – then he ran away up the beach towards the car, his long legs covering the distance in easy strides. When he returned, he was dragging two long pieces of driftwood. A coil of rope hung from his shoulder.

He worked quickly and efficiently, crossing the poles and binding them to form a litter. He spoke only to ask Stella to hold ropes while he tightened knots. When he was ready, he gestured for Stella to take William's legs while he grasped the man's shoulders. After two attempts they managed to lay him over the wooden frame. Zeph lashed the body in place.

Standing side by side, they took up a pole each, and lifted the frame.

'Are you all right?' Zeph asked.

Stella nodded. She could not stop her teeth from chattering.

'Let's go, then.'

Leaning forward to brace themselves against the weight, they managed to drag the litter slowly over the stony beach.

Stella kept her eyes directed forward, not wanting to see William's head rolling from side to side as they bumped along. But Zeph, she saw, kept looking back over his shoulder to check that his ropes were holding.

When they reached the boobyalla, they laid down the litter and Zeph went ahead, breaking down the bushes to clear a wide path. As he did so, the back hatch door of the station wagon became visible through the gap.

Zeph picked up his pole and gestured for Stella to start pulling again.

The interior of the wagon was empty, its load of driftwood pulled out onto the grass. Zeph used one hand to brush out some loose flakes of paint and broken scraps of wood. Then they moved the litter alongside the open back of the vehicle. Zeph untied the ropes that held William in place.

William almost fell as they tilted the frame, but Zeph managed to steer the weight forward into the wagon. Then he climbed into the front of the car. Leaning over the seat, he pulled the shoulders until the body was laid out inside.

Stella stood still, her gaze travelling up William's body, towards his head. Then she saw that he'd come to lie with the pale side of his face exposed. She closed her eyes, hiding from the ravaged flesh.

When she looked again, Zeph was shaking out a piece of folded cloth – a sarong printed with yellow and blue flowers. He laid it over William's body, drawing it up to cover the face. His hands moved carefully, gently – as though he wanted to make up for having dragged the man up here and bundled him in so roughly.

'Thank you,' Stella said, when he was finished.

'I'm glad I found you,' Zeph said. He spoke firmly, as if stating a simple fact.

Stella looked at him. She did not ask why he'd followed her along the derelict road. She was just grateful that he had come. If he had not, she knew she would be there still – unable to abandon her father's body. Sitting all alone on the empty stony beach.

CHAPTER FIFTEEN

Stella sat in the seat with her legs drawn up, her arms around her knees, hugging them close. She felt cold and shaky. She tried not to think of William stretched out under the cloth behind her, or of Zeph sitting next to her. Whichever way she let her thoughts turn, there lay a maelstrom of emotions. She just kept her eyes on the road and tried to empty her mind.

'We need to find Spinks,' Zeph said.

Stella nodded mutely.

When they reached the turn-off, Zeph headed in the direction of the wharf. Near the entrance to the car park, the wagon slowed to a crawl. The space was half-empty now – the volunteers were packing up their equipment and moving out.

'He's over there,' Stella said. She pointed to where Spinks could be seen squatting down by the front bumper of an orange four-wheel drive, reaching in under the chassis.

Zeph drove closer, and then stopped the car to let Stella climb out. She walked towards Spinks, her feet bare and her hair hanging dishevelled about her face. As she drew near him, Spinks seemed almost to sense her presence. He straightened up and turned around.

'What's happened?' he asked, putting down a spanner.

'I found Dad.' Stella's voice caught in her throat.

'What do you mean?' Spinks demanded.

Stella glanced behind her at the car.

The man's eyes widened. In three steps he was at the back window of Zeph's wagon. He opened the hatch door and lifted it up. He bent to peer inside. After a long moment he looked over his shoulder at Stella.

He seemed to be searching for something to say. Then he noticed Zeph climbing out of the driver's seat. He stepped towards him as Stella drew near, and began speaking in a low voice.

'Where did you find him?'

'Out past my place,' Zeph said.

Stella came to stand beside them. 'The *Lady Tirian's* there, too,' she said. Her voice sounded distant to her – as though she were a journalist on the job, reporting facts. 'Caught in an inlet. Sunk. Upside-down.'

Spinks raised his eyebrows in surprise. 'We checked up there.'

'The storm must have brought her in – last night,' Zeph said.

Spinks rubbed his hands over his face. 'She was at sea, then. All that time . . .'

He was motionless for a few seconds – then he returned to the rear of the car. He sighed and shook his head. 'He shouldn't have been moved from the scene, you know. He shouldn't have been touched. Still, I suppose – what else could you have done . . .' Spinks turned towards Stella again, his expression softening. 'I'm sorry it's ended like this. I really am.'

Stella nodded dumbly. Over Spinks' shoulder she saw that onlookers were beginning to gather around.

Then she saw Grace, weaving a path towards the car.

'Oh no,' Stella whispered to Spinks. 'Get these people out of here.'

The policeman began herding the bystanders away. Grace, moving past them, appeared oblivious to their presence. She seemed drawn, as if by a magnet, towards the back of the car.

Soon, she reached Stella's side. But she did not look at her daughter. She stared into the wagon, her eyes fixed on something there.

Following the direction of her gaze, Stella saw something blue protruding from the end of the sarong. William's sock.

Grace stood still, looking in over the draped body. A breeze stirred her hair and tugged at the end of her skirt. She reached for the bottom of the sarong and began to pull the cloth towards her – slowly, steadily, until her husband's face was revealed.

There was a long silence. Then a low animal howl broke from her throat – a chilling wail, tearing the silence. A gull sitting on a guide-post nearby launched itself, squawking, into the air.

Grace stared, wide-eyed, recoiling from the sight before her. Yet, at the same time, the magnet force still held her in its power. It drew her on, crawling on hands and knees up into the car. She crouched there beside the body, her limbs folded awkwardly. She dragged off the rest of the sarong, and then – grasping great handfuls of the fisherman's jumper – pulled herself down towards him.

'No. No. No,' she moaned. Her cries became louder and louder – an anguished weeping. Then she began beating her head against William's chest, as if she thought she could wake him up – bring him back.

Over Spinks' shoulder, Stella glimpsed faces in the crowd – looks of shock, fascination and revulsion.

Stella lowered the hatch door, pushing it closed. As she started round to the front passenger door, she saw Spinks stepping forward, shaking his head warningly; but she took no notice.

As she opened her door, Zeph was already back in his seat, turning on the ignition and pumping the accelerator. With Stella barely inside the car, he drove off – swinging the vehicle in a wide arc, escaping from the car park and speeding off up the road.

Grace's cries filled the car. The woman's grief sounded like fear – the terror of a child lost amongst strangers and expecting never to be rescued. Stella felt sick listening to it. She covered her face with her hands.

The car bounced off potholes in the road, throwing her body against the door. She felt a sense of relief – the distance from the wharf, the people, lengthening behind her. She had no thoughts in her head, no idea what to do next.

After several minutes, she lifted her face and swallowed hard. She summoned Daniel's voice. Let the fear wash past you, he'd taught. Breathe through it, like pain. Then level your gaze. And step forward.

'Take us home,' she said to Zeph. 'Please, just take us home.'

$$\backsim$$

Grace lay on the double bed, fully dressed but shoeless. The space beside her – William's half of the bed – looked wide and vacant. She stared up at the ceiling. Her arms were clamped at her sides, and her legs stuck out straight and rigid. Stella covered her mother with a blanket and then returned to her place by the window.

Looking out past the oak tree she could see Spinks standing by his van. Not far away was the red wagon – with the back hatch now closed again. Stella wondered if William was still there, inside, or if they'd moved the body already. She was not sure how long she'd been in here, holding Grace's hands and stroking her hair as the woman's sobs subsided slowly into silence.

Stella scanned the area that she could see, but found no sign of Zeph. If not for his car, she could almost imagine that he had not really been here. It seemed so impossible. She closed her eyes on a wave of questions. How long had he been in Halfmoon Bay? Why had he come? Did anyone know that he'd ever visited here before . . .?

She tried to remember what she'd said to him as she'd pulled Grace from the car and led her towards the path. He'd offered to accompany the two women into the house, but Stella had known that the last thing her mother would want at a time like this was a stranger in her home.

Stella's memory of the scene was confused and disjointed. She'd told Zeph to go away, she knew. But she did not recall what words she'd used. She should go out and find him now, she thought. At the very least, she owed him her thanks.

'I have to go outside,' Stella said, looking over to the bed. Grace lay there, her hair falling back from her face, draping the velvet-covered mound of the pillow. She looked like the carved stone statue of a knight's lady stretched out on her coffin.

Grace showed no sign that she had heard. As Stella watched the motionless figure, despair crept over her. The agonised weeping had been frightening to witness. But this retreat into stillness was even more unnerving.

Stella paused at the door, her hand on the brass knob. 'I'll come back soon.'

Stella walked toward Zeph's car. Weak sunshine played dully over its faded red duco. She looked around, but there was no sign of him. She could see Spinks talking into his car radio. The policeman caught her eye, and signalled for her to stay there until he'd finished his call.

Stella stood by the wagon, resting her hands on the roof, looking inside to where William still lay, shrouded again in Zeph's sarong. Whoever had replaced the cloth – Spinks or Zeph – had left one of William's hands uncovered.

Stella stared down at it. If she half-closed her eyes she could avoid seeing the work of sea lice: the small holes pitting the flesh. She tried to imagine that the hand belonged to someone who was just sleeping and would soon awake. But it was impossible. In some way that could be felt deep inside, rather than simply observed with her eyes, the hand declared itself to be utterly bereft of life.

Stella cast her gaze over the rest of the veiled body. William, her father, was not here. He had departed. The essence of him – all his knowledge, his strength, his tastes and dislikes – was gone.

The iron will with which he ruled his small world – and himself – was no more.

Stella felt something stirring deep inside her – an emotion that felt foreign and wrong. It lay behind the shock, the grief, the pain. With a sense of horror, she recognised what it was.

Relief.

Spinks came to stand beside her. 'I called in one of the volunteers. They gave Zeph a lift back to his place.'

Stella looked at the policeman in confusion. 'Why didn't he wait for his car?'

'The thing is, he can't have it back straightaway.' Spinks paused to take a deep breath. 'Look, Stella – there are procedures coming into play here. They've got a new sergeant in St Louis. He's one of those up-and-coming types that want to make their mark. He doesn't like the fact that you found the body.'

Stella frowned. 'What do you mean?'

'Well, when someone who's not involved in the police search finds the missing subject, it looks like we've not done our job. It's even worse that it was a family member. We've already got reporters onto us, wanting the story. And then you moved him from the scene.' The policeman sighed. 'The sergeant's got his police manual out on his desk. I could hear him turning the pages. He's going to follow the rules down to the last letter.'

Stella opened her mouth to speak, but Spinks waved his hand to ward off any words.

'I tried to tell him this is not how we do things around here. I'm the Police Forward Commander – in charge of the search – and I should have some say in how we handle the situation. But at the end of the day, he's the boss.'

Spinks turned at the sound of a vehicle approaching along the track. 'That'll be Probationary Constable Brown of St Louis police station, reporting for duty,' he said with a wry twist of his lips. 'He's been sent to guard the vehicle until the mortuary ambulance arrives. I'm afraid your father's body will have to remain where it is until then. When the deceased has been removed, the vehicle will be impounded, pending advice from the coroner's office.'

Stella stared at him. The meaning of his words settled slowly in her head. 'Do you think something else happened out there – that it wasn't just an accident?'

Spinks shook his head. 'The sergeant wants to go by the book, that's all. Your father wasn't in any trouble. He had no enemies.' He looked across to where the garden bordered the foreshore. 'The sea is a dangerous place, Stella. We all know that.'

Stella twisted her fingers in the woollen threads of William's jumper.

'What's going to happen to him?' As she asked, she already knew. Memories came to her, of interviews with coroners back in her days as a young journalist in Melbourne. She had a vision of William's body sliced open, his lungs pulled out and his heart laid bare.

'They'll want to determine the actual cause of death. They'll test his blood for alcohol or toxins and look for wounds – things like that. Shouldn't take more than a day or two. They'll contact St Louis – say it was an accidental death, no suspicious circumstances. Then it will all be over.'

Stella met his gaze. His last words echoed hollowly in the air.

It would not be over. They both knew that.

'How is Grace?' Spinks asked.

'She's calmed down,' Stella said. She pressed her lips together to hold them steady. 'She's in the bedroom, resting.'

Spinks nodded. 'Well, that's good. I'll radio the doctor for you. And I'll ask Pauline or my sister to come out here. Everyone will want to help.'

'No,' Stella said firmly. 'Please just leave us alone.'

Spinks turned at the sound of footsteps coming up behind him. A young policeman was approaching. He was thin, an Adam's apple sticking out from his throat. He walked with his head held high, like a soldier on parade.

'Stella, this is Constable Brown,' Spinks said. 'Brown, this is Miss Birchmore.'

Brown ducked his head briefly before turning to Spinks. 'I've got further instructions,' he announced.

'Yes?' Spinks asked.

Brown looked meaningfully at Stella.

Spinks glanced at her. 'You could wait in the house. I'll come in when we're finished.'

'No,' Stella protested. 'I want to stay.'

Brown offered her a condescending smile. 'I think you'll find it upsetting . . .' He looked to the older man for support.

'It's up to her,' Spinks said. 'She's not a child.'

Brown gave no reply. He just handed Spinks a pair of latex gloves.

The two policemen fitted plastic bags over William's hands, taping each one tightly at the wrist. Then they manoeuvred the body into a black canvas bag. They stuffed in the sarong. Stella watched the blue and yellow flowers disappearing as Spinks pulled up the zip to close the bag.

The three stood in silence for a moment, then Brown shut the hatch door. He placed himself in front of it, as if he feared that Stella might open it and steal her father away.

Spinks drew Stella aside, out of the young man's hearing. 'I'll have to get a full statement from you later. I'll head out and speak to Zeph first – that'll give you a bit more time to see to Grace.' He waited for a response.

'Okay,' Stella offered. 'Whatever you want.'

'But I just have to check something with you now. The sergeant asked me to find out if you are – associated – with the man who arrived on the scene.' Spinks gave Stella a reassuring smile. 'It's a standard question in a situation like this – straight out of the manual. I told him I didn't see how you could know Zeph at all. He only came here a couple of years ago. And until yesterday you hadn't been home for fifteen years.' Spinks scratched the side of his face. 'It's just that – once the question was asked – I began to wonder. There was something about the way he – worked with you – there at the wharf. You shut the hatch, and he just knew you wanted to get away. It stuck in my mind . . .'

Stella looked down at her feet. She pushed the toe of one boot into a tuft of grass.

Tell the truth. That's all you have to do.

She took a breath. 'I knew him – years ago. But not for long.'

Only seven days . . .

'It's nothing to do with – now.'

Spinks watched her face as he took out a notebook and opened it, ready to write. 'So it was just chance that he found you there, with William.'

Stella looked at his pen, poised over the page. She shook her head. 'He followed me there.'

Spinks raised an eyebrow.

'Just one thing,' he added. 'Was it here that you met Zeph, years ago? At Halfmoon Bay?'

Stella nodded, but did not speak.

Spinks snapped shut his notebook. 'Good. That's covered, then. I'll tell the sergeant that you are not known to be associated with one another. We'll try and keep this case as simple as possible.'

Stella looked into his eyes. 'Thank you.'

Spinks' face tightened with concern. 'Are you going to be all right?'

She lifted her chin. 'Yes.'

The man reached out a hand and touched her shoulder. 'Just remember, Stella. It's not always a good thing to be strong.'

A radio crackled in Spinks' pocket. As he reached to pull it out, Stella turned and walked away.

As she passed through the garden, she paused, her gaze settling on lily plants pushing up through the soil. Amidst the stormy weather, she'd not registered that spring was on its way. The trees, she saw now, were beginning to bud. The stalks of the berry canes were fuzzed with green. She lowered her eyes and hurried inside – to where Grace, the gardener, awaited her; lying silent and still – as if her soul had turned inward, towards death.

CHAPTER SIXTEEN

B right spring sunshine leaked in around the edges of the kitchen curtains. Stella swept them open and stood blinking in the sudden light. She put on the kettle and then returned to the window, looking out over the garden at the neat ranks of plants, all bristling with green shoots. Small birds pecked at the mulch that had been spread over the beds, then flew off towards their nesting places with wispy strands of gum bark held in their beaks. Beyond the fruit bushes Stella could see the ocean – a glittering plain of azure blue. Everything looked friendly and safe. It was hard to imagine that there had just been a whole week of wild winds and dangerous seas.

In contrast to the scene outside, a heavy stillness lay over the house. It crept like a fog out from the main bedroom, where Grace still lay motionless. A night, a whole day and another night had passed since the woman had seen her husband's body, and finally understood that he was dead. In those long hours, nothing had changed. Grace seemed deaf, mute and numb with grief.

As she moved around the kitchen, Stella felt the dense silence entering her lungs with each breath that she took. It made the beat of her heart sound too loud; and the tick of the clock on the mantelpiece too soft. She rattled the crockery as she prepared a breakfast tray – laying out a plate, cup and saucer on a starched linen cloth; adding a fine-china egg-cup, salt shaker, teaspoon, and a pat of butter in a saucer. She dropped a slice of white bread into the toaster. As she did so, her elbow caught on a cake-tin, toppling it onto the floor.

The loud clatter seemed to linger, trapped in the air. Stella picked the tin up and searched for somewhere else to put it – but almost every surface in the kitchen was already stacked with food. There were Tupperware containers full of biscuits and sandwiches; casserole dishes full of stew and soup; pies and quiches wrapped in tea-towels; and even bottles of milk and loaves of bread.

During the previous day, gifts of food had kept appearing on the front doorstep of Grace's house. People had respected Stella's request for privacy – no one had knocked; they had contented themselves with leaving small notes with their offerings.

With deepest sympathy. Sylvia and Ted Barron

Let us know if there's anything we can do. Everyone from the fish factory

I thought you might need some more honey. Joe

I'm worried about you, Stella. Please call. Pauline xxx

Stella pulled a piece of crust off a quiche and took two bites before tossing it into the sink. She felt hungry, but didn't seem able to think clearly enough even to choose what she wanted to eat – let alone to heat it up and set it out on a plate.

When the tray was ready – with its soft-boiled egg and toast fingers with no crust – Stella carried it into Grace's room. As she walked down the hallway, she pictured her mother lying in her bed – neither asleep nor awake, but hovering somewhere between.

At the bedroom door, Stella's step faltered. Sheets and blankets were draped onto the floor. There was a faint hollow in the mattress where Grace had lain. But her mother was gone.

Stella put down the tray and hurried into the sea room and then the bathroom, looking for her. Finally, Stella found her in the toilet. Grace looked as though she'd forgotten why she'd left her room. She just stood there, one hand resting on the cistern, her head bent, tangled hair covering her face as she gazed down into the bowl.

'Do you want to go?' Stella asked. She spoke slowly, as if to a foreigner who barely understood the language she was speaking. 'You want to go to the toilet?'

Grace gave the vaguest of nods.

Stella took the woman by the shoulders and turned her round. Grace moved like a puppet with loose strings, her limbs gangly, her balance uncertain. Stella hitched up the nightdress, bunching the flannelette around her mother's hips. She glimpsed lean white thighs rising to the triangle of dark hair, and, hanging above, the soft belly freed of its girdle.

'Sit. Sit down,' she commanded. She wondered if she should stay or leave. Then she heard a distant sound filtering through the silence of the house. A vehicle was coming up the track.

'I'll check who it is,' Stella said.

She moved quickly to the front door – to a place where she could see out, but where she would not be noticed by anyone who arrived. She waited, watching.

Against her will, she imagined it: a borrowed car – Laurie's Jeep, perhaps – bumping up the track, coming to a halt outside the house. Zeph climbing out – his hair falling across his face, a veil of sunlit gold . . .

There was no reason why he would come, Stella told herself. Whatever had brought him to live here, at Halfmoon Bay, was nothing to do with her.

She laid out facts like playing cards chosen from a deck.

Even if Zeph had hoped to see her again when he returned after all these years, he'd soon have found out that she was gone.

And that she never returned, even for brief visits.

Laurie could have told him that, or Mrs Barron.

Yet still, Zeph had bought the land and built himself a house.

He loved the coves, Stella told herself. That was it.

Back then, she remembered, he'd said the hidden cove where he'd moored *Tailwind* was one of the most beautiful places he'd ever seen. He must have kept sailing on, he and Carla, and found no better place to make his home.

To settle down, raise a family.

That was what people did . . .

A voice inside Stella argued against this careful reasoning but she refused to listen to it – opening herself up to more pain and disappointment was a risk she dared not take. She concentrated on peering out through the narrow window beside the door.

Before long a vehicle came into view – a dark blue sedan with a white checked pattern along the top and 'Tasmania Police' printed on the side.

Spinks climbed out. He smoothed down his uniform then reached back into the vehicle and lifted out a clear glass casserole dish. He did not carry it to the front doorstep, as everyone else had done – instead, he went round towards the side door. Stella heard him knock briefly, then let himself in.

As she entered the kitchen, Spinks greeted Stella by holding out the casserole dish. She looked down through the lid, onto a bubbly golden topping of melted cheese and circles of sliced hard-boiled egg – round yellow moons inside white ones.

'Tuna mornay,' he said. 'My sister's specialty.' He scanned the kitchen, looking for a place to put down his dish. 'You look like you're well-supplied.'

Stella gave no response. Anxiety twisted inside her. She knew the policeman had not just come to bring them food.

'How's Grace?' Spinks asked.

'She's a bit better,' answered Stella.

Spinks looked at her. 'You managing okay?'

'Yes,' Stella said.

'Good. Pauline's worried about you. I think you should have her up here.'

Stella pictured Grace, dirty and dishevelled; all trace of her careful manners gone. 'Not yet.'

Spinks cleared his throat. When he spoke, he used his official policeman's voice. 'I just came to let you know that the coroner's office has sent their report to St Louis. They've determined that the cause of William's death was hypothermia. The report says it was "probably following an accident at sea".' Spinks' fingers made marks in the air to show when he was quoting. 'They didn't seem to come up with anything more than we already guessed – compound fracture of the leg, dehydration . . .' Spinks sighed. 'What actually happened out there is anyone's guess. He probably got thrown across the boat by a rogue wave, or something fell on him. He was injured. Then, after that, he couldn't keep the boat on course. She broadsided into a wave, engine flooded. That's how these things happen – one thing begins it, and it just goes on from there.'

Stella nodded. She'd already run through the scenario a thousand times herself. She knew enough not to expect that the real story of the tragedy would ever be uncovered. That was the way with things that happened at sea. They remained a mystery.

Taken by the Sea.

Lost. Fell.

The words were always simple, and vague.

'Anyway,' Spinks continued, 'the main thing is that the coroner is satisfied there are no suspicious circumstances. They've released the body for burial.'

'That's good,' Stella said. She should be relieved, she told herself. But she only felt empty.

'Zeph's got his car back, too,' Spinks added. He gave Stella a searching look. 'I took a statement from him for the sergeant. When I asked the question – did he know you prior to the incident of discovering William's body – he said the same as you. Almost to the word.'

Stella looked down at the floor. She remembered the answer she'd given.

I knew him years ago.

It's nothing to do with now.

Lifting her gaze, she forced a quick smile. 'Well – that's good. Keeps it simple.'

'I suppose it does,' agreed Spinks. He was quiet for a time, looking thoughtfully around the room. Then he spoke again. 'Shall I get the rector to come out so you can plan the funeral?'

'No. I'll drive in and visit him. Thanks for coming to see us. And please pass on our thanks for the casserole.'

Spinks raised one hand in farewell, and then stepped out into the sunshine.

Stella propped Grace up on two pillows – her own, and one taken from William's side of the bed. Then she perched beside her mother with the breakfast tray on her lap. She sliced off the top of an egg and dipped a spoon into the soft yolk. She carried a loaded spoonful towards Grace's lips. She caught a glimpse of her reflection in the dressing-table mirror – noticing that as she willed her mother to eat, her own mouth opened.

Here comes the aeroplane.

She remembered how Grace used to fly the spoon towards her – a small craft circling in the sky.

Open the hangar. There's a good girl.

Grace looked at Stella's open mouth, then parted her own lips. Stella slipped the spoon between them. Her mother chewed and swallowed. And opened her mouth for more.

'Why don't you get up after this?' Stella suggested. 'It's a beautiful day outside.'

Grace didn't seem to understand what her daughter was saying at first. Then she shook her head – slowly, like someone who was deeply tired or ill.

'You can't just stay here, in bed,' Stella said. She adopted a motherly tone – gentle yet firm. 'Spinks has been here. The coroner has released the body. We need to arrange the burial.'

Grace turned her head away, burying her face in the pillow. 'I can't face it.' The voice was muffled but clear. 'I can't manage without him.'

'You can.' Stella hardened her voice. 'You have to.'

Grace raised her head. 'I won't know what to do. I won't know . . . anything.' Her face was a mask of fear and pleading.

Stella stared down at her. Something about that look – the strange blend of childish emotion laid over a mature woman's features – banished the tenderness she had felt. Darkness rose up in its place. She remembered how Grace had hidden behind that look as she'd sat on the bed – this bed – and mouthed the words that William had wanted to hear.

She remembered how Grace had betrayed her a second time. How the woman had knelt in front of her daughter less than a week later, holding the baby in her hands. Stella had thought her mother would understand how precious he was. Yet, when William had demanded her to, Grace had ignored Stella's pleas and relinquished the little boy to his grasping hands. To be taken away and never seen again . . .

Stella stood up, sending the breakfast tray crashing to the floor. The egg rolled in a long curve, disappearing under the bed. She took a breath.

'Dad was too strong, too hard.' Her words burst out into the quiet air. 'But you let him be. You gave up too much.'

Grace closed her eyes, as though blindness would offer her a shield.

'Listen to me!' Stella's voice rose, sharp and thin. She felt like a little girl – a sixteen-year-old child. 'You should have stood up to him. You should have been stronger. You let me down.' A gasping sob strangled her voice, but the words struggled out. 'You were my mother.'

Grace did not open her eyes, but a tremor passed over her face. Her hands clamped, white-knuckled, onto the edge of the blanket.

Stella stared at her for a moment. Then she turned and walked slowly from the room.

Stella sat on one side of a wide desk covered in a green felt cloth. The rector sat opposite her, his head bent over a book.

'You are correct,' he said. 'Your father purchased a family-sized burial plot back in 1963.' He smiled kindly at Stella. 'It makes things so much easier when people have made preparations like this. Did he leave instructions about his funeral service as well? In the will, perhaps?'

Stella shook her head. 'He wouldn't want a funeral service. He never went to church – at least, he never used to.'

'I must admit, I haven't seen him there,' the rector responded. 'But I've only been here six months. I don't think I've met your mother either.' He gave Stella a serious look. 'She really should be here to discuss this.'

'She's not well,' Stella said.

'We could wait a day or two . . .' The rector fixed Stella with a gaze that was almost suspicious. 'The wife is usually involved.'

Stella looked past the man's shoulder at a line of empty vases, pale with dust. She pictured Grace, back at Seven Oaks. Her mother was still lying on her bed, all day and all night. She refused to eat now, and would only sip water when it was poured between her lips.

'I think it's important to get it over with,' Stella said. 'Then we can get on with our lives.'

The rector raised his eyebrows briefly. Then he opened a prayer book and began turning the pages. His fingers were long and pale. 'There are several orders of service to choose from. Then hymns must be selected.'

'We don't need a service,' Stella said. 'Just a burial.'

The rector's hands became still, resting on the open book. 'It's important to consider the feelings of others at a time like this – his friends, his extended family –'

'There's no family,' Stella broke in. 'And his friends all know that he wasn't a churchgoer.'

The rector nodded slowly, looking down at the prayer book as if seeking wisdom. When he lifted his face it was a vision of sympathy and forbearance. 'It's not quite that simple, Miss Birchmore.

There are rules about how things must be done on consecrated ground. They are there to remind us of the sanctity of all human life.' He paused, eyeing her intently. 'If you attach no value to them, then – if you will excuse my bluntness – you might just as well put him in a hole in the garden.'

Stella pushed back her chair and stood up. 'Do what you have to do. But keep it as simple as possible – no eulogy, no singing.'

The rector looked at her in silence for a moment, then he offered her a faint smile. 'I think I understand what's required.'

Bees buzzed in busy clouds around bright bunches of garden flowers that had been placed on the ground beside the open grave. Stella stood looking down at the plain coffin – at the narrower end, where William's feet would be. She pictured the man there, dressed in his suit behind the nailed-down wood. He would be pleased, she knew, by the large crowd that had gathered to pay their respects. The fish factory, the shop and the pub had all been closed. Everyone was here.

Except Grace.

When Stella had gone into the bedroom this morning to say goodbye, her mother been lying so still that she seemed hardly to be breathing. With each day that passed Grace was becoming more withdrawn – now she would not even speak. Stella blamed herself for this. What had she been thinking of, she asked herself – bringing up pain and anger from the past, when Grace had enough to deal with already.

Stella shook her head, wanting to break free of the image of Grace all alone out there at Seven Oaks.

'You all right, dear?' Pauline asked.

The woman stood at Stella's side. Ever since Stella had arrived in the churchyard, Pauline had remained close to her. She'd said little; she just touched Stella's shoulder or elbow from time to time, letting her know that she was not alone.

Stella looked up at a movement in the crowd. The rector made his way to the head of the grave and stood there, gazing solemnly over the gathering. He wore a long, white robe and a black stole draped around his neck. A sheen of sweat lay over his bald head.

He held out his prayer book. Spreading his fingers over the covers, he let the book fall open to a place that he had marked.

'Man that is born of woman is of few days, and full of trouble,' he read. His voice was confident and clear. 'He comes forth like a flower and withers. He passes like a shadow and does not stay.'

He looked up then – his eyes travelling slowly over the crowd. He paused on Stella's face and smiled sadly. She looked at him blankly. The words he'd just said made no sense to her.

'Dear friends,' he said. 'We have come here today to give thanks for the life of our brother, William Charles Birchmore, who was so tragically taken from us. He was a man of many admirable qualities. He was a skilled fisherman who loved his work, and had a great respect for the sea.'

Stella stared at the rector, but he did not look at her again.

'William Birchmore possessed those qualities of leadership that are valued by any community . . .'

His voice went on and on. Then it slowed and deepened, gathering emphasis. Stella bowed her head as the man's words flowed past her.

'William had two great loves in his life: his adored wife Grace – who is unfortunately not able to be with us this morning – and his beloved daughter, Stella. As a father, and a husband, he was an example to us all.'

Stella closed her eyes. William's words of remorse came back to her.

If only I could be someone else. Someone good.

'He was a man of principle,' the rector continued. 'A simple, honest man.'

Stella looked up. People were nodding their agreement with the picture the rector was painting. Many of the women had tears in their eyes.

Only Spinks seemed unmoved. Stella saw him standing not far from the rector. He had been watching her, she realised. When she met his gaze, he nodded faintly, as if he understood – things were not as simple as they seemed.

She closed her eyes again, afraid, suddenly, of what lay ahead: all the tangled feelings that kept closing in around her – about William, Grace, Zeph. And the little boy whose voice still came to her, carried in the wind. And who visited her dreams with the strange pale face of the zeru zeru child. Lost. So lost.

She thought of the tiny body, buried in a hidden grave that was unmarked. Unholy. He had no coffin to protect his skin from the cold touch of the earth. Only the dress, and a cloth wrapping, perhaps.

Or did William just drop him down into the dirt . . .?

Stella fixed her attention on the flowers laid out on the ground. There were bunches of early spring flowers – daisies, poppies, lady's bonnets, baby's breath and jonquils – all mixed with sprigs of bluegum and wattle. Some of the more fragile blooms were already wilting in the sunshine. At the back of the pile was a bunch that stood out from all the others. It had a simple striking beauty. Stella took a moment to work out why this was. Then she saw: it contained no flowers. It was made only of different kinds of foliage in contrasting shades of green.

A single long parrot feather of gleaming emerald was tucked in amongst the branches.

She knew, somehow, as she looked at it, whose work it was. She stared at the green feather. What did it mean that Zeph had laid the wreath here? Had he known William as a friend? Or was it just a gesture of respect? Perhaps it was meant to speak to her . . . She felt light-headed in the hot sun. Confused. She sensed herself poised on the brink – in danger of falling prey to emotions that she could not afford to face.

Suddenly, Pauline was nudging her arm. 'It's time to do the soil now, dear.'

Someone pushed a handful of earth into Stella's hand. She closed her fist on its warm dampness.

'Earth to earth, ashes to ashes, dust to dust,' the rector was intoning.

Stella threw the soil down. It landed with a dull thud against the coffin.

She wished then that she could cry. For William, for her baby, for Zeph, and Grace – all that she had lost, and all that she had never possessed.

She imagined a river flowing out of her eyes – leaving her clean and open. Reborn.

But her eyes were as dry as ashes, as barren as dust.

The tea was tepid and milky. Stella swallowed it quickly to wash down a mouthful of chocolate lamington. She kept the rest of the cake on her saucer, so that it would look as though she were eating.

She smiled at Laura's parents. Then she greeted Jamie's father. The man looked uncomfortable in a jacket and trousers. Pauline had him at her side now. At the burial he had stood with all the other fishermen. They'd formed a guard of honour, paying their respects as a group. They'd looked strained and uncertain, hovering close to one another. Stella sensed their fear that a fate like William's might one day await them, too – and no precautions, no planning, could protect them.

'It's not as if William was an idiot,' one had said to Stella. 'He played safe, the poor bugger. Always played safe.'

Stella took the last sip of her tea. As she lowered her cup, she looked around the room, her gaze passing over all the faces, both familiar and new. Searching for Zeph . . .

She was about to give up, when – through a gap in the crowd of bodies – she glimpsed a tall figure with streaked sandy hair. He wore a dark suit and pale grey shirt. Stella stepped forward to see more clearly.

Her lips parted as she drew in a breath. It was him.

Zeph looked like a stranger in his formal clothes – a man who would be at home in a boardroom, an art gallery or a downtown street anywhere in the world. And yet, something about him still reminded Stella of the seafaring boy wrapped in a faded sarong.

He had not seen her – he was talking to a man whom Stella did not know. She watched Zeph for a few seconds longer, and then she tore her gaze away. Against her will, she scanned the hall again – searching now for a face she did not know. The face of a woman, dressed like Zeph in expensive city clothes. A woman with children at her side, perhaps. Or a baby in her arms.

Stella stared down at the wooden floor – at the scuffed remains of white painted lines, laid out to mark the boundaries of badminton and basketball courts. Played by generations of children coming after her.

She lifted her eyes, as a smudge of colour swam into the edges of her vision. A certain shade of mauve – distinctive and instantly familiar. A mass of gerberas appeared before her: a large cluster of perfect blooms – every one of them an even tone of lilac.

A young man in a taxi driver's uniform held the bouquet out to her. 'Special delivery,' he said. He bowed his head respectfully, then walked off.

Stella recognised the Interflora logo on a small card pinned to the cellophane. Beneath it was a typed message.

Our thoughts are with you.
Lorna and all the team at Women's World.

Stella touched one of the gerberas – it looked like an oversized daisy. This was no coincidence, she knew – the flowers would have been chosen carefully to match the company motif. They may even have been specially dyed – up in Sydney, or wherever it was that Interflora had found a florist able to meet Lorna's demands.

She longed suddenly to go back to being a part of Lorna's team – taking her place in a world where everything meant what it was intended to mean. There was no confusion.

Just tell the truth. That's all you have to do.

She wanted to be an outsider again. Looking in on the lives of strangers. Finding the facts, and keeping her feelings at bay.

She pictured her typewriter waiting for her behind Mr Berhanu's desk at the Ethiopian Hotel. Soon, she told herself, she would be back there. Tapping out a new story, swearing at those three keys that always stuck. She could see it – her bag unpacked on her hard, narrow bed.

And the stone angel sitting beside her – the sign that she was home.

CHAPTER SEVENTEEN

Sparks rose in the firebox as Stella poked another log into place. She glanced at the temperature gauge. It was nearly hot enough, but she wanted to be sure.

Behind her, Grace's recipe book lay on the table, opened at the page for Josephine's Canary Cake. As far as Stella knew, it was her mother's favourite. She told herself she was making it to encourage Grace to eat. But she knew as well that it was a gesture prompted by guilt over the decision she had made: to leave Tasmania just as soon as she could arrange it – even if it meant engaging a visiting nurse from St Louis to look after Grace.

Stella followed the recipe meticulously, reading the spidery hand-written instructions over and over again.

Stir in unbeaten egg.

Sift into basin all dry ingredients.

Do not over-mix . . .

She made certain she smoothed off measuring cups and weighed out the ingredients exactly. She even cut out kitchen paper to line the cake-tin. She had not baked anything for so many years that the actions, though once familiar to her, were now awkward.

It seemed a long time before the mixture was ready in the tin.

Looking around her, Stella was amazed at how much flour

seemed to have been spilled, how the eggshells had somehow rolled onto the floor, and how butter was smeared on the table. A fly sat on a sticky spoon, rubbing its front legs together. Thick yellow sludge dripped down the outside of Grace's blue and white mixing bowl, and pooled on the table.

Stella glanced over the rest of the kitchen. All the food that people had brought – now stale and spoiled – was still stacked up everywhere. Grace's neat kitchen had been transformed into a place of dirt and chaos. Once the cake was in the oven, Stella told herself, she would clean everything up.

As she slid the tin onto the oven shelf and closed the door, she noticed that the woodbox was nearly empty. There was enough wood there to keep the fire up to temperature for the baking, but more would be needed if there were to be any hot water later on.

She went out to the woodpile and began splitting pieces of timber. As she did so, she looked at the remains of the stack. Most of it was made up of large sections of trunk, which would need to be chopped before use. This had always been William's task. While he was home from the sea, he split enough wood to fill all the wood-boxes, and left an extra pile by the laundry. Stella tried to think about who would cut it now. And who would clean the guttering twice a year. Or fix the pump when it broke down . . .

Leaving the woodpile, she began walking around the exterior of the house, and then the laundry and shed, making mental notes of all the tasks that would need to be carried out. There were the regular ones, and the ones that would crop up from time to time without warning. Stella checked the state of the paintwork, the pipes, the roof iron. She was relieved – but not surprised – to see that William had kept the whole place in good repair. It would be a few years before any major maintenance work came up.

Then Stella went into the shed to carry out a quick survey of spare paint, timber supplies and tools. Satisfied that here, too, William had left everything in good order, she went back outside.

As she walked down the path, she noticed the faint smell of

burning. At first she could not think what it was. Then she saw smoke filtering out through the open back door.

'Damn! The cake . . .'

Stella ran towards the house. As she passed the kitchen, she glimpsed a haze of blue-grey smoke filling the room. She cursed her carelessness. The cake she'd made for Grace was ruined. And the smell would stay in the house for weeks, she knew, lingering in the curtains.

Reaching the side door, she swung round into the house. Then she stopped and backed away.

A figure stood in the hall, on the threshold of the kitchen – a pale wraith in a long, crumpled nightdress, grey-gold hair sticking out around her face.

As Stella watched from behind the lintel, Grace shook her head as if to wake herself. Then she sprang into action, grabbing a tea-towel and yanking open the oven door.

Black smoke billowed out. Grace coughed as she bent to reach inside the oven. After a few seconds she drew back, shaking burned fingers into the air. Scrunching the tea-towel into a thicker wad, she tried again to retrieve the burning cake. This time she succeeded. A dark plume of smoke poured from the tin as she pulled it from the oven and swung round with it towards the side door.

Stella ran back behind the woodpile, out of sight. She saw the smoking cake-tin sail through the air from the direction of the doorway and land in the middle of the lily bed. Moments later, the kitchen window swung wide open. The tea-towel fluttered into view, as Grace tried to fan out the smoke.

Stella heard Grace's voice, calling inside the house.

'Stella? Are you there?'

Stella stayed in her hiding place. Through a gap between pieces of wood she saw Grace come to the side door. With her hands on her hips, she stood there, scanning the garden and looking up the track. Rising onto tiptoes she peered down to the foreshore.

'Stella!' she called again. 'Where are you?'

After a short pause, Grace went back inside. Before long, Stella heard water gushing into the sink and the scrape of a chair-leg across the floor. Then came the clatter of dishes being moved, and the clang of the dustbin lid being lifted and replaced.

Stella stood with her back to the woodpile, resting her hands lightly over the splintery wall of logs. She felt the tension ease from her body. It was a small step, she knew – Grace getting out of bed and back into her kitchen. There was a long way to go. But the journey had begun.

She gazed out over the foreshore to the open sea. She did not see the gleaming blue water. Instead, she saw the highland plains of Ethiopia – red earth, barren hillsides, and the harsh beauty of deep gorges, inky purple in the last light of the day.

Stella leaned against the door of the phone box, gazing out over the car park towards the Seafarers' Memorial, where dozens of seagulls were lined up like troops awaiting orders. She found her eyes seeking the part of the wall she knew so well. The plaque of David Grey . . . Turning her back on the scene, she focused instead on the fish factory – the doors stained with fish blood and engine oil, and the stacked crates printed with blue letters: 'Produce of Tasmania'.

She could hear the international operator dialling through to London – and then asking Lorna's secretary if she would accept a reverse-charged call from Halfmoon Bay, Tasmania.

'Where on earth is that?' the secretary asked.

'Australia,' the operator added. 'I have Stella Boyd here.'

'Oh – Stella! Yes. Yes of course we'll accept the call!'

Stella felt a small thrill of warmth at the knowledge that she was still wanted, still important . . . The next moment, Lorna was on the line.

'Stella! How wonderful to hear your voice. You sound faint. Are you all right? Did the flowers arrive?'

'Yes, thank you,' Stella said. 'They were very nice.'

'Good. I am pleased. Everyone was terribly upset for you.' The woman gave a brief respectful pause. 'We were talking about you just this morning. We need you back on deck, Stella. I'm not pressuring you. You must take as long as you need. I understand what a difficult time you must be having . . .'

'I'm ready,' Stella broke in. 'I want to get back to work straightaway. I've already booked a flight to Dubai, leaving next Wednesday. '

There was a short silence. 'Dubai? Why Dubai?'

Stella frowned. She'd have expected Lorna to remember that Ethiopian Airlines flew from there. 'It's the best way back to Addis. I want to cover the end of the war from there – then head north into Eritrea.'

'Stella, I've got a fantastic new idea for you,' Lorna said, smoothly skirting what Stella had just said. 'Alaska. Avon ladies in Alaska. Can you believe it? Visiting igloos with cosmetic catalogues?'

Stella pressed the receiver to her ear. 'What did you say?'

'I'll call it "Women Who Sell Lipsticks to Eskimos" – or something like that . . . I'm not saying don't go back to Ethiopia. Just do this first. We've got to have variety, after all. Stella? Are you there?'

'Yes. Yes, I'm listening to you. But I've got things left there, in Addis.' Stella shook her head, struggling to catch up with the meaning of Lorna's words. 'My typewriter's at the hotel. And I kept my room there.'

'Leave it with me.' Lorna adopted her problem-solving voice. 'I'll give Reuters a call – they'll have a stringer there. I'll arrange for them to pay your bill and send me the typewriter. Meanwhile, why don't you just hop on a plane to London. We'll work everything out from here. You can stay at the flat.'

Stella pictured the office flat with its sparse Scandinavian furnishings – everything white on white, plus lilac. She had last stayed in it on the way between a jungle camp in Sri Lanka and an assignment in New York. She had felt uneasy there – she'd had to keep all her possessions in the bathroom to avoid leaving stains on the white carpet. Now she imagined the flat like a refuge – neutral and uncomplicated.

'I'll need an advance,' she said, 'to cover the air ticket.'

'Of course. Get me the name of your travel agent. Is there one in Tasmania? Let me know. Bye, darling. Bye. Take care of yourself.'

Stella put down the receiver. She pushed aside her misgivings about Lorna's plan – reminding herself that she had agreed only to travel to London. It was still up to Stella to decide where she would go and what she would write. She was still free.

The ute was parked by the telephone box. Stella reached in through the open passenger window to pick up a cardboard box. It was filled with the dishes and other containers people had brought to the house. Grace had emptied them all – tipping out the spoiled food into the compost bucket. As she'd done this, she'd examined each offering with interest. She had even lifted up the dishes to look at the bottoms, where pieces of tape had been stuck bearing the owners' names. Stella had been struck by the look of surprise and pleasure that had appeared on her mother's face.

Stella carried the loaded box across to the shop. Holding it in front of her, she pushed through the coloured fly strips that hung in the open doorway. Inside, she paused to look around her, breathing in the familiar smell of soap powder and old bananas. The place had hardly changed at all. The community noticeboard was still there by the door, covered with handwritten notes offering secondhand furniture for sale, or ute-loads of cut firewood. In its old spot near the freezer was the Fishermen's Wives Association stand. Amongst the knitted toys and pots of jam on offer there, Stella noticed a softbound book with a faded cover. It bore the emblem of the Association, and the words *Thirtieth Anniversary Cookbook 1976*. As Stella read the title, she remembered the day when Mrs Barron had told her of the book's planned publication and asked her to get a recipe from Grace. It felt, suddenly, so recent . . . Stella moved on towards the counter, occupying herself by scanning the other contents of the shop. She noticed that the range of tinned food had increased – a section of new shelves had been built, and they were stacked high with tins of baked beans, Spam, braised steak and onions, and Irish stew.

Stella put her box down on the counter and pressed a buzzer mounted by the till. She heard movement in the private sitting room. Since her return to Halfmoon she had only glimpsed Mrs Barron – at the wharf, and at the burial service. From a distance, the woman had looked completely unchanged by the fifteen years that had passed.

Stella caught the flash of bright red hair approaching the doorway – then Mrs Barron emerged.

'Stella!' The woman's face lit up instantly with warmth and interest. Her double chin had acquired more layers, and her cheeks were wreathed with wrinkles, but her hair was still dyed the same shade, and her eyes looked just as keen.

'Hello, Mrs Barron,' Stella said.

'You poor thing,' Mrs Barron declared. She fixed Stella with a frank gaze. 'You look tired.'

Stella shrugged. 'I guess I am . . .'

'You look good, though,' Mrs Barron said. 'I'd have recognised you anywhere. You haven't changed a bit.'

'Neither have you,' Stella said generously. She gestured towards the box. 'I need to return all these dishes. I thought if you put them near the counter, people could take them.'

Mrs Barron cast her eyes over them. 'Of course, dear – anything to help. How's your poor mother getting on?'

'She's a bit better,' Stella said. She handed over a shopping list written in Grace's neat hand.

Mrs Barron raised an eyebrow. 'She's cooking again! That's a good sign. I've missed William bringing me her orders. It's always a challenge, getting everything right . . .'

Stella smiled politely. Before long, she thought, Grace would be coming in here herself. Stella planned to discuss Grace taking driving lessons as soon as she felt the timing was right. When she had left Grace, an hour ago, the woman had looked almost a replica of her old self – neat hair, tied back; fresh shirt; polished shoes. She seemed to have made a miraculous recovery – stepping back into her normal routines; devoting herself to cooking, cleaning, gardening . . . But still, Stella didn't want to risk pushing her too quickly.

Mrs Barron began collecting the items on Grace's list and stacking them into a plastic bag.

'You've been away a very long time,' she said, shooting a glance at Stella. There was only a hint of accusation in the woman's tone. 'Nothing much has changed really. There are new people at the pub – mainlanders. They've closed the dining room!' Mrs Barron pointed towards the new shelves. 'I've had to bring in extra supplies. It's not so bad for the people who ate at the pub just to have a night out – but a lot of folk really relied on it. I get them in here – fishermen from other ports, or blokes doing the roadworks. They're hoping for a hot meal – and all they can get at the pub is a packet of chips.' She shook her head. 'It's a real shame.' Mrs Barron spoke in short bursts, pacing her words to match the movements of her hands – from shelf to counter to bag. 'Now, what else? The Nielsens moved to St Louis. Laura's just had her second girl – she's not here, though. She's up north. Jamie . . .' She threw Stella a quick, searching look. 'Jamie never came back, you know. He's in the Northern Territory now. Nice wife – I've seen a photo of her. Three kids.' She took a breath before continuing. 'There are a few newcomers. A retired couple from South Africa. And there's Zeph.'

Stella picked up an apple from a basket on the counter, and rubbed away a small spot of dirt.

'Of course, you've met him,' Mrs Barron continued, her tone now low and solemn. She was quiet for a moment – then went on. 'Anyway, he's a nice young fellow, Zeph. He's built a place out by the convict road. I haven't seen it, but I hear it's quite unusual.'

Mrs Barron bent down behind the counter to find a box of matches. She dropped it into the plastic bag.

Stella tightened her fingers around the apple. Her lips seemed to form the question all on their own. 'Does he live out there by himself?'

She kept her eyes fixed on the apple, turning its glossy skin to catch the light from the window.

'Yes, he does,' Mrs Barron said. 'No wife, no girlfriend either.' She shook her head, stiff red curls bouncing against her temples. 'You'd think he'd be lonely.'

Stella shrugged. 'Some people like spending time on their own,' she said.

Mrs Barron gave her a piercing look. 'Yes, well, they may. But I think it's bad for you.' She ticked off the last item on Grace's list and handed the note to Stella. 'There you are – you can check it if you like.'

Stella pushed the note into her pocket.

Mrs Barron leaned comfortably on the counter. 'Where were we? That's right – Zeph. He hasn't got a job, you know. Laurie told me – apparently he doesn't need to work. He made a fortune out of something he invented – to do with boats, I think. He lived in Sydney before he came here. Big house, his own business – everything he could want. Two years ago he gave it all up and came to live here, at Halfmoon Bay.' Mrs Barron smiled, as if she had just reached the happy end of a fairy tale. 'Simple as that. Just turned up in a yacht one day, and didn't leave.'

Tailwind.

'Where is the boat now?' The question slipped out of Stella's mouth.

Mrs Barron looked surprised by the query. 'It's usually here at the wharf. But he's had it out at Bennett's slipway through the winter. Must be about time he put her back in the water. He's probably waiting till he's finished helping Joe. They're fixing the roof on his wheelhouse. That's what Zeph does, instead of working – lends a hand around the place.' Mrs Barron chuckled. 'I don't know how everyone managed without him now. Anyway, that's enough about him.' The woman paused, eyeing Stella thoughtfully. 'You did well for yourself. Must have been that English ladies' college. Gave you a good education. We all read your magazine, you know.'

Mrs Barron pointed towards the magazine stand. There, between a glossy *Four-wheel Drive* magazine and a thick pile of *New Idea* was a copy of last month's *Women's World*.

'I'm glad you find it interesting,' Stella said. It was the response she usually gave to people who mentioned her work.

Mrs Barron shook her head. 'You've seen some terrible things. Sad things . . . I don't know how you can face it.' Her voice brightened. 'So, what are you going to do now that you're back?'

'I'm not staying long,' Stella answered. She picked up the bag of groceries. 'I'll make sure Mum's managing all right, of course. But then I have to get back to work.'

'They need you, I suppose,' Mrs Barron said. 'They need you to write your column.'

Stella paused. It was not a serious comment, she knew – just a passing remark. Yet it unnerved her. The truth of the matter was that Lorna would be very glad to have Stella's next article – whatever it was about. And there were plenty of important stories waiting to be told – more than any magazine would ever find room to print. But how much would it really matter if Stella Boyd were never to reappear? There were dozens of good, brave writers out there, just waiting to step into her shoes.

'I need to get back,' was the best response she could manage.

I need to get away.

Grace knelt on her gardening cushion, an apron tied in place to protect her clothes. She pulled tiny weeds from the lily bed and laid them in a basket at her side.

Behind her, the compost heap was almost hidden by gulls, still fighting over the mound of stale cakes, lamingtons, scones, pastries and sandwiches. The air was filled with their flapping wings and shrill cries of greed.

Stella called out a greeting over the racket.

Grace looked up, nodding approval at the sight of the bag of groceries hanging from Stella's hand.

Stella headed for the kitchen door. She almost stepped on the charred cake-tin – now full of murky grey water – that had been placed near the step. Stella could see remnants of white powder on the ground beside it, where Grace had sprinkled over bicarbonate of soda, to help lift the burned remains of the cake.

The kitchen was shadowy and cool, the curtains drawn closed to keep out the heat of the sun. Stella stepped inside, breathing air fragrant with beeswax polish and the smell of baking. She was about to put the bag down on the table when she saw – laid out on wire racks – a whole line of freshly made cakes. She recognised the colour and shape of Aunt Sophie's Good Pound Cake.

William's favourite cake, for taking to sea.

There were six of them – more than enough for a week-long voyage. Grace already had squares of silver foil laid out on the bench to wrap them in as soon as they were cool.

Stella drew in a slow breath – then turned her back on them. People found many different ways of dealing with tragedy, she knew. Cooking food for someone who was no longer here seemed harmless enough. The cakes could be given away. Joe, for one, would be glad to have some. Or they could be added to the stand in the shop – sold in aid of the Fishermen's Wives Association. She picked up the new box of matches and carried it to the sea room.

She paused in the doorway. The wide view of the sea, broken only by the lines of the window frames, still took her by surprise. The image never looked the same, so you could never take it for granted. When the ocean was turbulent and dark, you felt like drawing some of the curtains across to shield yourself from its power. When the water was just flat and grey, its bleakness seemed to demand that you offer it a touch of warmth – a fire glowing in the grate. On sunny days the sparkling blue was so bright that it dazzled your eyes. At sunset it was a picture of heaven. You felt yourself drawn towards the horizon. You longed to be able to walk over the water, like Jesus, and enter a land of unimagined glory . . .

Today the sea was a pastel blue, and the sky a painting on silk. Muted light drifted in over the quiet room.

Stella's gaze wandered slowly over the familiar details of furniture, paintings, ornaments. Then it stopped. On top of Aunt Jane's sideboard a candle was burning – a small orange flame dancing in the stillness. It cast a glow over a framed picture that had been propped up there. Stella moved to have a closer look. It was a black and white photograph of William – an image that she had never seen before. He looked about twenty years old. He wore a white coat, and a stethoscope hung around his neck.

His eyes were bright. A warm smile curved his lips. His spirit seemed to reach out of the frame, carefree and light.

He looked happy.

Stella picked up the picture and touched it with her fingers, almost wanting to check that it was real. This was the man Grace had married, Stella realised – William Birchmore, before his dream had been shattered.

She returned the picture to its place. Laid out around the candle was a collection of documents: William's cray-pot licence, his skipper's ticket, his driver's licence, an old passport. Petals were scattered between them – papery and dry. Stella recognised them as remnants of the bunch of flowers that she had seen in the sea room when she'd first arrived back – the last flowers Grace had picked before William went missing.

The HMS *Victory* coffee mug had been added to the shrine, along with William's last newspaper and a folded handkerchief with WCB embroidered on the corner. His bottle of brandy was there as well – with a glass set out beside it, as though William might visit at any time and seek refreshment.

Stella stared at the empty glass. More than any of the other relics, it brought a wave of loss washing over her. Pain ached in her throat. She found herself looking down at the damaged left-hand drawer where the weather journal was kept. She wanted to take the book out and open it up at the entry where William had expressed his remorse so deeply. They were his last words to her. They belonged out here with the other symbols of his life.

But she knew she could not. She had repaired the drawer as best she could, and said nothing to her mother about the things William had written. He was dead. Gone. It seemed pointless – and risky – to open up the past.

Least said, soonest mended.

Stella picked up a petal that had fallen onto the floor, and placed it next to the candle. The flame flickered in a slight breeze. It was burning unevenly, she saw – wax running away down one side. She rotated it to let the other side burn for a while. Then she turned and walked away.

CHAPTER EIGHTEEN

S tella picked up the ragged directory from the floor of the public phone box. Balancing it on one raised knee, she flicked
through the torn and dog-eared pages until she found an entry
for the Tasmanian Bank for Savings. Then she ran her eye down the
list of branches until she found the one in St Louis.

As she did so, she thought back over all the information she'd
gathered over the last few days. First, she'd made enquiries about
the widow's pension – and had found out that Grace was eligible to
receive a modest monthly payment. She'd then ascertained from the
council how much Grace would have to pay each quarter in rates.
She'd added this to an estimate of what would need to be spent on
power, food, petrol, and the cost of keeping the ute on the road. It
had become clear that Grace would be able to manage on the
pension – but that she would have very little to spare for luxuries or
unplanned expenses. Stella was not alarmed by this – she knew her
father had a savings account. She hadn't been able to find a pass-
book in any of the sideboard drawers, however, and Grace knew
nothing about William's financial arrangements. Phoning the bank
was the only way to find out how much capital Grace had been left
with.

Stella dropped a coin into the slot and dialled the number. Her call was answered by a young woman, who offered to put Stella straight through to the manager, Mr Wilson.

Stella recognised the name immediately – Mr Wilson had been in charge of the bank for years. She remembered him coming to her school to talk to the children about the importance of saving their pocket money. In his suit and tie he had looked as solid and dependable as the building he worked in. The bank premises – two storeys high and made of brick and plaster – towered over everything else in St Louis except the Town Hall.

When Mr Wilson picked up the phone he sounded bright and brisk. But his tone changed when Stella said who she was.

'Ah – yes. Excuse me for a second.' Stella heard the man getting up from his desk, and the sound of his office door being pushed shut. Then he returned to the phone. 'Let me begin by offering my deepest sympathy to you and Mrs Birchmore. It was a terrible tragedy. If we can help in any way . . .'

'Thank you,' Stella said. 'I'd just like some information about my father's savings.'

There was a brief silence. 'Can you come in for an appointment? I'd really prefer to speak to you in person.'

'I'm afraid I'm very busy,' Stella explained. 'I have to get back to work, and there's a lot to do . . .'

'I understand,' Mr Wilson said. 'Well, I can give you that information – if you can just hold the line.' The man returned after a few minutes. 'I have checked the file. Your father has – had – one savings account. It contains nine hundred and fifty-six dollars and twenty cents.'

Stella's hand tightened around the earpiece of the phone. 'That can't be all he's saved!'

It made no sense. William had never earned a large income from fishing, but he had always made a point of saving a portion of each cheque from the fish factory. He liked to remind his family that – unlike the local people, with all their cousins and uncles and aunties – the Birchmores had only themselves to rely upon.

'He used to have considerable savings, of course,' Mr Wilson said. 'But about ten years ago he decided he wanted to convert the crown lease on his property to freehold. The valuation was rather higher than he expected. Then there were legal fees, surveyors. It took him years to get it finalised.'

'You mean he didn't own Seven Oaks?' queried Stella. 'I thought he bought it from the man who built the house.'

'What he bought was a hundred-year lease. Lots of people round here have got them. They don't give it a second thought. But it bothered William. He just wouldn't be happy until he got a freehold title.'

Stella nodded to herself. She knew it was William's plan for Seven Oaks to be Birchmore land forever – not just for a hundred years.

'Well, thank you,' she said. 'I'll work out a budget with my mother. She should be able to manage on the pension, even without any savings.'

Mr Wilson's chair creaked. Papers rustled on his desk.

'I'm afraid it's not that simple,' he said. He spoke gently and slowly. 'His savings only covered a small part of the price he had to pay to the government. He took out a substantial loan. That means there are repayments to be made. They will exceed the amount of a widow's pension. I'm sorry. I hate having to tell you this.'

Stella stared at the grimy metal of the phone. She thought quickly, running back over everything he had said.

'What are the options?' she asked. 'Perhaps you could you waive payments for a while?'

'If that would help, I will certainly consider it,' Mr Wilson said. 'But I'll need to know what the long-term solution is going to be. I'm assuming William left no other assets. If he'd had any, I imagine he'd already have sold them. At the time we arranged finance for the loan he had no life insurance.' Mr Wilson sighed. 'Fishermen never do. I think they believe it's tempting fate – throwing down a gauntlet to the sea. Or something of that sort . . . What about you? Perhaps you have some resources?'

'No,' Stella said. 'I've got nothing.'

Just a typewriter, left behind in a foreign hotel. A few old clothes. A niche angel from a French garden . . .

'Are there any relatives who could help?' Mr Wilson asked.

Stella thought briefly of Daniel. He would offer assistance if he could, she felt sure. But he, like Stella, had never made much money. He lived with Miles in a grand old home in Melbourne – but the building, and even the furnishings, belonged to Miles' family. The two men scraped by – they managed to save enough each year for a holiday away, but that was all.

'I'm afraid not,' Stella said. 'There's no one.'

Mr Wilson sighed again. 'I've been in this situation before, Stella. It's a very hard road – battling with debt on top of bereavement. I advise against it. William was a smart man. Since he got his freehold title that property has more than doubled in value. Tourism is really taking off in St Louis. Ocean-frontage properties – even out your way – are at a premium. My advice is – sell up.'

'No, no. That's impossible,' Stella said. 'I couldn't even suggest it to my mother . . .'

'She may be upset by the idea now,' Mr Wilson said kindly. 'But sometimes it's actually easier for those left behind if they make a fresh start. I haven't done the figures, but as a rough idea – consider this: you sell the property and buy your mother a nice little unit in St Louis. Warm, easy to maintain, close to services. Then you invest the remainder. She's got an income for life. Instead of just scraping by on the pension, she can afford to go to the hairdresser once a week, even take the occasional cruise. It's not a bad scenario.'

'I don't think you understand,' Stella said. 'My mother's whole life has been built around that place. She could never part with it.'

Mr Wilson cleared his throat. 'I'll be plain with you, Stella. There may not be much choice. The repayments are about a hundred dollars per week. Look, I'm not going to push you on this. Take a few more days to think about the situation – look at your options. One piece of good news I have for you is that William had the title in both his and your mother's names, which means there won't be a delay with probate and all that. She's free to sell any time she decides to.'

Stella leaned her head back against the glass wall of the cubicle and closed her eyes. Everything the man was saying made sense to her. No one could live solely on a pension if they had a mortgage to pay. And it was not as though Grace were going to go and get a job in the fish factory or the pub . . .

'Look, Stella – I happen to know someone who would be very interested in the property,' Mr Wilson added. 'I could send him out to see you if you like. No obligation. I'll explain the situation to him. I'll tell him to keep it confidential.'

Stella rubbed a hand over her face. She hunched over the phone, as if to hide her words from the watching gulls or the listening wind. 'Okay. Let him come. I might as well find out what he's prepared to offer.'

'That's very sensible,' Mr Wilson said.

Stella agreed with him. It was the right step to take, she was certain – to gather all facts.

It never hurt to know.

Wallabies grazed in the paddocks to each side of the track. Stella steered the ute with her left hand. She hung her right arm out through the window, letting her hand lie against the outside of the door. The metal was warm and smooth. Cool air brushed her skin. As the car came up over a small rise, she slowed – looking ahead at the house.

Her eyes travelled over the familiar lines of the building. The roof – rising up against a clear sky – threw a long mid-afternoon shadow over the shed and water tanks. The oak tree stood near the front door, its branches dotted with small clumps of fresh spring leaves, just beginning to unfurl.

Further along the front wall of the house, a red smudge caught Stella's eye. Driving closer, she saw that it was Grace's cardigan. Her mother was standing there with bucket and sponge in hand – hard at work, cleaning windows.

Stella parked the ute, then climbed out and walked slowly over towards Grace. As she came near she could see the woman's face reflected in a pane of spotless glass. Grace was studying her handiwork intently – standing back with a small smile of satisfaction on her lips. She looked like a mother gazing upon her child: proud and critical at the same time.

Watching her, Stella felt a deep sense of misgiving at the prospect of having to pass on Mr Wilson's bad news. As Grace turned round, Stella made herself smile. Grace raised a hand in greeting, then picked up a sponge and began sloshing water over the next pane of glass.

Stella sat at the table, peeling apples. They were the last ones left from the winter stock and were difficult to peel. The waxy skins were slippery, and the flesh beneath it was shrunken and soft. But Grace hated to waste anything. The apples were to be made into sauce, to be served with My Own Roast Pork. Jars of the thick yellow brew – neatly labelled and dated – would be added to the rows of uneaten preserves that already stood on shelves in the shed.

Stella had seen them there while looking for a tin of oil for the ute. The colours had arrested her attention, burning behind glass in the dusty light: ruby-red raspberry jam; ink-black pickled walnuts; sunny yellow marmalade; flecked-orange tomato relish . . . Stella tried not to think about how they would all have to be given away or emptied out into the compost when the time came for everything at Seven Oaks to be packed up and taken somewhere else.

She went on with her task – pausing now and then to watch her mother at work. Grace moved back and forth between the recipe book on the table and the stove. Without taking her eyes off her frying she grabbed an oven mitten from its hook on the wall and slipped it on. She reached into the oven and turned round a pie that was cooking on the middle shelf.

She looked so comfortable and at ease, here in her domain.

Stella tried to picture her mother in a different kitchen – somewhere smaller, more compact, new. But the scene she conjured reminded her of a child's book she'd once been given: the illustrations were not on the same page as the story to which they belonged. The characters looked pointless and lost.

But Grace could adapt, Stella told herself. If she had to, she would . . . Stella had seen refugees left with nothing, forced to begin again in a new country. She'd seen prisoners facing life terms locked in foreign jails. People were always stronger than they appeared. Often, they surprised even themselves.

A heart torn in two did not stop beating . . .

A tapping sound broke in through the noise of Grace's cooking. Stella looked around, trying to find its source. A face appeared at the kitchen window – a man that Stella did not recognise: dark-haired, wearing a cream polo-necked jumper. His sunglasses glinted in the late afternoon sun.

She stood up and moved quickly to the back door. Fortunately, Grace was still bent over the stove and had not noticed the newcomer. Regardless of who he was and what he wanted, Stella preferred to deal with him herself. Opening the door, she stepped briskly outside and closed it behind her.

'I hope you'll forgive me for calling without an appointment,' said the stranger, holding out his hand. 'I'm Clifford Beaumont.'

Stella offered her own hand, and felt his fingers press warmly against her skin.

'Mr Wilson told me you have no telephone. I was in the area, so I took the chance to drop by. I understand the property is for sale.'

Stella's lips parted in surprise – she had not expected the bank manager to act so quickly. She glanced towards the kitchen window, then she beckoned the man to follow her round behind the woodpile. He appeared a little nonplussed, but when she looked back,

Stella saw that he was following her lead. He stepped cautiously over the uneven ground in a pair of cowboy boots. As soon as they were hidden, Stella spoke.

'My mother doesn't know anything about this yet. I have to break it to her in the right way. If you leave me your phone number, I'll contact you, but I'm afraid you can't possibly look at the house now.'

The man smiled, showing off white, even teeth. He had the smooth-skinned, carefully fed appearance of a wealthy man.

'I don't need to look at anything,' he stated. 'Wilson showed me the title.' He turned to scan the foreshore – taking in the whole sweep of the view. Stella watched his face, waiting to see his expression soften as the beauty of the scene touched him. Instead, his mouth thinned, his lips turning down in the corners. He nodded to himself. Stella tried to look through his sunglasses, to read his eyes – but the glass was shiny and dark. She felt her stomach tighten. She did not like talking to men who kept their gaze concealed. They reminded her of soldiers, bodyguards, secret police – men whose cars had blacked-out glass to match their blacked-out eyes and darkened souls.

'The property includes the whole point, down to the high-tide mark – right?' Clifford asked.

'Yes,' Stella said, 'from the fenceline at the front gate. There is a small dam as well. We're on a septic system out here, and tank water. The house hasn't been renovated, but it's been very well maintained.'

Clifford waved one hand as if a fly were annoying him. 'I'm not interested in any of that.'

'What do you mean?' Stella asked.

'The house will go, of course.'

Looking past the woodpile, Stella could just see the front of a silver sports car. Of course, she realised, a man like this would not want to live in a simple house like theirs. He would pull it down and rebuild.

'I can see eight – maybe ten – beach houses here,' Clifford continued. 'Each has a great sea view, outdoor entertainment area, carport. The road runs in behind them – through here.' Clifford drew a line in the air with his finger, showing how the new road would go straight through the existing house and pass right down the middle of Grace's garden.

Stella stared, mute with shock. In the midst of the moment an image came to her, detailed and vivid: she saw the bulldozer arriving at the picket fence, its blade raised, ready to move through, crushing everything in its path. It was like a military tank – the kind that soldiers drove over pits piled with bodies, only some of them dead . . . She saw timber splintering; plaster cracking into a powdery mess; the oak tree snapping at its base. Mangled lilies were squashed into the earth; bushes tumbled over, their roots in the air. As the water tanks burst, a small tidal wave swept out over the debris.

'You can't do that!' she said. Her voice sounded thin and high.

'I'm sorry – I thought Wilson would have told you. I thought you knew.' Clifford whipped off his sunglasses and fixed Stella with a sharp look. 'There's only one reason I can make you such a good offer. This is a prime development site. It's worth nothing as a home.'

Stella did not look at him. Her eyes travelled over the garden – the place that the man planned to see razed to the bare earth. She saw it scarred with the tracks of the bulldozer – then covered with concrete and tar.

Somewhere lay the bones of a tiny baby – just a fragile tracery of white in the earth. Too small even to be noticed as they were dragged up by the blade and churned into nothing . . .

'It's not for sale.'

Stella said the words quietly, as though trying them out for shape and meaning. Then she lifted her chin and repeated them, clear and strong. 'I've changed my mind. Seven Oaks is not for sale.'

Clifford touched her on the shoulder, then drew back his hand as Stella flinched away. 'I understand. You need time to get used to the idea. It was your childhood home, after all. But when you receive my formal offer, you'll see – you cannot refuse. I'll give you a few days and then come back.'

'No, you needn't bother,' Stella said. 'You'll be wasting your time.' She kept her voice low, so as not to attract Grace's attention.

Clifford took a step back. His eyes flicked from side to side, as if he wanted to keep hold of the coveted views. 'I'd like to meet your mother next time – and talk to her.'

'Don't come back,' Stella said. She felt suddenly angered by the man's insistence. 'I don't want to see you here.'

Clifford opened his mouth to speak again. Then he snapped his sunglasses back into place and walked off towards his car. A minute later, Stella heard the engine start – a throaty purr, soon lost in the sound of wheels spinning in dirt.

Stella took a deep breath, calming herself. She looked out at the sea, lapping against the grey boulders adorned with orange lichen. Emerald-green boobyalla grew down almost to the waterline. Beneath the foliage she could see the twisted branches, sculpted by the onshore winds. The trees had been growing here for generations, she reminded herself, undaunted by storms and droughts – untouched by the comings and goings of humans.

The sea, the rocks, the land had looked just like this when families of Aborigines had camped here centuries ago.

And when the house had first been built.

And on that night when William had walked out into the moonlit garden with a small bundle in one hand and a spade in the other. The night when – unwittingly – he'd sealed forever his family's bond with this little piece of land.

Stella turned to look out over Grace's garden. As she watched the dwindling sunlight playing over the trees and shrubs, she knew.

This was sacred ground – like the rector's churchyard.

However long it took, whatever it cost – Stella had to stay here until she was sure that Seven Oaks was safe.

Grace turned from the stove as Stella entered the kitchen.

'I heard a car,' she said.

'It was just a man who came to the wrong place.'

Grace picked up her wooden spoon, ready to stir the stew.

'Wait, Mum. I need to talk to you. Leave the cooking,' Stella commanded. She saw a look of surprise cross Grace's face. Stella knew she sounded like William – using words as implements to push people around. Grace pulled the stewpot over to the cooler edge of the stove-top. Stella waited until her mother was facing her, then she spoke.

'Do you know . . .' Her words petered out, and she began again. 'Did William tell you where he buried my baby?'

Grace stared at Stella in shock. The woman's lips moved silently as she struggled to frame words. Finally, she just shook her head.

'If you know, tell me,' Stella demanded. 'You have to.'

'I don't know,' Grace said. 'He never told me.'

'Please. You must know – something,' Stella whispered. But already she felt the chill of loss. What had made her hope that Grace could answer her question? Knowledge was power. William would have wanted to keep his secret. And Grace . . . Grace would have let him. Stella backed away from her mother. Her boot caught the leg of a chair and scraped it harshly over the floor. Anger sparked inside her, but then died under the weight of her despair. 'You didn't want to know! You didn't care!'

There was a long silence, broken only by the murmuring sea. Then Grace drew a deep, ragged breath. She looked down at the floor – at her feet, placed side by side on the edge of a woven mat. When she spoke, her words were drawn out and slow, as if being dragged up across a great span of time.

'After you left, I stopped working in the garden. Every time I dug in my spade and lifted the earth, I was afraid of what I would find. I asked William to tell me where the grave was – so that I could stay away from it. But he refused.' She studied her hands, twisting the soup ladle between her fingers. 'The truth was – I wasn't really afraid. I just didn't want to harm the grave. I wanted to leave him in peace. Either that, or plant flowers there for him. But I knew William would never allow that. Your father couldn't bear anything

that reminded him – of what happened. What we did to you . . .'
Grace lifted her face, gathering shreds of strength around her. 'I
stayed indoors for a long time. In the end, William gave in. But he
would only tell me one thing. He said I could be sure – he could
promise me – I would not find the place by accident. After that, I
dug only in the places where my plants already grew.'

Grace looked away towards the window. Her eyes were red and
shiny. Stella followed her gaze. Late sun shone over the garden, turning everything into stark shapes – half shadow, half light.

The two women hardly spoke as they worked their way slowly
around the garden. Like Spinks' orange-suited volunteers, they
divided the space into sectors and carefully examined every piece of
land that lay outside the fruit and vegetable plots. They trod quickly
over the parts where native grass and plants still grew. They looked
for the places where the ground was covered with weeds – the
foreign plants that invaded whenever the soil was dug up.

It was these sturdy weeds that Grace and Stella had to pull out or
drag aside, searching for some sign of the burial. They looked for a
stone or a heavy piece of wood – something laid there by William
to cover the broken earth. Even inside a fenced garden they knew no
one would risk leaving a grave unprotected from devils or stray
dogs – gates could be left open, or a picket could come loose.

The air became laden with the smell of fresh earth, bruised stems
and torn leaves. Weeds were piled up on top of the beds, along with
pieces of old glass, cracked seed trays and a yellow plastic duck that
Stella had once played with in her bath.

Stella straightened up, stretching out her spine and rubbing blis-
tered palms together. The sun had disappeared into the sea, and the
air was growing cool. The last of the gulls had wheeled their way
across the sky to find their rookeries. Soon, Stella told herself, it
would be too dark to see clearly the ground ahead of their feet. Yet
she did not want to abandon the search, now that it had begun.

As if reading Stella's mind, Grace went into the shed – returning after a few minutes with two kerosene lanterns. Blue-yellow flames burned low inside the smoky glass covers.

They worked on. As the sky darkened, the lamps shone bright – casting a yellow glow over the earth. Near the back fence they reached a blackberry thicket. A few canes had been planted there decades ago, to provide berries for Aunt Jane's Summer Pudding. But, since Grace had stopped working in parts of the garden that lay outside her plots and beds, it had run wild and colonised the whole back corner. Stella brought leather gloves and secateurs from the shed and they began to snip the thick stems. As they ripped them free and threw them aside, thorns caught the skin of their arms, leaving long scratches beaded with bright blood.

Stella slapped at a mosquito that was whining in her ear. Grace moved ahead of her, cutting a swathe into the thicket. Suddenly, the woman stopped. For a long moment she did not move. Then she stepped slowly back.

A small cross lay on the ground.

Stella pushed past Grace and knelt by it, pressing her shoulder into the thorny bushes. Grace bent over her, holding up the lantern.

The cross was crudely formed from two pieces of bare wood, joined with a rusty nail. Faint markings could be made out on the crossbeam – the remains of numbers. 1976.

Grace's faint voice drifted down over Stella's shoulder. 'William did that. He must have . . .'

Stella shook the gloves from her hands and reached towards the little cross. Carefully, she pulled it free of the tangled vines. Beyond it – half-concealed by low growing weeds – lay a large stone.

With trembling hands, she snatched the weeds away, revealing an egg-shaped piece of granite. The stone had come from the beach, Stella knew – it had been tumbled into shape by the waves. But here, in the shadows of the blackberry bush, the earth had begun to take possession of it: moss and lichen crept up the sides, colouring the grey stone with silver green.

The egg lay there, cradled in the damp soil. It was about the same size as a baby. Not the tiny boy buried beneath it – but the baby he should have become. Stella's fingers brushed the mossy surface. She waited, bracing herself for the sadness to sweep over her – the sense of loss, the rising fear, the guilt . . . But instead she felt a weight being lifted, as if the stone beneath her hands were able, somehow, to draw her burden down into its own mass and hold it there.

A hand touched her shoulder. Stella glimpsed Grace's long fingers laid over her shirt. As their grip tightened, pressing her flesh against her bones, Stella looked up. Her mother's eyes were brimming with tears.

Grace leaned over and placed the lantern down beside the stone. Then she pushed in next to Stella. The two knelt there, side by side, arms pressed together as they looked down at the grave. Grace picked up the wooden cross and put it back by the stone.

Stella turned to her. Grace's face, painted with yellow light, was beautiful. She looked young again – the woman who had made a tiny jacket for her daughter, yet unborn. A woman with hopes and dreams . . .

Grace's lips quivered as tears fell from her eyes. She smiled at Stella.

'We found him,' she said, in a voice that was soft with wonder.

They waited there in silence. A gentle wind ruffled their hair. The sea lapped quietly at the rocks on the shore. And the moon rose above them, sending down a silver veil to blend with the gold light of their lamps.

Grace sat at the sea-room table, her head bent over the open weather journal. The standard lamp had been pulled close to her so that it cast its light down onto the handwritten pages. The woman flipped back and forth between the two entries – a year apart – that Stella had marked.

From the opposite side of the table, Stella watched as contrasting expressions passed over her mother's face – pain and confusion, and a slowly dawning amazement.

'You didn't know, did you?' Stella asked her mother. 'That he was sorry . . .'

Grace shook her head. 'When you ran away, he was devastated – but he still insisted that we'd done the right thing. I didn't see it that way. I regretted my part in it – even before you left. But there was nothing to be done . . .' Grace gripped the edge of the table with her hands. 'I was so angry with him – and myself – that I didn't want to talk to him about it. I avoided the subject completely. We discussed you, of course – the news we heard from Daniel, and the things you wrote in your letters. But we didn't go back over the past. It was like a wound that was scarred over on the surface, but still raw underneath. It was all right if you left it alone – but it hurt too much to touch . . .'

Grace's voice trailed off. She met Stella's gaze with eyes that were dark with pain.

Stella looked at her in silence. She felt pain, too – but it was sharp and alive, not like the deadening ache that she had lived with for so long. She imagined her own wound being torn open – the thick scar being stripped away, leaving the flesh bleeding and raw.

'I didn't know he'd ever written an apology to you,' Grace said. 'Or that he'd tried, at least . . .' She shook her head again. 'I never imagined he'd come to see that he had been wrong.'

The woman looked away towards the dark glass of the windows. There was a long silence, broken only by the sound of a branch rubbing against the outside of the house.

When Grace spoke again, she turned back to Stella, leaning forward over the table. 'I used to blame William for how our lives – and yours – turned out. But you were right – what you said to me when I was lying on the bed in my room. I was the one who failed you. I was the one who should have understood. I don't expect you to forgive me. I've never forgiven myself. But I want you to know how sorry I am.'

As she finished, she lowered her eyes. Her shoulders slumped, as though the weight of her regret was too much to bear. Stella looked away, torn with emotion. Hearing all this, after so many years – she did not know what to say, what to feel . . . .

Movement drew her gaze back to Grace. The woman's hand was reaching across the table towards her. It waited there, the fingers outstretched, trembling. Stella stared at it, motionless. Then her hand crept out to meet it. Grace lifted eyes that were bright with tears as the two sets of fingers entwined in a tightening grasp.

Grace stood up, drawing Stella with her – leading her along to the end of the table. There, Grace stepped forward, spreading her arms. But as her mother drew her close, Stella felt herself stiffen. She could not remember the last time Grace had held her like this. It was a long time since anyone had. Her arms hung rigid at her sides, but Grace only held her more tightly, pressing her cheek against Stella's hair.

Gradually, Stella found herself softening into the embrace. Her hands rose, timid and cautious, until they met Grace's body. Then, suddenly, they were hungry – grasping for comfort. Stella clung to her mother, lost in a vision of unhoped-for closeness.

After a long, time-frozen moment, Grace dropped her arms and drew away. The memory of her touch lingered on Stella's body, as if a bright pattern had been left behind.

CHAPTER NINETEEN

In the soft light of dawn, the wooden cross appeared small and fragile. Thorny branches seemed to press in around it – as though the blackberries had begun growing back last night, the minute Stella and Grace had departed.

Stella stood there quietly, looking down at the grave. She focused on the date William had painted on the cross – the carefully drawn numbers of even size.

She pictured her father making the little cross, and then coming out in secret to place it on the grave. She wondered if the blackberries had already been there, or whether they had grown up later over a jungle of long grass and weeds. She wondered if William had understood that it was not just a baby's grave he was marking, but the grave of his grandson. She felt again the sense of loss. He was gone. She would never know.

Kneeling in the dew-damp earth, she touched the smooth surface of the stone. She recognised with a stab of pain that William's death was crucial to her presence here. If he had not been lost, she might never have come home.

Stella stayed there on her knees as the sun rose behind her, casting long, pale shadows over the ground. A fresh breeze stirred, carrying the smell of salt and seaweed into the garden. Gradually she became aware of sounds behind her. She turned to see a figure approaching. For an instant she did not recognise it as Grace – her mother was dressed in trousers and a shirt, and wore a wide-brimmed fisherman's hat. As she drew nearer, Stella saw that the clothes, though old, were neatly pressed. Grace had taken them, she guessed, from the pile of carefully laundered clothes in William's wardrobe.

As she came to stand at her daughter's side, Grace hugged the shirt close to her body. Her fingers smoothed the fabric over her skin. She gazed down at the cross, as if still surprised to see it there. Then she scanned the earth around it.

'All the blackberries will have to go,' she said. 'We'll have to dig out the roots or they'll keep growing back.'

The two pulled on their gloves and began to tackle the task. Progress was slow and difficult. The new season's growth formed only the outside of the bushes; beneath that lay a decade's accumulation of dead branches – a dense tangle of brittle brown stalks and curled leaves. It was a place of sticky spider's webs, abandoned birds' nests, and fragments of snakeskin – papery husks stamped with a tessellated pattern of scales.

As the morning wore on, more and more of the earth was revealed. Untouched by the sun, it was dank and barren, dotted with white fungus and beetles' eggs.

Finally, all the bushes had been cut off at the roots. Grace began dragging the prickly branches into a heap, ready to be burned, while Stella turned to the task of digging out the stumps from the soil.

The roots were deep and stubborn. Stella had to lever them loose with a fork, then pull them out with leather-gloved hands. Sweat ran down her forehead into her eyes. She could feel the sun burning the back of her neck. But she kept on with her task, only pausing now and then to look at the stone egg and the wooden cross, standing at the centre of an ever-growing circle of cleared ground.

Around noon, Grace disappeared towards the house – returning after a few minutes with two cups and a glass jug full of lemonade that tinkled with ice-cubes as she walked.

Stella took three long gulps of the sweet sour drink, quenching her thirst. Then she sipped it slowly, savouring the tang of lemon backed by a touch of mint. It tasted fresh, alive – like the essence of spring. She emptied her glass before handing it to Grace to take back inside.

Left alone again, Stella looked out over the barren earth that surrounded the grave. She pictured the place as she wanted it to become – bright with flowers through every season of the year. There would be Grace's lilies, of course; and other blooms in bold, strong colours – yellows, reds, purple, orange. And blue . . . Stella found herself remembering a beautiful shade of cornflower blue.

The blue of Zeph's painted dome, rising up against the sky . . .

Stella closed her eyes on an image of Zeph's face. He was the Zeph of the past, with his long salt-bleached hair, the teardrop stone hanging on a leather thong around his tanned neck.

Stella felt a sudden longing for that Zeph – a need for him that rose up inside her with a fierceness that took her breath away.

He became alive again in her heart. She wanted to bring him here and show him the grave. To tell him everything that had happened. She imagined him taking her in his arms. How light and free she would feel, with the pain she still held inside her now shared between two . . .

But the boy had sailed away. A new Zeph had returned – achingly familiar, and yet a stranger.

Stella remembered what Spinks had said about his interview with Zeph the day they'd found William – that when Zeph had been asked if he knew Stella, he'd given the same answer she had.

They had known one another a long time ago.

But it was nothing to do with now.

Stella got to her feet, and dragged on her leather gloves. Grasping the long handle of her garden fork, she forced the prongs deep into the earth, wedging them under a thick-stemmed stump. Then she leaned hard, wrenching the roots from the earth. Without pausing, she moved to another stump, and bent again to her task.

By the end of the day, the work was done. Every fragment of the blackberries was gone, all the weeds had been pulled out, and the ground had been raked free of small stones and shells. Thick brown smoke rose into the air from three piles of burning branches.

Grace and Stella stood together, watching curious seabirds walk over the new space – printing the earth with triangle footmarks in long, criss-crossing lines.

'We should plant it as soon as possible,' Grace said. 'We can still catch the spring growth.'

Stella nodded, but said nothing. She was remembering how Clifford, the developer, had stood not far from here – looking out over the garden while he described his vision.

Eight – maybe ten – beach houses . . .

Stella peered sideways at Grace. The woman looked tired. This was not the time, Stella told herself, to tell Grace about the threat to Seven Oaks. Yet, now that they had stopped working, Stella felt a sudden urgency to address the problem.

She turned to Grace. 'Mum . . .'

Grace nodded absently, her gaze still following the wandering birds.

'There's no money,' Stella continued. 'William left no savings.'

Grace frowned, looking puzzled – and then she waved one hand in the air. 'Well, I'll manage somehow. I don't need to be able to buy expensive things.' She glanced at Stella. 'You said I'd get the pension.'

'You will,' Stella said. 'But it won't be enough.'

She paused to take a breath. Then she began to explain about William's debt – and the threat to Seven Oaks.

Grace kept shaking her head, seeming unable to take in the information. Finally, Stella decided to be blunt.

'The fact is, the bank will make you sell the property. Remember the car that turned up here yesterday? That was a developer. He wants to buy the place. And he was sent here by the bank manager. He plans to bulldoze the house, Mum, and the garden. Everything will be destroyed.'

Grace moved round to look straight at Stella. 'It can't be true,' she whispered. Her eyes grew wide with horror.

Stella stared past her at the grave garden. 'It is true,' she said.

Grace covered her mouth with her hands.

Stella waited for a few moments – then she touched the woman's arm. 'Could anyone in your family help? I know Daniel would, but he's got no spare money. Perhaps if you contacted your parents . . .'

'No. No. How could I do that?' Grace's eyes smouldered with mixed anger and sadness. 'William wouldn't allow me even to write. I couldn't possibly contact them after all these years – and ask for money!'

'Well, is there someone else you could turn to?' Stella asked. 'Anyone at all?' She tried to sound hopeful, but she was not expecting a positive reply.

Grace shook her head. 'There's no one.'

The woman looked down at the ground. She was silent for a long time. Stella sensed her battling to come to grips with all that had been said. It could not be easy for her, Stella knew. Grace had spent over thirty years living with a husband who had made every important decision. Now that he was gone, Grace was like an insect, freshly emerged from a cocoon. Her wings were still wet and fragile, her legs shaky.

When Grace finally faced her daughter again, her eyes were dark with anxiety but her voice was steady.

'What can I do?' she asked. 'There must be something I can do. You'll have to go away soon, I know. You've got your work waiting for you—'

'No,' Stella broke in. 'I'm not leaving. We'll face this together.'

Grace looked at her in confusion.

'I'm going to stay here for as long as it takes,' Stella added, 'to make sure you're all right – and that Seven Oaks is safe.'

Grace stared now, in amazement. 'You can't. You've got your own life to think about.'

'I want to stay,' Stella said firmly. 'I've decided – I'm going to call Lorna and cancel the ticket she's booked.'

Grace shook her head wonderingly, relief and gratitude flooding her face. Then a worried frown reappeared. 'Do you have any idea – what we can do?'

Stella sighed. 'I've been thinking about it ever since I spoke to the bank. So far I've come up with nothing. I could file a few stories from here and sell them, but that's not a long-term solution. I thought of trying to get a job. There's the fish factory, but they mainly use young girls – they don't have to pay them much.'

'There might be something in St Louis,' Grace offered.

'I thought of that, too,' Stella said. 'But I'm really not very employable. I can write. I can type. I can do a bit of shorthand. That's all.'

'No, I meant for me,' Grace said.

Stella smiled. She knew Grace had never had a job in her life. The woman knew only how to do the work of a housewife – gardening, cleaning, sewing, cooking . . .

Stella took her mother's hand. It seemed an easy gesture now – Grace's toughened skin rubbing comfortably against her own. 'Don't you worry, we'll think of a plan.'

The next morning, Stella went outside early to cut some kindling. The sun had not yet gathered its warmth – and as she crouched by the woodblock with a tomahawk she shivered in the chill coming in off the sea.

Splitting the kindling was a satisfying task – as the blade came down, the thin sticks broke neatly away. All Stella had to do was make sure she missed her fingers.

When the box was nearly full, Stella paused, the tomahawk poised in the air. Behind the wash of the sea and the chatter of birds in the poker flowers, she could hear the sound of a vehicle engine.

She went out to the driveway to wait for its arrival. She squashed a flicker of hope that it could be Zeph coming here – telling herself that it was probably the developer returning to make another attempt to buy Seven Oaks. She eyed the tomahawk, still in her hands. If it were Clifford, she decided, she would not even give him the chance to get out of his fancy car.

An old blue van lumbered into view. As it came towards Stella, an arm was thrust out through the window, waving a huge orange crayfish. Stella glimpsed Joe's face behind the steering wheel. He brought the van to a halt close to where Stella stood. The giant grasshopper legs of the crayfish almost brushed her face.

'Take this,' the old man called out. As he turned off the ignition, the engine convulsed a few times before stopping.

Stella grasped the spiky body of the crayfish with both hands. It must have weighed several kilos.

'One of the fellas gave it to me,' Joe said, climbing out of the van. 'Octopus got to it so the factory turned it down. But there's nothing wrong with it. I boiled it straightaway.'

He gave Stella a keen look. 'I know William never took crays home with him. Didn't like eating anything that came from the sea. But now he's gone, and I thought perhaps you and Grace . . .' He broke off, looking suddenly doubtful.

Stella smiled. 'Thank you. I love crayfish. And I haven't had any since I got here.'

Joe reached back into his van. 'I've got some scallops, too. You should eat them fresh. If I had to choose, I'd put the cray in the freezer.'

'Okay, I'll do that,' Stella said. Then she pictured the freezer, jammed with Grace's cakes, stews and pies – the crayfish would never fit in the small space that remained.

An idea came to her. 'Have you got a freezer on *Grand Lady?*' she asked.

'Course I do. She's a fishing ketch.'

'Good,' Stella said. 'Come with me.'

The sudden shift from sun to shadow as Stella stepped into the shed left her blind for a few seconds. She blinked in the gloom before walking over to the workbench and putting down the cray-fish. As Joe came in she grabbed an empty fish bin and beckoned him over to the freezer.

'Most of this stuff will never get eaten,' she said. 'Just tell me what you'd like.' Lifting the lid, she began reeling off the names written on the packages inside.

'Egg and Bacon Pie? Harvest Stew? Courting Cake? There are ten of them . . .'

Joe nodded eagerly. 'Oh, yes,' he said. 'Very nice . . .' He took the frosty bundles from her and stacked them in the fish bin. As she worked her way through the top layer, he peered over her shoulder – his eyes wide with wonder, as though the freezer were an Aladdin's cave full of unimagined treasures.

'This is my lucky day,' he said, more than once.

When the bin was full, Joe hoisted it up onto his shoulder.

'Get them straight back and into your freezer,' Stella advised him. 'If they start to thaw, you'll have to eat everything now!'

Joe chuckled at the thought as he headed for the door. He paused there to wave at Stella. 'Let me know what Grace thinks about the cray-fish,' he said. 'If she reckons it's any good, I'll bring you some more.'

Stella stood in the shed, listening to the van starting up outside. She smiled, remembering all the times she'd taken leftover food to Joe down at the wharf.

'Your mum's the best cook in Tasmania,' he liked to say.

The old man had not been the only one to enjoy William's left-overs, Stella recalled. Sometimes her father had asked her to take spare food to other fishermen as well – single men, whose vessels were provisioned with tinned stew and sacks of potatoes and onions. These men praised Grace's cooking, too. Apart from the meals they ate at the pub, they said, hers was the only decent food they ever got to eat.

And now the pub served only chips and nuts and drinks . . .

For a long moment, Stella stared thoughtfully into the grey shad-ows. Then she looked across to the other side of the shed, at the shelves loaded with jars of pickles, jams and preserves – dozens and dozens of them. She shifted her gaze towards the space next to the freezer, where she could see the stack of wooden panels – the spare leaves for the sea-room dining table. Striding over to them, she ran her fingers along the dusty edges, counting them. There were twelve. She pictured them all in place, side by side . . .

She turned, finally, to the back corner of the shed, where – so many years ago – she'd seen the Boyd family cutlery set hidden away. She recalled the rows and rows of knives and forks and spoons set into beds of velvet.

She drew in a slow breath as a vision came to her, clear and strong . . .

The long table, with all Grace's cutlery laid out, shining in the sunlight streaming in through the sea-room windows. Plates piled up, ready to be filled from steaming dishes and platters. An array of tender roast meat and garden vegetables; hearty casseroles, fragrant with herbs; golden-crusted pies with cut-out patterns of pastry; home-made bread, still hot from the oven.

A banquet spread out in full view of the ocean.

'A café.'

The words sounded loud in the quiet, dusty air. They hung there, mocking. But Stella fought against the echoes of doubt – and began to lay out a plan.

She was not picturing the kind of café a person would find in Sydney or Hobart, or even St Louis. She saw a place more like the ones she had visited in wayside settlements in remote corners of the world. They were not cafés so much as family dining tables opened up to strangers. There was no complicated menu – usually no menu at all. Guests just paid an agreed fee, and then sat down to eat as they would in their own home.

Some were dirty places, serving food that was unsafe for a traveller to eat. Others were clean and friendly – they offered meals that were simple and good. But, occasionally, Stella had eaten surprising, wonderful dishes in settings that had lingered in her memory.

There was the cave-café near a Hindu shrine at the source of the Ganges. Stella had sat under the steady gaze of an ancient sadhu with grizzled locks and a face marked with ash, while a young boy crouched next to her, grinding spices in a stone mortar, and then roasting them on an open fire. The child had cooked a fragrant curry of dhal and vegetables, golden with saffron. The flavours had been clean and fresh – linked somehow with the crystal headwater of the Ganges flowing past; and the peaks of the Himalayas lining the horizon.

Then there was the farm-café in outback Massachusetts. A hand-painted sign on the highway promised '*Good home-cooked food. Vermont maple syrup*.' The place was run by two old women dressed in matching frocks. One had prayed before the meal; the other had served the food. They had sat down with Stella and watched her eat – offering her food that was as plentiful and hearty as the furnishings were lean and bare.

In an oasis near the heart of an African desert, Stella had been offered wheat cakes toasted to a warm brown that mirrored the hue of the sun lying over the sand . . . In a tent made of felt she'd sipped sugary tea, and eaten mares' milk cheese, flavoured with herbs.

There were many more of these wayside cafés that Stella remembered – dotted around the globe. They thrived in places where they did not have to compete with real cafés and restaurants. Places where there was nowhere else to eat – like Halfmoon Bay.

Stella stood up, pacing the floor of the shed as questions circled in her head.

Who would come? How often? What would they be prepared to pay?

The lounge bar at the Halfmoon pub had been busy all year round. Many families used to eat there once a week; a few regulars would have counter meals every evening. Several times a week in the summer, groups of people came off the yachts that moored in the gulch, eager for a hot meal after weeks or months at sea. Other visitors would turn up as well – youth hostellers lashing out on a dinner to remind them of home; bushwalkers hungry after braving the wilds; and ordinary tourists who had ventured off the beaten track.

It could work, Stella told herself. There were lots of questions that would have to be answered, she knew. But as she headed for the doorway there was a lightness inside her, and a spring of excitement in her step.

William's photograph still stood on Aunt Jane's sideboard, along with the other tokens of his life that Grace had assembled. Stella smiled into her father's face. The bright look in his eyes seemed to match her mood.

She slid open the damaged drawer, revealing the weather journal. Lifting it up, she pulled out another book from underneath it. The cover was plain, but she knew what it was: William's ledger of household expenses. The man had been as diligent about keeping this book up-to-date as he had been about his fishing log and weather journal.

Stella opened it up. In ruled columns, William had listed amounts spent on items like diesel, rope, petrol; and the cost of council rates, dental bills and other services. In a column called 'Food and Groceries' he gave an account of every cent that was spent at the local shop. It was this last column that drew Stella's attention. She checked the cost of all the items that Grace noted down each week from her recipe book and then ordered from Mrs Barron.

As she added up the figures, Stella's heart sank. The costs were very high. If Grace started ordering in large quantities, all the prof-its of the café would be eaten up by Mrs Barron's bill.

Stella felt the dream – the means of saving Seven Oaks – ebbing away. Still holding the open book, she walked over to the window, staring helplessly out over the garden. As she did so, a sudden movement caught her eye – drawing her gaze beyond the picket fence. Out in the paddock, a wallaby was hopping past. It came to a standstill and – lowering its furry grey head – began nibbling on the leaves of a small bush.

Stella watched it for a while as it grazed slowly over the shrub, picking out the tenderest morsels. Her eyes narrowed thoughtfully. She closed the accounts book and perched it on the sill – then she hurried from the room.

～

A steep track wound up the side of the small mountain that lay to the south of Halfmoon Bay. Stella drove along it, the tyres of the ute slipping in surface mud. She peered ahead looking for some sign of a house. Mrs Barron had given her directions to Laurie's place, but Stella wasn't sure if she'd followed them correctly. She seemed to have been driving for too long. The coastal trees had dwindled and then disappeared, giving way to dense rainforest. Through the open window she could smell damp leaves, and the resinous fragrance of sassafras bark.

Finally she reached the place where the track ended in a parking area. And there, half-covered with a piece of frayed tarpaulin, she saw Laurie's Jeep.

Stella parked beside it and climbed out, wrapping her workshirt close to her body as she felt the chill of the higher altitude. She turned round slowly, searching for some kind of building. All she could see were trees. Then she looked up, scanning the side of the mountain. Glimpses of roofing iron and weatherboards showed through small gaps in the tree canopy.

She set off along a muddy path that led up towards it. She walked between slender myrtle trunks daubed with lichen. Now and then she had to duck her head to pass beneath branches draped with pale green moss. As a child, she remembered, she'd thought the hanging moss was hair, left behind by some magical forest creature as it ran through the trees. Like the track, the path seemed to go on for too long – then, suddenly, Stella emerged onto a flat grassland.

Laurie's weatherboard house stood in the middle of the clearing. Stella paused, surprised by the sight of such an ordinary family home set here, in the middle of the bush. It looked as if it had been plucked from a suburban street; she could imagine it surrounded by pruned roses.

As she drew nearer, Stella faltered again. Looking down the side of the building, she saw that the structure had been sawn in two – straight through the roof and the walls. The two halves of the house had been placed side by side, but there was a space between them. On the roof, pieces of timber and builder's plastic bridged the void, but the gap in the walls remained – a long, dark slit.

'Still working on it.' Laurie's voice came from behind where Stella stood.

She spun round. The man was over near the edge of the treeline. Dressed in khaki and grey, he blended in with the trees.

He came to stand next to Stella, looking across to the building.

'Paid a hundred bucks for it,' he said, 'when the mine closed at the Gap. Had to cut it in half, though, to get it up here.'

Stella glanced back at the narrow pathway. It was hard to see how the building could have been brought here even if it had been cut into twenty sections.

'Come on up,' Laurie said. 'I'll brew some tea.'

Stella followed the man towards the house. They passed a line of tanned animal hides draped over a wire fence; and a dead wallaby, not yet skinned, hanging by its tail from a clothesline. Two shirts flapped in the breeze.

Laurie waved one hand at the rusty remains of a vehicle, abandoned by the side of the house.

'That's how I get stuff up here,' he called back. 'I've got a hidden track through the trees.' He turned round and winked. 'This way I get to say who can drive up here, and who can't . . .'

He paused to let Stella catch up to him. She saw now that the vehicle was the remains of a Jeep – just a chassis with wheels.

The man led the way on round the side of the house to the back door. There, he pulled off his boots, revealing striped socks that had been hand-knitted from leftover scraps of wool. As Stella bent to remove her boots, he kicked the door open with his foot.

A smell of roasting meat greeted Stella as she stepped into a hallway. She breathed it in, picking up complex layers of flavour that she could not identify.

'I'm baking a piece of goat,' Laurie said. 'Young goat, it is. Too good to boil.'

He stopped, then, and looked enquiringly at Stella. 'After some meat, are you?'

Stella nodded. 'I know you sell it at the shop, but I want to see about getting some direct from you.'

Laurie grinned. 'That's what I like to hear. I've got plenty to spare since the pub closed their kitchen. Come on in – but watch your step.'

He guided Stella along the hallway. When they came to the place where the two halves of the house met, she could see where a chain-saw had chewed a rough path down through the plasterboard walls and across the wooden floor. A wide plank bridged the gap. As she stepped onto it, she looked down – glimpsing an underworld of bare earth and dead grass.

Up ahead, Laurie disappeared through a doorway to the left. Stella followed him, entering a room that was bright with sunshine.

Laurie already had the oven door open. 'Look at this.' He drew out a large covered baking pan and lifted the lid.

Steam billowed out. As it cleared, Stella saw a large piece of roasted meat. Hot fat sputtered from skin that had turned a deep rosy red.

'Mountain pepperberry – that's the secret ingredient,' Laurie said. 'Grind the berries over the meat – not too fine – rub it in. You've got the colour, then – and the spice as well.' He tilted the pan, showing Stella that the meat was sitting on a rack above an inch of thin stock. 'That's the most important thing. Keeps it all moist. The same goes for all game – cook it long and slow. You can't go wrong.'

Laurie covered the pan again and pushed it back into the oven. He motioned for Stella to take a seat at a table. As she pulled out a chair, she glanced around the kitchen. The place was surprisingly neat and organised. The furnishings were simple – just a table, two chairs, a few cupboards and a sink. The wood-fired oven dominated the room, along with an island bench topped with a piece of pine that had been worn in the middle by years of chopping. A set of knives was laid out there on a piece of folded cloth. They looked clean and very sharp.

'That'll be a good piece of meat,' Laurie commented. 'It'll have the taste of spring feed in it, so I haven't added too much to it. As I said – there's the pepperberry. Then I like to baste with a bit of honey. If you can get some from Joe – that's the best. It's got a touch of smoke in it. Sometimes I'll add some of that as well . . .' He pointed up to the ceiling where bunches of spiky-leafed herbs hung from a wooden frame. 'Lemon thyme. It grows in the bush, right where the animals are feeding. That can be a good guide to what will go with what.'

Stella listened to him carefully, storing the information away. The smell of the roasting meat made her feel hungry, even though it was not yet noon. She wondered who Laurie was going to share it with – or if he planned to eat alone.

Laurie came to sit at the table. 'So, how much meat would you like?' he asked. 'Is it just for you and Grace?'

Stella licked dry lips. 'No, it will be for lots of people. We're opening a café.'

Laurie raised his eyebrows. 'You're what? Tell me more.'

The man leaned forward in his chair, listening intently while Stella explained the simple facts of the plan she had in mind. She spoke cautiously, sounding out his reaction as she went. When she was finished, he was still for a moment. Then he nodded his head, pressing his lips together.

'It's a bloody good idea,' he said. 'I'll be right behind you. And so will everyone else. There's heaps of food around here that comes for free. Not just meat. Down there at the bay they've all been trying to think of ways to help Grace. Especially the fishermen. I'll put the word out. They'd be more than happy to throw an extra line over every time

306

they go out. You'll have all the fish you can use. And that's just the start of it. You'll have vegetables, fruit. As much as you want . . .'

Stella smiled. She felt the warmth of his response reaching out to her, enveloping her like a soft summer breeze. Wrapped in its arms, she felt all the questions and worries drifting away. She was sure, suddenly, that the café would succeed. Seven Oaks would be safe.

'You look hungry to me,' Laurie said. He gestured behind her. 'Grab a red wine from the cupboard. I know it's lunchtime – but this is a time to celebrate.'

Stella reached into the cupboard and pulled out a bottle. A hand-written label was stuck to the side. Spidery handwriting ran across it.

Halfmoon Shiraz 1987

'That's something to think about, too – for the café,' Laurie said. 'Ted Barron makes that out the back of the shop – from his own grapes. Drinks a bit too much of it himself, it's true. But it's a very good drop.'

Stella pulled out the cork and lifted the bottle to her nose. She breathed the warm, deep fragrance of full-bodied grapes and sunshine.

When Stella returned she saw Grace in the back corner of the garden, turning over the compost pile. Tension showed in every line of the woman's body as she bent over, stabbing her fork deep into the heap and then heaving it to one side. Catching sight of Stella, she straightened up – her face looking strained, as if she expected more bad news.

Stella called out to her. 'Come inside!'

Grace hurried over, brushing her hands clean on her trousers. Once in the kitchen, she sat at the table, looking anxiously at her daughter.

Stella drew up a chair opposite her. She was silent – torn between the excitement of her conversation with Laurie and her concern about how Grace would react to her proposal.

Grace picked up the sugar bowl and began digging at it with a silver teaspoon. She seemed unable to be still.

Stella took a breath. 'I've got a plan. A way to make some money.'

Grace looked at her with a mixture of hope and doubt.

'I started thinking about how you're a great cook,' Stella said. 'That's what we have to use. You!' She ignored the puzzled frown on Grace's face. 'We're going to open a café.'

'A café!' Grace's lips parted in surprise. 'That's ridiculous!'

'No, it's not. I've thought it all through. It will be a simple place, just serving evening meals. Casseroles, pies, vegetables, soups. Home-made relishes, bread, puddings. All the things you do so well. I know what I'm talking about. I've been in places exactly like what I'm imagining. Home-cooking cafés.'

'Home-cooking cafés.' Grace repeated the words slowly. Then there was a long silence. The tin roof creaked as it expanded in the sun. Stella watched a tiny spider spiralling from a strand of web that seemed to come from nowhere.

When Grace finally spoke again, small lines of concentration marked her brow. 'Where would it be – this "café"?'

'Here. At Seven Oaks.'

Grace's head jerked back. For a while she was speechless. 'You mean – have strangers coming into the house?' Her voice rose sharply. She waved one hand, wiping away her daughter's suggestion. 'No. Definitely not. This is our home!'

'If we don't find a way to earn some money,' Stella said, 'it won't be our home much longer. It'll be a line of beach houses, owned by mainlanders.'

Grace flinched at her words. Stella gripped the side of the table as she fought against a rising sense of panic. So much was at stake . . .

'Anyway,' Stella continued, 'only some of the customers will be strangers. Others will be from Halfmoon – the ones who used to eat at the pub. People you know . . .'

Stella's voice faltered. Her last words sounded hollow. Who did Grace know? Stella remembered what Pauline had said to her down at the wharf, when she had just arrived back – that Grace had hardly been seen by anyone for years.

Stella pushed back her chair and went to stand by the window. She felt her belief in the plan beginning to weaken – she could see now that opening up her home to strangers was too much to ask of Grace.

She gazed out over the garden. Away in the far corner she could see the little cross, propped up beside the stone. A shaft of sun, piercing the shadows, lit up the silvery bleached wood – making it stand out brave and strong against the dark earth.

'We have to do it.' Stella threw the words behind her into the quiet. Then she turned back to face the room, bracing herself for Grace's reply – the words of defeat, denial, weakness . . .

But, instead of speaking, Grace got up and walked over to the stove. Reaching up to the mantelpiece, she grasped her recipe book. Then she found her notepad – the one she used for planning meals and writing out shopping lists.

Returning to the table, Grace sat down. She smoothed back her hair, tucking away strands that had come loose from her ponytail. Then she began turning the pages of the book, and making notes.

Stella crossed to stand at Grace's side. Glancing at the notepad she saw the names of three recipes. She eyed them uneasily. Was Grace going to start cooking again – avoiding reality by losing herself in the comforting pattern of weighing, measuring, chopping, frying . . .

Grace looked up. 'When I was cooking for the volunteers,' she said, 'I found that some recipes worked better than others in very large quantities.'

Stella smiled, relief flowing through her as she realised that Grace was taking the café plan seriously. But there was still another hurdle to be faced. She leaned over Grace's shoulder and placed her hand on the recipe book. She closed it up and slid it away.

'That way of cooking won't work any more,' she said. 'If we begin by choosing recipes and then buy all the ingredients at the shop, we won't make a profit.'

Grace frowned at her. 'Then what are we going to do?'

'Start with ingredients,' Stella said. 'And they will choose themselves. We'll make dishes that use all the fruit and vegetables that are in season. We'll use Laurie's game. Fish that the factory won't take. Crayfish that have been damaged by octopus. Abalone. Joe's honey. Oysters and mussels from the lagoon.' Stella smiled, caught up in a vision of the bounty that awaited their harvest.

She spread her arms wide. 'We'll use whatever is wild. Whatever we can get for free.'

Grace stared in mute astonishment.

Then, a look of wonder broke slowly across her face.

CHAPTER TWENTY

Stella stood by the Sea Wall, grasping the driftwood frame firmly with both hands. Looking along the decorated panel – past all the bits and pieces she'd tied onto it years ago – she could see Grace at the other end.

'Ready?' Stella called.

Grace nodded. 'Let's go.'

Together they dragged the structure away from its place by the shed, holding it vertical as they slid it over the ground. Progress was difficult; the Wall was heavy and unwieldy, but they managed to make their way between the vegetable beds and past the apple trees – finally reaching the newly sowed soil of the grave garden. Once there, they rested the Wall against a line of posts that they'd spent the first hours of the morning driving deep into the ground.

It took some time to manoeuvre the Wall into exactly the right position and then to secure it properly. When it was at last in place, the two women stood back to look at their work.

The tracery of driftwood, with its criss-cross lines and graceful curves, reminded Stella of the carved screens that covered the windows of houses built by Moghul merchants in Rajasthan. Their patterns were more ordered, it was true; but they both gave the same impression: of a boundary that should not be crossed, and yet which did not make the onlooker feel closed out.

'It's perfect,' Grace said.

Stella agreed. The Sea Wall, in its new position, hid the grave from the house and most of the garden. When people started coming to Seven Oaks they would be free to wander amongst the vegetable beds and fruit trees – but this area was to be kept private; a place untouched by casual eyes.

Grace bent to pick up a barnacle-crusted fishing buoy that had fallen off. Stella watched her mother tying it carefully back on.

Into the quiet came the distant hum of a vehicle coming along the track. As it drew closer, Stella heard – behind the usual engine sound – a loud rattling that suggested the vehicle was old and being driven at speed over rough ground.

Before long, Laurie's Jeep came into view. With its camouflage paint it looked like a piece of the landscape jumping along.

Grace looked towards it with interest. 'Is he bringing us some meat already?'

'I don't know,' Stella said.

Leaving Grace in the garden, she went out to meet Laurie. He waved at her from behind the wheel and then began to climb out. As Stella approached the Jeep, she glanced into the open back. She faltered, mid-step. The whole tray was filled with birds. Amongst the feathery mounds of muted brown and grey – geese and turkeys – were splashes of brilliant turquoise blue. Coloured tail-feathers as long as her arm emerged here and there from between the piled bodies. Stella stared at them. The ends were decorated with the distinctive eye-pattern that belonged to just one kind of bird . . .

'Mrs Barron's been wanting those peacocks off her place for ages,' Laurie said, coming to stand beside Stella. 'They keep her awake at night and scratch up anything she plants. They're very good eating – if you know how to cook them. So are the others.' He waved one arm, taking in the whole array of birds. 'I've got you a heap of turkeys – they're farm turkeys that have gone wild – and a couple of native geese.'

Stella stood in silence, her gaze travelling over outstretched wings, beaks stained with blood, curled feet, glazed eyes. It was a daunting sight. Stella had been around people who killed and ate birds often enough – in foreign places, and here in Halfmoon Bay – but she'd never seen so many dead birds at one time. And the blue of the peacocks – so bright and strong – seemed shocking in the midst of such wholesale destruction.

She didn't even like to think about how Grace was going to react . . . 'It's very kind of you to do this,' Stella said to Laurie. 'We really appreciate it.'

She glanced in the direction of the garden, where Grace was waiting by the Sea Wall. Stella was already planning how she should best prepare her mother for what she was about to see. She would remind Grace where the butcher's meat came from – pointing out that trays of lamb chops began with blood being shed on white fleece, and that beef came from slaughtered cows . . .

Laurie got some fish bins from the front seat and began tossing the birds down into them.

'Where do we take them?' Stella asked. She made her voice sound brisk, her tone firm and practical.

'Some place where the ground's not too hard,' he said. 'We need to dig a hole.'

Turquoise feathers fluttered through the air, turning in slow circles as they settled into the pit. The bottom was already lined with slivers of the iridescent blue, dotted amongst fronds of speckled brown and grey.

Stella and Grace sat together, each grasping a floppy bird in one hand and using the other to tear out feathers and toss them into the hole. They had already plucked several birds each. It was a still day. The air was fuzzy with floating down, and tainted with the smell of fresh blood.

Laurie squatted on the far side of the hole. He had a pile of stripped birds next to him. He placed them one at a time on a chopping board.

With quick, careful movements of his knife, he cut off heads and legs and then slit open the bodies. Pushing one hand inside the carcass, he pulled out the entrails, flinging them towards the hole. As the purple-red intestines looped through the air, a crowd of gulls watched with avid eyes. Seeing them gathered there, Stella wondered if they were simply tempted by anything that might be food, or if they were drawn to the sight of a massacre of their own kind, as humans often are. Repelled, yet fascinated . . .

Stella kept her head down, plucking steadily. The blood was a red haze at the edges of her vision. She glanced up uneasily to assess how Grace was coping with the situation. Stella had not imagined Laurie would arrive so soon – and with all this . . . It would have been much wiser, she knew, to have begun the project by gathering shellfish, or even abalone. But – to Stella's surprise – Grace seemed unfazed. The woman watched Laurie's hands while she plucked her bird, as if she were trying to memorise every move that he made. She'd wiped her nose with the back of her hand, smearing blood across her face. William's clothes were stained and dirty, but Grace did not appear to care. Stella paused, her fingers closing on a tuft of feathers. Her mother looked alive and interested. She looked almost happy.

Laurie, too, seemed pleased. Looking over to check the women's progress, he grinned encouragingly. He jerked his head towards the fish bin still half-full of birds. 'We won't pluck them all. We can skin some of them, feathers and all. It saves a lot of time. They'll be good for stews or curries.' He turned from Grace to Stella and back. 'You can make a great curry out of native goose cooked in with a bit of wallaby. The Indians would be amazed! We can cut the skinned birds up now, before we freeze them. They'll take up less room.'

They went on working quietly for a time. Then Laurie spoke again.

'I should warn you, there's always the "Skippy" factor to be considered.'

Stella and Grace looked at him with puzzled faces.

'You'll get some people turning up who have a thing about eating wallabies – and other game as well. You just have to explain a few things to them. Animals running wild have a good life till the moment they die. That's more than you can say about most farm animals.' He shook his head. 'If you've ever been to an abattoir you'll know what I mean. Most people haven't, of course. And another thing . . .' He paused to give both women a serious look. 'I never shoot anything that's in short supply. That's a golden rule.'

Grace nodded. 'My father had that rule, too. He used to go pheasant shooting. Perhaps he still does . . .' She smiled, a distant look on her face. 'You know, I remember seeing a painting in our hunting lodge – it was of a medieval banquet. You could see all the food laid out on the table, and the centrepiece was a peacock, served up in its feathers. They were considered the greatest delicacy, I gather . . .'

'Wait till you taste one of these,' Laurie said. 'You'll know why.' He reached for another bird – then he became suddenly still. He looked past the women, in the direction of the track. 'There's a car coming.' He frowned. 'Looks like a cop car. Spinks! What the bloody hell does he want?' He jumped up. 'I might just make myself scarce.'

Stella put down her bird. 'I'll find out.'

By the time she emerged from behind the shed, wiping her hands against her jeans, the police sedan was neatly parked in front of the house. Spinks was standing at the back of Laurie's Jeep, peering down into the tray. He looked immaculate, as always – his hat level on his head, and his shirt-sleeves pressed into crisp lines.

Stella waited in silence for him to notice her. Fluffy down, trapped in her hair, tickled her cheek – she guessed her hair was layered with feathers. A fly kept landing on her cheek, which she suspected might be flecked with drying blood.

If Spinks was surprised at her appearance, he betrayed no sign of it.

'I came to see how you and Grace are getting on,' he said. 'But I see you already have a visitor.'

Stella felt an urge to look round and check whether Grace and the bins full of birds could be glimpsed between the bushes. She did not relish the idea of taking Spinks out to the pit. If he and Laurie got together, she suspected there could be trouble. She wasn't sure if it was legal to shoot peacocks – even ones that had gone wild and were causing a nuisance. Not only this: the presence of the policeman – with his symbols of law and order – somehow made the chaotic scene that surrounded the plucking and cleaning of the dead birds appear barbaric.

'Where's it all happening, then?' Spinks asked. 'You've dug a pit, I hope? Best thing to do – bury it all well where the flies can't get at it.'

'You know what we're doing . . .' Stella said faintly.

'Mrs Barron told me,' Spinks said. He smiled. 'She's looking forward to her first good night's sleep in years, with those birds gone. Let's have a look, then.'

Stella wasn't sure if it was an official demand or a request. Either way, she felt she had no choice but to obey. She led the way back past the shed and into the paddock.

When they reached the pit, Grace was squatting in Laurie's place. Her sleeve was rolled up and her arm was buried up to the elbow inside a huge plucked bird. As Spinks came to stand nearby, she dragged out a handful of innards. Catching sight of the man, she paused – a bloody mess dripping onto her feet. She seemed at a loss for a second – then she flung it away into the pit.

'Morning, Grace,' Spinks said. He raised his voice. 'Morning, Laurie! Come on out – I won't bite.'

After a few seconds, the hunter shuffled out from the bushes. He gave Spinks a cold look and offered no greeting.

There was an awkward quiet. In the stillness the gulls risked moving a few steps closer. Then Laurie picked up another bird and began cutting off its head.

Spinks directed his gaze to Stella and Grace. 'I need to talk to you two. About this idea of building a café.'

'How did you know about it?' Stella asked.

Spinks gestured towards Laurie. 'Once you've told him, everyone knows! But before it goes any further, there are a few things you need to consider.'

'Here we go,' murmured Laurie.

Stella looked down at the ground, where ants were gathering around a lump of dark red liver. She focused on their frantic movements as a chill of foreboding spread through her. Spinks was about to tell them, she sensed – perhaps in just a few blunt words – why it was that their plan could never work.

'I'd like to have a look at your kitchen, if you don't mind,' Spinks said.

Grace raised her eyebrows. 'Whatever for? I can assure you, it's very clean.'

Watching her mother, Stella was struck by the confidence that Grace seemed suddenly to have found. There was something almost regal in her manner – the way she held her head, and projected her voice. She might have been addressing an impertinent guest.

'I'd like to see the toilet facilities you plan for guests to use,' Spinks continued. 'And a few other things as well.'

Stella looked at him in confusion. She was not surprised that there would be rules about facilities in a place serving food to the public, but she did not understand Spinks' attitude. Ever since her arrival at Halfmoon Bay he had been so kind and helpful. Yet now there was an officious tone in his voice.

Laurie picked up on it as well. 'Agh – give them a break, Spinks,' he said. 'They're just trying to make a living.'

'That's why I'm here – to help,' Spinks responded.

Laurie muttered under his breath. He picked up his knife and began slitting the skin of a feathered bird. A few seconds later, he ripped the whole skin off in one movement and flung it away. Flies rose in a small cloud as it landed in the bottom of the pit.

Spinks stood in the middle of the kitchen, rocking back and forth on his toes. Grace and Stella eyed him from a place closer to the door. Laurie came to stand behind them, looking over their shoulders.

'It's not me you need to worry about,' Spinks was saying. 'The health inspector from St Louis will be on to you like a ton of bricks. He'll go through your kitchen with a magnifying glass – he'll make notes on your food-preparation surfaces, dirt traps, unsealed drains. The more problems he finds, the more particular he'll become. You'll end up with a list of tasks you could never pull off.'

Stella exchanged looks with Laurie. She could see that the man agreed with what the policeman was saying. Grace, too, was nodding her head. A gloomy quiet settled over the group. Stella looked at Spinks in dismay. She was surprised to see that he appeared completely untouched by the effect his words were having. In fact, the man's expression was almost bright – as if he were nursing some secret that brought him pleasure.

'So, I think the thing to do,' Spinks continued, 'is for me to have a look first. You make some changes. Then I'll call the inspector and ask him to come and check it all, before he hears about it on the grapevine. That way you can get everything ready. Bake a special cake.' He threw a glance over at Stella and Grace. 'Make sure you look clean and tidy.'

Stella glimpsed Laurie nodding his head again. He was looking at the policeman with grudging approval. 'I can see what you're getting at,' he said. 'It's not a bad plan.'

Spinks walked slowly around the kitchen, followed closely by Grace, who held her notepad in her hand. Stella and Laurie watched from the hall doorway.

'All the outside drains must be covered,' Spinks said. 'Flies will always find a way to get inside, so we need to make sure there's nowhere dirty for them to have been sitting beforehand.'

'Yes, that's a good point,' said Grace. 'What next?' She held her pencil poised above her notepad. Watching her, Stella saw again the Grace who had been raised in a family where cutlery bore coats of arms, and banquets for twenty were served in the dining room.

'The sink won't do,' Spinks said. 'You'll need a double sink.'

Grace eyed the spotless sink and draining board critically. 'It is small,' she agreed. 'And we'll be using big pots – they'll be difficult to wash in there.'

'But a new sink like that will cost a fortune,' Stella protested.

'It would,' agreed Spinks, 'except I'm pretty certain Joe's still got the one Griggs took out of the pub. There's nothing wrong with it. He'll give it to you, or sell it cheap.' He scanned the room for the third time. 'You'll need more space for food preparation. Joe's got the stainless-steel benchtops from the pub as well. The kitchens were completely renovated, you know, before the place was put on the market. Joe's got all kinds of things you could use.'

Stella listened with growing alarm. Spinks spoke casually, as though it were an easy task to install a new sink, make new benches. Next, she feared, he'd be talking about new cupboards, doorways . . .

'You'll need help to do all that,' Spinks stated. He scratched his head, looking thoughtful. Then he turned to Laurie. 'Why don't you ask your mate Zeph to give these women a hand?'

Laurie looked at the policeman in surprise. 'That's the best idea you've had in a long time! He'll be glad to help. I know he will.'

Grace turned from Spinks to Laurie, and then finally to Stella. 'Who is this man, Zeph?'

Stella felt Spinks' eyes watching her face as she framed her reply. 'He was with me when I found Dad. He was driving the car.'

Grace became still, painful memories crossing her face. 'I don't really remember him.' After a brief pause, she continued, addressing Spinks. 'We can't possibly ask him. We hardly know him. We'd have to insist on paying for his time.'

Laurie grinned. 'Just try,' he said.

'You could cook him a few meals,' Spinks suggested. 'A single bloke like that – he'd be glad of a good dinner at the end of the day. A meal prepared by the famous chef of Halfmoon Bay.' The policeman was addressing Grace, but he kept his eyes trained on her daughter. 'What do you think, Stella? Shall we ask him to come out here at least – and look at the work to be done?'

It was the moment of choice, Stella knew – to pull back and close the door, or step out and let everything begin . . .

She met Spinks' gaze. Behind the aura of confidence that the policeman always carried with him, she sensed uncertainty – as if he understood the implications of his seemingly simple suggestion.

'I'm not pushing you,' Spinks said. 'You could look at getting a tradesman from St Louis. The job's not huge, after all. Couldn't cost that much . . .'

'No,' Stella said quickly. 'Let's . . . Let's ask him.'

'That's the way,' Laurie said approvingly. 'I'll come and give him a hand, too. I'm not much good with jobs like that – but I can hammer a nail in straight.' He rubbed his hands together restlessly. Then he gave Spinks a little salute. 'I'll get back out to the birds now – if you don't mind – before the crows move in.'

Spinks smiled. 'Good plan.'

Stella stared blankly across the room. She felt she'd just made a crucial decision – but what it might mean, she did not know.

As soon as Spinks and Laurie were both gone – and all the birds were stacked away in the freezer – Stella retreated to the sleepout. There, she sat on her bed, resting her back against the wall and hugging her knees to her body. She fixed her eyes on a vase of yellow daffodils that stood on the chest of drawers, and tried to think calmly about what Spinks had proposed.

Laurie seemed certain it would happen – that Zeph would come here to Seven Oaks to work in Grace's kitchen. He would stay for hours, Stella realised. He might even stay for dinner.

She told herself that Zeph would just be coming here to help – nothing more. She reminded herself that they were different people now – both of them. And that the events of the past stood between them, a chasm that could not be crossed.

Yet the hope was there – the hope that a miracle would happen. Their love would be reborn, bright and strong.

She turned at the sound of footsteps approaching. Grace came to stand in the doorway. The late sun shone in from behind her, making her a dark cutout shape. As she stepped inside, Stella saw that she held a bundle of folded clothes cradled against her chest.

'I brought these for you.' Grace spoke almost shyly. 'They're from my trunk. When I was putting your washing away yesterday, I noticed you've hardly got anything to wear.' She lifted the bundle to her nose. 'They were a bit musty, but I aired them and washed them. They're fine now.'

She laid the clothes on Stella's bed. There were two shirts made of silk, and another of dark green twill. A pair of corduroy trousers. A pleated skirt. And a black jumper knitted from fine, soft yarn.

'That's cashmere.' Grace brushed a finger over the jumper. 'I bought it in Paris.' She smiled at Stella, her gaze travelling tenderly over her daughter's face. 'It will look perfect on you, with your dark hair and fair skin.'

'It's beautiful,' Stella murmured. As she looked up at Grace, she forgot about Zeph for a while. She felt a sudden rush of joy. For so many years after she'd left home, she'd dreamed of sharing a moment like this with her mother. It was something so simple – a gift of old clothes – yet so precious. She'd never hoped it could be real.

'I'll go and bake a cake now,' Grace said. 'We've got visitors tomorrow, remember. You know – Laurie and his friend. What was his name?'

'Zeph,' Stella said. His name seemed to linger in the air – sounding too loud, too big, in the little room.

'That's right – Zeph,' Grace said. 'They'll be hungry, I'm sure.'

When Grace was gone, Stella climbed off the bed. Pulling open a drawer, she added the new clothes to her small collection. As she cast her eyes over her well-worn trousers and shirts, she was reminded of all the adventures they had shared with her. Each stain that they bore – each ragged tear – had a story to tell. They were emblems of the life she'd made for herself. The strong, independent person she'd become, without Zeph . . .

She opened another drawer and looked at the rest of her possessions – the camera, notebooks, shoelaces. Daniel's emergency supply of bathplugs tied together like keys on a ring. She smiled at the memory of him handing them to her.

'Bathplugs, my dear. Essential. When things start to fall apart, they're the first items to disappear from hotel rooms for some reason. It's very difficult to wash when there's just a trickle of water and no plug.'

Stella wished suddenly that she could speak to Daniel – to ask his advice. Was this the time to retreat and build up a wall around herself? Or should she risk being hurt again?

Daniel had been right about so much, Stella thought. He'd brought her back to life, and shown her how to survive. She looked over to the corner of the room at the travel-worn backpack that had once belonged to him. Then her eyes moved across to where the stone angel sat on the table beside the bed. Stella thought of all the years when the carving had been her only symbol of belonging. Suddenly, she leaned forward to look at the angel more closely. There was a spider there – spinning a web between the two stone wings. As Stella watched the spider at work, it came to her that for all Daniel's wisdom there was one important lesson he had not been able to teach her. How to know when it was time to stop and let the dust gather for a while. To settle down and make a home.

There were some things, Stella realised, that you had to work out for yourself.

CHAPTER TWENTY-ONE

Sun gleamed off the round bowls of the soupspoons as Stella laid them out on the weathered planks of the back verandah. Since she'd come out here after breakfast she had polished nine of them. There were another fifteen to go. Then there were all the knives, forks, teaspoons, dessertspoons, bread-and-butter knives, and serving spoons . . . It was a daunting task, but Stella welcomed it. The repetitive movements – rubbing on the Silvo, then using a soft cloth to polish it away – made her feel calm. The gradual completion of one utensil after another helped tie the passing moments to the steady rising of the sun in the sky.

It was nearly ten o'clock. Laurie and Zeph were now due to arrive at any time.

Stella put down the spoon and reached for the next one. Her hair fell forward in a curtain, hiding her face. She had washed it this morning, and the smell of Grace's lavender and rosemary shampoo lingered in the silky strands. She had put on mascara as well, for the first time she could remember – just a very fine coat that darkened the sunbleached tips of her lashes, but could otherwise not be seen. She'd dressed in her usual jeans, but had added the green twill shirt given to her by Grace. She knew it looked good on her – the rich colour sat well against her skin, and the cut of the garment followed the shape of her body perfectly.

323

Stella gazed out to sea. Her thoughts kept wandering, restlessly. She tried to pick out the distant spire of the lighthouse on the horizon. Then she searched amongst the kelp weed flopping in the swell, in case there was a seal to be seen. Or the fin of a dolphin, further out . . .

She made herself pick up the next soupspoon and smear it with polish. She watched the grey cream turning dark in the air. Then, with a soft cloth she rubbed away the tarnish of years, bringing out a flawless shine. Holding up the spoon, she glimpsed her reflection in the bowl. A tiny Stella. A fairy's child . . . Turning to the handle, she polished out the last dull traces of Silvo from the lines of the Boyd coat of arms.

The lily. The star. The cat . . . A symbol of bravery.

Carla. Where are you, little cat?

Stella told herself the cat would most likely be dead by now. A cat's life was short, compared with a human's. Did Carla survive to old age, she wondered? Or did some disaster befall her? Stella remembered meeting a sailor at a party, years ago. She'd been drawn to him when she overheard heard him commenting that he liked to have a cat on board.

'I lost one recently, though,' he said.

'What happened?' Stella asked.

The sailor told how the cat had gone to sleep in a furled sail. When the wind changed, and he hauled the sail up the mast, the cat had been thrown into the sea.

Stella stared at him, imagining a desperate attempt to rescue the frantic creature. 'What did you do?'

'I got another one at the next port,' the sailor said. 'A cat is a cat, really. Something to cuddle when you're lonely . . .'

He let his eyes run over Stella's body then. She'd turned and walked away.

She'd met other sailors like that. Tough, lonely men who had spent long years at sea and who seemed to enjoy pitting themselves against the elements. She always wondered, as she listened to them speak, if they had been different when they were younger. If it were possible that loneliness and the sea crept into a man's soul in the end – and made it cold.

Stella did not hear Grace's footsteps as the woman approached the doorway – but then her mother's tall figure appeared in front of her, cutting out the sun.

'They're here,' Grace said. 'I'm going to serve tea in the kitchen before they begin making a mess.'

Stella approached via the side door, pausing in a place where she could not be seen and peered into the kitchen.

Zeph was facing away from her. He was wearing a worn shirt of faded sky-blue. He sat upright with his shoulders squared – as though he felt ill at ease in Grace's kitchen. Laurie lounged beside him, legs outstretched and his arms folded over his chest.

In the middle of the floor was a double sink coated with dust, and a pile of loose plumbing fittings.

By leaning sideways, Stella could just see Zeph's legs under the table – he wore jeans cut off roughly into shorts that ended just above his knees. His bare calves curved down to meet thick woollen socks. Stella's eyes lingered on his well-worn boots. They were elastic-sided ones: the kind used by every Tasmanian who worked hard on land or sea. The toes had been rubbed through, revealing the glimmer of steel caps. The whole surface of the leather was scuffed; the elastic sides sagged. It was a good sign, Stella told herself. Jamie's dad used to say you could tell a lot about a man from his boots. 'You can tell if he's for real,' the fisherman said, 'or just a poser.'

'Where's that Stella, then?' asked Laurie, looking around. He saw her hovering in the doorway. 'There you are. Come on. We're hungry.'

As Stella entered the room, Zeph stood up. Stella glimpsed Grace's look of approval at his action, and Laurie's raised eyebrow, in the seconds it took for Zeph to turn around . . .

Stella stopped mid-step as she met Zeph's gaze. His eyes seemed to burn with a green light – a wild fire, able to jump the gap between them.

She caught her breath. In that instant it was as if she had not seen him since the day he sailed away. The encounters they'd had – outside his house, at the beach with William, in the car – had been crowded by emotions dragging her in different directions. Now, here, there was only him.

Suddenly she became aware that Grace was speaking to her. She saw her mother put down a steaming teapot beside a plate of sliced cake. 'I'll pour some tea.'

Grace's voice sounded calm, light. Stella looked at her and then at Laurie. Was it possible that they did not see, did not feel – anything?

Stella sat beside Laurie. She licked her lips, though they were not dry. Without planning to, she started talking about the birds – how carefully she and Grace had washed and bagged and frozen them. How they had written the dates on tags, so that they would be used in the right period of time. Her words tumbled out too quickly. She felt sure she was speaking too loud.

She didn't care. She could feel Zeph watching her – picking up every movement of her lips, the tilt of her head, the wave of her hand and the swish of her hair as she lifted it back from her face.

Laurie nodded approvingly. 'That's good,' he said. 'It occurred to me that the health inspector might want to take a look in your freezer. I reckon if you're writing lists for him to see, it might just be best to call everything turkey. Keep it simple. It's the best way with those blokes from the council.'

As he spoke, Laurie took a piece of cake from the plate and then went to stand by Grace's sink. He rested his hand on the spotless draining board. He looked across to Zeph.

'What do you reckon?' he asked. 'Shall we just hoe into it, and rip out the old one?'

Grace paused in the act of pouring tea, turning to Zeph in alarm.

'I'll have to think about it first,' Zeph said. 'I need to work out a plan. Design the new cupboard.'

326

'That's what he's like,' Laurie said to Stella. 'Has to do everything properly.' He took a large bite of cake and chewed hungrily. 'That's beautiful, Grace,' he said with his mouth full. 'What kind of cake do you call that?'

'That's Aunt Eliza's recipe – for a cake called "Cut and Come Again",' Grace responded.

Stella looked at the table. She picked at a stray crumb with her finger. Did Zeph remember, she wondered. This was the cake she'd brought to the coves on Christmas Day.

'That's a funny name,' Laurie said. 'What's it mean?'

'You can guess,' Zeph said. 'If you share the cake, it means you will return.'

Stella stared down at her hands – unspoken words circling in her head.

But you didn't come. Not then, when I needed you.

She could feel Zeph's gaze fixed on her. Slowly, she lifted her eyes and met his. She tried to hide the darkness that stirred inside her, but as she looked at him, she thought she could see its shadow reflected in his face. Then, the moment passed. Zeph gave her a smile, and handed her the plate of cake.

'It's a family recipe,' Grace added. 'Not my family – William's.' She looked at the cake appraisingly, her head tilted to one side. 'I've always thought it was a bit too moist. And a bit sweet as well.' She looked between the two men. 'Have another slice,' she said. 'You'll need the energy.'

When they'd finished their tea, Grace washed up the cups and saucers. She did the task slowly, carefully – as if this last wash-up in her old sink were a ritual to be savoured and memorised. Stella dried the crockery with a tea-towel, piling it up beside the draining board.

Zeph sat at the table, making a diagram on the back of an old envelope. Stella stole snapshot looks at his hands – at long fingers cradling a pencil, fingernails cut short, skin toughened by weather and work. She saw that his old blue shirt was made of finely woven linen. When it was new, she guessed, it would have been very expensive.

Stella began to put the cups and plates away where they belonged. Wherever she moved in the room she felt Zeph's presence, like an axis upon which she turned.

Zeph got up from the table and asked Grace to move aside from the sink. Then he unreeled his measuring tape and checked lengths and heights. His movements were quick and sure, but Stella sensed in them a veiled tension that matched her own.

When his drawing was finished, Zeph began bringing in his tools, laying them out on the floor. He buckled a nail pouch around his hips and rolled up his sleeves. Soon he was crouched beside Laurie, helping to unscrew the pipes under the sink. Grace went outside, preferring not to watch the dismantling, but Stella stayed in the kitchen, rearranging one of the other cupboards to take the things they'd removed from under the sink. As she worked, she kept looking over at Zeph. When she could see murky water beginning to leak from the u-bend, she leaned over to give him a plastic bowl. He looked up at her as he took it, his fingers brushing against hers.

Soon the old sink came free and Stella helped Laurie carry it outside. The day had become hot – the sun beating down through the cloudless sky.

Laurie wiped a hand over his face. He asked Stella to go and bring a box of tiles from the back of the Jeep.

When she returned, Zeph was sawing timber while Laurie held the planks steady.

'Here,' Laurie said, 'take over from me. I'm going to work on the plumbing.' He pointed towards the pipes that ran along the outside of the kitchen wall nearby. 'I'll be right here if you need a break.'

Stella held the timber firmly in place, preventing any movement as Zeph continued sawing it into lengths. Though the timber looked grey and ordinary on the outside, it was honey-gold inside. Stella smelled the fragrant resin of huon pine.

Zeph squinted with the effort of following his pencil lines. Standing beside him, Stella took the chance to study his face. His hair – cut short – was thick and almost curly. His cheeks were leaner and marked with laugh lines. The scar on his chin was still visible – but had faded now, to white.

Muscles tightened under the rolled sleeves of his shirt as he pushed the saw through the wood. Sawdust floating in the air settled in a fine yellow dust on the skin of his arms.

Stella lifted a new plank up onto the sawhorses. Though its surface was deeply weathered, it had not been used before – it was free of nail holes. She recognised the look of milled wood that had been drifting in the sea: probably deck cargo, carelessly secured by the first mate, and lost to a wave in a storm.

'Where did you find the timber?' Stella asked, raising her voice over the sound of the saw.

Zeph stopped work. 'Down at the coves. I got a whole load. Enough to build my kitchen.'

Stella pictured his house, with its driftwood window frames.

'You must have had a good collection,' Stella said.

'It took me nearly a year to get all the materials together – after I decided to stay.'

The two looked at one another in silence – the air between them thick with unasked questions. Then Laurie called out from his place by the wall.

'I told you to use proper wood, Zeph. You could've been finished by now.'

Zeph smiled at Stella. 'I'm in no hurry to finish.' He looked into her eyes. 'Are you all right, holding that?'

Stella nodded. 'I'm fine.'

He began sawing again – working his arm steadily back and forth. Sweat formed on his skin, glistening in the sun.

When it was time for lunch, Grace called everyone round to the verandah.

'I've laid out a picnic there,' she explained. 'It's too messy in the kitchen.'

She led the way through the house, Laurie and Zeph following behind her. Stella came last. As she stepped out onto the open-sided verandah, she faltered in surprise. Grace had spread out a cloth over the floorboards – not a cheap cotton picnic cloth, but a large square of red plush edged with a gold fringe that Stella had not seen before. There were cushions from the sea room around its edges. The centre was covered with food. It was simple fare, but Grace had set it out like a feast. There were plates of dried fruit and salted nuts, hunks of cheese, sliced tomatoes sprinkled with chopped herbs, and early lettuce just picked from the garden. There was a large bowl of preserved apricots and peaches left over from winter. And two large jugs of lemonade. In the middle was a vase of spring flowers.

Stella smiled at Grace. 'It looks beautiful.'

'It does,' agreed Zeph. His gaze shifted from the food up to the view. He looked north, towards the coves. After a long moment, he turned to Stella. 'We could almost see each other.'

'It's further than it looks,' Stella said.

Zeph seemed about to speak, but Laurie drew his attention.

'Did you bring the bread?' he asked.

Zeph shook his head. 'I left it in the Jeep. I'll get it.' He moved round the edge of the picnic, towards the steps.

Laurie lowered himself onto one of the cushions. He looked up at Grace. 'You must come to my place next. I'll cook you a . . . turkey.'

Grace laughed. 'The blue-feathered kind?'

'That's the one,' said Laurie.

Stella sat down facing the sea, with her back resting against the wall of the house. Grace remained standing, hovering like a dinner-party hostess until Zeph reappeared.

He held a round loaf of bread in his hand. On the way, he'd picked up an offcut of the plank he'd been sawing. He placed the loaf on the board and added it to the spread. The smell of huon-pine oil and yeast mingled in the air.

Grace pointed to the cushion beside Stella. 'Sit there,' she said to Zeph, 'so that you can look at the view.'

Stella and Zeph sat cross-legged on their cushions, side by side. With the feast laid out in front of them, Stella imagined they looked like an oriental prince and princess looking out over their domain.

The sea was a vast veil of silk, encrusted with diamonds. Wisps of cirrus cloud hung high in a blue sky. Birds fluttered around the orange poker plants that grew near the granite boulders. Butterflies danced beside wide-winged dragonflies. Crickets sang in the grasses.

Stella smiled. The beauty of the scene seemed like a gift offered specially to her – to them. She looked sideways and found Zeph already watching her.

'Let's eat,' Grace said. She began passing food and pouring drinks.

They all ate with their hands, not bothering with plates. They scattered crumbs over the red cloth and dripped syrup from the peaches. Laurie sliced the bread and handed some to Grace and Stella.

'Try that,' he said. 'Best bread you'll ever taste.'

Stella chewed on the soft dough. He was right. The bread had a faint but distinctive flavour. 'How do you make it?' she asked.

Laurie pointed to Zeph. 'Ask him.'

'It's seawater bread,' Zeph answered. 'You use yeast, flour, seawater – and honey. I use Joe's honey.'

Stella looked into his eyes. A memory danced between them – a boy and a girl eating smoky honey, dipping their fingers into the jar . . .

'He's a sailor,' Laurie said to Grace. 'That's why he cooks with seawater.'

Grace laughed – a low, warm sound. She turned to Zeph. 'Tell us about your travels, then,' she said. 'Where have you sailed?'

Zeph told stories of some of the places he had been on his yacht – north to Greenland, and as far south as Heard Island. He'd not really settled anywhere, he said, until about eight years ago when he began his business.

'Very successful business,' Laurie added proudly. 'He's an inventor. I read about him in *The Australian* – before I even knew who he was.'

Stella gathered every snippet of new information, piecing them together like bits of a puzzle.

At the end of an account of sailing between ice floes, Zeph turned to Stella. 'And you?' he asked. 'Where have you been?'

It was Stella's turn, then, to tell about her own life – her work, and her constant travelling. Zeph listened intently, taking it all in. When she fell quiet, he nodded slowly.

'It sounds – good,' he said. 'Interesting work. Important work.'

'She's done well,' Laurie commented, 'that's for sure. She was a lucky girl – getting the chance to go away to school and spending all that time in England. It's not so easy to make something of yourself if you're stuck here in Tasmania.'

The man's words fell into a sudden stillness. Zeph's hand froze, a glass poised halfway to his mouth. Grace stopped chewing. Stella looked down at hands, clenched in her lap. She felt the darkness gathering again inside her – the pain of what really had happened to her all those years ago. She didn't know if Zeph was hearing this story for the first time – or if he'd already been told about her supposed trip to England. Either way, she wondered what his feelings were as he thought back to that time. Perhaps his conscience was eased by the knowledge that she would not have been here anyway, if he'd kept his promise and returned.

She glanced sideways at him. He was staring out to sea. There was a distant expression on his face – as if he had chosen suddenly to retreat from her.

Guilt made people do that, Stella thought . . .

Laurie went on eating, clearly oblivious to the tension in the air. But no one accepted the dishes he offered.

Then, Zeph stood up. After thanking Grace for the meal, he looked into the sky, squinting at the sun. 'If we're going to get that new sink in,' he said, 'we'd better get on with it.'

His voice sounded strained. Stella peered up at his face. There was no trace of the warmth she'd seen there earlier on. She began to wonder if she had only imagined it – if it had been nothing more than a projection of her own emotions. But what she'd felt had seemed so real . . . She looked away from him. With a sense of panic, she realised she could not trust her grasp of what was happening. Perhaps he had not changed towards her. It was just that the darkness of the past had risen up and coloured her view.

Grace began to collect the plates and bowls. Stella helped her – bending her head over the cloth to hide her face.

By the end of the afternoon the double sink was in place, with new stainless-steel benches stretching out to each side of the draining boards. Below the sink, a new cupboard had been built, perfectly matching the new dimensions of the sinktop. Instead of ordinary knobs, the doors had handles made of curved pieces of driftwood.

Laurie opened and shut them half a dozen times. 'Look at that,' he said. 'It fits like a glove – hugs your hand. Looks good, too.'

Zeph began packing his tools away inside a hinged wooden box with a leather strap. Stella helped gather them up. She felt a sense of despair as she picked up each hammer and screwdriver, feeling its solid weight in her hand. They were symbols of him. As they disappeared into the box, one by one, she knew his departure was drawing closer. She felt as though they'd been given a chance to come together – but that she'd let the darkness intrude and spoil it. Now the day was over – the opportunity lost.

Soon, the four stood out by the Jeep, late sun slanting across their faces.

Grace thanked the two men for coming, and handed Laurie a cake to take home.

Zeph went round to the passenger side. Stella followed him. She wanted to ask him if he would come back again, but she didn't want to risk hearing an answer that was polite, but vague.

'Thank you for coming over,' she said.

'I enjoyed it,' Zeph replied.

The words passed between them like dragonflies skimming a pond, all the deep water beneath untouched . . .

Laurie started the engine, and the old car jolted roughly away.

CHAPTER TWENTY-TWO

Stella stood in the doorway to the sea room. The space looked bigger and lighter. The newly exposed floorboards – freshly waxed – gleamed in the late morning sun that reached in through the long bank of windows.

Most of the furniture was gone – the couch with its row of cushions, the covered stool, the television, the standard lamp and bookcase. They had all been moved into Stella's old room, which was to become a private lounge. Stella had prepared the space by packing up her childhood possessions – filling a box with toys, books, dolls, old clothes . . . The last thing to go into the box was the doll, Miranda. Stella had dusted off the naked plastic body and nylon hair, and then dressed her in the little fisherman's jumper. She laid the doll in the box, smoothing the red hair down over the narrow shoulders. After closing the lid, she'd taped it down. Then she'd carried the box out to the shed.

The sea room was beginning to look like a café dining room. The table, with all its extra leaves in place, filled the middle of the space. Ten chairs were set out along each side. Only four of them were alike – they were the ones the family had used. The rest had come from Joe's shed – rescued by the man over decades from doctors' waiting rooms, people's kitchens, the church hall, as well as the pub.

The mismatched collection looked right, somehow. It seemed to hint at the varied characters that would soon be sitting there.

Stella heard footsteps coming down the hall. Seconds later, Grace wandered in. Standing beside Stella, she looked approvingly over the room.

'The chairs are perfect,' she commented. 'I've had an idea – about how we can repay Joe. I know he won't take any money, but we could give him something.'

'What did you have in mind?' Stella asked. She imagined a quantity of cakes, or the promise of a month's worth of pies. But Grace took her arm and pulled her round to face the far side of the room. She pointed a finger towards the one piece of furniture – apart from the table and chairs – that was still left there. It looked heavy and dark, a dominating presence in the liberated space.

Aunt Jane's sideboard.

Stella glanced at her mother in surprise – then followed her over to stand in front of it.

'Are you sure?' she asked. 'Perhaps we should store it in the shed.'

'I don't want to keep it,' Grace said firmly. 'Joe can sell it to a dealer. He'll get a good price for it.'

Stella nodded slowly. She liked the idea, too, she realised, of removing forever this link with Aunt Jane. It seemed to suit the beginning of a new venture.

The polished top of the sideboard still bore the framed photograph of William as a medical student – along with his last newspaper, the *Victory* mug, the candlestick, and the other pieces of memorabilia dotted across a large lace cloth.

Stella and Grace looked at the display in silence. Then Grace picked up the photograph and handed it to Stella.

'We'll keep that on the mantelpiece,' she said. She lifted the cloth by each of its corners, gathering up everything inside – and carried it all away.

When she returned, the two women squatted side by side, emptying the contents of the sideboard. First, they packed up the special plates that had belonged to William's family. Then they turned to the piles of embroidered napkins and tablecloths.

'We won't use any of these,' Grace said. 'I'll cut up a sheet to make napkins. Plain white ones. And we'll leave the table bare – it's such beautiful wood.'

Lastly, they carefully transferred the weather journal – and all the other things from William's private drawer – into a carton.

The sideboard was now completely empty. With its doors hanging wide and drawers pulled open, it appeared smaller, somehow – stripped of its authority.

Stella and Grace took an end each, and lifted up the heavy piece of furniture. They tried to move it towards the doorway, but found they could only manage a short distance before they had to put it down and rest. Stella had already tried to lighten the sideboard by removing the drawers, but she'd discovered they were designed with catches that prevented them being slid out too far. There was no choice but to just continue as best they could – stopping every few metres for a break.

It took a long time to manoeuvre the sideboard out to the driveway. Then they had to build a ramp out of two planks and push the bulky weight up it in a series of short bursts. When the object was finally in place on the tray of the ute, Stella and Grace sighed with relief.

Stella drove carefully away up the track, with Grace sitting beside her looking over her shoulder to check on the load. Stella glanced into the rear-vision mirror as well. The sideboard rocked slightly with each bump that they met.

As they turned onto the gravel road, the ride became much smoother. Grace gave up watching behind her, and Stella let the ute pick up some speed.

Grace scanned the edges of the road as they drove. Following her gaze, Stella saw the usual dark furry mounds appearing at regular intervals.

'I've never noticed before,' Grace commented after a while, 'how much roadkill there is. There must be a lot of wildlife about.'

The bush gave way to an open, marshy area with mudbanks and tall reeds. They peered up through the windscreen as a pelican flew over – a huge bird that looked much too heavy to be able to stay in the air.

Stella slowed down as Joe's boathouse appeared ahead of them. She turned off onto a short driveway – bringing the ute to a standstill as close as she could to the building. The door was wide open, wedged back with the broken end of an oar. As Stella climbed out, she called Joe's name – but there was no reply. He was probably at the wharf, she guessed.

She peered into the gloomy interior of the shed, in case the old man was in there – but there was no sign of him. The air smelled of diesel and tar, faintly backed with stale fish. The place was a maze of old furniture, fishing gear, tools, washing machines, bikes, building materials, prams – junk and treasure, all mixed together. The wooden spines of a half-built boat rose up amidst the chaos, looking like ribs of a long-buried whale emerging from the sand. She noticed a large stack of white dinner plates and bowls – the solid-looking crockery often used in hotel dining rooms. Moving closer, she saw that the top plate bore a small insignia. Southern Ocean Line. She pictured the crockery laid out on the long dining table, in the room with windows that gave an unbroken vista of sea and sky. It would be like dining on a ship.

She turned to see Grace standing behind her, pulling on a pair of gardening gloves.

'We'll just leave it inside,' Stella said.

Grace gave a small wave of agreement and went round to the rear of the ute. As she opened the back, Stella jumped up and stood next to the sideboard. Working together, the two shifted the object to the edge of the tray.

'The next bit is tricky,' Stella said. 'We need to slide it down. Not too fast.'

Halfway off the tray, the sideboard began to tilt. The drawers began sliding out, hanging on their catches.

'Push it back!' Stella yelled at Grace.

'I can't!' Grace shouted.

Grace jumped out of the way as the sideboard fell, crashing to the ground. There was a sound of splintering wood as the drawers were smashed off under its weight.

In the quiet that followed, the only noise was the peeping of water birds.

Stella climbed down and stood beside Grace, staring at the broken drawers. It was a shocking sight – in the past, the discovery of even a small scratch on Aunt Jane's heirloom used to send Grace scurrying for her tin of special restorer's wax. But as Stella stood there looking, she had an urge to laugh. Glancing at Grace, she could see that her mother felt the same. Grace was pressing her lips together, trying to look grave.

A smile spread across Stella's face – then a laugh broke out. A few seconds later, Grace joined in – first covering her mouth guiltily, then tipping back her head and laughing freely. The bright sound echoed between them, dancing in the quiet air before finally dying away.

Stella was about to ask Grace what they should do with the sideboard now that it was worthless, when something caught her eye amongst the broken timber.

She bent to look more closely. There was the corner of a brown manila envelope poking up from inside one of the damaged drawers.

'I thought we emptied everything,' she said.

Grace watched as Stella dragged the drawer out from under the corner of the sideboard. It was William's drawer, Stella realised – she recognised the marks she'd made with the poker. There was a false back on the tray, and the envelope was lodged in an extra compartment hidden behind it.

Pulling the envelope free, Stella paused for a second, looking at it. She glanced questioningly at Grace.

'Open it,' Grace said.

Stella ripped open the top and reached inside. She pulled out a thin bundle of smaller envelopes, held together with a rubber band. Her gaze travelled over the top envelope, brushing the red and blue airmail pattern printed around the edges, touching briefly on a big, coloured stamp – then fixing on the handwritten address.

Stella
Halfmoon Bay
Tasmania, Australia

Flipping through the other envelopes, she saw the same address repeated. There were five letters. Only the last one was addressed any differently. It said:

Stella
Daughter of a crayfisherman
Halfmoon Bay
Tasmania
PLEASE FORWARD

Grace leaned over Stella's shoulder. 'They're to you!'

Stella bit her lip as she shuffled back through the envelopes. Each had an identical stamp – an image of a kiwi, with New Zealand written above its head.

'From Zeph,' Stella said slowly.

As the knowledge settled in her head, her heart began to beat faster. She lifted the bundle closer, picking out the mailing date on the first envelope. It was stamped in the fuzzy purple of a post office ink-pad.

25 JAN 1976

She checked the dates of the others: *FEB FEB MAR APR*

'I was still here!' Stella said. The words were wrung from her throat. She looked up at Grace then, mute with disbelief.

The woman frowned in confusion. 'Zeph is Robert? Is that what you're saying?'

Stella clutched Grace's arm. 'Did you know about these?'

Grace shook her head. She struggled with her emotions – ripples of anger and distress passing over her face. 'William must have kept them from you.' She stared into her daughter's eyes.

Stella gasped, remembering with sudden clarity the moment – down at the wharf – when she'd asked William if a letter had come for her.

If it had, I'd have given it to you.

Those were the words he'd used . . .

For a few seconds Stella was overcome with shock and outrage. Then she dug one finger behind the flap of the first envelope and pulled it open. She spread out a flimsy sheet of airmail paper.

As she skimmed the page, words and phrases jumped out at her.

There was a storm off the South Island . . . the self-steering gear broke again . . .

We were almost wrecked . . . the mast is gone, two sails lost . . .

I have to earn money to pay for repairs.

It will be at least another month before I can come back . . .

But I am coming. I will be there.

Leave a message at the Memorial. Tell me where to find you . . .

Think of me. I'll be working night and day and saving every cent I can – to come back to you . . .

I love you.

I love you forever.

Zeph (and Carla) xxxx

Stella stared at the letter as the meaning of the words fell slowly into place. Waves of emotion washed through her. There was amazement at the discovery of the letters. There was a burning anger towards William, for keeping them from her.

But, riding over both was something even stronger. A wild, bright hope.

She looked up at her mother.

Grace nodded, as if she understood everything. 'Take the car,' she said. 'Find him.'

Stella ran to the ute, jumping in and turning on the ignition in one movement – pumping the accelerator with her foot. She swung the vehicle round in reverse. Then she sped off, throwing up a spray of gravel behind her.

A ragged sarong, faded to pastel tones, fluttered on a washing line stretched out between two trees. Pinned beside it were several pairs of socks, two T-shirts, a new pair of jeans, stiff and dark. And there – in the sagging middle of the line – was the blue linen shirt Zeph had worn the day he came to work on the kitchen. As Stella ducked under it, heading towards the house, the sleeve brushed her cheek.

She looked out past the boundaries of the garden, searching in all directions for a glimpse of the red station wagon. It had not been in the turning circle at the end of the track, but she had not given up hope that it was parked here somewhere. She already knew it was not at the wharf, or near the shop or the pub – she'd checked those places on the way from Joe's boathouse.

Stella stood by a curve-fronted door, made from a section of hull cut from an old wooden boat, framed with huon pine. She knocked quickly before she could begin to form words, make plans . . .

The sound rang out into stillness. The wind had dropped, Stella noticed. Rain was coming, but had not yet arrived. Everything seemed poised on the brink of action – waiting.

She knocked again. As she listened for a response, she peered in through the window. She could see part of the kitchen. It was as neat and carefully designed as *Tailwind*'s cabin, but the orderly impression was softened by the presence of some bush flowers in a jar; a bowl of walnuts; and a bottle of red wine, half-drunk and recorked. Beside the sink, the utensils of the last meal had been left to dry – a single dinner plate, wine glass, knife, fork and spoon. She studied the rest of the space that was visible – noticing the rich dark tones of the floor. It was made of old wood bearing the imprint of many past lives – nail holes, burns, stains . . . Suddenly, she leaned closer, cupping her hands around her eyes to cut the reflection. Between two chairs, she could see – on the floor – something yellow, dotted with tiny spots of light. She drew in a sharp breath, recognising one of *Tailwind*'s mirrored cushions.

A long, dark shape – a tail – draped over one edge.

The heavy door swung open as Stella turned the handle. She crept in, her gaze fixed on the cushion as she crossed the room.

She smiled at the sight of the creature stretched out there – a cat with a coat of striped orange and black. Carla's kitten, perhaps . . .

But then, as she came close, she saw that the brindled fur had been invaded by grey. And the left ear was torn – caught on a fishing hook . . . Her eyes widened with delight.

She knelt down. 'Carla?' she whispered. 'It's me. Stella.'

The cat opened green eyes clouded with age. Then she lifted her head, with effort. A loud purr erupted from her throat.

Gently, Stella gathered Carla into her arms. Beneath the soft fur she felt the creature's body, bony and thin. Closing her eyes, she rested her cheek against the furry head. Carla nudged her with a wet nose.

Stella stood up with the cat, cradling it against her breast like a child. The purring was an engine firing inside the frail body. Stella smiled. Carla, the little cat. Now as old as a cat could be – yet still brave and strong at heart.

She turned in small circles, rocking the cat gently in her arms.

When she looked up, she found herself facing an open doorway leading to a narrow flight of stairs. Before she had time to consider her actions, she was climbing up them, treading lightly on each step. She guessed where they would lead – and told herself she should not trespass on private space. Yet she kept on . . .

The first floor consisted of a single room – an airy study with a drafting table and an easel set up by the window. Stella let her gaze move over it quickly, glimpsing books, maps and stacks of photographs. She walked on, up another set of stairs.

As she reached the top step, the domed roof curved away above her. It was painted the same cornflower blue as the exterior of the minaret. To mirror a summer sky, Stella thought.

She stopped on the threshold. If she crossed to the double windows, she knew she would be able to look straight down into the coves. If the sea was clear, she'd see the fish as they swam by . . .

She allowed herself only to look from the doorway – at the double bed with its one pillow. The doona had been thrown back, as if the morning had been welcomed with vigour. A sarong draped onto the floor. The room was pleasingly bare of anything that might distract from the views of the sea. As she glanced around the space, Stella saw only a few small pieces of furniture – and one picture . . .

She froze, staring at it. Carla wriggled in protest as the woman's arms tightened around her.

The picture was a large pastel drawing of a girl standing on the deck of a boat. Long, dark hair fanned over her slender shoulders. She wore a shirt hanging open, and a brown striped bikini top underneath. She had been caught by the artist in the moment of tossing back her hair – a bold, carefree gesture. Yet her eyes looked vulnerable – as if she could see into the future and read the pain that waited there . . .

Strong light fell across the girl's features, making the image dramatic. At the same time, the colours were soft, evoking the sense of a dream.

Stella's lips parted in wonder. It was so like the girl she had been.

Yet it was unlike her as well. She glanced down at the signature, a tiny scrawl in the bottom corner.

Zeph.

It was his memory of her, she realised. A vision that had accompanied him over all the long years . . .

Something else drew her attention then. A blur of yellow on a small table set beneath the picture. Stepping closer, she saw that it was a bunch of everlasting daisies. They were old and faded, the petals all ragged. The stems were tied together with a piece of fishing line. Stella remembered how she'd wound it round and round; and how she'd tied the knot – a fishing lure knot – tight and strong. The flowers had looked so bright and welcoming, standing up in their driftwood frame . . .

Stella stared down at the little bunch of daisies. They could not have survived, she knew, for more than a few months out in the open. Warm joy flooded through her. They were the final proof – he had come back to her, just as he had promised.

Stella turned away, looking out through the window to the sea. She pictured Zeph arriving at the Halfmoon wharf after his long voyage. He'd have gone straight to the Seafarers' Memorial to look for her message – and would have found nothing. He'd have asked people how he could find her. They'd all have said the same thing. She's gone to England – to school. Lucky girl . . . When he sailed into the coves and saw the flowers, he must have hoped for a note, hidden there with them. But the flowers were the only message. An apology. A farewell. An ending . . .

Stella carried Carla downstairs, and laid her on the yellow cushion. 'Wait for me,' she said. 'I'm coming back.'

As she headed for the door, she thought of the other place where Zeph might be. *Tailwind.* She tried to remember what Mrs Barron had said about where the yacht was moored. A private slipway somewhere . . .

Joe would know.

As Stella drove along on the edge of the wharf beside *Grand Lady*, the old fisherman emerged from the wheelhouse. He rested one hand on a newly timbered roof. In the other he held a wide brush, dripping with red paint.

Stella opened the door to speak to him, but remained in her seat, the engine running. 'Can you tell me where Zeph's got his yacht?' she asked. 'I think I might find him there.'

'You won't,' Joe said. 'I just came from the slipway. I went to get the paint.' He waved his brush towards Stella. A drop of red flicked onto the car door. 'Zeph was there. Then your mother turned up with Spinks in the cop car. Looked like she gave him something – nothing big, it was in her hand. She spoke to him – just for a minute or two – not long. Then he got in his car and drove off.' He frowned. 'Made no sense to me. He was supposed to be coming back here, to help me paint.'

'Which way did he go?' Stella asked.

Joe swung an arm away towards the coast road. 'Out your way.'

Stella let the clutch out and the ute bumped away over the wharf decking.

Joe called after her. 'Don't you drive too fast! There's rain coming!'

The red station wagon was not parked but rather abandoned in the middle of the track, near the shed. The driver's door hung open.

Stella brought the ute to a standstill next to it. As she jumped out, the wind stirred, bringing the first light spots of rain. She hurried towards the house – up the path, through the garden. The wind grew stronger – a cold west wind. It tugged at her clothes and snapped her hair against her cheeks. She turned her face away from its icy touch.

The garden was a place of wild waving plants. Over on the Sea Wall, loose rope-ends and pieces of netting all leaned out sideways as they were caught in the gust.

Stella paused mid-step. It was as though the garden, the Wall, were dancing for her – wanting to draw her gaze . . .

346

Then, beyond the lattice of grey wood she saw a splash of foreign colour. She traced the outline of a figure standing there.

She walked straight towards it, her boots sinking into the soft soil of garden beds.

Nearing the Wall, she faltered, but the wind was at her back, nudging her on . . .

As she stepped into the lee of the wooden screen, the air was suddenly still.

Zeph stood with his back to her, looking down at the little cross surrounded by the first pale spikes of new-sprung seedlings. In one hand he held the bundle of letters that he'd sent so long ago. The other hand was clasped stiffly at his side.

He turned, as if sensing Stella's presence there. He did not speak, but just stared into her eyes – a long, searching look that seemed able to reach deep inside her, to where all the secrets were hidden.

She felt, in that moment, that he could see – and feel – it all.

A girl alone in her room, watched only by the distant eye of the moon. Her cries heard only by the sea.

A row of tiny furled fingers pressed against a filmy sac.

A wedding gown made for a doll, smeared with blood.

A perfect, peaceful face with sealed-shut eyes.

A mother showing off her child to the stars.

Everything . . .

Zeph was still for a few seconds – then he spread his arms wide.

Stella took a step towards him. She was weak, suddenly – her legs barely able to hold her up. She felt the walls inside her beginning to crumble as a force stirred within her: a tide of tears – surely as wide and deep as the ocean. It rose up and flowed out, cleansing and pure.

Stella sobbed freely – not an anguished cry, but one that gasped out long-held pain.

Tears ran down Zeph's face, too – over his cheeks, onto the bow of his lips.

He reached out for Stella, pulling her against him. She let her face fall on his shoulder as he wrapped his arms around her and held her close to his heart.

The rain fell, mingling with their tears.

A blessing sent by distant clouds – or angels.

Acknowledgements

I am greatly indebted to my husband Roger Scholes for his vital role in the writing of *The Stone Angel*. He has, once again, spent countless hours at my side applying his filmmaker's skills to the manuscript – untangling storylines, challenging characters to become more real, paring back scenes or helping them grow stronger. At the same time, he has been an inspiring companion in all the other realms of the life that we share. It is a miracle for which I am always grateful.

I would like to thank everyone at Pan Macmillan Australia – especially my publisher Cate Paterson – for continuing to support me as an author. I am grateful to Karen Penning for her astute and careful editing.

Many thanks go to my agent Fiona Inglis, to Pippa Masson and others at Curtis Brown Australia, to Kate Cooper and Ali Gunn of Curtis Brown London, and also to Agence Hoffman.

I wish to express my appreciation to Christine Steffen-Reimann of Droemer Knaur, Germany, and Françoise Triffaux of Belfond, France, for the enormous encouragement they gave me throughout the writing of the novel.

Many people were involved in the research and writing of *The Stone Angel*. I offer sincere thanks to them all . . .

Dr Dennis Humphrey – for detailed advice about Stella's pregnancy and miscarriage.

Janet Pendrigh – for sharing anecdotes from her decades of work as a midwife.

Maree Pyke and the women of Swansea – for telling me everything I needed to know about Tasmanian cooking, food and kitchen life.

Michael Pyke – for information about fishing, diving, hunting and preparing wild foods.

My brother Andrew – for more of the above, and for reading a draft of the manuscript.

Inspector John Arnold of the St Helens Police and the volunteers at St Helens Marine Rescue – for advice about search and rescue procedures.

Stuart Lester – for his book *Of Coastlines and Crayfish*.

My father Dr Robin Smith – for reading the manuscript and helping with forensic and maritime research.

My mother Elizabeth Smith – for sharing insights into the lives of women of her generation, for notes on traditional English recipes and housekeeping, and for reading the manuscript.

Cathy Hawkins and Ian Johnston – for telling me tales of offshore sailing adventures and helping me create the world of Zeph and *Tailwind*.

Elizabeth McKenzie – for offering me the use of her cookery library, and providing cake as well.

My sister Dr Clare Smith – for applying her knowledge of psychology and family relationships to several drafts of the novel, and for always suggesting lunch.

Julia Fisher – for answering questions about Grace's garden.

Jane Ormonde – for reminding me that emotion *is* drama, and for reading the final manuscript with such a keen and sensitive eye.

My sister Hilary – for believing in Stella's story from the very beginning, and for bravely agreeing to be one of the first people to read the full manuscript.

The Curry Club writers – for professional support and fun.

Claire Konkes – for being a great writing companion (and purveyor of wrass patties).

Vanessa Poole – for checking details of Tasmanian life in the novel.

Anna Jones – for always being there to share a drink and listen to the predicaments of a bookful of characters she had yet to meet.

Lynda House and Tony Mahood – for my Sydney writing safari, and for all the years we've spent seeking stories together.

Peter Whyte – for some great photographs.

My niece Kate Visagie – for reading the manuscript with a nineteen-year-old's eye.

Myra Tite – for sending parcels every single Christmas of my life, no matter where in the world the family was living.

John and Caroline Ball – for shedding light on Grace's family background and for the gift of many sojourns at Binalong Bay.

Jay Yulumara – for sharing her garden retreat with us and offering wisdom on many things.

My mother-in-law Pat Scholes – whose story of a lost child was an inspiration for the book.

And finally, my sons Jonathan and Linden – for showing me how unimaginably precious babies are.

If you enjoyed *The Stone Angel*, here is the prelude from
Katherine Scholes' bestselling novel, *The Rain Queen*

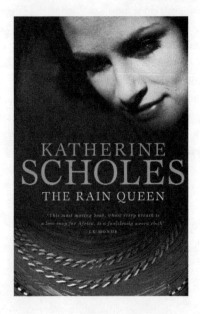

1974 Dodoma, Tanzania, East Africa

In the churchyard of the Anglican cathedral two coffins lay ready for burial. One of them was almost a foot longer than the other, but apart from that they were the same – simple boxes made from fresh-cut splintery wood, left bare. Bishop Wade stood beside them, a bulky figure draped in purple robes embroidered with gold thread. His pale skin was flushed with pink and sweat ran down his temples.

He looked out over a huge crowd. People lined the pathways and filled the spaces between the burial plots; they sat on the bonnets and roofs of Landrovers parked along the boundaries, and even hung from the limbs of the old mango trees that cast their shade over the cemetery.

The missionaries were grouped at the front, along with a scattering of other Europeans, and half a dozen journalists juggling cameras and note-books. Behind them stood the Africans from the town and the Mission, neatly dressed in Western clothes, and an enclave of Indians wearing tur-bans and saris. Village people made up the outer ranks – a sea of black skin dotted with bright cloths and blankets.

The Bishop raised his hand and waited for the crowd to grow still. Then he began to read from a book held out by one of his African clergy-men. His strong voice carried clearly over a blur of smaller noises: people coughing and shuffling, babies crying, and the distant sound of a truck being ground roughly through its gears.

'For we brought nothing into this world, and it is certain we can carry nothing out . . .'

He read on – a few more lines – but then faltered, sensing that some-thing was happening in the crowd: a subtle, silent shifting of focus. As he looked up, his gaze was drawn to a far corner of the churchyard. His eyes widened. A group of warriors had arrived there – long-limbed men with mud-daubed hair and necklaces of coloured beads. They were pushing forward, invading the ranks of the mission people, the tips of long hunt-ing spears rising above their heads and glinting in the sun.

Sheltered in their midst was a white woman. She was revealed in small glimpses, in between the men's bare shoulders – an impression of pale skin, steady eyes and striking red hair hanging loose. As she moved through the crowd, a low murmur grew, spreading out from where she was like ripples in water.

Not far from the Bishop, the warriors stopped. The white woman stood with them, silently facing the coffins, seemingly oblivious to the disturbance her arrival had created.

She was a strange figure. Tall and lean, she was dressed in khaki bush clothes stained with sweat and dust. Unlike any other woman in the crowd, she wore trousers. They were held in at the waist by a wide ammunition belt made of leather. She stood very still, her features immobile, eyes gazing blankly ahead.

The Bishop pushed on with his reading. When it was finished, he announced that the choir would sing a hymn. He turned deliberately to face the singers, hoping to draw the attention of the crowd with him. But at the edges of his vision he was acutely aware of the silent woman, still standing there . . .

'*Guide me, O thou great Jehovah, Pilgrim through this barren land.*'

The words rang out; strong clear lines drawing numerous harmonies into a single, complex voice.

'*Bread of heaven. Bread of heaven. Feed me till I want no more . . .*'

During the last verse of the hymn, the Bishop gestured to one of his assistants. Then a girl emerged from the crowd, guided from behind by one of the missionary wives. She wore a blue dress, crisply pressed. The full skirt brushed her knees as she walked. She kept her head bent, dark hair falling forward to hide her face. Cradled in her arms were two bunches of flowers. They were ragged collections of wild orchids, sunflowers, garden leaves and weeds – clearly her own creations.

As the slight figure edged towards the coffins, an African woman, some way back in the crowd, began to wail loudly. Others joined her and soon their cries drowned out the singing. It was as if, until now, the funeral had belonged to the Bishop and clergymen. But the sight of a child approaching her parents' coffins brought up a feeling of common pain that could not be owned, or contained, or organised into a liturgy. Grief rolled out over the crowd, deep and raw.

Kate stood between the two wooden boxes. She placed her first bunch of flowers down onto her father's coffin, positioning it carefully on the middle of the lid. Then she turned to the other coffin – the one that held the body of her mother. She looked down at the timber planks trying to see beyond them. Were the eyes open? she wondered. Or shut, as if sleeping . . .

She hadn't been allowed to see the bodies. They'd said she was only a child, after all. No-one had added that the bodies had been hacked by machetes, but Kate knew that this was the case.

Even the faces? she'd wanted to ask.

But no-one had seemed to expect her to speak. They'd wanted her to cry, to sleep, to eat, to swallow tablets. Anything, but ask questions.

'It's just a blessing that you weren't there,' was all they'd say. 'Thank God you were here, at boarding school. It doesn't bear thinking about . . .'

A journalist darted out from the crowd and squatted with his camera to catch the moment when the child laid down her second bunch of flowers. Kate stared at him, stony-faced, as he leaned closer for a better shot. Words circled in her head like a spell, keeping thoughts at bay.

Tighten your heart. It is the will of God.

Tighten your heart.

The phrases came to her in Swahili – with the voice of the African housemother who had led her away from the School Office, after she had been told. Told. Just like that. A man's mouth moving, words coming out.

'Something terrible has happened . . .'

Tighten your heart.

Looking up, over the crowd, Kate found herself meeting the steady gaze of the tall woman with red hair. She looked vaguely familiar, but the connection was not strong enough to penetrate the haze that dulled the girl's mind. After a brief moment, Kate turned her eyes away, looking beyond the churchyard. All the trees were in full growth. Harvest time was nearly here. She imagined the maize growing in the shambas. It would be over her head. The ears of yellow corn fattening inside their silken-lined shells. Only a few weeks now, and the time of hunger would be forgotten for another season . . .

Kate returned to her place beside the doctor's wife, and stood there quietly, her gaze looking down at her shoes – the shiny black leather dusted with fine red sand.

'Let's go home now, shall we?' Mrs Layton's voice buzzed close to her ear. Kate stared at her, confused. 'Back to my place, I mean,' the woman added. 'You don't need to stay any longer.' She tried to smile at the child, but her lips were trembling.

Taking Kate's elbow, Mrs Layton drew her back through the crowd. A young man holding a notebook and camera hurried after them.

'Excuse me,' he said as he reached Kate's side. He had a kind-looking face, but before he could say any more Mrs Layton waved him aside.

'Talk to the Bishop,' she said. Then she led Kate quickly away.

When the burial was over, and the final hymn sung, the congregation began to disperse. Reporters hurried to secure interviews, while the missionaries lingered in small groups as if unwilling to acknowledge that the service was finished.

The young journalist approached the Bishop. The man was still standing near the two graves, staring down at the mounds of crumbly earth.

'Bishop Wade, I've got a few questions . . .' the journalist began.

'The Mission has released a statement,' the Bishop cut him off.

The young man nodded. He'd read the document two days ago. It had simply confirmed the murder of two missionaries, Dr Michael Carrington and his wife, Sarah, at an outlying station to the west, near the border of Rwanda. It had said that there was no known motive for the killings. It had then added that a third European, visiting the station at the time of the incident, had not been harmed. That was all. No mention had been made of other 'information' that had nevertheless spread quickly around Dodoma. Apparently the female victim had been stripped naked before her death. More bizarrely, the rumour was that an egg had been stuffed into her mouth.

'There are a couple of points I'd like to get some details on,' the journalist said.

The Bishop glanced up, signalling agreement. Now that he had completed the task of conducting the funeral, he looked tired and distressed. The journalist guessed that he would not get the chance to cover too many questions.

'Can you confirm that there was an egg,' he began. The Bishop looked pained, but the young man pushed on. 'In the . . . in Mrs Carrington's . . . mouth.'

The Bishop nodded. 'As the attack took place during Easter, it seems reasonable to assume that it was meant as a reference to the eggs Christians give one another at this time.' He spoke in a flat voice as if reciting an answer that had been prepared in advance. 'The world over, wherever Christ's message of love is preached, there are those who respond with hatred.' He took a breath. The journalist checked his notebook and launched another question.

'How old is the girl?'

'Twelve.'

'What will happen to her?'

'She will return to Australia. There are no close relatives. The Mission Secretary will become her guardian. She will be well looked after. She will go to the very best school.'

The journalist scribbled notes. 'How is she coping?' he asked.

'She is strong,' the Bishop answered bleakly. 'We can only pray that her faith will sustain her.'

Another journalist appeared beside them – an older man with sparse grey hair and a flushed face. As he opened his mouth to speak, the Bishop shook his head.

'Enough. Please . . .' He turned away.

Undeterred, the newcomer fired off his question. 'And the other person there. It was a woman, wasn't it – a Miss Annah Mason?'

'Yes, that's right,' the Bishop answered, walking off.

Both journalists dogged his heels.

'She was a witness to the murder? She was right there?' the older journalist continued. Without waiting for a reply from the Bishop, he pressed on. 'So, how come they didn't even touch her? I mean, when you think what happened to the other two . . .'

The younger journalist looked shocked by this line of questioning. But he hurried along just the same.

'And this . . . Miss Mason . . . is it true that she used to be one of your missionaries? That she was forced to resign? Can you tell me why?'

The man's barrage of questions was cut off abruptly as the Bishop turned suddenly around. He was a big man, and his face was rigid with anger. Both journalists took a step back.

The Bishop strode off, leaving the two men standing alone.

'She was here, you know,' commented the grey-haired man. 'Miss Mason.' He licked his lips as if anticipating a move to find a drink.

The other journalist looked around him urgently. 'Did you talk to her?'

'Thought about it.' The man scratched his nose. 'Till one of her henchmen showed me the end of a very sharp-looking spear.' He shook his head. 'Pity.' Pushing the chewed stub of a pencil into his pocket, he shrugged and walked away.

Kate found herself in a sunny sitting room, with strangers offering her food. It entered her mouth, a cold leaden mass. When she had managed to chew and swallow a few times, she pushed her plate aside.

Next she was taken into a storeroom where several tea chests stood in a row. Mrs Layton explained to her that someone at Langali Station had packed up the family possessions and sent them here. The boxes would be shipped to Australia in due course. She handed Kate a few things that had been kept aside for her – things Mrs Layton thought the girl might like to have with her now. There was her father's Bible, and her mother's meagre collection of jewellery.

'Thank you,' Kate said. She barely glanced at the objects before putting them down on the floor. Crossing to one of the tea chests, she began looking at the things that had been packed away. She picked up one of her dolls – the one they wrapped in strips of white cloth each Christmas and used as Jesus in the manger.

'Keep her, too,' suggested Mrs Layton. Kate could see that she liked the idea of a comforting doll.

Dropping the toy back into the crate, Kate turned to look at a cardboard box full of old clothes.

'They're things I didn't think were worth keeping,' said Mrs Layton. 'Clothes mainly. They'll be given away to the Africans.' A frown crossed her face as Kate bent and picked up an old pair of shoes. They were Sarah's. Her everyday shoes – the ones she used to wear as she hurried about in the kitchen, the hospital, the compound. They were shiny clean, but soft and creased with wear. Kate leaned her face close to them, breathing the musky smell of long-dried sweat as she hugged them to her chest.

After a few moments, Mrs Layton came and laid a hand on her shoulder. 'Have a cry, dear. It's better to let it out.'

Kate kept her head down. She couldn't cry. The tears seemed to be locked away inside her, trapped in a hard lump of pain that felt as if it were stuck in her throat, half-swallowed.

Alone in a bare guestroom, Kate knelt by her bed to pray. Her lips moved but she could find no words. She couldn't think, couldn't feel. She felt lost and empty – as if she, too, were no longer alive. She wondered if it was because of the tablet Dr Layton had given her. After a few minutes, she got up. She found Sarah's shoes and put them on. They were much too big; if she'd tried to walk, they'd have fallen off. Instead, she sat still on the side of the bed, drawing comfort from the worn shapes, feeling the contours made by her mother's feet lying beneath her own. She could almost imagine that Sarah had just taken them off. That they were still warm . . . It calmed her, until the tranquilliser began to work, numbing the pain.

On the edge of sleep, Kate climbed into the bed, easing her way between tightly tucked sheets. Then she heard the door opening. Quickly she closed her eyes. Her limbs stiffened, awaiting another embrace – the touch of another stranger. Someone else's mother.

But the presence that moved to stand beside her wafted the smell of cold ash and butter. Kate peered between her lashes.

'Ordena?' Kate whispered her old ayah's name. No, she told herself, it was impossible. Who would bring her here? All the way from Langali . . .

'Was it not I who held you as a little child?' the woman answered.

'You have come,' Kate breathed, scarcely believing it.

'Truly, I have come.' Ordena bent and gathered Kate into her arms. Slowly, gently, she rocked her as if she were a baby again. Back and forth, the old nurse moved, to the steady rhythm of an African lullaby. Gradually the stiffness went out of Kate's body. She softened into the familiar embrace. At last the tears flowed out.

Katherine Scholes
Make Me An Idol

FROM THE AUTHOR OF THE INTERNATIONAL BESTSELLER
THE RAIN QUEEN

Ellen Kirby is 'Liberty' – American idol and ballet superstar. She has
fame and fabulous wealth, but the darkness of her past threatens to
overwhelm her. To escape the memories she must make the ultimate
sacrifice . . .

Twenty years later, Zelda Madison's safe and happy world is turned
upside-down by a shocking discovery. Leaving everything, she goes
in search of the mother she always believed to be dead.

From a remote Tasmanian island to the ashrams of India and the
foothills of the Himalayas, Zelda pursues the truth – about her mother
and about herself.

Make Me An Idol is a vividly compelling story of the power of the past
and the healing strength of love.

'Spellbinding'
NEW WEEKLY

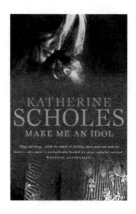

Photograph: Peter Whyte